D1562722

Since the whole town stood to inherit from the old man's will, everyone in it had a motive to kill him...

"How well did Rich know Mr. Withers?" Mev asked.

"Very well. Rich and Mr. Withers talked for a year about building a Senextra factory in Witherston. They became friends. Sort of. Mr. Withers was very old, you know. And not very talkative. But they did drink wine together. They drank Mr. Withers's fine wine."

"Why is Rich so interested in having BioSenecta build the Senextra factory here?"

"Because BioSenecta will bring jobs to Witherston and revitalize our town. Face it, Mev. Our town is dying. If Witherston does not bring in a big employer soon all of our young people will leave, and some of our older people too. And although you may not know it, we have a good number of unemployed and homeless people."

"Tell me, Rhonda. Did your husband sign a contract with BioSenecta?"

"Well...not exactly, though Rich and Martin Payne had an agreement. Mr. Withers had not finalized the $1 sale of his land to BioSenecta. Rich wanted to keep his negotiations with Martin secret until Friday's announcement. He knew that Lottie and Gretchen and all the other anti-progress folks around here who want to keep Witherston primitive would campaign against BioSenecta. And sure enough, they did."

"Rhonda, what's Rich's stake in BioSenecta?"

Rhonda hesitated. "What do you mean? Rich is the mayor. He wants a good future for Witherston. And Witherston needs the billion dollars Mr. Withers left our town in his will."

"Do you realize, Rhonda, that you've just offered a motive for Rich to kill Withers before Withers could change his will?"

At the celebration of his hundredth birthday, local billionaire Francis Hearty Withers announces to the people gathered on the front lawn of Witherston Baptist Church that he has finalized his will. In it he bequeaths $1 billion to his north Georgia hometown of Witherston and another $1 billion to be divided up equally among the town's 4,000 residents—in recognition of their support of a Senextra pharmaceutical factory. Senextra is a drug that enables individuals to lead healthy lives well into their second century, but it has some unanticipated consequences.

The group assembled to hear Withers's announcement do not all applaud. One person carries a sign that says SENEXTRA VIOLATES MOTHER NATURE. Another, KEEP SENEXTRA OUT OF OUR SYSTEM. A third, WE DON'T NEED MORE OLD MEN.

Withers flies into a rage. He vows to change his will and disinherit the community. Two days later he is found dead.

In Betty Jean Craige's first murder mystery a few humans die in unusual circumstances. A few others live in unusual circumstances. Who dunnit?

KUDOS for *Downstream*

In *Downstream* by Betty Jean Craige, billionaire Harty Withers is part of a clinical trial for a new drug, Senextra, which is supposed to prolong life in the elderly. In appreciation of his extended life-span, the billionaire decides to leave one billion dollars to the makers of Senextra in his will to build a factory on part of his land in the town of Witherston. In addition, Withers also leaves one billion dollars in his will to be divided among the residents of Witherston, which would net each of the 4,000 residents about $250,000. However, when a number of the residents reject the idea of having the Senextra factory built on the site of the old-growth forest, Withers angrily proclaims that he is changing his will and the town will get nothing. Of course, that's as good as signing his own death warrant, and less than 48 hours later he ends up dead. I thoroughly enjoyed Downstream. Craige makes some good points not only on conservation and what medicines and other human chemicals do to our environment, but also what greed can do to otherwise good people. Craige has a unique and refreshing voice and the book is not only thought-provoking but fun to read. ~ *Taylor Jones, Reviewer*

Downstream by Betty Jean Craige is the story of small town USA knocked on its head by big pharma, murder, money, and greed. In Witherston, Georgia, population 4,000, a town named after its founding family, Harty Withers is celebrating his 100th birthday by revealing the contents of his will. He tells those assembled for his birthday party that he intends to leave them all the sum of $1,000,000,000 to be divided among the equally, netting each resident $250,000. However there is a catch. Harty also leaves another $1,000,000,000 to the makers of a new drug called Senextra for them to build a factory on a 31-acre plot of land containing old-growth trees...*Downstream* will not only keep riveted from beginning to end, it will make you think about the consequences of human arrogance and greed. ~ *Regan Murphy, Reviewer*

ACKNOWLEDGEMENTS

After beginning *Downstream* I discovered that writing a murder mystery was hard. Really hard! I needed all the help I could get. And thanks to generous, smart, kind, wonderful friends I got lots of help. So...

Thank you, Susan Tate, for answering my legal questions, helping me figure out the plot, reading my manuscript at various stages of completion, and finding ever so many mistakes, ever so many, so many.

Other dear friends carefully read the first draft and observed that it was "message-heavy," in Wyatt Anderson's words. So to Wyatt and Margaret Anderson, who have encouraged my writing for many decades, I thank you for your extremely useful and utter frankness. I've tried to make the novel message-lighter.

To my fellow mystery lovers Valerie Greenberg, Tom and Karen Kenyon, Linda Schramm, Nelle Shehane, Barbara Timmons, and Hugh and Tricia Ruppersburg, I appreciate your telling me how I might make a better story.

Thank you, Mary Jo Johnson, my sister, for your thoughtful criticism of the book early on. We've loved mysteries since grade school, when we admired Nancy Drew, Trixie Belden, Judy Bolton, the Dana Girls, and the Hardy Boys and wanted to have adventures like theirs.

Thank you, Dana Bultman, Javier Zapata, and Eliot and Guillermo Zapata, for inspiring the characters Mev and Paco Arroyo and their twins Jaime and Jorge. I suspect you all will recognize yourselves in my book, even though I must say:

Thank you, Holly Marie Stasco, for doing the excellent maps of Witherston and North Georgia.

And thank you, Chuck Murphy, for photographing me with great skill and kindness.

I must also thank my friend the late Eugene Odum, ecologist and environmentalist, who taught me to see the world as an ecosystem whose parts are interactive and interdependent. I learned from you, Gene, that when we humans recognize our interdependence with all the other organisms on Earth we must acknowledge our need for cooperation.

And I thank Terry Kay who told me I could write fiction when I thought I couldn't. Were it not for you, Terry, I would have never tried.

I got the idea for *Downstream* from the book *Our Stolen Future*, first published in 1997, by Theo Colborn, Dianne Dumanoski, and John Peterson Myers. I learned from *Our Stolen Future* that our planet is medicated.

Downstream

A Witherston Murder Mystery

Betty Jean Craige

A Black Opal Books Publication

GENRE: COZY MYSTERY/WOMEN'S FICTION

DOWNSTREAM ~ A WITHERSTON MURDER MYSTERY
Copyright © 2014 by Betty Jean Craige
Cover Design by Jackson Cover Designs
Author photo by Chuck Murphy
Maps by Holly Marie Stasco
All photos and artwork copyright © 2014
All Rights Reserved
Print ISBN: 978-1-626942-01-1

First Publication: NOVEMBER 2014

Published by Black Opal Books **http://www.blackopalbooks.com**

DEDICATION

To Cosmo
and my other dear friends

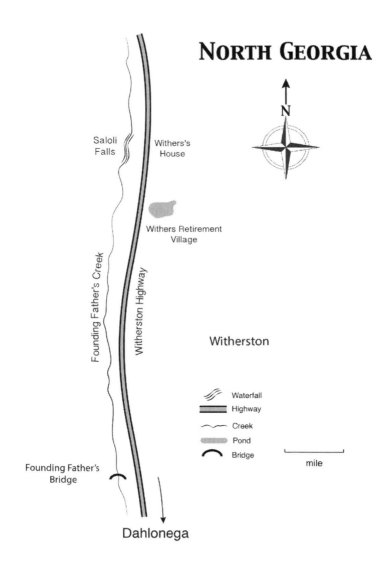

NORTH GEORGIA

N

Saloli Falls

Withers's House

Founding Father's Creek

Withers Retirement Village

Witherston

Witherston Highway

Waterfall
Highway
Creek
Pond
Bridge

mile

Founding Father's Bridge

Dahlonega

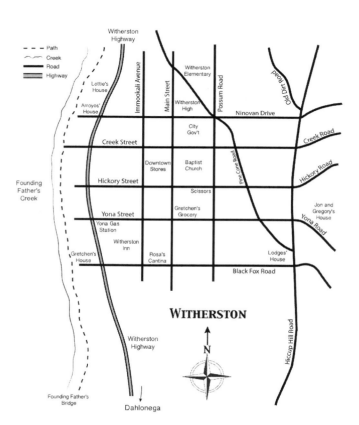

Path
Creek
Road
Highway

Witherston Highway

Lottie's House

Arroyos' House

Immookali Avenue

Main Street

Witherston Elementary

Witherston High

Possum Road

Old Dirt Road

Ninovan Drive

Founding Father's Creek

Creek Street

City Gov't

Creek Road

Downtown Stores

Baptist Church

Pine Cone Road

Hickory Road

Hickory Street

Scissors

Gretchen's Grocery

Jon and Gregory's House

Yona Road

Yona Street

Yona Gas Station

Witherston Inn

Gretchen's House

Rosa's Cantina

Lodges' House

Black Fox Road

WITHERSTON

Witherston Highway

N

Hiccup Hill Road

Founding Father's Bridge

Dahlonega

When we try to pick out anything by itself,
we find it hitched to everything else in the universe.

~ John Muir, 1869

PREFACE

He heard the strains of "Old Man River" before he saw the red pickup. It was empty. The engine was running. He reached into the cab to turn the engine off but changed his mind. He didn't want to announce his approach.

Instead he grabbed the deer rifle on the right front seat. It was loaded.

The sky was darkening with black rain clouds, but he spotted a man on the bridge. The man held something in his hand, a beaker of creek water. The man was obviously testing the water. The EPA would investigate.

He couldn't allow that to happen.

He got down on his knees and fired one shot through the man's back. He got him. He wiped the rifle clean of fingerprints with his handkerchief and shoved it deep into the brush along the creek.

He returned to the truck and wiped it clean of prints, too.

Now what?

Well, he'd use this occasion to warn off others. He found a pencil and a yellow post-it note pad in the glove compartment and left a message.

Then he returned to his car parked by the road.

PART 1

STATE OF GEORGIA
COUNTY OF LUMPKIN

LAST WILL AND TESTAMENT
OF
FRANCIS HEARTY WITHERS

I, FRANCIS HEARTY WITHERS, of said State and Lumpkin County, do make and publish this my Last (and Only) Will and Testament.

ITEM I

(a) I wish my body to be buried on the site I have chosen on the grounds of Withers Village. I desire and instruct that a funeral service be held at Witherston Baptist Church. The costs of my funeral service and burial shall be paid out of my estate. My casket has already been purchased.

(b) All of my due and payable debts shall be paid out of my estate as soon as is practicable.

ITEM II

I give and bequeath the sum of ONE BILLION DOLLARS ($1,000,000,000) to the municipality of WITHERSTON.

ITEM III

I give and bequeath the sum of ONE BILLION DOLLARS ($1,000,000,000) to the present LEGAL RESIDENTS OF WITHERSTON to be divided equally among them in appreciation of their support of the Senextra factory.

ITEM IV

I give and bequeath the remainder of my estate, including my home on 1 Withers Hill Road, the contents of said home, the 40 acres designated as tax map/parcel 184 001H on which the home stands, and the 31.7 acres designated as tax map/parcel 182B 007T on Founding Father's Creek in Lumpkin County to BIOSENECTA for use in the construction of a Senextra factory on the site.

If BioSenecta should not use the property for construction

of a Senextra factory, the remainder of my estate shall go to the municipality of Witherston.

ITEM V

(a) I hereby appoint RICHARD RATHER as Executor of this Will.

(b) If for any reason Richard Rather should be unable to fulfill this responsibility, I appoint DR. NEEL KINGFISHER, JR., Director of Withers Village, as Successor Executor of this Will.

IN WITNESS WHEREOF, I have hereunto set my hand and affixed my seal to this my Will, this 20th day of May, 2015.

Francis Hearty Withers
FRANCIS HEARTY WITHERS
1 Withers Hill Road, Witherston GA 30534

Signed, sealed, published and declared by FRANCIS HEARTY WITHERS as his Last Will and Testament in our presence. We, at his request and in his presence, and in the presence of each other, have hereunto subscribed our names as witnesses the day and year above set out.

WITNESSES/ADDRESSES:

GRANT HEMMINGS GRIGGS:
Grant Hemmings Griggs
47 Pine Street, Witherston GA 30534

GEORGE FOLSOM, MD:
George Folsom, MD
3300 Mountain Pass, Witherston GA 30534

WITHERSTON ON THE WEB
Friday, May 22, 2015

LOCAL NEWS

At 4:30 pm today, on the steps of Witherston Baptist Church, Mr. Francis Hearty Withers will celebrate his hundredth birthday. He is expected to make an announcement regarding his will. The event is free and open to the public. Witherston Baptist Church members will provide food.

Dr. Martin Payne, CEO of BioSenecta Pharmaceuticals, will come from Atlanta to honor Mr. Withers, who is the majority shareholder of BioSenecta stock and a member of its Board of Directors.

Dr. Payne will reveal the construction timetable for the planned BioSenecta plant in Witherston. BioSenecta manufactures the experimental drug Senextra, which has been developed to prolong healthy life.

~ Catherine Perry, Reporter

ON THIS DAY IN HISTORY
By Charlotte Byrd

On Monday, May 22, 1899, Witherston celebrated the completion of Founding Fathers' Covered Bridge, which crossed Founding Father's Creek two miles downstream from Witherston. Like Elder's Mill Covered Bridge in Watkinsville, upon which it was modeled, Founding Father's Covered Bridge spanned 100 feet.

After the covered bridge burned on July 4, 1910, the narrow bridge was rebuilt "uncovered," as it presently stands. Unable to support the weight of automobiles, Founding Fa-

ther's Bridge is used today primarily by hikers, picnickers, and fishermen.

POLICE BLOTTER

Witherston Police Officers were called to Rosa's Cantina at 8:15 pm yesterday to stop a fight between two underage men over a scantily clad young woman. The three were arrested for underage drinking and taken to jail. The bartender said he hadn't realized that the woman was scantily clad because he was concentrating on his job.

CHAPTER 1

Friday, May 22, 2015, Labor Day weekend, Witherston, Georgia:

Old Withers is gonna make us all rich!"
"I heard he plans to give everybody in Witherston a million dollars!"
"But that's when he dies. And he looks pretty healthy to me."
"He turns a hundred today. He'll be dying soon!"

"Oh my God! Georgia's beauty queen Rhonda Rather looks pregnant! Isn't she a bit long in the tooth to be carrying a foal?"
"She must be over fifty! God in Heaven! I didn't know that Mayor Rather—I've always called him Rotund Rather—was such a stud."
"Dear Rhonda doesn't want to be pregnant, and her daughter Sandra does. I heard that Sandra and Phil are getting fertility treatments."
"Faith Folsom has a bulge in her belly too, and she's older than dirt. Do you all think she's pregnant?"
"Probably. She doesn't have the sense God gave geese."
"Oh, but she does."
"Jesus God, I pray it doesn't happen to me."
"Honey, bless your heart and don't get me wrong but you

are way too old, way, way too old! You're almost old enough to go to Withers Village!"

"But they don't accept girls there."

"Lottie, come here! Look at Francis Hearty Withers all dressed up on stage acting holier than the High and Mighty just because he's going to bless us with his unearned money. He thinks we'll clap for him when Scorch unveils his statue."

"Gretchen, did you know he paid Scorch $50,000 to make that statue?"

"I'm not giving Withers a single clap. The old geezer is an environmental criminal. He thinks he can use our town and our creek and our land for *his* toxin-producing Senextra factory."

"Who's that hunk in the blue suit?"

"The man talking to Dr. Folsom? He's the CEO of Bio-Senecta, Dr. Martin Payne."

"Well, good gracious, I'll be darned! He's sure easy on the eyes!"

"Francis Hearty Withers talked him into building a Senextra factory here."

❧❧❧

Detective Emma Evelyn Arroyo, "Mev" to her friends, heard these conversations as she walked through the crowd. She was on duty until 5:00, and her assignment was crowd control on the front lawn of Witherston Baptist Church. Rumors abounded that today Witherston's local billionaire would announce the construction of a pharmaceutical factory on Founding Father's Creek upstream from Witherston and that Witherston's KEEP NATURE NATURAL environmentalists would protest. The Witherston Police Department, for which she worked, was on alert.

Mev spotted a group of teenagers wearing KEEP NATURE NATURAL T-shirts.

"Ladies and Gentlemen!" Mayor Rather bellowed into the microphone. "It's 4:30 and time for a grand and glorious party! We're here to celebrate the hundredth birthday of Witherston's most famous citizen, actually Lumpkin County's most famous citizen, Francis Hearty Withers. Thanks to all you folks for turning out for the occasion. Let's give a big hand to Mr. Withers, the last of five generations of Withers residing on Founding Father's Creek."

Mev was relieved to hear only clapping, polite and restrained as it was. She was too preoccupied with her own immediate problem to share in her fellow Witherstonians' excitement.

"Fellow citizens, I didn't hear you. Let's give a big, big, big hand to—let me drop a hint—Witherston's most generous benefactor."

More clapping.

Francis Hearty Withers sat smiling on stage in his navy Armani suit with his aqua Salvatore Ferragamo silk tie, holding his ivory-inlaid mahogany cane. He was flanked on one side by the tall, solemn, well-dressed Dr. Neel Kingfisher, who stood, and on the other by the overall-clad Scorch Ridge, a giant of a man, who also stood.

"Now let us sing 'Happy Birthday!'"

Mayor Rather led the crowd of some three hundred men, women, and children in a spirited version of the song, which included the second verse usually sung for the very young:

> "How old are you?
> How old are you?
> How old, how old
> How old are you?"

Mr. Withers stood up and raised both arms in triumph. "I'm one hundred years old, and going strong!"

"Congratulations, Mr. Withers!" exclaimed Mayor Rather. "We're so glad you are still with us. We thank you from the bottom of our hearts for honoring us with your presence on this special day. In just a moment we will unveil our monument to you, a statue created by our own Witherston sculptor Scorch Ridge. Then we will partake of the green beans, black-eyed peas, ham, fried chicken, and cole slaw that the fine ladies of Witherston, Georgia, have prepared. Plus cold beer, the hot dogs that our fine gentlemen are grilling, and—need I say it?—the best birthday cakes known to mankind. But first, Mr. Withers, I understand you have an announcement to make."

Withers quickly approached the microphone, barely leaning on his cane. He looked healthy, and not a day older than eighty.

"Hello, dear friends of Witherston," he said, opening the black loose leaf binder that held his prepared speech and putting on a pair of wire-rimmed glasses. "In my lifetime I have accumulated great wealth. Now I want to make it yours."

Withers paused as if awaiting applause. Hearing none, he turned back to his script.

"But you will inherit not only my money. You will inherit the mission of our great civilization. And if you accept my gift, you must accept responsibility for advancing this mission."

"We will," said Mayor Rather. "We will make you proud."

Withers went on reading. "So what is the mission of our great civilization? It is to bring mankind power over his destiny. It is to bring order to wilderness and discipline to wildness. The land we stand upon today was once wilderness, occupied by animals and Indians. It was once wildness, where nature ruled the lives of animals and Indians alike. The land we stand upon today remained unchanged for ten thousand years until our ancestors brought civilization to this place. What did the Indians do who lived and died here during those ten thousand years, who inhabited the woods like animals, who left no permanent mark upon the world? Not much."

"Whoa!" cried Gretchen Hall Green, whom Mayor Rather usually called Gretchen Whole Grain. But then she referred to him as Mayor Rather Round.

Withers glanced momentarily at Gretchen and asked her, "Will you permit me to continue?"

Gretchen said nothing.

Mev looked at Neel Kingfisher. He was scowling.

Withers continued. "What did the Europeans do? A lot. Our ancestors developed writing and mathematics. Built the printing press, the steam engine, the telephone, the phonograph, the light bulb, the train, the automobile, the airplane, the computer. Created cathedrals, symphonies, novels, newspapers. Discovered penicillin, vaccines, and other drugs to overcome the diseases that would have killed us too young. To achieve all this, our ancestors acquired wealth and used it wisely. Witherstonians will acquire wealth too and will have the chance to use it equally wisely."

"You forgot to mention the atomic bomb, Mr. Withers!" shouted Gretchen. "And you forgot to mention DDT and asbestos!"

"And bullets!" shouted Lottie Byrd.

Withers held up one finger. He continued to read. "And now, in the twenty-first century, we—BioSenecta Pharmaceuticals, to be specific—have developed the drug Senextra, the most life-changing achievement for the individual in the history of mankind. Senextra exemplifies our civilization's mission: to control nature for the benefit of humanity. And that is the mission I ask you to carry out.

"For the past five years I have been kept alive and healthy by Senextra. And I thank BioSenecta for the privilege to test Senextra on myself. For the past four years the twenty-three residents of Withers Village, all of whom happily signed on to the FDA-approved pilot study, have also been kept alive and healthy by Senextra. We are grateful to Dr. George Folsom for conducting the pilot study.

"So on my hundredth birthday, I announce the date of our groundbreaking ceremony for a BioSenecta factory on my land in Witherston. It's July 30. I've hired loggers to begin clear-cutting the site on June 15. "

Withers grew more and more enthusiastic. "My mission, my own personal mission, is to give every citizen of the United States the same opportunity for longevity that I have had."

Withers paused for applause. A good number of people clapped.

Withers continued. "Now I will disclose my gift to you. Just last Wednesday, on May 20, 2015, I signed my will—I confess, the only will I have ever made—bequeathing each of you citizens of Witherston an equal portion of $1 billion. I will read to you from my will.

> *"I give and bequeath the sum of ONE BILLION DOLLARS ($1,000,000,000) to the present LEGAL RESIDENTS OF WITHERSTON to be divided equally among them in appreciation of their support of the Senextra factory.*

"I've filed my will at the Dahlonega courthouse, and I've appointed your mayor, Mr. Richard Rather, to be my executor representing both the town of Witherston and the residents of Witherston."

The Witherstonians gathered on the lawn roared with pleasure, or at least two thirds of them did.

A third did not. Gretchen Green held up her hand-made sign: SENEXTRA VIOLATES MOTHER NATURE. Lottie Byrd held up hers: KEEP SENEXTRA OUT OF OUR SYSTEM!

Lottie Byrd was Mev's favorite aunt and her next-door neighbor. She was also Mayor Rather's nemesis. Lottie was fearless in expressing her environmental opinions publicly.

Gretchen, owner of Gretchen Green's Green Grocery and president of Eat Locally, was Lottie's accomplice. Gretchen's rescued Great Dane, whom she'd named Gandhi, was at her side, as usual.

Lottie and Gretchen were the founders and funders of KEEP NATURE NATURAL.

"In addition to the $1 billion I am bequeathing to the citizens of Witherston," Withers hastened to say in his baritone voice, "I've also bequeathed $1 billion to the municipality of Witherston for your support of the Senextra factory. Witherston will become world famous as the home of Senextra."

Cheering erupted: "We love you, Mr. Withers!" and "Bless you, Mr. Withers."

But suddenly other signs popped up: SENEXTRA = SENILITY; DON'T FELL TREES TO BUILD FACTORIES; WE DON'T NEED MORE OLD MEN.

Mev smiled when she saw THIS LAND'S NOT OUR LAND, THIS LAND'S NOT YOUR LAND, THIS LAND IS CHEROKEE LAND. Her Cherokee friend Gregory Bozeman would love it.

Mev watched Withers sit down. He looked old, tired, and confused. The anger she'd always seen on his face returned.

Ignoring the protest, Mayor Rather took the mic and shook Withers's hand. "Thank you, thank you, Mr. Withers, for your extraordinary generosity! Thank you! You are Witherston's gift from God. You are a great American. We will put your wealth to good use. And now it's time to unveil the sculpture that is our tribute to you! Please pull the cord, Mr. Ridge."

Amid the shouting Scorch Ridge moved to the podium, yanked a cord, and unveiled a ten-foot-high Elberton marble statue of a handsome, much younger Withers with his right arm outstretched.

A teenage girl wearing a pink KEEP NATURE NATURAL T-shirt threw an egg at the statue and splattered yoke across the forehead. Other KNN members chanted *"Withers must go!"*

A middle-aged man in a suit and tie yelled, "Eat mud, KNN!"

Another yelled, "Go back underground, you moss lovers!"

Suddenly everybody was yelling something at someone.

Mev chased the egg-thrower into the woods behind the church, while Witherston's three policemen blew their whistles, ordered the crowd to disperse, and arrested one young KNN protester, who went limp when cuffed, forcing two of the three to drag him to their car.

Withers returned to the mic. "What's wrong with you people?" he asked. "I thought you'd be happy. I've given each of you an opportunity to be rich, to do something good for the world. And I've given your town an opportunity to be famous, to advance the mission of civilization."

Someone hollered,"We don't want your drug factory in Witherston!"

Another hollered, "Or your drugs in our bodies!"

"Or your civilization in our nature!"

Withers's demeanor changed. He struck the ground with his

cane. "Whose side are you on, young man? Our great civilization? Or this...this...this *nature*?" He spat out the word "nature" and pointed angrily at the woods behind the church.

"Okay, young man, you *won't* get my drugs." Withers was
yelling into the mic. "You won't get a Senextra factory here to
make Witherston prosperous. I'll change my will. You'll have
your wish. But you won't have your precious nature. I will log
every tree in my woods. I will clear-cut my land, the thirty-one
acres on the creek and the forty acres where my house stands.
It's my land! Mine! To use as I please. It's not your land! And
it's not the damned Cherokees' land!"

Withers seemed to lose control. He punctuated his remarks
with his raised cane. "And you won't get my money! I will
change my will. I will change my will immediately. Not a one
of you Witherstonians will ever see a penny of my fortune.
You have destroyed Witherston's future."

Mayor Rather grabbed the microphone. He was beside himself with fury. "You protesters have killed Witherston!" he
bellowed. "You want to keep nature natural? You want to keep
Witherston in the nineteenth century? You want to live like
Indians, padding through the woods in moccasins, paddling up
the creek in canoes? You want a life span of thirty years?
Without modern medicine? Well, that's where you're taking
us!"

Withers descended the stairs leaning heavily on his cane,
walked slowly down to Hickory Street, climbed into the driver's seat of his long black Chrysler, and drove away. Harry, his
Chow Chow, peered out the back window.

ꙮꙮ

"God damn it. This can't be happening!" said George Folsom, Withers's doctor. "Damn it, damn it, damn it! How can
those aging hippies defeat an idea whose time has come?
Won't someone stop them? Won't someone stop Withers? We
can't let him change his will! Not now, not ever!"

"Those aging hippies won't defeat anything," said Grant
Griggs, Withers's lawyer. George and Grant were watching the
police disperse the crowd. "They are on the wrong side of his-

tory, the wrong side of the law, and the wrong side of God. They are blocking our town's progress, depriving us of prosperity. Trust me, they won't escape punishment for their actions."

"What do you think Withers will do?"

"Probably change his will, like he said. He's a cantankerous, stubborn old man, Harvard-educated and intelligent but stubborn, and motivated by one hundred years of resentment."

"You've got to talk him out of it, Grant. Witherston's future and your future and mine depend upon the execution of his will, this will, the will you wrote for him."

"Trust me, George. This will will be Withers's only will.

ε⁄ͻε⁄ͻ

Professor Charlotte Byrd—Lottie to her friends and relatives—saw George huddle with Grant. She discerned their distress, and she felt their rage against the KNN protesters, Gretchen, and her. Their rage was not new. Like some other folks of her acquaintance, George and Grant viewed environmentalism as an attack on capitalism and hence on their way of life. For them it was either/or. Either capitalism or environmentalism. Either cars or trees. Either Christianity or atheism. Never neither. Never both. Never anything in between.

Why did some people, like George and Grant, get so angry at advocates for a clean environment? They needed a clean environment for their health just as much as the environmentalists needed it for theirs. But with an either/or outlook, the anti-environmentalists saw the world as a zero-sum game in which humans and Earth were in competition. They must be afraid that advocates for a human-friendly Earth might take away their stuff.

Well, how well would they do without a human-friendly Earth?

Lottie was aware of what George and Grant thought of her. Behind her back they called her Hickory Nut. She took it as a compliment. She loved hickory trees, especially when their leaves turned bright gold in October. Hickories surrounded her house.

Lottie thought back on the afternoon. Withers too seemed full of anger and fear. That was odd. What did that billionaire have to fear? Not poverty. Not starvation. Not homelessness. Not loss of health insurance. Not unemployment—he'd never been employed but he'd never needed to be.

Not loss of an only child gone off to war. Not the everlasting pain a child's death inflicted upon his parent, and the guilt over things said and unsaid. Lottie feared nothing. At the age of sixty-four she'd probably never fear anything again. She'd already faced what she'd feared the most. She'd already lost what she'd loved the most.

Evidently Withers had not. So what could he fear? From Lottie's perspective, Withers was standing atop a pyramid of assets and power obtained at the expense of others. He possessed more than his share of Earth's bounty. Did he feel guilt? He should. He probably did. His billions protected him from want but not from guilt. Had he wanted to assuage that guilt today? Or had he wanted to extend his power beyond his death?

Lottie knew Georgia's past. She knew that the wealth Withers had offered Witherstonians had been built upon a theft. A theft committed by her state against the Cherokees less than two hundred years ago.

But then, wasn't much private wealth in these parts built upon original thefts? Thefts of land and gold from the Cherokees and labor from the Africans. Lottie knew about these thefts. She was an historian of the South.

Lottie was suddenly sure that Withers's anger arose from guilt, guilt he'd inherited with his wealth, guilt that the land he owned had been stolen, that the gold that was the source of his wealth had been stolen. And the guilt was accompanied by fear, fear that the injustice his forebears had perpetrated would be avenged.

❧❧❧

Gretchen put down her sign and leaned against a church pillar. She felt she'd been protesting all her life. She'd held her first sign—MAKE LOVE NOT WAR—in a demonstration against the Vietnam War with her mother when she was eight, after her father, Sergeant Keith Hall, had been killed in the battle of Khe Sanh on January 31, 1968. She'd never forget the arrival of the Army officers at their home in Fort Benning to inform her mother of his death. The officers' refusal to provide details turned her mother against the war. Her mother, whom Gretchen had always called Ann, got a job in a Columbus book store, read everything she could about the war, and taught Gretchen a life lesson: that the powerful will always act to perpetuate their power.

On April 22, 1970, her tenth birthday, Gretchen and her mother went to Athens for the first Earth Day celebration. Gretchen learned from the teach-ins at the University of Georgia that humans were polluting the planet and upsetting the balance of nature. When she returned to Columbus she told her friends she'd become an environmentalist.

In 1973, Gretchen demonstrated with her mother in favor of the Equal Rights Amendment in Atlanta. When she returned to Columbus she told her friends she'd become an eco-feminist.

She remembered a conversation her mother had with her Uncle Hodge over the dinner table one evening.

Uncle Hodge asked her mother, "Well, Rachel, if you favor the ERA you must think that women are superior to men."

Her mother had answered sweetly, "No."

"Then you admit that men are superior to women."

"No, just different."

"Then if men and women are different from each other," Uncle Hodge asked impatiently, "who is superior?"

As a teenager, Gretchen realized that some folks, like her Uncle Hodge, ranked everything. They thought that if you were different from someone you were either superior or inferior. And if you were the superior one, you got to dominate the inferior one. Eventually she saw that humans mistreated Earth out of their assumption of superiority to other species.

In 1981, the same year her mother died of lung cancer, probably from smoking, Gretchen had married Smithfield Green, whom she'd met in a journalism class at the University of Georgia. Her love for him was born in loneliness but was nonetheless real, for a while. When Smitty got the offer to edit the *Witherston Weekly*, Witherston's short-lived print newspaper, she and Smitty came to Witherston, where they'd stayed, but not with each other. They divorced amicably the next year, and Smitty had remarried. Gretchen had not, and she'd never quite buried her sadness over not having borne a child.

"A dollar for your thoughts," said Martin Payne.

"Hello," Gretchen said, surprised that the good-looking CEO of BioSenecta had approached her.

"I am Martin Payne, of BioSenecta," Payne said. "I noticed you among the protesters."

"I'm Gretchen Green. What did you think of my sign?" she asked him.

"What did you mean by nature?" Payne responded.

 espero

Dr. Neel Kingfisher headed up the Witherston Highway on foot. He had walked the two miles from Withers Village to the church, and he would walk back. He thought about Withers's speech.

Neel couldn't dispute Withers's argument that Western civilization had exceeded his own civilization in its lasting achievements. His own civilization had not produced symphonies or cathedrals or novels. But was Withers's civilization inherently superior to his? What did superiority mean, anyway? Did the achievements of Withers's civilization give it the right to dominate all other civilizations?

Withers had mocked the Cherokee civilization's ten thousand years of living in the woods and not leaving their mark upon the land. But the woods had lasted ten thousand years. Was that not an achievement of his people? They'd sustained their culture—their way of life, their care for each other, their reverence for nature, and their environment—for ten thousand years. Was that not worthy of respect?

Withers's people no longer intimidated the Cherokee with bullets. They no longer considered the Cherokee an enemy. Instead, Withers's people absorbed the Cherokee into their midst and instilled in them their Western values.

Withers's people had conquered the Cherokee by integration, assimilation, conversion. Just as they'd conquered nature, by converting land into asphalt and steel, and drugs. Withers's people's lifestyle would destroy the planet for everybody. Their lifestyle was not sustainable. The human species would go extinct, because humans would foul the nature that supported them. Humans would then become one, once again, with the valleys and the rivers, the seas and the deserts, the soil, the rocks, the clouds, and the vegetation as their bones disintegrated, fossilized, vaporized. Their civilization's achievements—the symphonies, the cathedrals, the novels—would vanish in the cycles of time.

Contemplating Earth's future, Neel felt no sorrow.

Earth would survive, because Earth did not exist for humans. Ten thousand years from now, a hundred thousand years from now, a million years from now, who would populate the planet? Not humans.

Neel was lonely. He had acquired education in philosophy and training in medicine. He was successful by Western civilization's measure of success: money. But he'd lost all that he'd ever loved. Perhaps that was why he pondered the crime Withers's forefathers had committed against his people.

Perhaps that was why he contemplated revenge.

༚༝༚

Now off-duty, Mev wandered through the crowd in search of her family. A light rain was falling on the uneaten green beans, the untouched cakes. She wanted to be with her husband and children. Late yesterday she'd gone to see her doctor, Jim Lodge, her gynecologist and obstetrician, to examine the lump she'd found in her left breast. With obvious distress, Jim told her she likely had breast cancer.

His office made an appointment for her to see a Gainesville physician on Tuesday.

Jim, one of the few African Americans in Witherston, was the beloved husband of Lumpkin County probate judge Lauren Lodge, Mev's best friend. Their handsome son Beau, who resembled his dark-skinned father more than his blonde mother, was Mev's fourteen-year-old twins' best friend.

Mev found her boys Jaime and Jorge and her husband Paco
drinking cokes with Jon and Gregory in rocking chairs on the
porch of Scissors.

Jon Finley, a cosmetologist, and Gregory Bozeman, an
ecologist retired from the Environmental Protection Agency in
Athens, owned the hair salon.

They'd been life partners for sixteen years. Renoir, their
white Standard Poodle, lay on the bench.

Jon and Gregory were not fans of Francis Hearty Withers,
nor was Paco. Nor were Jaime and Jorge, who had turned into
environmental activists under the influence of her Aunt Lottie.
Jorge was wearing his green KEEP NATURE NATURAL T-
shirt.

"Would you like a coke?" Gregory asked, getting out of his
rocking chair.

"Thanks so much, Gregory," she replied, "but I'm all tuckered out and I need to take my family home to dinner. We'll
see you all soon." She felt tuckered out indeed.

As they walked home, Mev commented: "I bet old Mr.
Withers will be dead by Tuesday."

"Mom!" said Jaime. "Why do you say that? He looks like
he works out. He's healthy!"

"Unfortunately," muttered Jorge.

"Because," Mev continued, "he can't change his will till
Tuesday, since Monday is Memorial Day. If he dies before he
changes his will, the 4,000 residents of Witherston will inherit
more money than they've ever seen in one place. About
$250,000 each. If he dies after he changes his will, nobody
here will get anything."

"I don't care," Jorge said. "I don't want a Senextra factory
on Founding Father's Creek."

"Me neither," Jaime said.

ᏮᏮᏮ

Francis Hearty Withers opened the carved mahogany door
reluctantly.

"I thought you might show up tonight," he said to his visitor.

"Hello, Mr. Withers. I know how distressed you are. Let's talk. Talking will make you feel better."

"I don't want to feel better. Or to talk. Now's not a good time for you to pay me a visit. Not a professional visit, not a personal visit. I want to be alone."

"Very well. I'll be back tomorrow."

After shutting the door Francis Hearty Withers uncorked a bottle of 2011 Syrah from Terry Hoage Vineyards to eat with the perfectly broiled steak the maid set before him. He ate in silence, as he had for decades. He used the time to think.

After dinner he went upstairs to his bedroom, sat down at his computer, and began to compose a new will. He wrote:

> *I, Francis Hearty Withers, wish to rescind my will of May 20, 2015. Instead of bequeathing the amount of $1,000,000,000 to the citizens of Witherston, I would like every penny of my estate to go to—*

Then his phone rang. He answered it.

"Mr. Withers, this is Abby Ridge. Are you still up? I've made a rhubarb pie for you. May I bring it now?"

"Yes, Mrs. Ridge. I'm still up."

He went downstairs and sat in his favorite chair. In a few minutes the maid showed Abby into the living room, took the pie she'd brought to the kitchen, and then disappeared up the staircase. "You saw those environmentalists insult me, Mrs. Ridge. You did, didn't you?"

"Yes, Mr. Withers."

"You were there for the whole riot?"

"Yes, I was there for all of it. I felt bad for you. That's why I baked you the pie."

"I have lived on this hill my entire life. My great grandfather founded this town. I deserve respect. I got none today."

"I'm sorry, Mr. Withers."

"I'd planned to give a lot of money to Witherston. A lot. I'd planned to give a lot of money to every one of you residents of Witherston. I wanted to make Witherston famous as the home of Senextra. My father thought I'd never do anything important in my life. But he was mistaken. He underestimated me. I made more money than he did, and he was pretty wealthy. I was going to give it away to you people, to be remembered in history for my generosity. Now I won't."

"Mr. Withers, most of us respect you very much. Only a few carried signs today."

"Enough to make me a laughing stock. I won't be an object of ridicule for ungrateful people. I'm changing my will. I'm leaving everything to BioSenecta for a foundation in my name. BioSenecta will get my money, and they can do with it what they will. Let Witherston watch."

☙☙☙

Back in his study at Withers Village, Dr. Neel Kingfisher wrote in his journal:

> *What should I have expected? That Mr. Francis Hearty Withers would change his view of the Cherokees after one hundred years of contempt for my people? He speaks of advancing the mission of civilization. Civilization to Mr. Francis Hearty Withers means HIS civilization, as if there were no other. And what is the mission of his civilization?*
>
> *To judge by its achievements—the automobile, the plane, the computer, and drugs like Senextra—I say it's to engineer nature for the benefit of humans. Engineer nature. For humans. And what is the goal? To control all of nature, as he sees it. Well, imagine taking on that responsibility! The Cherokee civilization, and I will always call it a civilization, had no such ambition. I guess that's why we were defeated by Mr. Francis Hearty Withers's civilization.*
>
> *Mr. Francis Hearty Withers assumes there's only one right way to live, his own; only one right way to think, his own; only one right culture, his own. Is there no room on this planet for multiple ways of living, multiple ways of thinking?*

*Mr. Francis Hearty Withers does not deserve a
long life.*

❦❦❦

That night after the boys had gone to bed, Mev told Paco
about her visit with Jim. They held each other for a long time.
"*Te quiero más que nunca*," Paco said. "I love you more
than ever. We'll get through this together. And we'll tell the
boys tomorrow morning."

WITHERSTON ON THE WEB
Saturday, May 23, 2015

LOCAL NEWS

Yesterday, at 4:45 pm, in front of Witherston Baptist Church, a riot erupted that probably determined the course of Witherston's future.

At the public celebration of his hundredth birthday, local billionaire Francis Hearty Withers disclosed the contents of his will to a crowd of three hundred gathered in front of Witherston Baptist Church. Mr. Withers announced that he was bequeathing $1 billion to the present residents of Witherston, to be divided equally.

When he mentioned BioSenecta's proposal to build a Senextra factory just north of Witherston, teenage members of the environmentalist group KEEP NATURE NATURAL protested. Some threw eggs and others shouted insults at Mr. Witherston.

Mr. Withers, who appeared surprised by the demonstration, then declared he would change his will to disinherit the Witherston community. He also said that he would clear-cut the 31.7 acres he had planned for the Senextra factory.

~ Catherine Perry, Reporter

ON THIS DAY IN HISTORY
By Charlotte Byrd

On May 23, 1932, Hearty Harold Withers purchased 100,000 shares of Lawrence Company stock at $3.80 a share, when the share price was at an all-time low. HaHa Withers, as he was called, became majority shareholder in the company *and at his death in 1960 bequeathed his stock to his son Francis Hearty Withers.*

When the Lawrence Company became BioSenecta Pharmaceuticals in 2002, it was already a multi-national corporation. Francis Hearty Withers continued to buy shares of Bio-Senecta to maintain his position of majority shareholder.

We may speculate that his stock in BioSenecta motivated Withers to arrange for the men at Withers Village Retirement Community to participate in Senextra's pilot study.

POLICE BLOTTER

Witherston Police arrested Thom Rivers, age 18, at 5:30 pm yesterday after a demonstration against BioSenecta Pharmaceuticals in front of Witherston Baptist Church. Police accused Rivers, a member of the environmentalist organization KEEP NATURE NATURAL, of placing an I AM A DIRTWORSHIPPER bumper sticker on the blue BMW convertible of Dr. Martin Payne, CEO of BioSenecta.

Dr. Payne, invited to Witherston by Mayor Rich Rather, was attending Francis Hearty Withers's birthday party, at which Withers announced his intention to build a BioSenecta plant in Witherston.

Rivers was charged with defacing private property and fined $50.

Witherston Police arrested four inebriated under-age Witherston High School students for drinking White Russians last night on Founding Father's Bridge. A White Russian is a cocktail made of vodka, Kahlua, and cream. The girls said they were celebrating the end of the school year and weren't aware of the alcoholic content of the drink. They were fined $50 each and released.

CHAPTER 2

Saturday, May 23, 2015:

Every morning before the rest of her family came down to breakfast, Mev got her news on her tablet. She read the *Atlanta Journal-Constitution* at AJC.COM; the *Dahlonega Nugget* at THEDAHLONEGANUGGET. COM; and Witherston's news source, *Witherston on the Web*, edited by her friend Smitty Green, at ONLINEWITHERSTON.COM.

Over coffee Mev reread carefully Catherine Perry's brief account of Withers's public birthday party and promptly called Lauren.

"Good morning, Lauren! Have you seen *Webby Witherston* today?"

"I have, Mev, and I paid particular attention to Catherine's report that Withers plans to disinherit us. Darn!" Lauren laughed.

"As probate judge, Lauren, would you say that Withers invalidated his present will when he declared he'd, quote, change his will to disinherit the Witherston community, unquote?

"You mean, if he dies before he finalizes a new will?"

"Yes."

"I'll have to get back to you on that, Mev. But I'm inclined to think not. What we have is only a newspaper account of an oral declaration. Are you thinking he'll die soon?"

"It could happen, Lauren. He just gave every resident of Witherston a motive for murder."

இை

"*Hijos,*" Paco said, as Jorge and Jaime sat down to the orange juice, scrambled eggs, and toast Mev had prepared for their breakfast. "Your mother and I have something serious to tell you."

Then Mev told them that she'd found a lump in her left breast, that she'd consulted Dr. Lodge who said it was in all probability malignant, and that she'd find out more on Tuesday when she'd have some tests at the Northeast Georgia Medical Center in Gainesville.

Paco told them the recovery rate for breast cancer was excellent these days.

There were questions, tears, hugs.

"We're here for you, Mom," said Jaime.

"We'll take care of you," said Jorge. "We'll be good boys."

"You all are always good boys," said Mev. "Now let's go swimming."

e/ɔe/ɔ

"Grant. This is Francis Hearty Withers calling."

"Hello, Mr. Withers. How are you today?"

"Not happy, if that's what you are asking. I want to change my will as soon as possible."

"Of course, Mr. Withers. We can do it on Tuesday. Would you like to come to my office Tuesday morning?"

"Can't you do it right now? I can tell you how I want to change it. It's simple."

"How would you like to change it, Mr. Withers?"

"I'd like to remove my $1 billion bequests to Witherston and to Witherstonians. Instead, I would like to establish a Withers Foundation at BioSenecta. Can you do it today?"

"Well, no. No, I can't, Mr. Withers. No, I can't. I can't do anything until Tuesday. How about coming to my office Tuesday morning at 11:00? I will have a draft of a new will to show you then."

"Okay. But I'm working on a new will myself. I will show it to you on Tuesday."

e/ɔe/ɔ

"Mayor Rather? This is Francis Hearty Withers calling."

"Hello, Mr. Withers! Great to hear from you! How are you doing today?"

"Not well, obviously, Mr. Mayor. I was publicly humiliated yesterday by your Witherstonians, whom you did not control. I am changing my will. I won't be leaving anything to Witherston. And I won't be building a Senextra factory in this town."

"Oh, Mr. Withers! You don't really want to do that! Don't you want to live on in the minds of your fellow Witherstonians as our town's most generous benefactor?"

"I want to live on in my own flesh, Mr. Mayor! And thanks to Senextra, I can."

ფფ

"George? This is Francis Hearty Withers calling."

"How are you, Mr. Withers?"

"Not happy, George. I've called you to tell you that I'm changing my will on Tuesday. I'm not putting up a Senextra factory here."

"Don't act so quickly, Mr. Withers! Don't do anything in haste. You should take time to think this through."

"I've had enough time, George. And you've already gotten enough from me. And from BioSenecta."

ფფ

"Martin? This is Francis Hearty Withers. I called to tell you that I'm revising my will."

"What will you change, Mr. Withers?"

"You'll see."

ფფ

"Rich? Martin Payne here. What's going on up there?"

"Mr. Withers is rescinding his will. Says he won't be building the Senextra factory in Witherston. This is a terrible turn of events. Just terrible."

"Can you change his mind?"

"I'll do what I can. What I can. Witherston's future is at stake."

"So is Senextra's future, Rich. And BioSenecta's future. Withers was funding the pilot study at Withers Village."

"I'll do what I can, Martin."

"So will I."

❧❧❧

Lottie entered Gretchen Green's Green Grocery with her blue Pacific parrotlet Darwin perched on her left shoulder. "Good morning, Gretchen!" Lottie greeted her friend and patted Gandhi, who jumped up to give her a juicy kiss on the mouth and sent Darwin flying.

"I came to join you for lunch," Lottie said, returning Darwin to her shoulder. "I made us a potato salad with smoked trout. We can have some of your fruit for dessert. What do you think?"

"Good morning, Darwin! And good idea, Lottie! I love your nice surprises."

Gretchen put placemats, plates, forks, and bottles of water on the small table at the back of her store. The two women sat down to eat.

Gandhi settled himself by Gretchen's feet.

"We've got to stop old Withers from clear-cutting his land," said Lottie. "As the founding mothers of KEEP NATURE NATURAL we have to protest. Got any ideas?"

Gretchen had ideas to spare. "Let's protest so loudly that we make preservation of old-growth forests a cause for environmentalists everywhere. Let's put up billboards all over north Georgia asking 'Which do you prefer: old-growth forests or old-growth men?' We could have a picture of Withers's forest on one half of the billboard and a picture of Withers's face the other half!"

"Whoa, Gretchen! I didn't mean to get you started…"

"And on KEEP NATURE NATURAL's Facebook page we could let people vote. I'll bet 'old-growth forests' would beat 'old growth men' by a landslide!"

"Gretchen!"

"And we could make a YouTube video with the first half showing Withers screaming 'I will clear-cut my land' and the second half showing his forested land with squirrels jumping from tree to tree and birds singing on the branches. I'll bet we could find a doe with her fawn to star in the video."

"Gretchen!"

"And we could get FM radio stations in Dahlonega and Gainesville and Athens to play clips of birds chirping followed by Withers ranting."

"Gretchen!"

"I'm so glad you dropped by, Lottie! Let's do it!"

"Gretchen! Think about this seriously. We need to persuade Withers to our way of thinking, and we won't succeed if we make fun of his way of thinking."

"Okay. I'll try to think like the geezer."

"Be serious, Gretchen."

"Okay. Withers believes he can do what he wants with property he owns. And he's paid taxes yearly on the 31.7 acres. He believes that ownership of the land means ownership of the trees on the land, and that ownership of the trees gives him the right to sell the trees as logs. So he thinks he has the right to clear-cut the forest. He believes that anybody who tells him what to do with his property is violating his freedom."

"Right," said Lottie. "So what's our position?"

"We believe that land is not just a flat piece of soil with trees and bushes on top. It's an ecosystem, and it's a home for squirrels and deer and birds and bees and worms. It's selfish of humans to take away other critters' homes."

"That argument, Gretchen, is not effective against the argument that humans are special."

"Okay." Gretchen thought a moment. "So we'll have to show that we humans must preserve the forest for our own survival."

"That's the only argument I think would work. Withers is promoting Senextra to help humans have longer healthy lives. We have to show him that preserving our natural environment will help humans have longer healthy lives without drugs."

"Do you think we can get our KEEP NATURE NATURAL kids behind that argument?"

"I do."

ɔ⌒ɔ⌒ɔ

At 3:30 Annie Jerden called the meeting of KEEP NA-TURE NATURAL to order at their usual meeting place, on the east bank of Founding Father's Creek at the west end of Hickory Street. Present were Thom Rivers, Sally Sorensen, Jorge Arroyo, Jaime Arroyo, Beau Lodge, Mona Pattison, and Christopher Zurich. They were all wearing KNN T-shirts of different colors, some of them cleaner than others.

Absent were the group's two behind-the-scenes sponsors Charlotte Byrd and Gretchen Green.

"I called this emergency meeting of KEEP NATURE NATURAL to see how we can stop Francis Hearty Withers from clear-cutting his woods," said Annie, president of the small group of teen-age environmentalists.

"We sure made our point yesterday!" Sally said, laughing.

"You have good aim, Sally! Your egg smacked that statue right between the eyes," said Thom.

"I wish I'd hit him in the mouth. The statue of him, I mean."

"I think the old man took it personally."

Jaime and Jorge were quiet.

"Do you think our actions made the situation worse?" Beau said. "We got Mr. Withers mad, and now he's going to clear-cut his land just to spite us."

"We had to protest," said Christopher. "If we hadn't protested yesterday, we'd be getting the Senextra factory here this summer!"

"Beau," said Annie. "You've asked a good question. A few minutes ago I got a text message from Miss Charlotte. I'll read it:

> "Annie, please persuade your fellow KNN members that you can catch more flies with honey than with vinegar. Gretchen and I suggest that KNN write

letters to Webby Witherston showing how forests are good for the health of humans. Try to inform your opponents rather than beat them up for their ignorance. Good luck. Charlotte."

"What did you text back to Aunt Lottie?" asked Jaime. "I texted her this message:

"Dear Miss Charlotte. You seem to be a wise lady. I will try. We are all good writers. We are all A students. But we are passionate. And we like to make signs. Thank you for your advice. Sincerely, Annie."

Jorge held up his hand. "Some of us could make signs, and others could write letters to *Webby Witherston*. I want to write a letter."

"I want to make a sign," said Mona. "I can draw. I'll draw pictures of Mr. Withers's forest."

"Where will we put the signs?"

"On all the street corners of Witherston," said Thom.

"But the signs have to be like honey and not vinegar," said Beau.

"No. No censorship," said Thom. "Not from Miss Charlotte, not from our parents, not from the fat mayor. With all due respect to your influential aunt, Jaime and Jorge, I say that the old should not control the young. And the young, like us, need to do what we think is right, not what the old tell us is right."

"Let's make the signs funny," Jorge said. "Like a picture of a squirrel running away from a chain saw."

"That's not funny, Jorge," Jaime said.

Annie stepped into the discussion. "Let's everybody do what they think is right."

"And if we get arrested, so much the better," Thom said. "I've been arrested before, lots of times. It's no big deal. This is my last summer in Witherston, so I want to make it count."

∽∾∽

With their boys gone to the KNN meeting, Mev and Paco sat together quietly on the back porch of their hundred-year-old, two-story red brick house. Here they could listen to the wind whistle through the pines and watch the squirrels eat seed from the birdfeeder.

"We have a good life, Paco," Mev said. "I don't want anything to ruin it."

"Nothing's going to ruin it, Mevita! We're together. We love each other."

"I'm afraid I'll lose my breast."

"You probably won't. But I really don't care how many breasts you have, if any," Paco responded. "I didn't marry you for your breasts. I married you for your *corazón*. Your heart." And then he added, "and for your *huevos revueltos*." Scrambled eggs.

He made her laugh, no matter how dire the situation.

"And if I lose my hair?"

"I'll shave my head, and we'll both look pretty. *No hay problema.*"

"What will Jorge and Jaime think if I lose my hair? I don't want to embarrass them in front of their friends."

"They'll shave their heads too. Listen, *guapa*, you can't worry about your hair when you're busy getting well. Besides, there's no shame in having breast cancer."

"I remember my grandmother whispering about a neighbor who had breast cancer. My grandmother never called her, never asked her if she needed help, never went over there. My grandmother acted as if Mrs. Rickle had done something awful. I once asked my grandmother, 'Wouldn't Mrs. Rickle like some company if she's sick?' My grandmother said, 'No. She doesn't need any company. She doesn't need to be talking about her cancer to other people. And I don't want to embarrass her by mentioning her situation.' Paco, that's what can happen to me. People may be afraid to talk to me if they know I have cancer."

"Mevita, your grandmother is dead, so you don't need to think about her any more. And she was probably just expressing her own fear of cancer. Anyway, times have changed. I say, be open and honest about whatever is happening to you.

That way other people won't feel that they have to hide any illnesses they have."

"Well, that's what I'll have to do. I work for the Witherston Police Department, and I have to do my job in public. So I can't really hide my condition, whatever it is."

"*Querida*, you will be a model for others. You always have been."

"I love you, Paco."

"*Te quiero mucho*, Mevita."

୧∕୬ଫ∕୬

Dr. Neel Kingfisher sat on his favorite bench by Withers Village Pond. It was 4:00 pm. He threw a few sticks into the water for Swift to retrieve. Swift, his five-year-old white German Shepherd, was his companion and his best friend, actually his only friend.

Neel turned to his journal:

Why did I leave Oklahoma? I had to leave. I could not stay where every aspect of my life reminded me of what I'd lost. I had to leave to forget. Yet I'll never forget.

I have to think about the bigger picture, in which my pain is minor.

I left Oklahoma, where I belong, to come to north Georgia, where I don't belong, but where I should belong, for my Cherokee ancestors' blood reddened Georgia soil. This is the land of my Cherokee ancestors, or rather this was the land of my Cherokee ancestors before Governor Wilson Lumpkin took it from the Cherokees, gave it to white settlers in the Georgia Land Lottery, and banished the Cherokees, or most of them, to Oklahoma. In 1838, every one of the 16,000 Cherokees forced to march a thousand miles suffered mightily, at least as much as I suffer now. 4,000 of them died.

That was 180 years ago, when Hearty Withers

got rich from Cherokee gold and land and passed his wealth down through four generations of descendants. But not to me, his great, great, great grandson.

I did not inherit Withers wealth.

Why did I come here—to the land where my great grandfather, Witty Withers, disinherited my grandmother? Just because she loved a Cherokee, Mohe Kingfisher, my grandfather. Did I want to feel the pain she felt, when she had to choose between her father and her husband, between her father's civilization and her husband's? My grandmother, Penance Louise, made her choice in 1930. I've heard the story again and again, from my Cherokee aunts and uncles, from my Cherokee parents.

Penance Louise Withers did not inherit the Withers family's wealth.

Mr. Francis Hearty Withers did. And he inherited the Withers family's contempt for Cherokees.

And I, Mr. Francis Hearty Withers's first cousin once removed, inherited my grandmother's pain, her hatred of the Withers family, her outrage at the Withers family's racism. But I also inherited my grandfather's Cherokee pride. I hope I inherited my grandfather's Cherokee wisdom.

Yes, I took this job as director of Withers Village to understand what my grandmother had rejected. And now I do understand it. She rejected not just an inheritance but a vision of the world, the vision of the world that Mr. Francis Hearty Withers expressed yesterday, when he celebrated one hundred years of a life of luxury on stolen soil.

I must admit it. I want revenge. I want to show the Withers of the world what they lost when they destroyed the Cherokee nation.

∽∾∽

"Come in, come in. I was expecting you."

"Good afternoon, Mr. Withers."

Francis Hearty Withers ushered his visitor into the living room.

"It's 6:00," he said. "I've just finished supper. Would you like a glass of wine? Then I'll tell you why I am changing my will."

"Let's talk about it, Mr. Withers."

の

I never dreamed that murdering Withers would be so easy. Do I feel bad? Not very. Well, perhaps a little. Withers trusted me. He invited me into his home. He gave me a glass of his fine wine. I offered a toast to the future of BioSenecta. He raised his glass, clicked mine, and drank. How I despised him.

I killed him, exactly as I'd planned. He died quickly. I watched him fall to the floor.

I should have killed his dog while I was at it. The dog bit my leg.

Just hours ago I was a moral person, a church person, re-spected by the community, or at least by the people who mat-tered. I was what you'd call upstanding. Little did they know.

Now I am a murderer, a killer. I have defined myself for the rest of my life as a murderer, a killer. But I didn't kill Withers for his money. I killed him for a good cause. If I'm ever put on trial for this crime, I will tell the jury that I killed one man for the benefit of many. Withers will do more good in death than he ever did in life. He'll become the benefactor he promised to be.

That's why I don't feel guilty.

I knew I was capable of murder. I tried to kill somebody when I lived in Savannah, for a good cause. But I failed.

Is everyone capable of murder? When I look at other hu-man beings, I will always wonder whether they too are capa-ble of murder.

Will I kill again, now that I know I can? It was so easy. Revenge is sweet.

WWW.ONLINEWITHERSTON.COM

WITHERSTON ON THE WEB
Sunday, May 24, 2015

EDITORIAL

Historically peaceful Witherston has become divided in the last few days over the prospect of a Senextra factory here. Witherstonians who witnessed the anti-BioSenecta protest on Friday need to know more about BioSenecta Pharmaceuticals.

BioSenecta Pharmaceuticals is a multi-national corporation headquartered in Atlanta with research facilities located in Atlanta, Chicago, Dallas, and Los Angeles. It has branch offices in London, Paris, Mumbai, Shanghai, Tokyo, and Beijing.

BioSenecta emerged out of the Lawrence Company, which was founded in 1901 as a manufacturer of skin care products. In the first seven decades of its existence, the Lawrence Company increased in size until its revenues exceeded those of Proctor and Gamble. In 1980 Lawrence opened a division of pharmaceutical research aimed at developing anti-aging products.

By the time Lawrence Company became BioSenecta Pharmaceuticals in 2002, the stock had split six times and a share was worth $118. The stock split again in 2011, and today a share is worth $84.

When Lawrence became BioSenecta, our own Francis Hearty Withers joined its board of directors. In 2010, BioSenecta developed the anti-aging drug Senextra, which Mr. Withers, at the age of ninety-five, requested permission to begin taking.

In 2011, BioSenecta initiated a five-year FDA-approved pilot study on the residents of Withers Village. All twenty-three of them signed consent forms.

Mayor Rich Rather and many of Witherston's business leaders support construction of the Senextra factory because of the economic prosperity it would bring to our community. The local environmentalist organization KEEP NATURE NATU-RAL claims that the factory would pollute our natural environment. Some of them oppose Senextra itself for prolonging life unnaturally.

~ Smitty Green, Editor

LETTERS TO THE EDITOR

To the Editor:

Let us have a huge celebration on June 15, the day Francis Hearty Withers clears his land for the Senextra factory. I invite anybody willing to join a Celebration Planning Committee to come to Fellowship Hall in the Witherston Baptist Church at 10:00 a.m. on Saturday, May 30. We will have coffee and doughnuts.

~ Signed, Ruth Griggs

To the Editor:

Witherstonians who love trees should know that within a month Francis Hearty Withers will log 31.7 acres of old-growth forest to build a BioSenecta Pharmaceuticals plant to make Senextra.

BioSenecta will kill healthy 300-year-old trees to keep alive 100-year-old humans long past their ability to work. Think of the significance of this choice, folks!

We humans are destroying our natural habitat to keep ourselves alive artificially. Is it our destiny to use all of nature for the benefit of us humans?

Remember: Forests are not trees alone. Forests are ecosystems with multitudinous plants and animals living together symbiotically.

Aren't we humans being selfish if we convert all these plants and animals into pills for our medicine cabinet?
   ~ Signed, Gretchen Green

ON THIS DAY IN HISTORY
By Charlotte Byrd

According to Witherston courthouse records, on May 24, 1857, Harold Francis Withers, known as "Harry," and his wife Patience Gray Withers gave the name of Founding Father's Creek to the stream that flowed on the east side of their forty-acre lot. The Cherokees had called it Saloli Creek. Harry wanted to honor Abraham Baldwin, a delegate to the Constitutional Convention from Georgia and the first president of the University of Georgia. Harry had briefly attended UGA. Harry was the great grandfather of Francis Hearty Withers.

POLICE BLOTTER

An officer arrested a seventeen-year-old man at the corner of Main Street and Creek Street at 10:15 pm on May 23, for underage intoxication. The young man, wearing a chicken suit, said to him, "Eat my eggs, cop!" When taken to jail the juvenile apologized for his behavior, Witherston Police said.

CHAPTER 3

Sunday morning, May 24, 2015:

"Oh, my God! I can't believe it! Yes, I can believe it! I predicted it!" Mev held her cell phone to her ear and listened intently. "I'll be there in twenty minutes."

It was shortly after 9:00 a.m. on Sunday. Mev and Paco were still eating breakfast, and the boys were still sleeping. They had planned to spend the day at Tallulah Falls.

"Withers is dead," Mev exclaimed. "I knew it! I knew he was a corpse the moment he said he'd revoke his will. His housekeeper, Amy Woods, found his body this morning."

"*¡Caramba! ¿Fue asesinado?* You think he was killed?" Paco asked.

Although he had not learned English until he'd left Madrid to join Mev in Georgia, Paco spoke English well. He'd earned his Master's degree at the University of Georgia and was now teaching biology at Witherston High. Mev, with her degree in criminal justice from UGA, held the rank of Detective in the Witherston Police Department.

Mev and Paco tried to speak both Spanish and English at home, but the longer they stayed in Witherston the more they spoke English together. Jaime and Jorge felt more comfortable in English.

"Yes. It seems obvious to me. Now I have to go to that old coot's mansion and look at his body."

"What a delight," Paco said.

Mev loved Paco's accent. She kissed him.

"Don't take his clothes off," Paco advised.

"You all hike without me. I'll probably be stuck with Withers for a few hours. If there's even the most minimal evidence that he did not die of natural causes, I'll start an investigation."

"*Adiós, guapa.*"

"I'll call Lauren, since she'll have to probate the will. Maybe she's free for lunch." Mev kissed Paco good-bye.

Probate Court was in Dahlonega, but Lauren and Jim made their home in Witherston. They loved the small community spirit.

തൈൻ

Pastor Paul Clement greeted his parishioners as they entered Witherston Baptist Church.

"Hello, Grant and Ruth. How are you today?"

"Fine, thank you, Pastor Clement. I look forward to talking with you after church in Fellowship Hall," replied Grant.

"Good morning, George. Good morning, Faith. Faith, you look lovely. When will your baby join us in the world?"

"My due date is August 25, Pastor. We're having a boy. I will name him Walter, after my father."

"And I will name him George, after me. We're still discussing the issue, Pastor," said George with a little laugh as they passed into the sanctuary.

"Good morning, Rhonda. Good morning, Mayor. How are you all today?"

"Just fine, just fine," said Rich.

"Fine, thank you. How are you?" replied Rhonda.

To Pastor Clement, Rhonda did not look fine. Pregnant and pretty, beautifully dressed, but pale. She looked unhappy. He did not ask about her due date. He spoke to their daughter Sandra and her husband Phil Anders.

"Good morning, Pastor," said Jake McCoy, Police Chief of Witherston. Jake was with his cute wife Josephine and their son Billy, age 15 and obviously reluctant to be seen with his parents.

"How are you all, Chief McCoy, Josephine, Billy?" Billy hung back so that he could sit with his friend Sally Sorensen, who was reluctantly following her parents Col. and Mrs. Ed Sorensen.

"Good morning, Benningtons." Pastor Clement returned Carolyn Bennington's hug and shook hands with Trevor, Sr., Trevor, Jr., and Trevor, III.

Several young couples with grade school children, a twenty-year-old woman with a crying baby, a few unescorted older women, and the church secretary Linda Favors entered. Not many teenagers, though. Pastor Clement figured that his sermons must not appeal to teenagers.

Finally, the busload of elderly men from Withers Village arrived. The driver dropped off Art McCrakken, Asmund Jorgensen, Frederick Whitney, Pete Piper, Delbert Maron, Frank Black, Tim Ayers, and Snuffy Parrett, all of them in apparent good health.

Where was Francis Hearty Withers? Pastor Clement couldn't remember him ever missing a Sunday.

Pastor Clements then closed the door to the church and walked into the sanctuary. Today he would preach about repentance.

ოჲო

Repentance? Do I want to repent? No! To repent I'd have to admit guilt. I don't feel guilt. I have committed a crime, but not a sin. A crime is an act against society. A sin is an act against God. I don't respect society. I respect God. God will understand an act committed for the greater good.

Society's values are superficial. Just look at the people in this church listening to the pastor. They've never had to think deeply, never. They've not had to make the decision I had to make. They are shallow. So is the pastor.

Yes, I have killed one person, but I did it to save many persons. Do the arithmetic.

Repentance? I'm not about to confess my crime, not to anybody.

Murder is an act of amazing power. You murder one person and you affect the lives of hundreds, maybe thousands in Withers's case. You murder a dog and you don't affect anybody. Well, actually, you don't murder a dog. You kill him.

Murder is the killing of a human being, the premeditated, illegal killing of a human being.
I should have killed Withers's dog. Would he recognize me if he saw me again? I'll kill him if I get a chance.
I won't get caught. I won't let myself get caught.
Anyway, Miss Mev will have a hard time proving murder. The autopsy will show nothing abnormal.
I have to show nothing abnormal too.
I bow my head in prayer like all these shallow people.
Amen.

$\wideparen{\mathcal{C}}\mathcal{C}\mathcal{C}$

¡Dios mío! Por favor permítele que se mejore y se ponga buena. Déjala vivir. ¿Qué haría yo sin ella? ¿Y qué harían nuestros hijos sin ella? Oh, God. Please make her better. Please let her survive. What would I do without her? What would our boys do without her?

Paco was not religious. But when he suffered—which was rare these days—he reverted to Spanish. And in Spanish he prayed, though to whom he prayed he had no idea. Prayer came to him automatically in Spanish. It was built into the language.

Paco had no knowledge of English when he met Mev in Madrid in January of 1995. They bumped into each other at the Prado on a Saturday morning and exchanged ideas about Goya. Their conversation was superficial, for she was not fluent in Spanish, not yet. But he could tell she was smart, and he loved her American accent. He still did. He took her to lunch that day. And to the movies a few days later. She was learning Spanish at the Universidad Complutense de Madrid where he was learning biology. They spent the spring together studying in Madrid and the summer together traveling to Spain's other great cities and towns.

She finished her degree in Georgia, he finished his in Madrid, and they married two years later at the home of her parents in Gainesville. At their wedding, a dear friend sang Paul Stookey's "Wedding Song." He recalled the song as if he'd just heard it:

Well a man shall leave his mother
and a woman leave her home,.
They shall travel on to where the two shall be as one.
As it was in the beginning is now and till the end.
Woman draws her life from man and gives it back again.
And there is Love.
There is Love.

In marriage, he and Mev had become one.

Paco had taught Mev to think in his language, and she'd taught him to think in hers. They loved each other in a realm that transcended language. Now they were a unit, interconnected, interactive, and completely interdependent. They were a bi-cultural whole, greater than the sum of their parts. Paco had gotten his life lessons from ecology. This one was the most important.

And now she was more than half of him, and he was more than half of her, for they'd integrated each other's soul into their own.

Jaime and Jorge were born in 2001. Never could Paco and Mev have imagined the joy their children would bring them, the pleasure of their intelligence, the hilarity of their humor, the depth of their affection.

Would he lose all this? Paco was scared.

৶৶৶

Jaime and Jorge came down to breakfast in their pajamas. The good-looking twins were identical to most people but not to their parents or close friends. Jaime's curly and unruly brown hair parted naturally on the right, Jorge's on the left. They were the same height, five foot six, and the same weight, 125 pounds.

Their interests differed. Jaime loved science, especially ecology, and Jorge loved politics, especially environmental politics. Jaime, who could tell you the names of all the mollusks to be found in Founding Father's Creek, was the naturalist in the family. He had a terrarium and two aquariums in his and Jorge's bedroom.

Jorge was the political activist. He collected political bumper stickers of the liberal, environmentalist variety. Jaime was the musician. Jorge was the writer. Both boys were brainy, and each was the other's best friend.

Paco told them that their mother had gone to investigate Withers's sudden death. "Your mother wants us to go hiking without her. Shall we? It's Sunday, a good day for a walk."

"Dad," Jaime said after a few seconds of silence, "if Mom has cancer will she keep on working? Won't she be very sick? Will she'll die?"

"She's not going to die, Jaime. She'll just have to go through surgery and maybe some treatments."

"Dad," said Jorge, "Jaime and I can take care of her all summer."

"We don't have to go back to school until the middle of August," Jaime said. "And neither do you, so we can all look after her."

"Will she have a massectomy?" Jorge asked.

"Mastectomy," Jaime corrected.

"*Hijos*, we won't know anything till the end of the week. Anyway, even if she does take chemotherapy or radiation, she may not get very sick."

"Dad, I don't want to go to Tallulah Falls without Mom," said Jorge. "Let's just follow the creek downstream to Founding Father's bridge and have a picnic on the rocks. We haven't done that since last summer."

"I can add to my mollusk shell collection. And I can bring some live mussels to Aunt Lottie. I'll take my net."

"Let's get Beau to go with us," Jorge said.

Beau Lodge, their playmate from childhood, loved the creek too. His passions were Indians, Georgia history, and fish. He read everything he could about the Cherokee clans that once lived in Lumpkin County, he looked at old newspapers, such as *The Southern Banner*, on the web, and he caught fish, studied fish, drew fish, and ate fish.

"You know Mom's prediction was right," Jaime said thoughtfully. "Withers was ripe for the pickin.' And someone picked him. I bet he got poisoned."

"It would be perfect if he overdosed on Senextra—or was given an overdose of Senextra." Jorge responded. "That's what he deserved for trying to turn Witherston into a Senextra factory."

ᘓᘓᘓ

As she sped north along the winding Witherston Highway in her green Honda CRV, Mev thought about her possible mastectomy. She knew the disfiguring surgery would not change Paco's feelings for her. In the nine months she'd spent in Madrid at the age of twenty-one she'd become fluent in Spanish and fortunate in love. When she was with Paco she always felt safe, as she did yesterday afternoon when she told him she might lose her breast.

After dinner the boys had looked up breast cancer on the web, and they now knew the differences between ductal carcinoma in situ and invasive ductal carcinoma. They'd also read articles about breast cancer and estrogen. Jaime had asked her if she'd used birth control pills. She told him the truth. She had, since their birth fourteen years ago. She said that she and Paco could not imagine more wonderful children than the twins, so they'd decided not to have more.

At 9:20 Mev drove up Withers Hill Road to find Withers's Chrysler parked perfectly in the spotless garage and two Witherston Police vehicles parked behind it. She got out of her car, breathed the sweet scent of the pines, listened to the roar of Saloli Falls not far away, and paused before ascending the front steps. She'd never been inside the multi-gabled hickory log house that Withers had inherited from his father, Hearty Harold Withers, when HaHa had passed away. Francis Hearty Withers had occupied the century-old mansion for fifty-five years alone, alone, that is, with only a series of Chow Chow dogs for company. Harry, whom he must have named after his father, was his most recent Chow. Harry was still a puppy at the age of one.

Poor Harry. Mev found Harry sitting by his master's body in the living room. Withers, elegant even in death in expensive navy silk pajamas, was lying face down on the Oriental rug.

Harry whimpered and wagged his tail when Mev allowed him to smell her hand, and then he obediently moved aside.

Mev greeted the three police officers on the scene: Pete Senior, Pete Junior, and Ricky. Ricky was taking photos.

In the dining room, a crystal wine goblet that had held red wine, a half-full crystal water goblet, and a china plate with a partially consumed piece of rhubarb pie were on a beige linen place mat at one end of the long mahogany table. Knife and fork were still on the plate. Mev deduced that Withers had just finished eating dinner when he died.

In the kitchen, separated from the dining room by a swinging door, a small Formica breakfast table held an empty bottle of 2010 Ramey Napa Valley Cabernet Sauvignon and a white Corningware bowl with the remains of a morel mushroom-and-wild-rice casserole. An unwashed large china plate was in the sink. A washed wine goblet was on the counter.

Had Withers had company before he died? Mev wondered. Who had drunk out of the second wine goblet, and washed it? Who brought the casserole? And who brought the pie? She couldn't picture Withers as a chef.

On the plastic kitchen chair was a sack full of groceries from Food Lion.

Lined up on the shelf above the sink were a bottle of Celebrex capsules prescribed by George Folsom, MD, a bottle of potassium chloride tablets also prescribed by George Folsom, MD, a bottle of orange-flavored Centrum Chewables, a bottle of Sundown Naturals iron tablets, and an opened box of MiraLAX packets. The array of medications gave no indication of serious health problems.

Mev put samples of the pie, mushroom casserole, and wine into test tubes and dumped the medications into a plastic baggy to send to the lab in Dahloniga. She asked the officers to dust the casserole dish, the pie dish, the water and wine goblets, the wine bottle, and the utensils for fingerprints. She knew the officers would probably dust the whole kitchen, but she was especially curious about the origins of Withers's dinner.

Mev reentered the dark living room. Heart pine floor. White walls. Heavy blue curtains. Lots of beautiful Appalachian antique wood furniture. Coffee table and cabinets made out of wormy chestnut, which would be prized by antique collectors now but were probably quite ordinary when Withers's ancestors acquired them. An elm buffet cabinet. Another couple of oak ladder-back chairs that matched the ones in the dining room. An oak rocking chair with a wicker seat. An oak desk chair pulled up to a maple roll-top desk. An oak trunk, with a new brass lock. A double-wide, floor-to-ceiling bookshelf holding mostly nineteenth-century novels and histories of Europe, but also a paperback *Rosemary Gladstar's Medicinal Herbs*, a couple of dictionaries, and a black leather-bound Bible. A blue Scotch-plaid dog bed to the side of the fireplace. And a very out-of-place maroon leather recliner facing a small television.

Not the living room she would have imagined for the billionaire.

Mev searched for the key to the trunk in the shallow desk drawers. She noted little of interest: utility bills, a check book, stationery, stamps, pens, pencils, peppermint lifesavers, four pairs of eye glasses, a bottle of aspirin, a hardback *Autobiography of Andrew Carnegie*. No trunk key. She'd bring a screwdriver with her next time to pry open the lock.

Little evidence of an exciting life, at least not from Mev's viewpoint.

Why was Withers taking Senextra when he apparently had no friends other than his dog and no hobbies other than his books and his investments, no family, no work, no evident pleasures? Why did he want to live so long? What had he accomplished in his life? He'd accumulated wealth, of which he'd given little away. He'd dressed up with nowhere to go. Now he was gone. Like dust in the wind.

If she lost her life to breast cancer, she too would be dust in the wind. But at least she would have left her dear sons to the world. And maybe the traces of whatever good work she could do before she died. She wanted to leave a mark on the world, a mark to indicate she'd lived.

Enough ruminating. Mev returned to Withers's body in the living room. Perhaps Withers too had wanted to leave a trace of his existence on the earth he trod when he arranged to bring the Senextra plant here. Was that his way of doing good—

enabling others, such as the nonagenarians and centenarians at Withers Village, to live as long as he had?

Mev's motto for life was "Have fun, and do good." In her view, Withers had done neither.

Mev's cell phone rang. It was Mayor Rather. Odd.

"Hello, Mayor Rather. How are you?"

"Not well, Mev, not well. I know that Mr. Withers is dead. Sad. So sad. Chief McCoy told me. He told me you'd be up at his place looking around. Found anything?"

"Nothing to indicate homicide, Mr. Mayor. Nothing yet."

"Natural causes. That's what I think. He was a hundred years old, for god's sake. Even Senextra couldn't keep him alive forever."

"You may be right, Mr. Mayor."

"I know Mr. Withers's place well. Been there many times. I even have a key to his front door. How about if I come help you look around? I could be there in half an hour."

"Thanks, so much, Mr. Mayor. But there's no need. Even though we haven't found evidence of murder yet we're handling this as a crime scene. But I appreciate the offer."

"Any time, Mev. Any time. Just keep me informed. I need to stay informed."

As Pete Junior and Ricky put Withers's body on a gurney and moved it out of the house, Mev sat down with Amy Woods at the far end of the dining room table.

"Tell me your name," Mev gently asked the thin gray-haired woman, probably in her early fifties, who was trembling from fear.

"Amy Woods."

"And where do you live?"

"I live in Mr. Withers's maid's room downstairs. When my husband died thirteen years ago I came to Witherston to clean and cook for Mr. Withers. I don't know what I'll do now. I don't know where I'll live. I don't know where I'll get a job."

"Mrs. Woods, Mr. Withers died last night. Where were you last night?"

"Mr. Withers gives me Saturday off. I spent last night with my sister in Dahlonega."

"He didn't give you the whole Memorial Day weekend off?"

"No. He doesn't give me holidays off."

"What did you find when you came to work this morning?"

"I found Mr. Withers dead on the living room floor. I didn't touch anything. I called 911."

"What time did you arrive this morning?"

"About 9:00."

"So you didn't cook him the mushroom casserole?"

"No, ma'am."

"Or the rhubarb pie?"

"No, ma'am. I've never cooked either mushrooms or rhubarb for Mr. Withers. I thought he didn't like mushrooms. And I don't know anything about rhubarb."

"What did Mr. Withers do in the evenings, Mrs. Woods?"

"He just read. He read all the time, morning, afternoon, evening. Occasionally he watched television. Sometimes Mayor Rather would come to have wine with him. Sometimes somebody else, but not very often. Mostly Mr. Withers just read, with his puppy Harry lying beside him. Mr. Withers loved Harry."

℘℘℘

Paco watched Jaime, Jorge, and Beau from the granite outcropping above the bridge. The boys were dipping their bare feet into the cold, rapidly flowing creek after having devoured their bacon, lettuce, and tomato sandwiches. Jaime dangled his net in the water.

Paco had stayed up on the granite outcropping to finish Daniel Quinn's *Ishmael*. He borrowed most of his books from Aunt Lottie, as did the boys, and Lottie had been trying to loan him *Ishmael* for years. Lottie had a sizable collection of books about the natural environment, a good percentage of which focused on the harm humans did to non-humans. Paco noticed that she always took the side of non-humans in their lively conversations.

Paco loved Lottie for her eccentricities. Lottie fed the birds, squirrels, raccoons, possums, deer, and all the other furry and feathery creatures she spotted in the woods behind her house. She put out deer corn for them. She gathered mushrooms to use in the phenomenal dishes she concocted. She went everywhere with Darwin on her shoulder or in her apron pocket—to Gretchen Green's Green Grocery, to Eat Locally meetings, and to Scissors, where Jon cut and brightened her short, curly silver hair. She entertained her friends with fabulous dinners and fine wines, frequented Witherston's art galleries where she regularly purchased paintings and wood sculptures from Georgia artists, and wore purple silk blouses. In fact, she always wore purple, come to think of it. She didn't want to take Senextra because, she said, "You lose your looks at ninety."

Lottie was not your average aunt. She wrote a daily history column for *Witherston on the Web*. She knew the history of north Georgia well. She had retired at sixty from Hickory Mountain College a couple of years after her son Brian was killed in Iraq. She said she'd lost her will to keep teaching history to bright students who could have been Brian's friends. So she bought the little yellow brick cottage next door to their house and moved to Witherston. Paco loved her wit, her wisdom, and her wackiness, knowing that her *simpatía*—her genialness, niceness, desire to have fun—masked deep sorrow. She never went looking for fun. She didn't need to. She brought fun wherever she went.

Paco turned back to *Ishmael* and reread the sentence "The world was not made for any one species." As a biology teacher he knew that the world was not made for humans, but as a consumer he behaved as if it were. How could he behave differently?

∞

"Why is this stream called 'Founding Father's Creek?'" Jaime asked his companions.

"Because that sounded better than 'Floundering Father's Creek,'" Jorge said, giggling at his own humor.

"I know! I read about it in your Aunt Lottie's column today," Beau answered Jaime seriously. "Because old Withers's great grandfather Harry Withers named the creek after Abraham Baldwin, who was one of our country's founding fathers."

"Why'd Harry Withers get to name this creek?"

"Because he was rich," said Jorge. "If you're rich you get to name anything you like. Woods, creeks, towns, colleges, whatever. If you're poor, you get to name only your children and your pets."

The boys listened to the sound of the whitewater.

"Beau," Jaime said. "We've got something to tell you."

"Our mother has cancer," Jorge said. "She went to see your father on Friday."

"Oh no! Oh no! What kind?"

"Breast cancer," Jaime said. "Last week Mom found a lump in her left breast when she was in the shower. She didn't tell Dad until Friday night, after she'd gotten the diagnosis. She and Dad told us on Saturday morning. They say not to worry, but we're worried."

"How old is she?'

"Forty-two."

"Does my mother know?"

"She's probably telling her right now. She's gone to your house for lunch.

೧೨೧

"Dad, come here," Jorge called. "Look what Jaime found."

"A bullfrog," Beau shouted. "It's deformed!"

Jaime had captured an adult male bullfrog with three back legs. Jorge photographed the frog with his smartphone, and Jaime released him in the creek.

Jorge emailed the picture to *Witherston on the Web* for its "Nature" page, to which he and Jaime regularly contributed. He titled the picture "Fancy Frog with Superfluous Foot Found Floating in Founding Father's Creek near Founding Father's Bridge." He was proud of his alliteration.

WITHERSTON ON THE WEB
Sunday, May 24, 2015

LATEBREAKING NEWS!
(11:15 a.m.)

Officers from the Witherston Police Department were called to the home of Francis Hearty Withers at 1 Withers Hill Road this morning, Sunday, May 24, at 9:20 am, in response to a 911 call by Amy Woods. Mrs. Woods, Withers's housekeeper, said that she found Withers dead on the dining room floor with his dog Harry lying at his side when she arrived at the house about 8:55 am. She had had Saturday off.

Detective Emma Evelyn Arroyo, on the scene, reported that Withers, age 100, had apparently collapsed and died on Saturday evening.

Withers's body was taken to Chestatee Regional Hospital in Dahlonega for a routine autopsy.

~ Catherine Perry, Reporter

CHAPTER 4

Sunday afternoon, May 24, 2014:

Gretchen was surprised to get the text message that afternoon. It came from Martin Payne. *Would you like to have dinner Tuesday night?*

Gretchen answered, perhaps not as graciously as she might have. *Okay. Why?*

Martin replied. *I'll pick you up at your grocery store at 6.*

And Gretchen replied. *Okay. Thnx. Bye.*

How odd, Gretchen thought. Now why would Dr. Martin Payne want to talk with her? What in the world did they have to say to each other? She was a fifty-five-year-old hippy with braided gray hair, no make-up, sandals and long skirts who lived with a brown dog named Gandhi and a black cat named Barack. She was a pescatarian, anti-war, feminist environmentalist who rode a bicycle. She sold organic fruits and vegetables for a living. She'd carried an anti-BioSenecta sign—SENEXTRA VIOLATES MOTHER NATURE—in the protest.

He was a wealthy, exquisitely groomed younger man who wore $1,000 suits and drove a $50,000 BMW convertible. CEO of BioSenecta. Probably a Republican. Most CEOs were. And he probably ate meat. Yuck.

Friday Dr. Payne had noticed her sign and had asked her what she meant by nature. Well, that was easy. Nature was the planet's ecosystem without humans' interference in its normal operation. Humans created bombs, poisons, and Senextra. Humans constructed things that made everybody—humans and other animals, and plants, and water, and air—sick. Dr. Payne was probably on the side of everything that made humans sick, because he was making a profit from the medicine BioSenecta manufactured to make humans well again.

She was prepared to argue with him. Now she looked forward to dinner. Should she take Gandhi?

❧❧

Mev and Lauren had finished their good cry. Mev smiled. "You're the best, Lauren. I don't know what I'd do without you." They hugged.

"We'll get through this together, Mev. Besides, you have a job to do. You've got to figure out who killed old Withers."

"Whether or not someone killed him—and I'd bet my small salary some blessed soul did—you'll be probating his will." Mev sat back. "You know, this is my first big investigation. I can't wait to get started, cancer or no cancer."

"Will you be talking with the county coroner, Mev?"

"I think I'll await his report." Mev leaned back from the table and patted Harry, who lay at her feet. Harry wagged his tail and licked her hand with his black tongue.

"Mr. Withers is dead, and I got you, babe," Mev said to Harry.

"Lucky you!" said Lauren.

"Lucky Jaime and Jorge!" Mev rose to go. "You know, I had to adopt Harry. If I hadn't the puppy would have gone to the pound and probably been euthanized. Now I get to deliver him to Paco and the boys. They will be thrilled."

❧❧

Lauren told Jim about her visit with Mev.

"I'm worried," Jim said. "Mev is facing a traumatic event, however it turns out. She'll need us to lean on."

"She'll have us to lean on, Jim, as well as her loving family. But Mev is strong. As long as I've known her, she's never let anything get her down, not even that disastrous foot surgery. You watch: Mev will keep us all smiling. I saw her cry today for the very first time ever, but I doubt I'll see her cry again. She's already focused on her case."

Lauren remembered something her yoga teacher had given her that she'd put on her fridge. It was a message from Swami Satchidananda: "When you fill your system with vitality, with health and happiness, you become contagious. People will sit with you and feel happy and laugh."

That was what she and Lauren did for each other. They made each other laugh. Lauren was the yoga enthusiast, but Mev fulfilled its promise of vitality instinctively. Because she brought joy to her friends, her friends brought joy to her, and would continue to bring joy to her no matter what happened.

$$\backsim$$

Paco and the boys were thrilled indeed to have a puppy. And so was Harry, who wagged his whole body with excitement when Mev made the introductions. Mev had brought home from Withers's house a case of canned dog food, a new leash, and a brand new collar with neither a rabies tag nor a name tag.

She had not brought home any vaccination papers for Harry because she hadn't found any.

"So will you all take Harry to the vet's tomorrow morning?" Mev asked.

"Yes, we promise," Paco said.

"We'll all go," Jaime said.

"I want to change his name," Jorge said. "I don't think he should live with the name that Withers gave him."

"Let's call him Barry."

"I say Terry."

"Larry."

"Gary."

"Perry."

"Mary. Hehe."

"I say let's talk about it tomorrow, boys. Time for bed." Mev ended the discussion.

$$\backsim$$

Neel wrote in his journal:

> *Mr. Francis Hearty Withers is finally dead. His century of wealth has come to an end. And the power his wealth gave him.*
>
> *How will his death affect Witherston? The billionaire on the hill cast a long shadow over Witherston. Nobody—not I, not his doctor, not his lawyer, not anybody with an address in Witherston—escaped his shadow. Not anybody with ambition to inherit his wealth. Not anybody with an investment in BioSenecta. Not anybody taking Senextra.*
>
> *I lived in Mr. Francis Hearty Withers's shadow. And my ancestors lived in his ancestors' shadow. Those conquered always live in the shadow of their conquerors. That's an unspoken rule of civilization. And if you're one of those living in someone else's shadow, you can't make decisions in the light of the sun, because you get no sun. You have to scurry from bush to shrub in the shade, making decisions that affect your immediate survival only. You do what you can to survive.*
>
> *But now the billionaire's shadow is gone. And the people of Witherston can see clearly now. The people of Witherston can make decisions free of his influence. The people of Witherston can decide on their own whether to allow BioSenecta to build a Senextra factory on the banks of Founding Father's Creek.*
>
> *Did the people of Witherston hate Mr. Francis Hearty Withers? How could they not? People hate those who have power over their lives. The police must know he was murdered. I'm glad he's gone. I hated him, and his father, and his grandfather, and his great grandfather, and his great, great grandfather.*

એએએ

I can't sleep. What did I leave at Withers house that could incriminate me? I washed my wine glass. I wish I'd put it away, but I was afraid to stay there any longer. If anybody had seen me, I'd have had to kill him too. I could not leave any witnesses.

But there was one witness I left alive: the dog.

WITHERSTON ON THE WEB
Monday, May 25, 2015
Memorial Day

LOCAL NEWS

In view of the sudden death of Francis Hearty Withers, Mayor Rich Rather has cancelled the traditional Witherston Memorial Day Parade, originally scheduled for 4:00 pm today. The float created to carry Miss Teenage Witherston will lead the Fourth of July Parade instead. Sponsored by the Witherston Roundtable, that float will feature Mona Pattison standing in front of a replica of Founding Father's Bridge made of pine cones.

Two posterboard signs with amateur lettering and cartoon figures appeared in town yesterday morning. They protested the clearcutting of Francis Hearty Withers's old-growth forest. One sign, tacked to the telephone pole on the southeast corner of Creek Street and Main Street, depicted a chainsaw on legs chasing a squirrel through the woods. The chain saw said "WITHERS IS GONNA GET YOU!" The other sign, taped to a bus stop bench on the southeast corner of Yona Street and Main Street, depicted an older gentleman standing on cleared land holding logs in his left hand and a big capsule in his right hand that said "SENEXTRA."

In view of Mr. Withers's sudden death Mayor Rather removed the signs last night.

The funeral service for Mr. Withers will be held at 2:00 pm on Tuesday, May 26, at Witherston Baptist Church. Pastor Paul Clement will officiate. A reception will follow. The burial will take place afterwards on the grounds of Withers Village.
~ Catherine Perry, Reporter

LETTERS TO THE EDITOR

To the Editor:

Don't Witherston's police officers have anything better to do with their time than arresting children wearing chicken suits?
~ Signed, Gretchen Green

To Gretchen Green:
No.
~ Smitty Green, Editor

ON THIS DAY IN HISTORY
By Charlotte Byrd

On May 25, 1787, Abraham Baldwin, after whom Founding Father's Creek was named, joined fifty-four other delegates from twelve states to draft the Constitution of the United States.

And on Memorial Day, May 25, 2009, one day before his nineteenth birthday, U.S. Army Corporal Brian Remington Byrd, my beloved son, was killed in Iraq.

POLICE BLOTTER

At 6:10 pm on Sunday, May 24, Witherston Police re-

sponded to a 911 call from Hilda Burrough on Wayback Road, who said that a man she knew had hit her over the head with her frying pan. She said she didn't know why. After thinking it over, she declined to press charges.

At 1:10 am on Monday, May 25, Witherston Police officers ticketed Trevor Bennington, III, age 21, of Athens, Georgia, for traveling in his 2013 Land Rover at the speed of 80 miles an hour down Hiccup Hill Road. Mr. Bennington said he'd seen a ghost.

CHAPTER 5

Neel Kingfisher and Swift walked up the path that followed Founding Father's Creek. Neel carried his journal in his backpack. They were heading to Saloli Falls, where Swift liked to swim and Neel liked to think. After a few minutes of human-canine play, Neel opened his journal and wrote:

Mr. Francis Hearty Withers died without acknowledging our kinship. He gloried in his family's history, explained his heritage at every opportunity to anybody who would listen. So he must have known who I was. He must have known we were cousins. He had a role in hiring me, because he was the benefactor of Withers Village and a member of the board.

Mr. Francis Hearty Withers's curiosity about me may have equaled my curiosity about him. Yet his Withers pride never let him reveal that his aunt had run away with an Indian, at least not to the public. And he would not have wanted to give me, a Cherokee, a cent of his wealth. That would have been an admission of the original crime his ancestors committed against my ancestors: exiling mine from their homeland so that they could enjoy the land's riches.

But now I wonder: When does a land become a

*homeland? For how many years, for how many cen-
turies must a people occupy a territory before it be-
comes rightfully theirs? Is Lumpkin County now the
homeland of its present occupants? Their people
have lived here since the 1830s. And almost all land
claimed by one people originally belonged to another. What constitutes 'original,' anyway?*

*I wish I'd dared to ask old Francis Hearty Withers
what he thought of his aunt. He was fifteen when
she married Mohe Kingfisher and went to Oklahoma. Mohe and Penance Louise had to leave Lumpkin
County. Nobody here would speak to them. Another
trail of tears.*

୧∽୧∽

Mayor Rather arrived at Rather Pre-Owned Vehicles in
Dahlonega at 10:00 in the morning. Memorial Day was always
a good day for selling cars and winning votes. To bring customers to his lot he'd hired the Four Fire Crackers to play pat-
riotic tunes and Nomadic Grill to serve hot dogs and beer. Rich
treated holidays as opportunities for parties on the premises.

Rich was accustomed to friends and acquaintances dropping by for music and food, even when they had no intention
of buying anything, so he was not surprised to see Grant
Griggs approach.

"Rich," Grant said. "I have a suspicion that Mr. Withers
was murdered. What do you think?"

"Well, I don't know, Grant. I don't know. If Mr. Withers
was murdered, who do you think did it?"

"I didn't do it, but I'm afraid the police will think I did.
They're going to find my finger prints there. I visited him Saturday afternoon."

"They're going to find mine too, and Rhonda's. She
brought him a mushroom casserole on Saturday."

"I think that the maid, Amy Woods, killed Mr. Withers.
She needed money and had asked him for a loan. He told her
no."

"Amy wouldn't have done it. She was devoted to him. She worked for him for thirteen years."

❧❧❧

Lottie had awakened with memories of her son, as she did every morning. But this morning, because it was Memorial Day, she was flooded with sadness. Six years before, on Memorial Day of 2009, Brian had been shot and killed outside of Baghdad. He was just one of 4500 Americans to lose their lives in a war whose stated purpose varied from punishing Iraq for 9/11 to saving the world from Iraq's weapons of mass destruction to removing Iraq's president for his inhumane treatment of Iraqi citizens.

Brian had joined the Army for two reasons. He felt unready for college, and he wanted to prepare himself for a career in politics. He thought that serving his country for two years would mature him and give him the credentials to stand for election to Congress one day. He had a long-term plan. He would go to Iraq or Afghanistan or wherever he was sent and then return to Georgia, study political science at the University of Georgia, focus on environmental law in law school, and ultimately run for local, state, and national office. Although he'd inherited his mother's skepticism of war as a means to establish peace, Brian had enlisted the week after he graduated from high school.

One year later he was dead.

Lottie was glad that Jon and Gregory had invited her over for a Memorial Day cookout. With Gretchen and of course Gandhi and Darwin. Jon and Gregory knew the pleasure of living with animals. Lottie put Darwin into her apron pocket.

This afternoon they would honor Brian's memory and enjoy each other's company, without hoopla since none of them had children now. She picked up Gretchen and Gandhi at 1:00. Gandhi squeezed into the back of Lottie's electric Smart Car.

Jon and Gregory occupied five wooded acres with Renoir the dog, a goat, a donkey, and countless wild animals who ate the corn Gregory put out for them by the pond. As Lottie and Gretchen pulled into their driveway off Yona Road, Sassyass and Vincent van Goat greeted them with Jon and Gregory following close behind.

"Hello, sweet friends!" Jon called out. "We're so happy to have you with us today!"

Gregory helped them out of the car—they appreciated the assistance—and led them onto the wrap-around porch of the old white farmhouse. Jon had set four glasses and a pitcher of lemonade on the table by the four rocking chairs. The day was hot and the lemonade refreshing.

Renoir settled down beside Jon. Gandhi settled down beside Gretchen. And Darwin perched on Lottie's shoulder.

"First, let's remember your son, Lottie," said Gregory. "Tell us about him."

Lottie did. She described their lives together after Rem had died. Brian was only five years old at the time of his father's awful automobile accident. She told them of Brian's passion for politics, his athletic ability and love of sports, his impatience with school, his decision—difficult for her to comprehend—to join the military. She recalled the arrival at her home of the two Casualty Notification Officers who had given her the awful news. She'd wept for a week.

Lottie was grateful for the opportunity to share her grief with friends who were unafraid of her tears.

After a few minutes of silence, Jon said quietly, "I'll never understand the logic of sixty-year-old politicians sending twenty-year-old men and women to the battlefield because the politicians have a grievance against each other."

"Old folks make the decisions," said Gregory, who had survived a year in Vietnam before the pullout in 1973. "Young folks carry them out. The young are proxies for the old."

"I think that the old should sacrifice themselves on behalf of the young," said Jon. "The old should go to war. They're not contributing much to the economy any more, not like the young, and if they die on the battlefield it's no big deal, since they're going to die soon anyway."

Lottie was grateful as always for Jon's ability to raise everybody's spirits.

Gretchen joined in the fun. "That's a fantastic idea! And those elderly soldiers with Alzheimer's who wander off on the battlefield can be honored as Missing in Action, a much more prestigious designation than Senile Dementia."

"And those elderly soldiers who have fatal heart attacks or strokes on the battlefield can be honored as Killed in Action," rejoined Jon.

"And then our country won't be risking its most valuable resource, young people. In the long run it would be much cheaper to wage war employing old folks than employing young folks who need to support their families, contribute to the economy, and pay taxes for roads and bridges," Gretchen said.

"And care for their aging parents," Gregory added.

"And if the young lose their limbs at twenty they suffer for sixty years, whereas if the old lose their limbs at seventy they suffer for only ten years," Jon said. "Unless they're taking Senextra."

Gregory grew serious. "Think of the irony. Pharmaceutical companies develop drugs to keep old folks alive till they're over a hundred years old at the same time that politicians send young folks to be killed or maimed."

"Right," said Lottie. "Francis Hearty Withers gets Senextra, and Brian Remington Byrd gets a bullet."

The four friends grew quiet. Gandhi and Renoir took off for the pond. Finally Lottie broke the silence.

"Every day I remind myself that the twenty-year-old Iraqi who shot Brian was following orders to kill the enemy very similar to the orders my son was following. I must remind myself of that or I would go mad with hatred of the person who shot him."

"How many generations does it take for the prejudices engendered by war to disappear?" Gretchen wondered aloud. "I suspect at least two."

"Maybe only one," Gregory said. "The Vietnamese are now our friends."

"At least the Vietnamese government is friendly to our government. But it would have to be, wouldn't it? The Vietnamese government wouldn't want another American invasion," said Gretchen.

"You're Cherokee," Jon said to Gregory, "and yet you live

with me. My north Georgia ancestors were hateful to yours, but you're not bitter."

Gregory thought a moment and replied, "No, because I was fortunate economically. I didn't grow up on a reservation. I grew up in Dahlonega with parents who were teachers. But I suspect my distant relatives who grew up in poverty on a reservation inherited from their elders some resentment toward their conquerors."

"Neel Kingfisher grew up in Oklahoma," Jon said. "Do you all think that he'd stored enough resentment to kill Withers?"

 espeso

Early in the morning Mev, Paco, Jaime, Jorge, and Beau had driven up to Cherokee, North Carolina, two hours from Witherston. The boys had read about the Oconaluftee Indian Village, modeled on a Cherokee village of 1760, and they'd talked Mev and Paco into the road trip. After three hours in the village and two in the Cherokee museum learning the history of the Cherokee nation they were on the way home.

"Boys, what will you remember most about the Cherokee traditions?" asked Paco, turning around in his seat to talk to the boys. Mev was driving.

"I will remember that the Cherokee Indians want to be called Cherokee Indians and not Native Americans," Jorge said, "because a Native American can be anybody born in America."

"I will remember that in 1821 a Cherokee named Sequoyah created a written language for the Cherokee," Jaime said. "He created a symbol for each syllable in their spoken language, so the Cherokee people could use those symbols to write what they heard or said."

"And to pass on information," added Mev from the driver's seat.

"What I will remember," Beau said, "is the philosophy of Cherokee medicine. I can't wait to talk to my father about it, since he's studied only Western medicine."

"What did you find important?" Paco asked Beau.

"That Cherokee traditional medicine is prevention-based, in

contrast with Western medicine which is cure-based. Cherokee medicine focuses on wellness, and Western medicine focuses on disease. I also liked the idea that you can be well only if you are connected to the natural world."

"I liked the fact that the Cherokee word *tohi* means both *health* and *peace*," Jorge said. "Wow. Isn't that cool? When your body is at peace, you are healthy!"

"I liked learning about all those herbs they used as medicine," said Jaime. "The Cherokees must have been great botanists."

"They used witch hazel for sore throats and laryngitis," said Beau.

"What's witch hazel? Sounds scary," said Jorge.

"Witch hazel is a large shrub whose bark has lots of medicinal uses," Mev said. "When I was a child my mother used it on me to stop bleeding when I had a cut."

Jorge said, "Mom, I appreciate Cherokee medicine, but for your cancer I want you to be treated by Western medicine."

"And I will be, honey. If I have cancer I'll be treated immediately. That's because I'll have already contracted the disease. Western doctors are good at fixing us up if we get sick. But I still think it's better not to get sick in the first place!"

"I'd hate to have to choose between Cherokee medicine and Western medicine."

"We don't have to choose, Jorge," Mev said. "We can do both. We can try to stay well by connecting with nature and then go to Western doctors if we get really sick."

◦◦◦

Amy Woods sat at her sister's bedside. Amy was eight years younger than Sharon, but in the last few months Amy had assumed responsibility for Sharon's welfare.

Three weeks ago Sharon had learned she had stomach cancer and could no longer clean houses, as she'd done since she was sixteen. Sharon lived alone in a tiny yellow clapboard bungalow on the outskirts of Dahlonega, and she soon would need full-time home care. She had no job, no source of income other than her unemployment insurance, no savings, and no children to help her in her last few months of life. She had only Amy.

Amy had no savings either. And now she had no job. But she still had her car, a twenty-five-year-old Honda, and she still had her health, for which she was thankful. She'd find another job, but not as a live-in maid.

For years Amy had supplemented Sharon's small food budget by pilfering from Francis Hearty Withers's well-stocked freezer. The duties the old man had assigned her included not just cooking and cleaning but also grocery shopping. At Dahlonega's Food Lion, where she shopped on Sunday morning before returning to Withers's mansion, Amy always bought a little more than would be needed for the week, and every Saturday morning, after leaving Withers for the day, she would take her sister a few packages of frozen vegetables, a package of frozen meat of some kind or another, a piece of fruit, and perhaps an onion or a potato. Mr. Withers never noticed.

Amy herself ate well during the week, for she ate what Mr. Withers ate, which was good. After preparing and serving Mr. Withers's dinner at the dining room table—steak, lobster, stews of various kinds—Amy would sit alone at the kitchen table in front of the small television and eat her own dinner, but without the wine that Mr. Withers enjoyed with his meal.

After doing the dishes, Amy was allowed to retire for the night to her room in the basement, where she kept her few possessions: a framed photograph of her late husband Paul; an extra uniform; her street clothes and shoes, which she purchased from the Salvation Army store; some paperbacks, mostly murder mysteries, and some magazines she'd retrieved from Mr. Withers's waste basket; and her make-up, shampoo, and soap. Mr. Withers had furnished the room with a twin bed, a dresser, a small book shelf, an old lamp, an old rug, an old curtain, an old television, an old radio, and old linens. Here was her home. She was allowed to leave it on Saturdays only.

"How are you feeling?" Amy asked Sharon. "I've brought you some cod, which I can sauté and serve on rice. That would be easy to digest."

"Thanks so much, hon. The good Lord blessed me with a wonderful sister. I'm fortunate."

Amy didn't see it that way.

She often thought about the choices she had made in her life. At the time they seemed minor, but they could never be undone. Like deciding to work for Mr. Withers after Paul's death. She thought she'd benefit financially from working for a billionaire. She thought she'd save money by being a live-in maid. She had not anticipated the loneliness of the job. No opportunity to have visitors, no opportunity to go out at night, no opportunity to make friends, no opportunity to talk with anybody.

Not even Mr. Withers. Mr. Withers never talked with her. He never thanked her for cooking his meals, ironing his clothes, folding his underwear, changing his bed sheets, scrubbing his bathroom floor. He never discussed Senextra with her. He never asked her about her views on local events. Did he assume she had no thoughts, no opinions, no feelings? Did he think she was happy cleaning up after him?

More likely Mr. Withers did not think about her at all.

Amy had been Mr. Withers's servant, and he'd paid her little. He said she didn't need much money because he fed her, lodged her, and bought her uniforms. Why would she need money?

But she did need money. That's why she stole from him. Just a little cash now and then from the pockets of his pants when she was hanging them in his closet. Never more than a few dollars. Still, she was a thief. She could go to jail if she were found out.

And on Friday night she'd done something worse. She'd erased a document from his computer when she was upstairs pulling down his bedspread.

Amy hadn't killed Mr. Withers, but she'd wanted to, many times. She'd fantasized about putting rat poison into his *coq au vin*, or Freon into his *boeuf bourguignon*, or Ambien into his *bouillabaisse*. It would have been so easy to take the old man's life. She hated him.

And now, thank the Lord, he was dead. Would she get a share of his billion dollar gift to the residents of Witherston?

Please, God, she prayed. Please, please, please, let me have my fair share.

But she knew she was not a legal resident of Witherston. Mr. Withers had made her keep her sister's address in Dahlonega as her official address.

She didn't kill Mr. Withers, but she had an idea who did. Mayor Rather.

ᐁᐁᐁ

Strange that I am not afraid of being caught.

I see the big picture now. I see a history of the world in which courageous men killed to influence their people's destiny. Some get revered and others get reviled. Depends on your viewpoint.

Harry Truman, who ordered the dropping of the atomic bomb twice got revered in America but reviled in Japan. Osama bin Laden, who ordered the destruction of the World Trade Center, got reviled in America but revered by al Qaeda.

Both Truman and bin Laden influenced the course of history. So will I.

We remember some killers as good and some as bad. But that's only local opinion. Fleeting, in the long run.

I wonder how I'll be remembered. I'll probably be revered. I have killed one man to benefit many. And not just the residents of Witherston. I have acted to bring Senextra to mankind. I will influence the course of history.

If I get caught it won't matter to history. But I won't get caught. My picture—side view, front view—will never go up on Webby Witherston. No, there won't be a mug shot of me.

WITHERSTON ON THE WEB
Tuesday, May 26, 2015

LOCAL NEWS

Detective Emma Evelyn Arroyo and Chief Jake McCoy of the Witherston Police Department have not indicated whether they believe Withers's death to be a homicide. Detective Arroyo has adopted Withers's Chow Chow puppy, Harry.
~ Catherine Perry, Reporter

LETTERS TO THE EDITOR

To the Editor:

We are shocked and saddened by the sudden passing of our dear friend and benefactor Francis Hearty Withers. I say, we have ourselves to blame for his death.

I believe that Withers died of heart break—because some of his fellow Witherstonians rudely protested the establishment of his Senextra factory at the very time he was announcing his generous gift to our community. Withers was a great American who wanted to make Senextra available to everybody who desired a long life. I urge that we build the Senextra factory here, fulfill Withers's dream, and secure Witherston's future.
~ Signed, Rich Rather, Mayor

To the Editor:

Let us honor Francis Hearty Withers by speaking kindly of

him as a human being, but not by welcoming BioSenecta to
Witherston. Let us not exchange clean air and water for an
allusive economic prosperity that a polluting pharmaceutical
factory claims it will bring.

Why sacrifice our health for money we'd use for medicine
to cure us of ills we'd suffer from the toxic pollutants.
Say NO to BioSenecta. Say NO to Senextra.
~ Signed, Gregory Bozeman, Ph.D.

To the Editor:

I urge all Witherstonians to recognize the medical and financial benefits that a Senextra factory will bring to every citizen of our community, as well as the prestige and prosperity it
will bring to Witherston, Georgia.
~ Signed, George Folsom, M.D.

To the Editor:

Almost two hundred years ago Hearty Withers became rich
by taking gold and land from the Cherokee Indians. Now his
great, great grandson, Francis Hearty Withers, is using his
inherited fortune to enable similarly greedy people everywhere
to live beyond their natural lifespan.

The Cherokee civilization lasted more than ten thousand
years because the Cherokees lived in harmony with the forces
of nature. Their great civilization was destroyed in the 1830s
by a people who, like the Withers, saw nature as nothing more
than a source for material wealth, a people who lived—and
continue to live—in defiance of the forces of nature. Senextra
symbolizes Western society's mission to control the forces of
nature. Think: If the seven billion humans consuming Earth's
bounty all live as long as Francis Hearty Withers, our de-
mands will exceed Earth's bounty. And we humans will perish
by the forces of nature. Let's keep BioSenecta Pharmaceuti-

cals out of Witherston. Let's go further. Let's expose Senextra for the threat it poses to humankind.

~ Signed, Anonymous

OBITUARY
Francis Hearty Withers

Billionaire Francis Hearty Withers, age 100, of Witherston, died on Sunday, May 24, 2015, apparently of natural causes. He left no survivors. Francis Hearty Withers was the great, great grandson of Hearty Withers and his wife Penance Hearty Withers Withers, who made their fortune in gold in 1829 and passed on their wealth to their descendants.

In 2005, Francis Hearty Withers, always called by his full name, endowed the Founding Father's Retirement Community and changed its name to Withers Village.

He was unanimously praised by Withers Villagers for arranging for them to take the drug Senextra, which he credited for his own longevity, in a BioSenecta pilot study.

On Friday, May 22, Francis Hearty Withers announced at his hundredth birthday party that in his will he had bequeathed $1 billion to the present legal residents of Witherston to be divided equally among us. In his will Withers also bequeathed $1 billion to the town of Witherston.Withers bequeathed the remainder of his estate to BioSenecta Pharmaceuticals, in which he held the majority of stock shares, with the proviso that BioSenecta build its Senextra factory on his property in Witherston. Francis Hearty Withers's funeral service will take place in Witherston Baptist Church today at 2:00 pm today.

His burial service will be held afterwards on the grounds of Withers Village.

~ Smitty Green, Editor

ON THIS DAY IN HISTORY
By Charlotte Byrd

On May 26, 1830, the United States Congress passed the

Indian Removal Act, which President Andrew Jackson signed on May 28. The law gave the President the authority to buy land from Native Americans east of the Mississippi in exchange for "Indian Territory" west of the Mississippi outside the borders of the United States. The discovery of gold on land occupied by the Cherokee Nation in Georgia made the law popular among white settlers.

It must have pleased Hearty Withers, who was becoming wealthy from gold he had panned in Yahoola Creek the year before. The Indian Removal Act led to the "Trail of Tears," in which 4,000 of some 16,000 Cherokees died in the fall of 1838 during their forced march westward to what is now Oklahoma.

The Congressmen who voted for the bill, including Wilson Lumpkin who would become Georgia's governor in 1832, intended to protect Georgia's white settlers from Cherokees unhappy over the settlers' seizure of their land and gold.

President Jackson, Representative Lumpkin, and the other Congressmen must have viewed the Cherokees as lower than Anglo-Saxons on the hierarchy of humans.

They probably felt that they were fulfilling their destiny of bringing civilization to the American continent.

NATURE

Deformed Frog Caught at Founding Father's Bridge

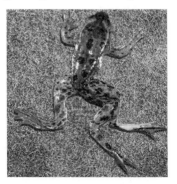

Photo by Jorge Arroyo

CHAPTER 6

Tuesday, May 26, 2015

Jorge and Jaime had arisen at 7:00 Tuesday morning in time to kiss their mother good-bye as she climbed into Lauren's white Prius. Lauren was driving her to Northeast Georgia Medical Center in Gainesville for the tests Jim had ordered.

When the twins returned to the kitchen they found the note their mother had left them on the table:

> *Your mission, Jaime and Jorge, should you choose to accept it, is to attend Francis Hearty Withers's funeral this afternoon, wearing a tie and clean white shirt, mingle with the crowd in the reception afterward, and report back everything you have heard or seen. Be at Witherston Baptist Church by 1:45.*

"We've been deputized!" exclaimed Jaime.

"We're detectives!" exclaimed Jorge.

By 10:00 Jorge and Jaime were with their father at the vet clinic for Harry's checkup. Dr. Ralph Elders, Paco's and Gregory's fishing buddy, had given them an appointment as soon as Paco had called. Ralph gave Harry a series of shots, vaccinations against rabies, distemper, and parvovirus. He looked at Harry's black tongue, which proved Harry was a purebred Chow Chow. He took a stool sample to Harry's dismay. Now he was examining Harry's private parts.

"There's something peculiar here," Dr. Elders said. "Harry

has either anorchism, which means no testicles, or bilateral cryptorchidism, which means undescended testicles. Hard to tell right now. This is not a problem if you don't want to breed him. He'll still be a great pet, but he won't become a father. And he won't be very aggressive."

"Okay by me," said Jorge.

"Perfect!" Jaime said. "He'll be the last of the Withers Chow Chows."

"I took care of Harry's mother," Dr. Elders continued. "Maud Olive—that's what Mr. Withers called her—was sixteen years old when she had her last litter. I was astonished that she'd gotten pregnant, or that she'd even lived that long. She gave birth to four puppies, but only Harry survived. She died six months later."

"Maud Olive? Her name was Maud Olive?" Jorge giggled.

"Are anorchism and cryptorchidism unnatural?" asked Jaime.

"I don't consider anything unnatural. But medically, anorchism and cryptorchidism are viewed as congenital defects. I'd say that Harry has an unusual variation of genital development," Dr. Elders said.

"Let's name our dog Varry—for variation," said Jaime.

"Good idea!" Jorge said, kissing his puppy on the nose. "Hi, Varry! You're my man!"

"You're our nearly-man," Jaime said.

❧❧❧

After the funeral, Paco, Jaime, Jorge, and Aunt Lottie hovered over the table of sweets and lemonade in the Witherston Baptist Church Fellowship Hall.

"Time for mingling," Jaime said, and so he and Jorge mingled, fully conscious of their responsibilities as undercover detectives. This is what they heard:

Faith Folsom, wife of Dr. George Folsom, speaking with Gregory Bozeman: "I read your online letter to the editor,

Greg. Is that your Indian blood or just your lovely leftist spirit speaking?"

Gregory Bozeman: "Probably both, dear Faith. I like Witherston the way it is now, with deer in our woods and turtles in our creek and even the occasional skunk in our midst. I do not want to see a drug manufacturer destroy all that."

Faith: "What do you have against drugs, Greg?"

Gregory: "I view drugs as pollutants, whether in our creeks or in our bodies."

Faith: "So you take no drugs, Greg? Not ever?"

Gregory: "Not often, dear Faith."

Faith: "Well I do, Greg. And I need something today. It's hot as forty hells, and I'm ready to pass out.

Mayor Rich Rather, speaking to Grant Griggs, Withers's lawyer: "Did you see that outrageous anonymous letter to the editor in *Witherston on the Web* this morning? I'm going to make sure that Smitty never publishes another such letter as long as he is editor. That Mr. Anonymous—or Ms Anonymous—has insulted all of us. Mr. Anonymous must be some Cherokee-loving, tree-hugging, civilization-hating, left-leaning liberal who wants to destroy Witherston."

Grant Griggs: "I'd say that Lottie or Gretchen wrote the letter. Maybe one of them killed Withers. Those rabid environmentalists would do anything to keep BioSenecta out of Witherston."

Mayor Rather: "They prefer trees to humans."

Grant: What's the point of having trees if people don't have money? BioSenecta will bring Witherston some good jobs. That will benefit everybody."

Scorch Ridge, speaking to his wife Abby Ridge: "Can we leave now? I prefer the company of Oprah, Hillary, Lucille Ball, and our other chickens to these bitching hens."

Abby Ridge: "Do you think Dr. Folsom could have poisoned Withers? He certainly had access to Withers's pills. Think of Michael Jackson's doctor."

Scorch: "Folsom could have done it, maybe. But if you want a motive, look at Gregory Bozeman. He's Cherokee, you know, and Withers's factory would have poisoned the land where the Cherokees lived for a millennium."

Abby: "Neel Kingfisher may be Cherokee too. He's got a Cherokee name.

Scorch: "But he's director of Withers Village, so he probably didn't have a motive. And he's a doctor. Doctors take a vow to heal, not to kill."

Abby: "Everybody in Witherston has a motive. It's money. Even Neel Kingfisher. Even you. You might have killed him."

Scorch: "I would have used a chisel, not poison."

Pastor Paul Clement, speaking to Smithfield Green, editor of *Witherston on the Web*: "Yes, Smitty. Our dear friend and neighbor died suddenly but naturally when God called his soul to Heaven."

Smitty Green: "You conducted a beautiful ceremony, Pastor. Thank you. I know Francis Hearty Withers would have been pleased."

❧❧❧

Paco, Jaime, Jorge, and Beau stood under an old oak tree listening to Dr. Neel Kingfisher welcome people to Withers Village for the burial of Francis Hearty Withers. The crowd included not only the attendants at Withers's funeral but also the twenty-three residents of Withers Village, all men, all over ninety years of age, five or six of them over a hundred.

The pallbearers, Mayor Rather, Grant Griggs, George Folsom, and a fourth man they didn't recognize, carried to the open grave the highly polished mahogany coffin. A replica of Leonardo da Vinci's "Last Supper" was carved into the side that Paco, Jaime, Jorge, and Beau could see. The gold hinges reflected the afternoon sun.

"The worms crawl in, the worms crawl out," Jorge whispered.

"Jorge! Behave yourself," Paco whispered back.

Jaime giggled. "No way will worms get into that coffin! Withers will be preserved in his wrinkly old body for eternity."

Dr. Kingfisher stood on the steps of the building's entrance and spoke into a microphone. "Greetings, ladies and gentlemen. We are pleased to have you here at Withers Village today. Francis Hearty Withers was our benefactor. So it is fitting that he be buried here. The statue unveiled on his birthday will designate his resting place. Now Pastor Paul Clement will lead our prayers."

Pastor Clement did, for way too long according to Jorge. Finally Pastor Clements arrived at the point of the ceremony. "Almighty God, our heavenly Father, we praise you for the sure and certain hope of the resurrection to eternal life for all who die trusting in the Lord Jesus Christ. We now commit the ashes of Francis Hearty Withers to the ground: earth to earth, ashes to ashes, dust to dust; rejoicing that on the last day Christ will transform the bodies of all who trust in him into the likeness of his own glorious resurrection body. Amen."

"Amen," repeated the hundred people listening to the pastor.

"Amen," repeated Dr. Kingfisher, who moved to the microphone: "Dear guests, not all of you are Baptists, but you honor the faith of your neighbors when you join Pastor Clement in this ceremony. Not all of you are Christians, but you honor the faith of your neighbors who are. Not all of you believe in a god above, but you honor those who do. I say we are all of us residents of Earth, like the birds in the sky, the fish in the sea, and the animals that walk upon the ground. And though we may be different from each other we live together. We humans come from the land, belong to the land, and return to the land.

"I hope that the death of one of us reminds all of us that our lives are linked, and that we should use our time on Earth to help others. When we die our separate beings will blend once again into the universe from which we came. Let's think of this when we bid Francis Hearty Withers farewell."

"Amen!" said Lottie, with Darwin perched on her shoulder.

"Amen, amen, amen! What a beautiful speech! What a beautiful soul Dr. Kingfisher must be," said Gretchen, with Gandhi at her side. Gandhi barked once. Gretchen turned to Lottie. "I want to talk with him."

"Wow!" Jorge grabbed his brother and hugged him. "That's the way I see things!" Jorge, Jaime, and Beau raced over to shake Dr. Kingfisher's hand.

Gretchen followed with Gandhi. "Dr. Kingfisher," she said, "if I went to church I'd want you to be my pastor! But my church is the woods. So I don't need a pastor. Anyway, thanks for your remarks."

"Ms. Green, I hope we can find an occasion to talk," Dr. Kingfisher responded.

Other witnesses to the burial did not approach Dr. Kingfisher. They approached Pastor Clement instead, and they addressed their questions to him.

"Who is that Dr. Kingfisher? Some non-believer?"

"He's an Indian from Oklahoma."

"Obviously."

"He might as well have worn moccasins."

"He's an atheist."

"He's an infidel."

"He's just insulted Pastor Clement."

Pastor Clement chimed in: "Dr. Kingfisher is a good man, ladies and gentlemen. But he lacks a Christian education. He does not understand the superiority of the spirit to our natural world. We must invite him into our church."

"Of course Dr. Kingfisher does not understand the superiority of the spirit to our natural world, Pastor!" Lottie interjected. "He is an Indian. Indians don't separate spirit from nature, or at least they didn't until white people invaded their land and Christianized them. Traditional Cherokee Indians don't worship a god in heaven the way you do. They don't need to. They revere nature here and now. You don't."

"Shut up, Lottie," said Grant Griggs. "Could you please, for once, keep your atheist views to yourself?"

"Yes, Grant," Lottie replied sweetly. "But just this once."

⟨✦⟩

"Hello, Rich. How are you on this sad occasion?" Grant and Ruth Griggs joined the circle around the mayor.

"Fine, thank you, Grant. And hello, Ruth, George, Faith. Yes, the occasion is sad indeed. Sad, sad. It's the end of an era. Witherston no longer belongs to a Withers. The Withers House no longer belongs to a Withers. Withers Hill Road no longer belongs to a Withers. What do we have left of the Withers?"

Faith answered the mayor. "We have Withers names. Withers Village. Witherston. Witherston Baptist Church, Witherston High School, Witherston Highway. Five generations of Withers named the landscape after themselves. That's what they left us: their names on things."

"I guess they wanted immortality."

"Don't we all?"

"Francis Hearty Withers left us Senextra," said George.

"That he did. And he left us a statue of himself," Faith said.

"And money. Lots of money."

"Do you think someone killed him?"

"No. No. He just died. It was time."

"It was."

"It was indeed."

⟨✦⟩

He's in the ground. Good. If there was an autopsy it's already been performed. If the autopsy was routine, the potassium chloride would not have been detected. And if it was, so what? Withers always had a bottle of potassium chloride tablets on the shelf above his sink. Everybody could see it. He took it as a supplement.

Do I look guilty? I probably don't look guiltier than every other hypocrite here. They're all hypocrites, pretending to be sad while being secretly happy that Withers is dead and they'll get his money. They should be thanking me. If they find out, they will.

I'll bet that every one of those so-called mourners would have killed him if they'd had the opportunity and they'd recog-

nized the need for his death. Look at his pallbearers, each of whom had a motive to kill him. I was the one to kill him because I was there at the critical time. And I was smart enough to figure out how to do it.

I don't feel bad. Probably because Withers was old and useless. Would I feel bad if I'd killed somebody younger? I wonder.

I can't worry about my crime. I can't worry about having committed it or being caught for it. The future of Senextra has to be uppermost in my mind. That's what will be expected of me. I will focus.

Funny. I went to church Sunday morning. I greeted Pastor Clement, went into the sanctuary, smiled warmly at my fellow parishioners, sat down in the pew, bowed my head to pray, and sang that hymn "How Great Thou Art." My voice rang out loud and clear: "Then sings my soul, My Saviour God, to Thee, How great Thou art, How great Thou art!" Nobody saw into my soul. Nobody knew what I had done.

I committed murder, what ordinary men never contemplate, and now I am free to do anything I need to do. Anything. I have crossed the line that separates those who see law as order and those who see law as constraint. I have escaped the constraint of law. I have escaped a cage. I can see clearly now. I can do good for the world.

಄ನ಄

Mev and Lauren were on their way home. They'd spent the day inside the Northeast Georgia Medical Center in Gainesville, where Mev had gotten a mammogram, a slew of tests, and a painful biopsy. Jim had been convinced that Mev had a tumor. The mammogram showed he was right.

"Does it strike you—" Mev turned to her friend. "—that a whole lot of folks in Witherston are getting sick lately?"

"Who else besides Wanda Clement, who died in March? I think she had ovarian cancer."

"Well, there's Gretchen Green. She had a small lump removed from her breast at Christmas, but she didn't have to go through chemo, so hardly anybody knew. Aunt Lottie told me. They're best friends."

"Hmm," Lauren said. "I didn't know. My sweet profession-al husband never discusses his patients. By the way, do you count pregnancy after menopause a sickness?"

"I would if I contracted it! Who's pregnant?"

"Rhonda Rather and Faith Folsom. Jim says there are more in town. He won't tell me their names."

"What a world, what a world! Fifty-year-old women get pregnant when they don't want a baby. And thirty-year-old women who want a baby have to do in-vitro fertilization to get pregnant.

"Jim says he knows two couples here in Witherston who are going to Athens to get pregnant."

"Ha!"

"You know what I mean, Mev! They're getting fertility treatments there. I guess some folks have to buy fertility these days. It's become a commodity."

"In our society today, everything is a commodity. Clean water, which we buy in bottles and give profits to the corpora-tions that own the source. Health, which we buy with insur-ance. And land, of course."

"You know, Mev, the Cherokees who once lived in north Georgia didn't own land as individuals. Beau talked about the Cherokee culture non-stop last night. By the way, thanks so much for taking him with you to the Oconaluftee Village. Beau said the Cherokees had communal fields and communal gardens. They didn't turn everything into commodities. At least not until the white people, quote, civilized them, un-quote."

"You're right, Lauren. Our ancestors thought the Cherokees were primitive, since they didn't own property like us white people."

"If you spent your time looking at wills, as I do, you'd know that everything under the sun is claimed by someone as property."

"Do we share anything in our society?" Mev wondered aloud.

"Yes, diseases."

"But not the cure."

☙❧☙

When Mev got home she received an earful from the boys about the funeral. Having seldom entered a church, they'd been fascinated by the cross on the altar, the images of Jesus in the stained glass windows, the recitation of the liturgy, the lighting of the candles, and the minister's sermon about the afterlife. But Mev hadn't sent Jaime and Jorge to the funeral to get educated in Baptist ritual.

"What did you hear from the people at the reception afterward?" she asked them.

"Not a lot," Jorge replied. "Mr. Griggs and Mayor Rather don't like Aunt Lottie and Gretchen Green. They plain don't like environmentalists. They accused Aunt Lottie and Gretchen of killing Withers to stop the Senextra factory."

"At the burial Mr. Griggs told Aunt Lottie to shut up," said Jaime, laughing.

"That's because she was giving Pastor Clement her views of religion," said Jorge. "Aunt Lottie was defending Dr. Kingfisher who was speaking about everybody blending into the earth when we die. I like Dr. Kingfisher's ideas about death, Mom. And Aunt Lottie's ideas about nature too."

"You know, Mom, Aunt Lottie's always saying that European-Americans worship a god separate from nature," Jaime chimed in. "So they don't understand the Cherokees' reverence for nature. They think that Indians see spirits in trees. They think that Indians are like children who will believe in God in Heaven when they grow up."

"Aunt Lottie says that Indians don't see spirits in trees," Jorge said. "They just see trees spiritually. European-Americans don't. Indians revere their land. European-Americans treat land as real estate, to be bought and sold."

"Aunt Lottie could be a Cherokee with her views—"Jaime said.

"Boys, boys!" Mev interrupted. "Let's focus. We've got a mystery to solve that's not about European-Americans and Indians."

Jorge looked thoughtful. "May we go with you tomorrow to Withers's house to look around?"

"Okay, if you all will promise not to touch anything, not a single thing."

"We promise," Jorge said.

"I suppose you want to invite Beau along?"

"Of course!"

"That's fine. I'm consulting with Beau's mother about Withers's case," Mev said. "And, come to think of it, I'm consulting with Beau's father about my case."

"Oh, Mom, we forgot. What happened at the hospital? What did you find out today?"

"A lot of tests and not a lot of information. Except for the mammogram, which showed the tumor. I'm supposed to get the results of my biopsy by 5:00 Friday. Jim will call me."

"Oh, Mom!"

"It's okay. I'll do what the doctors recommend for my physical health, and I'll do what the Witherston Police Department requires for my mental health."

"We'll help with both," Jaime said, giving her a hug.

"We love you, Mom," Jorge said.

Mev engaged both boys in a group hug. "I'm so happy we've got a really good mystery to think about. Probably a murder mystery. My first!"

"Ours too," said Jorge.

"By the way, Mom," said Jaime. "Harry's new name is Varry."

"Very what?"

"Very long story." Jaime giggled.

"Mom," Jorge said, "Varry is spelled "V-A-R-R-Y," he explained.

☙◆❧

Mev checked her email. One day out of the office and twenty-one emails. She read the most recent one. George Folsom had sent it at 4:10 pm.

Hello, Mev. I would have talked to you at Mr.

Withers's funeral today, but I didn't see you. As you know, I've taken care of Mr. Withers for more than a decade, and for the last five years I've administered his Senextra.

Would you like me to accompany you to his house tomorrow to go through his medications? I could be helpful. George

Mev wrote back.

I appreciate your offer, George, but I really have all the help I need from the Witherston Police Department. Thanks anyway. Mev

Mev read the other emails, replied appropriately, and then looked at George's again. Hmmm. First, the mayor. Then the doctor. Who else wants to help? The lawyer? The Indian chief? The butcher, the baker, the candlestick maker?

She wasn't counting Jaime and Jorge. They were part of her.

૭൦௸

Martin Payne came by Gretchen Green's Green Grocery at 6:00 pm sharp. He was still wearing the navy suit he'd worn to the funeral, but he smelled of seductive after-shave lotion.

Gretchen had dressed up, Gretchen-style. A black cotton sundress that hit mid-calf, black Birkenstock sandals, long copper earrings with dangling brown feathers, and a wide copper bracelet engraved with a Kokopelli figure. Her black lace shawl covered the Picasso dove tattoo she sported on her upper right arm. She wore her two long gray braids loose. No perfume. No make-up.

No Gandhi either. Gandhi would stay home with Barack.

Martin held the car door open for Gretchen. He was positively courtly, Gretchen thought. In his BMW convertible with the top down they descended the mountain road to Dahlonega. The wind made conversation difficult, but the ride thrilled Gretchen.

Gretchen and Martin sat down at a table for two in the Back Porch Oyster Bar. He ordered their appetizer: White Tuna Ceviche. They both ordered Sea Scallops Florentine. Their wine, which came immediately, was a Rombauer Carneros Chardonnay. Expensive, Gretchen thought, but delicious.

The conversation started with the normal preliminaries. Where are you from? Are you married? Do you have children? How old are they? Gretchen learned that Martin was from Illinois, where he'd gotten an MD/PhD from the Pritzker School of Medicine at the University of Chicago. That he'd been recruited to Atlanta in 2010 to be BioSenecta's CEO. That he'd come alone, having recently divorced. And that he had two children, thirteen-year-old Ellen and eleven-year-old Patricia who lived in Chicago with his ex-wife. From other comments he made about his education and work, Gretchen estimated his age to be forty-five. She asked him and he told her that he was a Republican.

"How did you learn that Francis Hearty Withers had died?"

"Mayor Rather called me yesterday afternoon and told me what happened," Martin replied. "So I drove up from Alpharetta this morning. I'm only seventy-five minutes away. I felt obliged to pay my respects to Mr. Withers, since he was BioSenecta's major stockholder. I'd met with him and the mayor a few times at his house to discuss plans for building the Senextra factory in Witherston."

"Why didn't I know about the plans?"

"What would you have done if you'd found out?"

"Protested!"

"Right."

Then Gretchen posed the question that had been on her mind since he'd texted her. "Why are you taking me to dinner after I carried a sign saying Senextra violates nature?"

"I wanted to know what you meant by nature."

"I thought about it. Nature, I'd say, is our planet's ecosystem as it functions independently of human control. When humans use technology to advance our own species's interests at the expense of other species's interests, then we are violating nature."

"So we humans are not part of nature?" Martin replied.

"Isn't that an antiquated view, a pre-Darwinian view? Darwin showed that we humans are not unique as a species."

Gretchen was startled to have a Republican CEO of a pharmaceutical company call her viewpoint pre-Darwinian.

"Of course we humans are part of nature!" she responded. "I simply meant that Senextra violates the laws of nature. The laws of nature bring both life and death to individuals—individual birds, squirrels, fish, bees, worms, and humans. And the death of individuals in the present makes way for the life of individuals in the future. The laws of nature keep the whole biosphere balanced. Senextra unbalances the biosphere by keeping humans alive longer than the laws of nature would normally allow."

"But as an individual, don't you want to stay alive as long as you can?"

Gretchen recalled her feelings six months ago when she chose surgery to remove the malignant lump in her breast. She'd wanted desperately to live. She was only fifty-four at the time. The laws of nature would have put her in the ground, but surgery and drugs had kept her alive.

"I do. If I had a life-threatening disease, I'd probably choose medicine over nature's laws," Gretchen answered. "She didn't want to tell him that she'd already had cancer, at least not yet. She didn't want to tell him that her left breast attested to the savagery of the scalpel, that she no longer felt pretty, that she wondered daily when she'd suffer another life-threatening disease. He was only forty-five. He was handsome, fit, self-confident. He wouldn't understand.

"So medicine and nature's laws are opposed to each other?"

"They must be," Gretchen said. "Medicine fights nature on behalf of the individual. Nature ignores the individual."

"So whose side are you on?" asked Martin. "Nature or the individual?"

"Gee, Martin. Now you've tricked me into saying some-thing that's not in keeping with what I advocate. I don't want to think of sides and oppositions and battles against nature. I want to think of humans as part of nature's ecosystem. We humans won't live long if we don't live in harmony with na-ture."

"Go on," Martin said. "I didn't mean to trick you."

"When you pit medicine against nature, you're saying that humans are in a battle with nature," Gretchen continued. "You're implying that humans are special. That's why you're working for a pharmaceutical company that makes Senext—"

"Easy," Martin interrupted, putting a hand on her arm.

"The attitude that humans are in a battle with nature and that humans are superior to everybody else on Earth led to our species' mistreatment of other species. It led to the deforestation of our planet. It led to the poisoning of our land. It led to global warming. It led to destruction of our home!"

"Easy, Gretchen, easy! Let's be calm," he said, putting both hands on her arm.

"I'll try."

"Will you let me tell you how I think of things?"

Gretchen smiled. "Okay."

"I believe that humans are distinctly different from other species. We humans have consciousness. We humans can think—"

"That's arrogant! We humans are not the only animals who have consciousness. Neurobiologists say that all mammals and all birds, and even octopuses, are neurologically capable of consciousness. My friend's bird Darwin has consciousness."

"Please, Gretchen, let me finish. We humans can think of ourselves as individuals. I studied medicine to enable individuals to have healthier lives, longer lives."

"But what if the medicine that is good for the individual is bad for our whole web of life? By the way, what's in Senextra?"

"Synthetic estrogen, and some other compounds that I'm not at liberty to disclose."

"Synthetic estrogen as in oral contraceptives?" Gretchen asked.

"Yes."

"But oral contraceptives help control our population. Senextra does the opposite. How is that?"

"Again, I'm not at liberty to disclose the secret of Senextra to you, Gretchen."

"Well, maybe Senextra is good for the individual human,

but it may keep alive too many humans for our planet to support."

"That may be true, Gretchen. But don't you yourself try to extend human lives by urging your customers to eat organic foods, exercise, and do yoga?"

"You're right. I do want to keep people healthy. I want to stay healthy myself, naturally. That's why I do yoga. Do you know that the word *yoga* means *union* in Sanscrit? Yoga reveals to me that we are all part of the same web of life, that we all have the same spirit within us. When I practice yoga every morning I shed my individual *I* and become *we* with all other living things. I reach this state of spiritual peace without drugs—though I admit I tried a few mind benders in my youth. Well, actually, more than a few."

"I can't imagine doing yoga. I'm too busy."

Gretchen grinned. "If you and if all your fellow CEOs of big corporations and all our Congressmen and all the world's political leaders and everybody who ever picked up a gun did yoga, we'd have world peace."

"I guess nobody would have time for war if everybody were sitting cross-legged on the floor humming OM.'"

"What a wonderful world it would be!" said Gretchen. "I see trees of green..."

"And if everybody ate organically, we'd have no need for medicine? And no need for doctors?"

"Pesticides on fruits and vegetables harm us humans, and pesticides in our environment harm fish, birds, and all the other animals that ingest them. Pesticides kill the bees that pollinate plants. Pesticides disrupt nature's balance. So do synthetic hormones. And other drugs that get into our water supply."

"Go on," said Martin.

"When we put pesticides and synthetic hormones into our environment we're putting them into ourselves, and making ourselves sick. And when we put drugs into ourselves to get well, we make our environment sick. We aren't separable from our environment."

"So where do you stand on anti-biotics, anti-depressants, oral contraceptives, analgesics, and vaccines? And speaking of medical attention to individuals, where do you stand on tubal ligation, abortion, and heart transplants?"

Gretchen had had an abortion when she was seventeen years old. If she hadn't had it, she would never have gone to college.

She'd used oral contraceptives through her short marriage and thereafter until she reached forty. At the age of forty she'd had a tubal ligation to make sure she'd never get pregnant, and then she'd gone through a depression when she realized that she'd deprived herself forever of having children. But she wasn't about to reveal all that to Martin, not on their first date.

"Oh my god, Martin! You're making my brain tired. Can we talk about something else? Like your taste in movies?"

"Of course, Gretchen. But first let me say that our country's founding fathers wrote the Constitution to protect the individual, not the environment. Our Bill of Rights protects the individual, not the environment. And as a doctor I'm concerned with the individual, not the environment."

"I know that," Gretchen snapped. "You're disconnecting the health of the individual from the health of the environment. I'm not. So what's your favorite movie?"

"*Out of Africa*," Martin said.

"Wow! That's mine too!" Gretchen said.

They talked about *Out of Africa* and Mel Streep and Robert Redford.

Martin quoted his favorite line from the movie, "God made the world round so we would never be able to see too far down the road."

"So you, a maker of drugs, don't want to see too far down the road?" Gretchen said. She regretted her remark immediately. She wanted Martin to like her.

Martin poured her a third glass of wine and ordered their coffee. "I'm spending the night in the Witherston Inn. I have a meeting tomorrow morning with Grant Griggs and another one late tomorrow afternoon with Rich Rather. So may I take you to lunch tomorrow?"

"I'll fix you lunch at the grocery, if you will eat organic vegetables."

"I guess organic vegetables won't kill me, unless you serve me poisonous mushrooms."

Gretchen smiled. "You don't want any Destroying Angel with your morels?"

Gretchen and Martin drove back up the mountain in comfortable silence. When he walked her to her door, he kissed her good night.

On the forehead.

ℰↄℰↄ

Mev, Paco, Jaime, and Jorge sat happily at the round table in Aunt Lottie's dining room. Varry lay under the table resting his head on Mev's feet.

With Darwin perched on her left shoulder Lottie presided over the meal she'd prepared using local organic foods from Gretchen Green's Green Market. Cold beets drizzled with thick Balsamic Vinegar of Modena—well, that was imported—surrounded by basil leaves and slices of lemon. Rainbow trout sautéed in Georgia Olive Farms Extra Virgin Olive Oil and garlic, garnished with lemon zest and served on a bed of spinach. Asparagus with a slice of lemon. Strawberries and blueberries. Seltzer water with a slice of lemon. A 2010 Napa Valley Cabernet from Whitehall Lane for Mev, Paco, and Lottie. Lottie liked lemon with everything and fine red wine with anything.

"We had a special wine tonight," Lottie explained, "in case Mev has to go without wine for a couple of months."

"God forbid!" said Mev. "Will I have to choose between saving my life and drinking your fine wine? I don't know which I'd prefer!"

"You can have both. For each week you're feeling poorly, I'll put on the fireplace mantle a very special wine for our post-cancer celebration. Or celebrations."

"Can't wait," Mev said.

"Me neither," Paco said.

"Now I don't know whether I want the treatment to be short or long!"

"Aunt Lottie," Jorge interrupted the frivolity over his mother's cancer. "Jaime caught a deformed frog in Founding Father's Creek near Founding Father's Bridge. You can see my picture of him on *Webby Witherston*."

"I saw it," Lottie said. "You're a good photographer, Jorge."

"Anyway," Jorge said, "Dad, Jaime, Beau, and I hiked down the creek on Sunday for a picnic. Jaime took his net to get some live mussels for you, Aunt Lottie, but he didn't find any. That was strange. And Beau was looking for a few minnows for his aquarium, but he didn't find any minnows either. Then Jaime saw this strange frog and captured it. Lo and behold, the frog had three hind legs. We call him Leggy Froggy."

"He'll do well in Frog Olympics," Jaime said. "If he doesn't get disqualified for taking a performance-enhancing drug."

"The officials won't need to do a blood test. They'll just count his back legs." Jorge stood and looked official. "One...two...three. Wait! Let me count again: one...two... three. Yup! Three back legs. Disqualified!" He sat down amid the laughter.

"Anyway, Jaime released him," Jorge continued. "Jaime likes to grow his own frogs from tadpoles."

"To make sure they're locally grown!" said Jaime.

"All Jaime's frogs are locally grown," Jorge said. "Aunt Lottie, you could eat them. The tadpoles come from Founding Father's Creek, which has the best-tasting water in Georgia—"

"According to *Webby Witherston*," said Lottie.

"Yes. We could bottle Founding Father's Creek water and get rich like the Perrier people. We could even advertise it on TV as 'Local water. Makes frogs grow three legs. Who knows what advantages it can give you!'" Jorge mimicked a television advertiser.

"I wonder who owns the creek," said Jaime.

"It once belonged to the Cherokee people. But our ancestors sent the Cherokees far away so they could have it. Now we consider the creek ours. I say it belongs to everybody, like the air," Lottie said.

Paco changed the subject before Lottie could begin a rant

on injustice. "I wonder who killed Mr. Withers, if he was killed," he said. "What's your thinking, Lottie?"

"Many folks may have wanted to kill Withers. Withers was ready to flatten thirty-one acres of old-growth forest to build the Senextra factory on the creek. That would be another insult to the Cherokee people, and to all of us who choose to live in north Georgia because of the beautiful land. Withers would have paved paradise and put up a parking lot."

"Where have I heard that?" Mev said.

"Right here in my house, love. 'Big Yellow Taxi,' by Joni Mitchell."

"Lottie, who do you really think killed Withers?" Paco asked again.

"Maybe Neel Kingfisher. Maybe Gregory Bozeman. Those two would have done it for honorable reasons, to save our land and to keep a pill factory out of Witherston. You know, the Senextra factory would have taken clean water out of the creek upstream from Witherston, used it to make Senextra, and then flushed it back into the creek for the rest of us to use. Not fair."

The boys were paying rapt attention. "Neel or Gregory? Really, Aunt Lottie?" asked Jaime.

"However," Lottie continued, "most murderers have dishonorable reasons for committing their crime, such as greed. If greed's the motivation, then the murderer could be any Witherstonian who'd enjoy a little more money. But I think that the murderer is not just your standard average Witherstonian. I'd advise Mev to focus on the Senextra connection."

"Why?"

"Withers' birthday party was all about the Senextra factory. Since Withers died before he changed his will, Witherston gets the Senextra factory. Remember what Withers said to us protesters? He said he'd change his will, that he'd not give his money to Witherstonians, that he'd not bring the Senextra factory here, and that he'd mow down his woods. So anybody who wanted money, anybody who loved woods, and especially anybody who wanted the Senextra factory here would want to kill the malicious old man. I for one am glad he's dead and incapable of doing more damage to the world."

"Me too," Jorge said.

"And I'm glad he didn't have kids," Jaime said. "They'd make our lives witherable."

The boys giggled."

"Do you all realize that Withers lived for 36,528 days?" Jorge said, looking at his smartphone.

"How did you figure that?" asked Jaime.

"One hundred times 365 equals 36,500 plus 25 leap year days equals 36,525 plus the 3 days he lived after his birthday."

"Wow, think of all he could have done with so many days! I think I'll calculate the number of hours he lived." Jaime got out his smartphone. "Then I'll do the minutes!"

"You all, I have a bad feeling about this murder," Lottie said. "I imagine that Withers was killed by somebody who had never before committed murder, maybe some respected member of our community, probably somebody we know. That person is now a murderer who may kill again to cover up his first crime."

Mev stayed silent.

"Don't worry, Mev. I'm going to keep watch over my favorite people. I'm an insomniac, you know. And insomniacs evolved to keep watch over their tribes at night. Only the insomniacs heard the enemy's footsteps while everyone else slept."

❧❧❧

While he mulled over the day's events, Neel sipped a Tiger Mountain Malbec. He liked many Georgia wines. Then he wrote in his journal:

> *Why did Mr. Francis Hearty Withers struggle so mightily against death?*
>
> *And to acquire that outrageously expensive, outrageously tasteless, airtight coffin to spend eternity separated from the elements! He must have viewed Earth as his enemy. He certainly viewed death as his enemy, as mankind's enemy.*
>
> *So selfish. He used his money for only two pro-*

jects: Withers Village and the Senextra pilot study on the Withers Villagers. To make the old older. Why couldn't he have used just a little of the interest on his billions to make the young healthier? Couldn't he have supported the prenatal care unit at the hospital, or the maternity ward there, or the breakfast program for elementary school children here? Or research into childhood leukemia. Mr. Francis Hearty Withers, my first cousin once removed, valued one-hundred-year olds over ten-year olds.

At least that's what his money said. But then Mr. Francis Hearty Withers never had a child.

Here I am, working for Withers Village as its director when I don't want to make the old older.

And, more importantly, when I'm seeing side effects to Senextra that should be known. Am I the only one seeing those side effects? If the old men aren't complaining, should I raise the issue?

Or should I resign?

I will resign. Soon. And I will go far away.

WWW.ONLINEWITHERSTON.COM

WITHERSTON ON THE WEB
Wednesday, May 27, 2015

LOCAL NEWS

Yesterday, at 4:30 pm, Francis Hearty Withers was buried beside the entrance to Withers Village.

Withers Village director Dr. Neel Kingfisher welcomed guests to Withers Village, and Pastor Paul Clement presided over the burial service.

Pallbearers included Mr. Withers's friend Mayor Rich Rather, his lawyer Grant Griggs, his doctor George Folsom, and BioSenecta CEO Dr. Martin Payne.

In 2004, Mr. Withers had endowed Founding Father's Retirement Community and changed its name to Withers Village. In 2011, Mr. Withers arranged for Withers Villagers to take the anti-aging drug Senextra in a five-year pilot study sponsored by the drug's manufacturer BioSenecta of Atlanta.

Two new signs appeared on street corners some time yesterday afternoon.

One sign, nailed to the picket fence surrounding the City Hall, on the southeast corner of Main Street and Ninovan Drive, depicted a doe and her fawn sleeping on dirt surrounded by tree stumps.

The other sign, nailed to the same picket fence on the northeast corner of Main Street and Creek Street, depicted a long wrinkled arm reaching out of a coffin waving a chain saw.

Mayor Rather took down both signs when he got to his office at 9:30 this morning. He is keeping the signs as evidence against *Witherston's KEEP NATURE NATURAL* environmentalist organization.

~ *Catherine Perry, Reporter*

LETTERS TO THE EDITOR

To the Editor:

I too am sad that Mr. Withers passed away. As a long-term Withers Villager I have taken Senextra for four years, and now I am a happy, healthy 102-year-old man. I owe my long life to Mr. Withers and Dr. Folsom, who enabled me to take part in BioSenecta's pilot study.

I was a successful architect in Atlanta for thirty years until I retired at the age of 62. Having no children, my wife and I built a beautiful home on Lake Hartwell, where we golfed and sailed and enjoyed each other's company until her death twenty years ago. At the age of ninety-two, I sold our home and moved into the renovated Withers Village, which Mr. Withers had endowed in 2004.

Here my friends and I, all of us either over a hundred or approaching a hundred, lead good productive lives. Indoors we play bridge, pinochle, canasta, and mahjong. Outdoors we play golf, croquet, and horseshoes. We have cocktails before dinner and wine at dinner. We socialize with each other.

None of us has a serious illness. Few of us take drugs other than Senextra, an occasional aspirin, or an occasional laxative.

None of us has Alzheimer's or any other form of senile dementia. Some of us subscribe to the Wall Street Journal or the New York Times. One of us subscribes to Cat Fancy. Withers Village has four cats, named Goldilocks, Redskin, Brave, and J.C. Penny.

All Withers Villagers take Senextra. We have proven that Senextra can halt the aging process, which is the body's enemy. To me, Senextra symbolizes American medicine, which is obviously the best in the world.

I want every American who can afford it to have access to Senextra.

I hope that when you opponents of the BioSenecta factory get old you'll realize that you don't want to die either. And then you too will take Senextra, if you can afford it. I advise you to stop protesting and go to work, or you won't be able to afford it.

~ Signed, Asmund Jorgensen

To the Editor:

Young Jorge Arroyo's fine photograph of the five-legged frog that appeared in yesterday's Witherston on the Web is a pollution wake-up call. As most environmentalists know, birth defects in wildlife can signal environmental pollution dangerous to humans.

If nobody else does, I myself will get a sample of that creek water for the EPA. And if the water is already contaminated by toxic chemicals, then I myself will lead the charge to eliminate the source of the pollution.

~ Signed, Gretchen Green

To the Editor:

I learned a good reason for saving Mr. Withers's old-growth forest when my family visited the Oconaluftee Indian Village and the Museum of the Cherokee Indian in Cherokee, North Carolina, on Memorial Day.

The philosophy of Cherokee medicine is to prevent illness, in contrast to the philosophy of Western medicine which is to cure illness. The Cherokees believe that to stay well you have to have contact with nature. When you spend time outside in the woods or on the creek or in the mountains you develop harmony between your mind, your body, and your spirit. And that's what being well means for the Cherokee people.

So let's not clear-cut Mr. Withers's woods. We Withersto-nians need all the contact with nature that we can get.

By the way, the Cherokee word "tohi" means both health and peace. Isn't that cool?

~ Signed, Jorge Arroyo

POLICE BLOTTER

At 11:45 pm yesterday, Tuesday, May 26, a Witherston po-lice officer was called to the grounds of Withers Village by Dr. Neel Kingfisher to investigate an attempt to dig up the body of Francis Hearty Withers. Mr. Withers had been buried next to the entrance of the retirement facility. The officer spotted two individuals wearing stocking masks and dressed in black flee-ing into the woods with shovels.

At 1:00 am on May 27, a Sheriff's deputy was called to the home of Miss Mercy Calvin on North Possum Road who com-plained that there was a snake in her mailbox. The deputy checked the mailbox. The snake was a rattlesnake, a dead one.

ON THIS DAY IN HISTORY
By Charlotte Byrd

On May 27, 2009, Witherston Baptist Church hired Paul Clement from Augusta to serve as its pastor, beginning August 1. Pastor and Mrs. Clement moved into the old Lowry House on Black Fox Road.

Wanda Clement died of cancer on March 30, 2015, at the age of fifty-two. She was survived by her husband Paul, who remains here, and her son Nathan, who lives in Miami.

CHAPTER 7

Wednesday morning, May 27, 2015:

Mev kept her regular Scissors appointment. Every third Wednesday at 7:30 am, Jon shampooed her hair, cut it, and styled it. She loved the decor of Scissors—mauve walls that displayed Jon's photographs and paintings of north Georgia, navy leather chairs, and exotic orchids under growing lights. And she loved the classical music he played. Today it was Chopin.

Mev told Jon about her breast cancer worries, not just because he was a dear friend but also because he would be her beauty advisor if she underwent chemotherapy.

"Look good, feel better," he advised all the cancer patients who turned to him for comfort when they got their diagnosis. And then he cared for all their cosmetology needs free of charge.

Mev knew that if she needed chemo Jon would shave her head, order her wig, and make her feel attractive. Jon said that was his mission in life: "To make every woman who walks out of Scissors happy with her appearance."

Considering his alopecia areata, Mev found Jon's dedication to his profession truly admirable. Jon didn't have any body hair at all, apparently, and hadn't had any since high school thirty years ago. He was a nice-looking man, slender and tall, and he would have been handsome had he worn a toupée, but he didn't seem interested in making himself handsome.

"How are your boys handling your health news, Mev?"

"Better than I expected," Mev said. "On Sunday Paco took

them hiking down Founding Father's Creek to the old bridge. When they got home they were more excited about finding a deformed frog—a frog with three back legs—than worried about me. I was happy for them."

"I saw Jorge's picture of the frog on *Witherston on the Web*. By the way I've shot Founding Father's Bridge for my collection. He pointed to a beautiful black and white framed photograph at the back of the shop. Gregory and I've gone there many times. It's Gregory's favorite spot to fish."

Today Mev was eager to hear from Jon the opinions Witherstonians held about Withers's murder. Jon heard everything because his devoted clients relaxed and spoke to him intimately during their beautification process. He never revealed the source of his news, but if he hadn't received the news in confidence he usually didn't hesitate to disclose it. She leaned back in his navy leather shampoo chair and closed her eyes in pleasant anticipation of the sudsy head massage. "What have you heard about Withers, Jon?" she asked.

"I've heard—" Jon began his disclosure as always. "—that old Withers and his antique cronies in Withers Village aren't the only folks in this neck of the woods to be using Senextra. A few middle-aged ladies of your acquaintance, Mev, have been illegally taking the drug for some time. They want to feel younger than their fifty years. I guess all the work I do on their hair doesn't suffice."

"My gosh, Jon! Is Senextra on the black market?"

"Sure is, sweet baby. Senextra is sold, or at least distributed, by someone in Witherston. I don't know who, and I don't care. I've got no desire to live past ninety."

"I understand trying to look good—heaven knows I'm trying—but I don't understand trying to extend one's life artificially."

"But that's what people do, Mev. We take antibiotics and sulfa drugs to keep from dying of an infection. Medications to lower blood pressure, elevate thyroid function, regulate heartbeat. Antidepressants. Antacids. Antihistamines. Celebrex. And other prescription drugs to make us feel good and extend our lives."

"And I'm probably going to take chemo to keep from dying of breast cancer," Mev said.

Jon wrapped a towel around Mev's head and steered her toward his cutting chair. "And I hope you do everything your doctors recommend to keep from dying of breast cancer, sweet baby."

"Jon, what happens when everybody takes Senextra?"

"For one thing, we Americans will be the oldest folks on the planet."

"And the most medicated," Mev said. "And when we're buried, we'll bring our meds—the traces of them still in our bodies—with us, into the land. We'll have medicated land. Maybe we already do."

"You're done," Jon said, holding up a mirror so that Mev could appreciate his handiwork.

"I guess I don't want to give up my meds. I want to accomplish something before I take my dirt nap."

"Like what?"

Mev laughed. "Like solving this mystery."

As Mev left, Rhonda Rather entered Scissors. She was carrying her terrier Giuliani. Beautiful, sweet Rhonda always dressed elegantly, even when six months pregnant. And she dressed Giuliani elegantly too. Giuliani was wearing a pink ribbon.

"Good morning, Rhonda!" Mev greeted her. "Are you bringing Giuliani here for a hair cut too?"

"Yes, she is, Mev!" Jon said. "I give Giuliani a discount because she weighs only fifteen pounds."

"And I weigh ten times that!" Rhonda said.

Mev had heard that Rhonda's wealth came not from her husband's used car dealership but from her own investments. Like everybody else in town, Mev had heard that Rhonda had BioSenecta stock. Why in the world had Rhonda married Rich? Mev wondered. Maybe because she wanted a child. And she got lovely Sandra.

 espa

Jaime and Jorge were waiting for her with Beau when Mev

returned home at 8:30 to pick up a flathead screwdriver and take them to Withers's house. Actually, Jaime and Jorge were waiting for her with Beau and Varry. Mev told them that Varry had to stay home.

"But Mom," Jaime pleaded. "Varry knows Mr. Withers's house. Varry can find us clues to his death."

Mev relented. Jorge got into the right front seat of her CRV. He opened his tablet. Jaime, Beau, and Varry got into the back seat. Varry seemed delighted to be seated between the two boys, who promptly fastened their seatbelts. Jaime put his arm over Varry's shoulders.

When Mev brought the car to a halt at the end of Withers Road, outside the yellow CRIME SCENE ribbon, she gave the boys latex gloves and put a pair on herself.

"Don't touch a thing without asking me first," she called out as Jaime, Jorge, and Beau raced after Varry onto the front porch.

"Sure, Mom," Jaime yelled over his shoulder.

"Sure, Mom." Jorge yelled.

"Yes, Mizz Arroyo." Beau yelled.

Mev followed her young team and opened the front door with the key the Witherston Police Department had made for her use.

They were alone in the house. Varry walked in circles in the dining room, sniffing the floor and the two chairs at the table. Then Varry went upstairs to Withers's bedroom. Mev and the boys climbed the stairs after him, curious.

The bedroom was unremarkable. The bed was unmade, probably because Amy had had Saturday off. Withers's suits, jackets, shirts, and trousers were hung neatly in his closet.

A computer, still powered up, was on a table. Mev moved the mouse and brought the screen to life. Withers had been reading the *Wall Street Journal* online. She was impressed. At the age of one hundred he got his news online.

The top dresser drawer was open. Varry stood on his hind legs to investigate it. Looking where Varry sniffed, Mev discovered seven bottles of NatureMade Melatonin, each containing 120 tablets. Under a pile of handkerchiefs she found a well-thumbed book titled *Hormones and the Aging Process.*

Now Mev had something to think about. "Boys, have you all found anything?" she called.

The boys had followed Varry down the stairs into a sunroom beyond the living room.

"Nothing much, Mom," answered Jaime. "Just a bunch of plants."

"But we found a spiral notebook, Mom," said Jorge. "It has a name written on the first page: "Penny Kingfisher. Nothing else."

Hmmm, Mev thought. "The director of Withers Village is Neel Kingfisher. I wonder who Penny is."

✌✌✌

Mev descended the stairs into the living room. With her screwdriver she attacked the lock of the oak trunk. Success! She lifted the lid.

On the top of numerous papers and files was a diary from 1838 by Penance Hearty Withers Withers. Leafing through the diary she chanced upon the entry for May 30. On that page only one sentence was written:

My dearest husband was killed
this morning by an Indian.

Good god! Mev looked at the next page, which was blank, and the next and the next. Then on the page designated June 6 she found the story of Hearty Withers's death. That was the last entry in Penance's diary. She put the diary into her briefcase to show to Aunt Lottie.

Mev turned her attention to the other contents of the trunk. There was an old leather-bound black Bible. She opened it and found birth, marriage, and death dates for four generations of Withers on the inside cover. It had belonged first to Harry Withers, born in 1830. She put the Bible into her briefcase as well. Aunt Lottie could construct an historical narrative out of this information.

There were at least a dozen thick files. She opened one of the manila folders: old, very old, letters. She opened another:

newspaper clippings. Another: stock certificates issued by the Lawrence Company from the 1930s. And under the files a crudely framed certificate.

Mev took the framed certificate out of the trunk and examined it. Beneath the cracked glass it was yellowed and stained. Dear Lord! It was a deed to the forty acres of land she was standing on, the land that had once belonged to the Cherokee Indians of these parts, the land Hearty Withers had won in the 1832 Georgia Land Lottery, the land Francis Hearty Withers had inherited and occupied.

Mev read and reread the deed, issued by Governor Wilson Lumpkin to Hearty Withers on October 22 of 1832. Here was first-hand evidence of the state's crime against the Cherokee nation, from which Hearty's great, great grandson Francis Hearty Withers had benefitted until his death 183 years later.

STATE OF GEORGIA.

BY HIS Excellency Wilson Lumpkin Governor and Commander-in-Chief of the Army and Navy of this State, and of the Militia thereof:

To all to whom these Presents shall come—Greeting:

KNOW YE, That in pursuance of the Act of the General Assembly of this State, entitled "an Act to lay out the Gold region in the Lands at present in the occupancy of the Cherokee Indians, into small lots, and dispose of the same by separate lottery," passed on the 22nd day of December, 1831, I HAVE GIVEN AND GRANTED, and by these presents, DO GIVE AND GRANT unto Hearty Withers of Savannah District Chatham County, his heirs and assigns forever, all that Tract or Lot of Land, containing Forty Acres, lying and being in the Twelfth District of the First Section, in the County of Cherokee, in said State, which said Tract or Lot of Land is known and distinguished in the plan of said District by the number

Three hundred and ninety five having such shape,
form, and marks as appear by a plat of the same
hereunto annexed:

TO HAVE AND TO HOLD the said Tract or Lot
of Land, together with all and singular the rights,
members, and appurtenances thereof, whatsoever,
unto the said Hearty Withers, his heirs and assigns;
to his and their own proper use, benefit, and behoof
forever in fee simple.

GIVEN under my hand, and the Great Seal of the
said State, this twenty-second day of October in the
year eighteen hundred and thirty two and of the in-
dependence of the United States of America the fifty
nannetts—

Mev couldn't make out the last word, but she understood
well the certificate's significance. Hearty Withers had won his
forty acres in a lottery operated by the state of Georgia to dis-
tribute Cherokee land to white people.

Luck of the draw. Hearty Withers was twice lucky. In 1829
he panned for gold and found his fortune in a creek on Cherokee land.

Three years later he won the lottery, acquired his lot on
Founding Father's Creek, and built his log home there. Withers and his fellow white settlers of north Georgia, including
Mev's ancestors had acted as if the Cherokee land belonged to
nobody, as if the Cherokees were not people.

Mev would have liked to spend the rest of the day explor-
ing the trunk's contents, but she had a murder to solve. She
doubted that the diary, letters, clippings, bills, receipts, and
other documents would advance her investigation. But they
should not go unread before she turned them over to a library.
Aunt Lottie could study the diary and the Bible. The boys
could study the other documents.

"Boys," Mev called. "Come look at what I found!"

౼౩౬౷

Jaime, Jorge, and Beau sat at Withers's dining room table on ladderback chairs. Varry dozed at Jaime's feet. The boys faced three stacks of files, which they'd organized into categories: letters, newspaper clippings, and official documents.

Their mission, which they chose to accept, was to examine all the documents and learn from them who Francis Hearty Withers was. His genealogy, his heritage, his connections with other members of his family and his community, his tastes, his virtues, his vices. Who might want to kill him, and for what reason.

Jorge opened his tablet and clicked on the camera app. He would photograph all the documents and email them to Jaime, Beau, and himself to read together at home.

∽∾∽

Mev continued her inventory of the contents of Withers's house. Refrigerator: one bottle of soymilk; two unopened bottles of Frei Brothers Reserve Chardonnay; two bottles of Perrier, one of them half empty; three tomatoes; a Gouda cheese; a stick of butter; and so forth. Mev quickly grew bored making her list. She opened the freezer compartment: four packages of frozen peas. She opened the pantry: flour; sugar; extra virgin olive oil; expensive Balsamic vinegar from Modena; five other vinegars. Amy must be a good cook, Mev decided.

Then she entered the basement, actually, the wine cellar. Wonder of wonders! Case after case of fine wine, very, very fine wine—mostly from Napa Valley, mostly Cabs—piled on top of each other. She counted fourteen cases, plus some odd lots. There must have been close to two hundred bottles there. When was Withers planning to drink it? What was he saving it for? His 105th birthday?

Mev looked at several cases. They were from 2007. But the rest of the cases were of more recent vintages. So Withers had bought all this wine. He hadn't inherited it. Wine was his hobby. But what fun could he have counting his bottles, or even drinking their contents, all alone? He'd never be able to drink them all.

Mev counted the bottles to ensure that none of them would

disappear in the course of the police investigation. She noted 188 dusty bottles in all.

Her cell phone rang. It was Catherine Perry, the twenty-year-old reporter for *Witherston on the Web*. Mev knew Catherine's parents, Wyatt and Margaret. She'd watched Catherine grow up, edit her high school yearbook, and then major in mass communication at Brenau College in Gainesville, Georgia. Catherine had worked for *Webby Witherston* for the last three summers.

"Hello, Detective Arroyo," Catherine said. "Are you investigating Withers's death as a homicide?"

"Hello, Catherine. How nice to hear from you. I have to tell you no. At least, not now. I am simply looking through Withers's house to see whether the cause of death is suspicious. I have found nothing yet to prompt a criminal investigation."

"Can you tell me what you've found? I need to give my readers something to think about."

Mev talked with her for five minutes.

એજાજ

I am not going to let my life be driven by fear of discovery. I'm not. I killed one individual for the benefit of many. I killed Withers to further the research into Senextra. When it is manufactured for public sale, Senextra will become the most revolutionary drug in the history of the world. And I will be famous as one of its founding fathers. As famous as Alexander Fleming, penicillin's founding father. As famous as Jonas Salk.

I can't let Gretchen Green and her environmental vigilante comrades block the Senextra factory just because some kid found a deformed frog in the creek. She thinks there's industrial waste in the water. But it's probably Senextra. Senextra excreted by the old men taking the drug in Withers Village.

I've got to find out myself, before anybody else does.

And what if Senextra is in our water supply? So is Valium. So is Prozac. We all get each other's drugs, and we all share our drugs with each other. Everybody who takes drugs urinates drugs. These days almost everybody urinates drugs.

Fine.

If Senextra is in our water supply, then we'll all live longer. Witherston is downstream from Withers Village. So Witherstonians are in for a big treat! Long life. And that's thanks to me.

Still, it would be better for Witherstonians not to know that they're drinking Senextra in their iced tea. I need to know, but they don't.

ↁↁↁ

As she walked into the house with the boys, Mev's phone beeped, indicating that she'd received an email. She opened it on her computer. It was from Dirk Wales, Lumpkin County's Coroner. She read the attached letter. How perplexing.

Lumpkin County Coroner
Chestatee Regional Hospital
227 Mountain Drive
Dahlonega, GA 30533

Dirk Wales, M.D., Coroner
Case No.: 2015-0001

May 27, 2015

Detective Emma Evelyn Arroyo
Witherston Police Department
Witherston, Georgia 30533
RE: Francis Hearty Withers, white male, age 100
Date of Death: May 23, 2015

At 9:20 am on Sunday, May 24, 2015, Witherston Police Department officers summoned to the home of Francis Hearty Withers at 1 Withers Hill Road pronounced Mr. Withers dead on the scene. The body was taken by ambulance to Chestatee Regional Hospital where a routine autopsy was performed. The time of death was determined to be between 6:00 and 9:00 pm on Saturday, May 23.

The deceased, a Caucasian male, age 100, appeared to have died of natural causes.

Dr. John Morston, pathologist, found in Withers's body traces of red wine, morel mushrooms, mozzarella cheese, rhubarb pie, and the drugs Senextra and Celebrex. Dr. Morston reported elevated levels of potassium in the blood stream. He also reported a slightly inflamed site of an injection. Dr. Morston noted one oddity in the five-foot-ten-inch-tall, 160-pound body: slightly enlarged breasts.

Dr. Morston determined the cause of death to be cardiac arrest. Since the deceased was known to have been taking a potassium chloride supplement and monthly injections of Senextra, the Coroner discounts the findings of potassium in the blood stream, as well as the inflammation at the injection site.

The coroner declares that the deceased came to his death by natural causes.

Dirk Wales, MD
Dirk Wales, M.D., Coroner, Lumpkin County, Georgia

಄಄಄

"Boys," Mev said to Jorge, Jaime, and Beau, after showing them the Coroner's letter. "I have another bit of detective work for you all."

"Woohoo!"

"Would you all like to get on the web and look for poisons that are undetectable in an autopsy?"

"Sure," Jorge said. "I'll google how to kill a man with poison and not get caught!"

"I'll just google poisons that are undetectable in autopsy," Jaime said.

"And that cause cardiac arrest," Beau added,

"You've got the idea, boys. Now I have to go back to the office."

಄಄಄

From her office, Mev called Chief McCoy. "Hi, Jake. I just got the Coroner's report. The Coroner states that Withers died of natural causes. But I can't believe that Withers wasn't given a boost."

"Do you have any evidence that he was murdered?"

"Nothing other than motive—motives, I mean—to kill him before he had the opportunity to write a new will. According to his present will, upon his death every man, woman, and child presently residing in Witherston will inherit a huge sum of money. That's motive number one."

"What's motive number two?"

"According to his present will, BioSenecta will inherit the rest of his estate to build a Senextra factory. The factory would provide jobs for Witherstonians and tax revenue for Witherston. But Withers was already negotiating with BioSenecta to sell the company the 31.7 acres he owns on the creek."

"Is there a motive number three?"

"Withers had hired bulldozers to level the forested land he was going to sell to BioSenecta. Environmentalists might have thought that his death would save the woods and stop the construction."

"I read in the paper that Withers was the majority stockholder of BioSenecta, so he really did own the company."

"And there's a fourth possibility. Withers may not have been the only person in our community with stock in Bio-Senecta or with a stake in the success of Senextra."

"How interesting, Mev. Can you obtain stockholder records to find out who among us owns shares of BioSenecta?"

"I think so. But I have a question. What happens to Withers's fortune if his will is determined to be invalid?"

"If Withers has any living relatives, even distant relatives, those relatives would inherit his money."

"That would give his relatives a motive, if he has any relatives," Mev said.

"Be sure to look for any new will he might have written himself on Friday night or Saturday."

ぐろぐろ

Having finished their lunch of organic locally grown vegetables—asparagus, beets, morel mushrooms, and snap peas,
drizzled with extra virgin olive oil from Italy and roasted in the
oven—Gretchen and Martin moved to the oak rockers on the
front porch.

"That was an excellent vegetarian meal, Gretchen."

"You're extravagant with your compliments, Martin. Because I'm starting to like you I chose not to serve you fried
five-legged frog, which is available locally this week."

"What are you talking about?"

"The deformed frog that the Arroyo boys found at the
bridge. *Webby Witherston* published a picture of it yesterday.
Some folks are saying that the frog's deformity is proof of toxic waste in the creek.

"Oh."

"Anyway, what did you speak with Grant Griggs about?"
she asked.

"Mr. Withers's will, which Grant drew up. I wanted to
make sure that BioSenecta still inherits Withers's estate. By
the way, Mr. Withers was going to sell the 31.7-acre site to
BioSenecta for only $1. His heart as well as his money was
invested in BioSenecta."

"So what did you learn?"

"That we'll get it."

"So nothing will stop you from building your Senextra factory here?"

"Nothing," Martin said. "Or almost nothing."

೧౩౮౧

Jim Lodge called Mev at 2:15. "Hi, Mev. I've got the results of the tests. But first, Lauren asked me to invite you and
your boys to eat with us at the Smith House in Dahlonega tonight."

"We accept your nice invitation, Jim. But tell me. What's
my future?"

"Your future's bright. You have a fairly small cancerous
tumor, a ductal carcinoma in situ, which is estrogen-receptor-
positive."

"What does that mean?"

"That means that the growth of the cancer cells is stimulated by estrogen."

"Is that good or bad, Jim?"

"Your cancer is treatable, and you have a good prognosis. We're scheduling a lumpectomy for you on Tuesday. No mastectomy. Lauren will take you to Northeast Georgia Medical Center in Gainesville Monday morning for the blood tests. Paco will want to be with you on Tuesday."

"Will I have to spend Tuesday night at the hospital?"

"No. You won't feel very well after the surgery, but you'll be ready for Paco to drive you home by 5:00. Paco will be your nurse for a few days."

"Paco will be an excellent nurse," Mev said.

"After the oncologist and the surgeon get lab results from the extracted tissue, they will decide whether to prescribe chemotherapy and/or radiation. I have a hunch you'll need only radiation after the surgery."

"Tell me about the radiation."

"It won't be painful," Dr. Lodge reassured her. "You'll probably have 35 days of radiation focused on your left breast. The major effect you'll feel from the radiation is fatigue. You can get the radiation at Chestatee Hospital in Dahlonega at 8:00 in the morning, come back to Witherston to go to work at 9:00, and then go home for a nap at 3:30."

"At home I'll have the company of Paco, Jaime, Jorge, and Varry. By the way, the twins named Harry Varry."

"Very what?"

Mev laughed. "Very long story."

"You're taking this news well, Mev."

"I've had time to get used to it, Jim. And I've looked around. Everybody has some problem or other to overcome. This is mine, and I'll overcome it. Besides I have a mystery to solve. Probably a murder mystery. I'm going to think about cancer as little as possible and murder as much as possible."

"One last thing, Mev. No more birth control pills. Stop immediately. And no synthetic estrogen for the rest of your life. Estrogen is your enemy."

"Estrogen is my enemy," Mev repeated.

"I look forward to seeing you all tonight. We'll meet there at 7:00. Bring your Aunt Lottie."

ೲೲ

Mev told Paco, Jaime, Jorge, and Lottie about Jim's phone call on their way to Dahlonega.

"We love you, Mom," Jaime said.

"We love you, Mom."

"*Querida*, we all love you."

"Me, too, dear," Lottie said.

Mev turned around from the right front seat and sent virtual kisses to all.

CHAPTER 8

Wednesday afternoon and evening, May 27, 2015:

Dr. Martin Payne walked into the Mayor's office at 5:00 as the municipal government staff exited the building. He closed the door behind him.

"Rich, let's talk. I'm worried."

"You've nothing to worry about, Martin. BioSenecta gets Withers's whole estate, minus the $1 billion for Witherston and the $1 billion for Witherstonians."

"But what about Detective Arroyo's investigation of Withers's death?"

"I don't see the relevance of the investigation to Bio-Senecta's inheriting the estate."

"So the will will be probated soon? Might Judge Lodge delay probating the will because of the investigation?"

"No problem. I'm requesting that it be probated immediately. She'll do it."

"I sure hope you're right. BioSenecta has a lot of money invested in this project."

"Stop worrying, Martin. I've got things under control."

"Will there be any delay in clear-cutting the land? The clear-cutting was scheduled to begin on June 15th."

"No problem."

"You sure, Rich? I must keep the Senextra factory construction on schedule. I'm hoping to break ground on July 6. The price of our stock will plummet if we have to announce a delay."

"No problem, Martin. Leave it to me."

☙❧☙

"Hi, George. This is Martin calling. I've talked with Rich. There's no problem. We're on schedule to build the Senextra factory."

"The will will be probated right away?"

"Yes, soon. Rich is the executor of the will, you know."

☙❧☙

"Hi, Grant. Martin here. Rich says there will be no problem with executing the will. He foresees no delay."

"Thanks, Martin. And I can help you with any legal issues related to Withers's estate."

"I appreciate the offer, Grant."

"And thanks for all you're doing to make Witherston the site of the Senextra factory. That factory will transform Witherston from a town to a city, a very nice city."

☙❧☙

Neel wrote in his journal, sitting under his favorite oak by Withers Pond. Swift lay at his side.

Should I report Senextra's side effect of feminization? Or should I wait?

Or should I resign and move away?

If I resign now I won't be implicated in George's scientific deception. But if I wait, I can use my position to expose the deception. Also, there's too much hullaballoo over Francis Hearty Withers's death now to bring up an unrelated crime. I'll wait.

☙❧☙

Mev, Paco, Jaime, Jorge, and Aunt Lottie met Lauren, Jim, and Beau in the parking lot of Dahlonega's Smith House. The Smith House was built at the end of the nineteenth century about a block away from the 1836 Lumpkin County courthouse. Jaime, Jorge, and Beau loved the restaurant for its exhibit of a mine shaft sunk into a vein of gold deep in the ground. The boys raced ahead to the glass-enclosed shaft. They peered down the mine shaft and then looked up into the mirror that showed how far down it went.

"Wow," said Beau, "That is really, really deep!" Then he added, "I read that the original owner of this land, a Captain Hall, wanted to mine this gold but was not allowed to, so he just built his house here and kept the shaft."

"Why wasn't he allowed to mine the gold?" Jorge asked.

"The city didn't want a gold mine right by the town square."

"You told us that Withers's great, great grandfather made a pot of money mining gold in this town in 1829 or so. I wonder where his mine was," Jaime said.

"His name was Hearty Withers. But he didn't do mining," Beau continued. "He did panning. On Yahoola Creek. So he didn't have to invest in any construction. He just sat on a boulder in a stream and panned enough gold to get rich, really rich."

"Oh, right," Jorge said. "Isn't it amazing that one man's finding gold in a creek in 1829 means that for almost two hundred years none of his descendants has to work. And Witherston's own billionaire Francis Hearty Withers can live to be a hundred because he can afford Senextra."

"And the poor black slaves who worked in the mines had nothing to bequeath to their descendants," Jaime said.

"My dad was one of those descendants," Beau said. "My dad grew up poor, but he got a scholarship to the University of Georgia. My mom was in law school at UGA at the same time, and they met and married. Her parents got mad at her because she married a black man, but they like Dad now because he went to medical school and became a doctor."

"Just think," Jaime said. "This land belonged to the Cherokee Indians in 1829. So the white gold diggers stole the gold from the Cherokees."

"That's such a sad story," Beau said. "I read a book about it. Actually, white people took something from the Cherokees they cared for even more than gold. Between 1805 and 1833 the state held land lotteries and gave the winners, who were white of course, each a forty-acre tract of land. Cherokee land! That's how Hearty Withers got his forty acres on Founding Father's Creek."

"Then," Jaime said, "because the Cherokee were all upset, our government just moved them out to Oklahoma."

"That was in 1838. Trail of Tears."

"If I were Cherokee I'd still be outraged," Jorge said.

"Do you all know what the name Dahlonega means?" Beau asked. "The word *talonega* is Cherokee for *yellow*. As in gold!"

"So the whites took the Cherokees' gold and land, kicked the Cherokees out, and kept the Cherokees' word for their town."

છ૭છ૭

The merriment started when the waitress brought the ham, batter fried chicken, batter-fried okra, mashed potatoes, gravy, green beans, lima beans, black-eyed peas, and cole slaw to their long table. She commented to the twins, "Boys, you are getting harder and harder to tell apart!"

Jorge and Jaime had dressed identically in maroon KEEP NATURE NATURAL T-shirts, blue jeans, and black flip flops.

"That's because we wuz wombmates," Jorge replied.

"We shared a womb before we wuz born," Jaime said to the waitress. "You probably had your own womb."

Lauren raised her iced tea glass in a toast: "Here's to Mev. May she have little pain and lots of pleasure in the coming months."

They clicked their glasses. "*Salud*."

"And as Mev always says," Paco added, "May all of us have fun and do good."

"And may we solve the mystery of Mr. Withers's death," Mev said.

"*Pronto*," Jaime said.

"Now it's time to get serious," Lottie said. "We're going to pool our knowledge about the Withers case."

Suddenly Dr. George Folsom and his pregnant wife Faith appeared carrying their strawberry shortcake.

"Would you all like to join us?" Paco asked, always the gentleman.

"We'd be delighted," George replied.

They sat down at the other end of the table. In the Smith House you never knew who would become your table companions.

Mev was not delighted. She had always disliked George's arrogance. She knew that Lauren did too, for George always showed contempt for Jim.

Yet Lottie greeted the couple cheerfully. "How are you all this lovely evening?"

"Fine, thank you, Lottie." George turned to Faith. "Imagine, Faith. We're having our dessert and coffee with Detective Arroyo and her gang just minutes after our debate over Withers's death."

"Hi, George. Hi, Faith." Lauren leaned past Lottie to shake hands. "Do you think that somebody killed Francis Hearty Withers?"

"I do," Faith said. "His death was too convenient to be accidental. But George maintains that Withers died of natural causes. And George was his doctor."

"Faith, dear, Withers was a hundred years old," George said.

"I have three suspects," Faith said. "Amy Woods, because she needed money, didn't like Withers, and feared he'd rewrite his will before he died. And our friend Grant Griggs who knew how much he'd gain when Withers's will got probated. He was Withers's lawyer, you know."

"I think Grant has already made beaucoup from Withers, dear."

"And our friend Rich Rather, who has to live off Rhonda's money because Rather Used Cars is doing rather poorly," Faith continued.

"Please, Faith. It's Rather Pre-Owned Vehicles," George said. "Of course Dr. Kingfisher may have murdered Withers.

He's not rich either. Also, he's an atheist, and doesn't fear God. He's Cherokee, you know."

Lottie suddenly got irate. "Having no belief in God doesn't mean having no conscience, George! Do you think that only God-fearing Christians would refrain from murder? Are you saying that a church-going Christian like yourself is morally superior to an atheist? Morally superior to a Cherokee?

George then smiled patronizingly at Lottie. "No, dearest Lottie. Forgive my insensitivity toward atheists and Chero-kees. But I will say that you may have killed him. You don't like big business, and you don't want the Senextra factory to be built. You don't want to improve the living standards of Witherstonians."

Lottie didn't miss a beat. "And you may have killed him, George, because you not only had the motive to increase your wealth and maybe get another Jaguar or a condo on the beach but you also had the opportunity. And you're obsessed with Senextra. As his doctor, you injected him regularly with Sen-extra. Saturday night you could have injected him with some drug that wouldn't show up in an autopsy."

George chuckled. "But Withers was already paying me $100,000 as his personal physician, and BioSenecta was pay-ing me a handsome sum—I won't tell you how much—to ad-minister Senextra to Withers and to the Withers Villagers in the pilot study. I benefitted financially more from Withers's living than from his dying."

"Could your hippy friend Gretchen Green have killed him?" Faith asked Lottie sweetly. "She's into nature and all, and she carried a sign protesting the Senextra factory. I suspect she opposes every good thing that Withers stood for."

"What did Withers stand for?" asked Lottie.

"Old age!" exclaimed Jaime.

"And money!"

"Shhhh," Mev admonished Jaime and Jorge.

George answered Lauren's question. "Withers stood for the preservation of the life of the individual. That's one of our na-tion's noblest values. Withers recognized that the drug Senex-tra could overcome the forces of aging that disable the individ-ual, and so he invested his fortune in BioSenecta Pharmaceuticals to make Senextra for every American who wanted it. I admired him for that—"

"I didn't," Lottie interrupted.

"Well, you wouldn't, because you are still living in the 1960s," George said. "But for at least five hundred years in our culture, scientists and engineers and doctors have aimed to understand and control nature. That's our culture's great ambition. And mine too. As a doctor, I do all I can to keep my patient alive. If that is to violate the laws of nature, so be it. The individual human life is precious. Nature doesn't serve the individual. So as long as I have antibiotics at my disposal, I'll refuse to let nature take its course."

"In the case of individuals with health insurance," Jorge interjected.

"Do you feel the same way about cows, Dr. Folsom?" Jaime asked. "Farmers give antibiotics to cows. And growth hormones."

"Ha! That's because the individual bovine life is precious," Jorge said. The boys laughed uproariously.

George did not.

"Amen," said Lottie.

"Farmers give antibiotics to cows to keep them from getting mastitis," Jaime said.

"If farmers yanked your tits every morning, you'd get mastitis too," Jorge said.

"I'm glad I don't have tits."

"Be glad you're not a cow."

"If I were a bull, I'd get growth hormones to produce more sperm," Jaime said. "To get more cows pregnant. To make more calves that would get growth hormones to make more meat. For humans!"

"For rich humans," Jorge said.

"Hijos!" Paco shouted over the hilarity. "We're trying to have a serious conversation here."

"But Dad, this is serious," Jaime said. "We give cows antibiotics to keep them healthy for us humans to eat steak—or at least us humans who have money. And we give the cows growth hormones to make them big to make us more steaks."

"So everybody who eats beef gets hormones," Jorge said. "And everybody who eats chicken too."

Now Beau got into the fun with a song. He stood up.

"Who gets hormones?
You get hormones.
Who gets hormones?
I get hormones.
Who gets hormones?
We get hormones.
Who gets hormones?
We all get hormones.
And we all fall down."

"Beau, please!" Jim said.

Beau sat down.

George did not seem amused.

"Nobody's natural anymore, not in our society," Jorge said. "Humans, cows, chickens—we're all violating the laws of nature."

"Frogs are natural," Jaime said.

"Not if they live in Founding Father's Creek where our water makes them grow three back legs," said Jorge.

"What did you say?" George asked.

"Jaime found a frog with three back legs at Founding Father's Bridge. So I say there may be something in the water there to make leggy froggies."

"I saw your photo on the web, Jorge."

"I wonder if Senextra is in the water," Jaime said. "We'll find out soon because somebody will get the water tested."

"Boys, think about this," George said. "If we all lived in compliance with nature, some of us at this table would be already dead."

The group grew quiet. George had stopped the conversation.

"George," Mev said. "I may as well tell you, because you'll hear about it soon. I have breast cancer, and I will have to have a lumpectomy and possibly radiation."

"Mev," George said. "I am very sorry. Is there anything I can do?"

"Jim is supervising my treatment, since he's my gynecologist, but thank you so much. I feel fortunate to live in Witherston with so many good friends.

"Oh, honey," Faith said. "Please, I want to help too. I'll bring you a pie every week to make you feel better. That is, until I have my baby. You all know that I'm having a baby, don't you, at my advanced age of fifty-one. I'm embarrassed."

"We've very happy for you," Lauren said.

"It's a boy, a big healthy boy." Faith said.

George stood up. He was six feet, two inches tall, fifty years old, with a full head of sandy hair, an unlined face, and the fitness of the football player he once was. Faith, looking younger than her fifty-one years, stood up too.

"We've got to run now. It's almost 8:00," George said. "We've certainly enjoyed our evening with you all, but we must be on our way."

The Folsoms left.

"Do you all think George Folsom did it?" Jaime asked.

"No," Lauren said.

"No," Mev said.

"Of course," Lottie said,

"Lottie," Mev said. "You think that anybody who doesn't eat organic fruits and vegetables is capable of murder."

"I do," Lottie said, with a twinkle in her eye.

"Let's have some strawberry shortcake," Jim said.

❧❧❧

On their way home Lottie rolled down the back window of Mev's CRV to let in the cool air of the evening. It was 8:30 and still light, though dark rain clouds were forming.

Jaime was on his phone with Beau, whose family was following them back to Witherston in their Prius.

"Mom," Jaime asked. "Can we stop at Founding Father's Bridge where I found Leggy Froggy? If I find him again, I'm going to take him home. Beau says that his parents have time to stop."

"Yes, let's do," Mev said.

"*Muy bien*," said Paco, who was driving.

"Okay, Beau," Jaime reported to Beau over the phone. "They said yes. We're almost there."

Three minutes later the two cars pulled off the highway onto a barely discernible unpaved road, drove a quarter of a mile, and slowed to a halt when they neared a vaguely familiar red pickup parked by the old wooden bridge. They heard the strains of Paul Robeson singing "Shenandoah" from the truck's CD player.

"Who else could be here?" Mev asked.

Nobody bothered to answer her. Jaime, Jorge, and Beau eagerly led the way to the creek. Mev, Paco, Jim, and Lauren hurried after them. Lottie brought up the rear.

Suddenly Mev heard the boys yell. "Come here! There's a body on the bridge!"

"It's a man!"

"He's dead!"

"No, he's not. But he's unconscious. And he's bleeding through his mouth."

"Hurry, Mom, Dad!"

"Oh, no!" Jorge shouted. "It's Gregory!"

Mev ran as fast as she could. Oh, no! she thought. Another murder? Or attempted murder?

Jim took charge. Mev could see that Gregory Bozeman had been shot in the back, probably just minutes ago. The brown-skinned, good-looking, hefty sixty-three-year-old man was unconscious but still breathing.

∽∾∽

Two of the Witherston police officers Mev had met at Withers's home, Ricky and Pete Senior, arrived promptly in response to her 9-11 call. After directing the officers to the bridge where Jim was attending Gregory, Mev sent Paco, Jaime, and Jorge home. Jim sent Lauren and Beau home.

Jim had cleared Gregory's airway and had wiped some of the blood off his chin by the time the Chestatee ambulance from Dahlonega got there.

As the medics lifted Gregory onto the gurney, the rain came down, drenching everybody. Mev called Jon on her cell phone.

"Jon. I have terrible news for you. Gregory was shot at the old bridge on Founding Father's Creek." She paused. "Yes, he's alive. But he was shot in the back, so he's probably in critical condition. He'll be taken to Chestatee Regional Hospital. Jim and I are with him. Do you want to meet us there?" She paused again. "We can talk at the hospital. But drive carefully. It's raining hard. Gregory will want to see you when he regains consciousness." That is, if he regains consciousness, she thought to herself. She was not optimistic.

Jim found the keys to the truck in the ignition. "I'll drive Gregory's truck," he told Mev.

Mev climbed into the back of the ambulance, where she sat on the bench alongside Gregory. The medic put in an IV to give Gregory fluids and then checked his blood pressure and his pulse.

"He's stable."

∽∾∽

Mev and Jim sat with Jon in the hospital's waiting room. Jon was agitated. "I should never have told him where Jaime found the deformed frog," Jon said. "Gregory became obsessed with that frog. He went to the old bridge tonight to get a sample of the water to test. Gregory still works occasionally for the EPA on a contract basis. He has a small lab at home."

"Why did he want to test the water?" Mev asked him.

"Gregory said that frogs in creeks are like canaries in coal mines. If the frogs are normal, healthy, and plentiful, then the creek water is probably clean. If the frogs are not, and the deformed frog was not, then the creek water may be polluted with bacteria or toxic chemicals. The polluted water can bring harm to all the other creatures who swim in it or drink it, including us humans."

"Gretchen says that too. You must have read her piece in *Webby Witherston* this morning," Jim said. "If Founding Father's Creek is polluted, then our drinking water in Witherston may endanger our health. We should get Mayor Rather involved."

"You know Mayor Rather. He doesn't want to hear anything from an environmentalist that could affect the way Witherstonians carry on business. And he is not fond of Gregory. So Gregory had to find out what was in the water. Did you all find any test tubes around him?"

"No," Mev said.

"No, but I didn't look," said Jim.

After a few minutes of silence, Jon said quietly, "What will I do if Gregory dies? We've been together for sixteen years."

"I think Gregory will survive, Jon," Jim said. "The bullet may have punctured a lung, but it did not go through his heart."

"He has a big heart," Jon said. "I must see him. He'll want me with him, no matter what happens."

"I'll tell the hospital staff that you are his family," Jim responded. "When he's out of surgery you'll be allowed to stay in his room."

Mev's cell phone rang. It was Catherine Perry.

"Hello, Catherine. You sure get news fast."

"What news, Mizz Arroyo? I called you about Mr. Withers's investigation. Is there new news?"

"Well, yes, there is, Catherine." Mev had a soft spot in her heart for the young energetic reporter. She told her about finding Gregory.

ফ্রেফ্র

At midnight, the surgeon entered the waiting room. "Dr. Bozeman has survived his surgery," he said, "and he'll be taken to Room 312. You may meet him there, Mr. Finley."

Mev and Jim said their good-byes to Jon, returned to Gregory's truck, and climbed aboard. In the right front seat Mev spotted a yellow post-it note affixed to the dashboard. She held it up to the dashboard lights.

"Oh my god!" she exclaimed. "Jim, did you not see this?"

"No, Mev. The rain was coming down pretty hard, and I was focused on the road. What's the message?"

Mev read the note aloud.

"Whoever else stands in the way of Witherston's destiny will be likewise destroyed.

"Now we have attempted murder," she said.

She called Chief McCoy and requested a couple of officers to meet her at the bridge at 8:00 am. The heavy rain would make an investigation before then impossible.

℮ↄ℮ↄ

I didn't intend to kill Bozeman when I stopped here. I intended only to get a water sample. I didn't know anybody would be here till I saw the pickup and heard the music. "Old Man River," by that communist Paul Robeson. I took the rifle from the pickup for protection. It was on the front seat, fully loaded. I figured that somebody was hunting off season. Naturally I'd need protection from a poacher.

Then I saw Bozeman on the bridge with the beaker of creek water. I couldn't let him test the water. The EPA would discover Senextra in the water, and all the radical environmentalists in north Georgia would scream and yell.

The New York Times would come here. And CNN. And all those left-wing ecologists at the University of Georgia. Jesus.

Then BioSenecta would pull out of Witherston. Hell, BioSenecta would stop the Senextra pilot study. Senextra would never get on the market.

All this before we even had a chance to show the world Senextra's benefits. Very long life with very good health all the way. That's what Senextra can do for people.

So I shot Bozeman. I had to. I shot one man to help a million. I shortened the life of one man to lengthen the lives of a million.

Now he's dead. I'm twice a murderer.

I wiped off the rifle and buried it in the woods. It won't be found.

WITHERSTON ON THE WEB
Thursday, May 28, 2015

BREAKING NEWS

Dr. Gregory Bozeman, of Witherston, was shot in the back by an unknown assailant at Founding Father's Bridge sometime between 8:00 and 8:40 pm yesterday.

Dr. Bozeman was discovered unconscious at 8:45 pm by Captain Emma Evelyn Arroyo of the Lumpkin County Sheriff's Department.

Dr. Bozeman was taken by ambulance to Chestatee Regional Hospital, where he is listed in critical condition. His partner Jonathan Finley is with him.

Captain Arroyo and her family were returning to Witherston from Dahlonega and had stopped at the bridge where Jaime and Jorge had found the deformed frog pictured on this website on May 26. They were friends of Gregory Bozeman and recognized him immediately despite his bloody condition.

Dr. Bozeman is an ecologist recently retired from the Environmental Protection Agency in Athens. A much admired environmental activist, Dr. Bozeman acquired statewide fame for working with communities to detoxify their streams and ponds. In 2009, he joined University of Georgia faculty, staff, and students in a team effort to clean up the polluted Tanyard Creek, which runs under the stadium.

Witherstonians will want to know why Dr. Bozeman went to Founding Father's Bridge last night.

Captain Emma Evelyn Arroyo of the Lumpkin County Sheriff's Department was in the home of Francis Hearty Withers yesterday to investigate the circumstances of Mr. Withers's death. Captain Arroyo has not called for a criminal investigation because, as she said to this reporter, there is no evidence of homicide.

Yet Witherstonians have questions. Why did Mr. Withers die before he could change his will? Who knew that Amy Woods, his live-in maid, would be out of town Saturday night? Who disliked Mr. Withers? Who killed him and how?

Stay tuned.

~ Catherine Perry, Reporter

LETTERS TO THE EDITOR

To the Editor:

I would like to respond to Mr. Jorgensen's letter of May 27.

How "productive" has Mr. Jorgensen been for the last forty (40!) years of his life?

How "productive" is a man who spends the first thirty years of his retirement golfing and sailing and the last ten years playing bridge?

I'd say he has been unproductive since the age of 62. He is just entertaining himself at the expense of productive Americans.

Dear reader: Please think about the big picture and not just your individual self!

If nobody takes Senextra in the coming decades, still by the year 2050 twenty percent of all Americans will be over 65, and five percent of all Americans will be over 85. Another twenty percent of all Americans will be children.

That leaves only sixty percent of our population to work and support everybody else.

Now imagine what will happen if many of the over-65 set take Senextra.

Fewer and fewer productive young people will be supporting more and more unproductive old people, until our economy collapses under the intolerable burden of such Senextra-

centenarians as Mr. Jorgensen and his superannuated bridge-
playing pals.
  ~ Signed, Anonymous

POLICE BLOTTER

Witherston Police officers were summoned to Witherston
Bridge by a 911 call placed at 8:45 pm by Detective Mev Ar-
rollo of the Witherston Police Department.
  They encountered face-down on the bridge an unconscious
six-foot-tall male of Native American ancestry, 63 years old,
identified as Dr. Gregory Bozeman of Witherston. He had been
shot in the back on the right side. He was taken by ambulance
to Chestatee Regional Hospital.
  Heavy rain made collection of evidence difficult. The police
designated the area as a crime scene and returned to Wither-
ston.

ON THIS DAY IN HISTORY
By Charlotte Byrd

On May 28, 1830, President Andrew Jackson signed into
law the Indian Removal Act. The new law authorized him to
"negotiate" with the Cherokee, Chickasaw, Choctaw, Creek,
and Seminole Indians for their removal from their homelands
to federal territory west of the Mississippi River. Actually, the
tribes had little choice in the matter, and their leaders were
forced to agree to the relocation.

CHAPTER 9

Thursday, May 28

*G*ood god! *Bozeman is alive. I wonder whether he saw me. I don't think so. He didn't turn around. Will he start talking?*

If you read this morning's Witherston on the Web you'd think that Bozeman was some sort of public health hero. All he does, all the environmentalist lefties ever do, is say no. No pollution. No factories. No cars. No pesticides. No damn chicken trucks. No Senextra. No clear-cutting. No No No No No. The environmentalist nuts are the party of No, not the Republicans.

Well, Bozeman can't be a hero if he says no to progress. I will be a hero because I say yes to progress. Yes to medical research. Yes to BioSenecta. Yes to Senextra. Yes to long life. I am the hero.

I should have checked on him. I should have shot him again, in the head. Damn. But today I have to focus. I have to stay cool. I can't look back.

❧❧❧

Lauren called Mev's cell phone Thursday morning. Mev briefed her on the previous evening's discovery.

"What's on your schedule today, Mev?" Lauren asked.

"First, I'm taking Renoir to stay at my house until Jon and Gregory go home. Then I'll head to the Bridge. I'll probably spend a couple of hours this morning with the deputies looking for clues there. After that I'll return to Witherston. What's on your mind?"

"Mayor Rather, Withers's executor, petitioned the court yesterday to have the will probated."

"But Withers told all of Witherston at his birthday party that he intended to change his will. When he said that didn't he revoke it?"

"Not unless another will or a similar document turns up. So far, you haven't found one, have you? Just stating an intention to revoke a will doesn't constitute a revocation. A revocation would have to be in writing—unless it happened automatically because of some life event, such as birth or adoption of a child, if the testator hadn't provided for future children in the will."

"Hmm."

"Of course it is possible to revoke a will by destroying it or by obliterating major clauses."

"Now I remember," Mev said. "He told us he'd filed it in Probate Court. So he could not have gotten hold of it before his death."

"However, if you should discover that one of his inheritors wrongfully brought about Withers's death, then that beneficiary would not be allowed to inherit any part of Withers's estate."

"There are two crimes I have to investigate, Lauren. The first is Withers's death, for which I have to find evidence of homicide. And the second is Gregory's getting shot."

"Do you think that the two crimes are related?"

"I didn't until I read the shooter's note. There must be a connection. Withers was killed for his money, in all likelihood. Gregory was shot because he was probably doing something the shooter didn't like."

"Such as looking for five-legged frogs?"

"More likely sampling the water," Mev said. "That's the reason he went to the old bridge, according to Jon."

"So you have to figure out *why* that might have annoyed somebody. And *whom* that might have annoyed."

"I also have to figure out who else might be standing in the way of Witherston's destiny."

"If you knew Witherston's destiny—in the mind of Gregory's shooter—then you'd know whose life could be in danger."

"I have to go to Gainesville on Monday for blood tests and then back to Gainesville on Tuesday for the lumpectomy."

"And I'm taking you on Monday, honey," Lauren said.

"I think I should start by getting an education about mushrooms. I'll go see Gretchen this afternoon."

℘℘℘

Renoir squirmed out of the doggy door onto the front deck when Mev pulled up to Jon and Gregory's contemporary, cedar-sided home. He barked excitedly. Being a large poodle, large even by Standard standards, Renoir needed a large doggy door. But that was no problem in Witherston, for there was little crime here. At least not until Greg's shooting. And maybe Withers's murder.

Renoir gave Mev a big wet kiss, leaped into her CRV, and seated himself on the right front seat as if he were a person. Actually, in Mev's mind he was. A curly-white-haired, long-nosed, bright-eyed, intelligent person. When she arrived home and opened her car door, Renoir climbed over her in his eagerness to greet Jaime. Jaime was on the front walk trying unsuccessfully to teach Varry to sit. Paco sat in a rocking chair on the front porch watching.

Renoir stood on his hind legs, put his paws on Jaime's shoulders, and licked his face. Varry stood on his hind legs, put his paws on Mev's shoulders, and licked Mev's face.

Paco held his hands to his head. *"¡No me digas, cariño! ¿Otro perrito? ¡Ay!"* But he opened the front door and invited Renoir into their house.

℘℘℘

The sun shone brightly when Mev got out of her CRV at Founding Father's Bridge.

She saw the vehicles of Lumpkin County's Sheriff Weston Bearfield and Witherston's Police Chief Jake McCoy parked in the muddy road near the creek.

She found Jake and Weston on the bridge taking a cigarette break. Weston dipped his cigarette butt into the water and then put it into one of the innumerable plastic baggies he always carried. Neither Weston nor Jake ever littered the woods they loved. Mev liked both men, especially her boss Jake who had a master's degree in criminology from the University of West Georgia.

"Hi, Jake," Mev greeted them. "Hi, Weston. Have you found anything?"

"Hello, Mev, So good to see you," Weston said. "I'm sorry that we've found nothing. The rain has wiped out all the footprints and all the tire tracks. And the creek has swallowed the cartridges. All we have is the bullet in Bozeman's back."

"But we've got this note that the would-be killer left in Gregory's truck. Would you mind taking it to the lab, Jake? It says: 'Whoever else stands in the way of Witherston's destiny will be likewise destroyed.'"

"So Gregory was apparently standing in the way of Witherston's destiny," Jake said.

"What's Witherston's destiny? Is that like manifest destiny?" Weston asked.

Mev thought for a moment. "What a good question. Hmm. The killer's choice of the word *destiny* is interesting. As I recall, the term *manifest destiny* was used in the mid-nineteenth century by political leaders to support America's taking over the West. Politicians said that the United States had a divine calling to spread democracy and moral values, but they were really justifying conquest. To me, manifest destiny means imperialism. Even as intellectually immature as I was when in college I thought the notion was wrong. I still do."

"So we may have an ideological killer on our hands," Weston said.

"Either an ideological killer or a greedy killer, but I don't have much experience in murder," Jake said. "Mev, Witherston's never had a murder before, or even an attempted murder. And now we may have both within a week. Are you sure that Withers's death was a homicide?"

"I can't prove it now, but I will. His death seems too timely to be natural. I suspect poisonous mushrooms. I'm looking into that."

"What about the rhubarb pie?" Weston asked. "My wife

won't make me rhubarb pie because she says rhubarb contains oxalic acid, which can be toxic in large quantities."

"And you eat large quantities of everything put before you," Jake said. "Your wife is smart to keep you off rhubarb pie!"

"If I were a betting man, rather than a smoking, drinking, over-eating, cussing man," Weston said, "I'd bet that the old man overdosed on Senextra. And if he did, I'd say 'Yippee! Well done, Geezer! Live by Senextra and die by Senextra. Good bye, farewell, ciao, cheerio, adiós, au revoir, adieu, and bon voyage. You stayed at the party way too long, so thanks so much for making your exit now.'"

"Weston!" Mev exclaimed. "We should not speak ill of the dead."

"I forgot," Weston said. "My apologies to the deceased old coot."

✌✌✌

Lottie sat out on her back deck sipping her green tea and examining her two borrowed historical treasures. First she opened the old black leather Bible. Here on the inside cover, in a combination of almost illegible scripts and different colors of ink, was the Withers family genealogy.

Hearty Withers (1798-1838)
Married to Penance Hearty Withers in 1825.
Children: Hearty Edward Withers, born in 1826,
died in 1826; James Edward Withers, born in 1828,
died in 1835; Harold Francis Withers, born in 1830.

Harold Francis ("Harry") Withers (1830-1882)
Married to Patience Gray in 1857.
Children: Withers Francis Withers, born in 1858;
Walter Gray Withers, born in 1860, died in 1860;

Withers Francis ("Witty") Withers (1858-1931)
Married to Obedience Olmstead in 1881

Children: Hearty Harold Withers born in 1889;
Penance Louise Withers, born in 1900

Hearty Harold Withers (1889-1960)
Married to Maud Olive McGillicuddy in 1914
Child: Francis Hearty Withers, born in 1915

Francis Hearty Withers (1915-)

"Oh my god," Lottie said to herself. "Our Francis Hearty Withers had an aunt. HaHa had a baby sister. Penance Louise. I wonder what happened to her. I wonder whether she had heirs."

Inside the Bible, in Song of Solomon 1:2, Lottie found a handwritten note:

On June 1, 1881, Withers Francis Withers ("Witty," age 23) and Obedience Olmstead (age 20) were married in the Dahlonega United Methodist Church. In attendance were her parents Jedediah and Else Olmstead of Dahlonega and his father Harold Francis Withers ("Harry") of Witherston.

Then Lottie turned to the diary of Penance Hearty Withers Withers. Having looked at the family Bible, Lottie figured that Penance was both wife and cousin of Hearty Withers. The diary was half blank.The lengthy entries stopped on May 30, where Lottie read the single sentence:

My dearest husband was killed this morning by an Indian.

Then there was a final entry. On June 6 of 1838 Penance had written:

One week ago early in the morning a Cherokee Indian killed my husband. My husband was pulling up carrots in our garden when the Indian came out of the woods along Saloli Creek., grabbed him from behind, and slit his throat. Then he stabbed him, left his bone knife in my husband's heart, and ran back into the woods. Little Harry saw his father die. As did I.

Little Harry and I will never forget that young savage's murderous eyes. I can't imagine what my dearest husband could have done to make that Indian so vicious.

We have to get rid of the Indians. We will never be safe as long as there is a single Indian left in Georgia.

Fortunately, little Harry and I have our property. The Indian took my husband's life, but he didn't take our land or our gold.

My older brother John, who never married, has come here from Savannah to live with little Harry and me.

Lottie put down the diary. So a Cherokee had killed Hearty Withers in 1838, just months before sixteen thousand Cherokees were forced to leave Georgia. Hearty Withers stole their gold and occupied their land. And all his descendants—Harry Withers, Wittty Withers, HaHa Withers, and humorless Francis Hearty Withers—owed their wealth to that original theft.

Unlike Penance, Lottie could imagine what had made that young Cherokee murderous. He had witnessed Hearty Withers and all the other white settlers destroy his people's way of life.

෩෩෩

When Mev returned home at 11:30 to have lunch with her family, she found Jaime, Jorge, and Beau sitting on the living room floor poring over the copies of the documents she'd found in Withers's trunk. In the kitchen, Paco had put their lunch of tomato-basil-mozzarella bruschetta under the broiler and had set the table for five.

Varry and Renoir both leaped up to greet her, showering her with love and slobber. Paco gave her a kiss. "Hola, *guapa*."

But the boys hardly noticed her arrival.

Finally Jorge spoke up. "Mom, may we ride our bikes down to the bridge this afternoon? Jaime wants to catch Leggy Froggy again."

"No. I'm going to have to tell you no for two reasons. In the first place, the bridge is now a crime scene cordoned off with yellow tape. You won't have access to the creek from the road there. And in the second place, I don't want you all playing where Gregory was shot. Jim and I found a note last night in Gregory's truck that shows the shooter intended to murder Gregory."

"What did the note say, Mom?" asked Jaime.

"It said, 'Whoever else stands in the way of Witherston's destiny will be likewise destroyed.' I sent it to the lab in Dahlonega."

"What's Witherston's destiny, Mizz Arroyo?"

"That's for us all to figure out. The note reminded Sheriff Bearfield of manifest destiny. You know, the nineteenth-century concept that America's destiny was to conquer the whole continent and spread our morality to everyone already here, like the Indians."

"But what's Witherston's destiny?"

"I don't know," Mev answered Beau. "Maybe if we can find out, we'll know who the killer is."

"Mom," said Jaime. "We found something interesting here. We found Withers's birth certificate, his father's birth certificate, and his father's sister's birth certificate. They were all clipped together."

Mev looked at the three birth certificates. One was for a baby boy named Francis Hearty Withers, born in Dahlonega on May 23, 1915, to Hearty Harold Withers and Maud Olive McGillicuddy Withers.

Another was for a baby boy named Hearty Harold Withers, born in Witherston on April 15, 1889, to Withers Francis Withers and Obedience Olmstead Withers.

The third was for a baby girl named Penance Louise Withers, born in Witherston on July 4, 1900, to Withers Francis Withers and Obedience Olmstead Withers.

"There's the proof!" Mev exclaimed. "Penance Louise was

Francis Hearty Withers's aunt. Francis Hearty Withers must have known her."

"Auntie Penny Lou," Jorge said. He giggled.

Mev thought a moment. "I wonder what happened to her."

ᥫᥬᥫᥬ

Mev gazed at the motto inscribed on Gretchen's mailbox post:

If you do not change direction,
you may end up where you are heading.
~ Lao Tse

"I wonder where Witherston is heading," she said half to herself as she climbed the stairs of Gretchen Green's Green Grocery.

Mev shopped there often because she liked organic fruits and vegetables which Gretchen stocked in abundance. Today she sought information.

"Mev! So nice to see you!" Gretchen hugged her. Gretchen, fifty-five years old, would have looked no older than forty if she had dyed her long gray hair. Her vegetarian diet of organic produce and her health regimen of yoga, hiking, and meditating kept her young.

Gretchen brought out a pitcher of sparkling water and two glasses filled with lemon slices. The two women seated themselves on the front porch rockers. Gandhi dozed on the swing.

Mev turned to Gretchen. "I've come to pick your brain, Gretchen. Tell me about rhubarb and morel mushrooms."

"I love to talk about morels, Mev! I call them hickory chickens. Just last week your aunt Lottie and I found several pounds of beautiful morels near Founding Father's Bridge. Close to where Gregory was shot. Lottie took some home, and I sautéed a few for myself, and then I sold the rest to Rhonda Rather. By the way, she's really big with child!"

"Are there poisonous mushrooms that someone could have baked in the casserole that Withers ate before his death?" Mev asked.

"I know of many," Gretchen said.

"If someone intended to mix a poisonous mushroom with the morels, what would be his or her mushroom of choice?" asked Mev.

"Mine would be an Amanita mushroom, the one called Destroying Angel," Gretchen said. "And I would grind it up so that it would not be noticed in the casserole. But since Amanitas don't usually appear as early as May up in these parts, they'd be hard to find. The killer would have had to order them from elsewhere."

"That would require a bit of premeditation," Mev said. "More than two days."

"But if I were the killer and on a tight schedule," Gretchen continued, "I probably wouldn't do murder-by-mushrooms. Or by rhubarb either. Rhubarb leaves contain oxalate, which can be toxic depending on the quantity ingested. But rhubarb seldom kills. If I were the killer, I'd use a drug. What drugs was old Withers taking?"

"So far as I know, just Senextra and Celebrex."

"Oh, Lordy! Don't get me started on Senextra! Good god! Witherstonians take Senextra, a drug, and then shop in my grocery store for organic food. That makes no sense."

"But," Mev said, "it makes sense to those folks who want to stay healthy and live long."

"Maybe, but it's still weird. Most Witherstonians think that drugs keep people healthy. I think that organic foods keep people healthy. Some folks need drugs because we use pesticides, antibiotics, and hormones to grow foods that make us sick. And drugs cure sickness. If we stop eating foods laced with pesticides, antibiotics, and hormones, we won't get sick and we won't need drugs."

"I agree, Gretchen, but you must admit that Withers looked fit at his birthday party."

"Yes, and he probably still looks fit in his $25,000 coffin. You can probably guess: I don't like coffins."

"I don't either, because I don't want the living to go broke making the dead comfortable."

"That's not my reason, Mev. On our planet every non-human organism who lives reenters and replenishes the soil when he dies so other organisms can live. Only humans think we're so special, so superior to everybody else, that we must encase ourselves in a waterproof casket for eternity. We take up more than our share of space above ground, and we take up more than our share of space below ground."

"We don't give back," murmured Mev.

ↄ⌒ↄ⌒ↄ

After her visit with Gretchen, Mev interviewed Mayor Rich Rather and his wife Rhonda in their exquisitely furnished home on Ninovan Drive. Rhonda, wearing an aqua linen big shirt and navy linen cropped pants, ushered her into the living room. Pregnant as she was, Rhonda looked stunning. She held Giuliani.

Rhonda must be an animal lover, Mev concluded, hearing puppies in a back room and seeing a silver Persian cat on the loveseat.

Rhonda's tanned, quite large husband looked like he'd come right off Dahlonega's Achasta Golf Course, and he had. Rich Rather never missed an opportunity to play golf with the influential business leaders of north Georgia. Mev wondered what the other golfers thought of Witherston's crass mayor.

The interview went quickly. Mev learned that Rhonda had baked a mushroom casserole for Withers Friday night because she felt sorry for him after his disastrous birthday party. That Rhonda had taken it to him Saturday morning. That Rhonda and Rich had enjoyed an identical mushroom casserole for themselves Friday night without becoming ill. That Rich had cultivated a close personal relationship with Withers and that Withers had appointed him executor of his estate.

Mev figured out that Rich and Rhonda lived beyond Rich's income as owner of Rather Pre-Owned Vehicles because Rhonda had inherited wealth from her long-deceased parents. Rich turned over his hunting rifle to her. It did not appear to have been used recently.

"Let me ask you one last question, Rich," Mev said. "You knew Withers well. Did he ever mention an aunt? Her name would have been Penance Louise, or Penny Louise, or perhaps just Penny. Possibly Penny Lou."

"An aunt? No…Mr. Withers never mentioned any relatives. Never. He seldom even mentioned his father, although he got his house and his wealth from his father. He never talked about his childhood. I don't think he had happy memories. He didn't seem to have any friends, other than me, and obviously his doctor and his lawyer, though they weren't exactly friends."

"Did he confide in George Folsom or in Grant Griggs?"

"Mr. Withers spent a lot of time with them. He talked about George, because George was his doctor. He talked about Grant too. Grant's been visiting him every day. I think that Grant's made a pile of money off Mr. Withers. Grant drives a fancy silver Lincoln, pre-owned of course which he bought from me on time. And on Memorial Day he asked me to look for a pre-owned Porsche Boxter Spyder. That's one pricey vehicle. I guess he wants to look really wealthy."

"What did you and Withers talk about?" asked Mev.

"We talked about our country. About politics. Mr. Withers believed in the American dream. He believed that America should spread democracy around the world, even if we had to wage war to do it. He believed that there would be peace on Earth when other countries adopted our way of life and our values. Our American values, not the values of socialist Europe. He hated our Europe-loving left-wing politicians who'd turn the United States of America into the Welfare States of America."

As she got up to leave, Mev said to Rich, "I know you've had a hard weekend, Mr. Mayor. I'm so sorry about your friend's death. And I'm sorry that the protest disrupted the beautiful birthday party you'd planned."

Rich Rather erupted. "Those protesters! They eat berries, live in the woods, read philosophy, play the guitar, and fish for a living, like Indians, while the rest of us work. They think that they're intellectual and the rest of us are dumb as rocks. They call themselves progressive, and yet they block progress. They're contemptuous of prosperity. They're contemptuous of capitalism. Don't get me started!"

Rhonda touched his arm. "Rich, please!"

Rich shook her off. "Mev, hear me out. Those protesters—and some of them are your friends and relatives and possibly your own children—may have ruined the future for everybody else in Witherston. They insulted our town's benefactor, fatally! Our town's only benefactor. We don't have a benefactor-in-waiting."

"I understand your feelings, Mr. Mayor. Thank you for visiting with me," Mev said.

Rich looked suddenly remorseful. "I apologize for my outburst, Mev. I do appreciate your attempting to solve this mystery. Thank you for coming." He walked her to the door and shook her hand.

❧❧❧

Mev had no sooner gotten home than the phone rang. It was Lauren.

"Mev! Something terrible has happened. Jim just called me. This morning Faith had a massive stroke. The ambulance took her to Chestatee Regional Hospital. George has been with her all day. Jim went there this afternoon. Jim's her gynecologist."

An hour later Lauren called her back. "Mev, Faith has died. Dr. Morston will do an autopsy tonight."

Then Jim called.

"Mev, I know Lauren has told you about Faith. A tragedy. But I'm calling to tell you about Gregory. Gregory is still in intensive care. Jon is by his side. Can you call Jon? You're his best friend."

Mev called Jon on his cell phone. "Jon, how are you doing?"

"Not well, sweet Mev. I feel so alone, more alone than I've felt in my entire life. For sixteen years I've made decisions with Gregory. We've shared everything. Not just a house, but thoughts, feelings, ideas, plans for our future. I never think of me anymore. I think only of us. And of Renoir. Jesus Lord! Who is taking care of Renoir?"

"Renoir is here with my family, Jon. You don't need to worry about him. I picked him up this morning. He and Varry are playing chase right now in my living room. I'll tell you about what happened to my lamp when you're up to it."

"Oh, sweet baby, thank you so much!"

"I'll do anything I can to help you and Gregory. You know that, Jon."

"Mev, do you suppose you could come to the hospital for just a little bit? I need a friend."

"Of course. I'll eat a bite of supper and then drive down. I'll see you in an hour or so."

Mev left her house at 7:00. Daylight lasted till 9:00 this time of year in Georgia. As she passed Founding Father's Bridge her thoughts turned to Gregory's shooter. Why, in the shooter's mind, would sampling the creek water stand in the way of Witherston's destiny? What was in the creek water that would affect Witherston's destiny? And what in the world *was* Witherston's destiny?

Driving into the Chestatee Regional Hospital's parking, lot Mev suddenly had the answer. She remembered what Mayor Rather had shouted at the protesters: "You want to keep Witherston in the nineteenth century?" For Mayor Rather, at least, Witherston's destiny was to build the Senextra factory.

Mev was still puzzled. If the creek was indeed polluted, as Gregory had thought, how would the test results affect the Senextra factory's construction? Well, obviously a pharmaceutical plant needed clean water. If it were to be built, the factory would get its water and energy from Saloli Falls, more than a mile upstream from Withers Village and two miles upstream from Witherston. And four miles upstream from Founding Father's Bridge. Was the creek polluted for all that distance? If so, what could be the source?

Mev made her way to the Intensive Care Unit. Jon was sitting on a bench outside the room leaning against the wall with his eyes closed. He looked morose. She sat down beside him and took one of his hands.

"I'm here, Jon."

"Oh, sweet baby. Thank you so much."

"You're not alone, Jon. You can always talk with me, and if you have to make any medical decisions you can always talk with Jim. He's very concerned."

"Why was Gregory shot? Just because he was sampling the creek water?"

"Think, Jon. What did Gregory tell you before he went to the bridge?"

"That if the water makes deformed frogs it probably harms humans."

"What did Gregory believe was in the water?"

Jon thought a minute. "He'd read about a chemical called BPA in plastic bottles—Bisphenol A—that gets into our bodies. It shows up in almost everybody's urine, everybody's, yours, mine, old people's, young people's. Some scientists think BPA can cause miscarriages and affect women's fertility. It acts like a hormone. Gregory wondered whether BPA had contaminated the creek and had caused the frog's deformity."

"Did Gregory talk about this to anybody besides you?"

"I don't know. Probably. Gregory was obsessed about the passing of pharmaceuticals through our bodies into our soil, into our water supply, and into our bodies again. He called it a toxic cycle. Some folks get hormones prescribed by their doctor from the pharmacy, and other folks get the same hormones not prescribed by their doctor from their tap water. Disgusting, isn't it. We're all on hormones." Jon smiled. "Maybe it will make more men effeminate."

"Everybody drinks water from a plastic water bottle, at least when we're on the go," Mev said. "I always carry one in my purse. I don't like the taste of tap water, and now I know why."

"Gregory doesn't use plastic water bottles. And he takes no medicines. He's like a pharmaceutical vegan. He won't even take aspirin. He takes wine instead."

"But now he has to take drugs," Mev said. "And we have to figure out why the shooter feared Gregory's testing the creek."

"Gregory wrote a letter to *Webby Witherston* opposing the Senextra factory. The shooter could have connected Gregory's investigation of the creek to his opposition to BioSenecta Pharmaceuticals. Maybe the shooter was afraid that the discovery of water pollution would scare off BioSenecta."

"Now we're getting somewhere," Mev said. "Did anybody tell you about the post-it note the shooter left on Gregory's

dashboard? It said: 'Whoever else stands in the way of Witherston's destiny will be likewise destroyed.' So the shooter must
have thought that evidence of a polluted creek would block the
building of the Senextra factory, which was Witherston's destiny."

"Oh my god, Mev! And the deformed frog was evidence!"

"Do you think that anybody else in Witherston might try to
test the water?"

"Your own kids might."

"And I might."

⌇⌇⌇

When Mev got home after dark, Paco was reading his book
in his recliner. Varry and Renoir occupied the two ends of the
sofa. Jaime was playing his guitar in the boys' bedroom, strug-
gling to learn Mason Williams's difficult "Classical Gas."
Jorge was on the living room floor studying a document from
Withers's trunk that he'd photographed on Wednesday.

"Mom," he said. "Look what I found."

Jorge showed her a picture from the *Dahlonega Nugget* of a
handsome young man putting a wedding ring on a pretty
young woman. Jorge read the caption aloud:

> *Penance Louise Withers, daughter of Mr. and
> Mrs. Witty Withers of Witherston, married Mohe
> Kingfisher, son of Mr. and Mrs. Atohe Kingfisher of
> Tahlequah, Oklahoma, at the Lumpkin County
> Courthouse yesterday. No family members attended
> the ceremony. The couple will make their home in
> Oklahoma.*

The date of the newspaper clipping was Saturday, February
15, 1930.

Mev sat down beside him. "Oh my god!" she said. "1930.
Our Francis Hearty Withers would have been fifteen when she
eloped. Since she was HaHa's sister, any children she had
would have been Francis Hearty Withers's first cousins."

"Whose last name would have been Kingfisher," Jorge said. "Like Dr. Neel Kingfisher."

"Yes. Oh my god. I wonder whether Withers knew they were related."

"Mom, Neel Kingfisher is way younger than old Withers. They can't be first cousins."

"Dr. Kingfisher could have been Withers's first cousin once removed if Withers's aunt was his grandmother."

"Now we have two questions," Jorge said. "Did Dr. Kingfisher know that Mr. Withers was his first cousin once removed? And did Mr. Withers know that Dr. Kingfisher was his first cousin once removed? I'll bet they both knew it and neither would admit to it. For sure, Mr. Withers wouldn't have blabbed that he was kin to a Cherokee!"

"You don't think that Francis Hearty Withers would have mentioned his aunt to someone? Like Mayor Rather? Maybe over a glass of wine?"

"No, Mom. Think! What a scandal this marriage must have been. Rich, lily-white, silk-clothed, high-and-mighty Penny Lou Withers was running off with a not-rich, red-skinned, moccasin-wearing Cherokee named Mohe Kingfisher. His red ancestors had probably aimed spears and arrows at her white ancestors for stealing Cherokee land and gold." Jorge giggled. "Do you think Penny Lou was pleasing her family when she married Mohe? She probably made them furious."

"Enough to disown her, do you think?"

"Enough not to have a wedding for her. They were Withers, Mom. They were millionaires. Snooty millionaires."

"Maybe they were worried that she would not have a good life with someone so different from herself."

"I think they were just prejudiced. Like a whole lot of people who won't mingle with people different from them. Mom, why did whites call Indians redskins?"

"I know," said Jaime, who walked in on the conversation. "Whites in the north called the Algonquian Indians redskins because the Algonquians painted their faces and bodies with red paint. After a while whites started calling all Indians redskins. It was a derogatory word."

"Penance Louise would have been twenty-nine years old, almost thirty," Mev said thoughtfully. "Old enough to make her own choices. She must have been rebelling against her parents, against her whole society."

"I'll bet her parents felt disgraced," Jorge said. "They made her marriage all about themselves. You know, parents give their daughters fancy weddings if they like the groom. And they don't if they don't like the groom. It's kind of obvious that Mr. and Mrs. Withers Francis Withers didn't like Mohe the Cherokee."

"Penance Louise must have loved Mohe passionately. Enough to abandon her family and possibly give up her inheritance."

"In our family we don't care if people of different races marry each other," Jaime said. "Lauren is white and Jim is black, and they're your best friends. And Beau is brown, and he's our best friend. But there are still lots of people just like the Withers. In our school, some of the girls don't invite Beau to their birthday parties. Beau pretends he doesn't care, but he does."

"You've never told me that, Jaime. Has Beau told his parents?"

"No, Mom. He just handles it."

☙❧☙

I don't feel guilty. But I feel lonely. Murder brings loneliness. Terrible, endless loneliness. Murder separates you from your victim. Of course. But it also separates you from everyone else, everyone you know, everyone you will ever know. You have a secret you can never disclose.

What's that line? "After the first death, there is no other." So true. But the poet had mourning in mind. Not murder. No murder affects the murderer as much as the first.

I have not finished. Now I know what I am for. Now I know my destiny. To do good in the long run I must do evil in the short run.

WITHERSTON ON THE WEB
Friday, May 29, 2015

LOCAL NEWS

Faith Murrow Folsom, wife of Dr. George Folsom, died yesterday, May 28, at the age of 51 after a massive stroke. She was pronounced dead at Chestatee Regional Hospital in Dahlonega at 4:55 pm. Dr. Folsom was at her side.

It was not a secret that Mrs. Folsom was pregnant. Dr. Folsom said that pregnancy had been difficult for her because of her age and that it was the probable cause of her death. The Folsoms were childless.

Mrs. Folsom will be buried on Monday morning in her home town of Savannah, where her mother, Mrs. Walter Murrow, lives. According to Dr. Folsom, there will be no funeral or memorial service in Witherston.

A fifth KNN sign, this one a ten-foot banner on butcher paper, appeared early this morning on the Town Hall picket fence facing Possum Road. In huge brown letters resembling logs, with red drops falling from them, the sign said "TREES DIE TO MAKE ROOM FOR YOU AND YOUR TOYS."

When he arrived at his office at 10:25, Mayor Rich Rather ordered Police Chief Jake McCoy to take down the sign immediately and arrest the signmakers, whoever they might be.

Mayor Rather has offered a reward of $100 to anybody who takes a photograph of somebody putting up a KNN sign.

Detective Mev Arroyo of the Witherston Police Department is investigating the attempted murder of Gregory Bozeman, PhD. Dr. Bozeman, a retired EPA ecologist, remains in serious condition at Chestatee Regional Hospital.

Detective Arroyo hopes that Bozeman can identify his assailant when his condition improves.

~ Catherine Perry, Reporter

LETTERS TO THE EDITOR

To the Editor:

I must reply to Mr. or Mrs. Rude Anonymous. I am not a burden to anybody! I made a lot of money working hard as an architect. I was successful.

I have savings because I saved, and I have health insurance and a pension because I contributed to my company's retirement plan. I don't even need social security, although I take it because I earned it too.

So Mr. or Mrs. Rude Anonymous, I am not a burden to you! And if I want to use my money to buy Senextra to live longer and to play bridge longer, that's my right. It's my money!

I would also appreciate it, Mr. or Mrs. Rude Anonymous, if you would sign your name next time you express your sorry opinion!

~ Signed, Asmund Jorgensen

To the Editor:

I think that fourteen-year-old Jorge Arroyo will change his mind about Western medicine the moment he or one of his family members gets a real illness.

Then he won't idealize life in the woods any more. He'll want drugs.

I am seventy-five years old, and I hope to take Senextra soon because I do not want to die.

I say let's build the Senextra factory on Mr. Withers's 31.7 acres. We humans need Senextra more than we need pretty trees.

~ Signed, Alvin Autry

ON THIS DAY IN HISTORY
By Charlotte Byrd

On May 29, 1829, Hearty Withers found gold in Yahoola Creek and became very rich.

Hearty Withers and his wife Penance Hearty Withers Withers (his first cousin) had moved to Dahlonega from Savannah during the 1828 Gold Rush. After winning 40 acres of Cherokee land on Saloli (Squirrel) Creek in 1832 in the Georgia Land Lottery, they built a log house that eventually became the lodge Francis Hearty Withers occupies today.

Hearty and Penance produced three children, of whom only Harold Francis Withers lived to adulthood. "Harry," as Harold Francis Withers was called by his friends, and his wife Patience Gray Withers named their settlement Witherston.

Harry Withers and Patience had one son who lived to adulthood, Withers Francis Withers, affectionately called "Witty." Witty Withers married Obedience Olmstead and in 1889 begat a son, Hearty Harold Withers, known to all as "HaHa." He also begat a daughter, Penance Louise, whom he apparently disinherited when she married a Cherokee named Mohe Kingfisher in 1930.

In 1914, HaHa married Maud Olive McGillicuddy, who on May 23, 1915, gave birth to Francis Hearty Withers. In 1932, HaHa invested more than half of his inherited wealth in the Lawrence Company, which in 2002 became BioSenecta Pharmaceuticals and made Francis Hearty Withers a multibillionaire.

CHAPTER 10

Friday, May 29, 2015:

Friday promised to be a hot day for Lumpkin County, and a humid one. The temperature had already hit seventy-five degrees by 8:00 a.m. But the TV weather lady predicted rain.

After Mev had left for her office, Jaime asked his father, "Dad, may we take Varry and Renoir to the creek this morning?"

"*Hijos*, I have to take the Civic to Shorty's Garage for an oil change."

The eleven-year-old Civic had 116,000 miles on it, but Paco kept the car for its economy. He'd covered the back with bumper stickers, among them: ILLEGAL ALIENS HAVE ALWAYS BEEN A PROBLEM—ASK ANY CHEROKEE, WE ALL LIVE DOWNSTREAM, and a tiny BOO!

Jorge had once asked his father what the tiny BOO! was for. Paco replied that the little sticker would scare drivers following too closely.

"Don't go to the creek," Paco said. "How about going to the pond behind Withers Village? The dogs can swim there. And I'll be back in a couple of hours. Then we can go to the pool together if you like."

As soon as their father had walked out the door, Jorge said to his brother, "Let's go to the creek." He leashed up Varry and Renoir, who were jumping up and down in excitement.

Jaime stuffed a couple of plastic baggies into his pocket and a small net. "Yes, let's."

Jorge grabbed his smartphone. "We might need to take a picture of another weird frog."

As soon as they got into the woods, Jorge let the dogs off the leash. Varry bounded down the slope toward the creek, barking at the top of his lungs and alerting squirrels and birds for miles around of his presence. So did Renoir. The boys followed. Varry and Renoir leaped joyfully into the water. The boys halted.

"Let's go skinny-dipping," Jorge said.

"I'm hot, but the water will be cold," Jaime said.

"I dare you to get nekkid."

"If you get nekkid, I'll get nekkid."

"We'll all get nekkid. Varry too."

"Varry's very nekkid."

The boys shed their clothes, left them in a heap on the bank with the backpack, and waded into the creek. To Varry's delight.

"Woohoo!" Jorge splashed Jaime. "Water's *cold*."

Jaime splashed Jorge and Varry. "Woohoo!"

"Woof, woof!"

The boys' laughter echoed through the woods.

"Now let's look for tadpoles," Jorge said.

"And eight-legged frogs."

They waded gingerly through the shallow water, each bent over double in search of water creatures.

"That's weird," Jaime said after a few minutes. "I don't see a single tadpole. I don't see any minnows either."

"They've been raptured! They've been taken to Heaven, all of them."

"Ha! But seriously, isn't it eerie that nobody's swimming in the creek but us humans?"

"And a dog, or an almost dog."

"Two dogs."

"Three otters."

"Four muskrats."

"Five calling birds."

"And a partridge in a pear tree."

Suddenly Varry growled and looked back up the trail. The boys stopped moving and listened. But they heard nothing.

Varry and Renoir scrambled up the bank, barking fiercely, and raced into the woods.

Then they stopped barking.

Another dog barked back.

Jaime and Jorge heard a man speak. "Good dog, Harry. Good dog."

"Oh, no! Where can we go?" whispered Jaime.

"Too late. Sit down." The boys quickly sat down on the stony creek bed so that the way-too-shallow water would conceal their nakedness.

Out of the brush appeared Dr. Kingfisher with Swift on a leash. Swift sniffed the boys' clothes. Varry sniffed Swift's privates, what was left of them. Swift was neutered. Renoir sniffed Dr. Kingfisher's privates.

"Hello, boys," Dr. Kingfisher greeted them.

"Hello, Dr. Kingfisher," Jorge said, startled. Jorge did the talking for the two of them.

Dr. Kingfisher leaned against a boulder near their clothes and let Swift off his leash. The three dogs jumped into the creek and headed in their direction, to the boys' chagrin.

"Are you boys having fun?"

"Yes, sir," answered Jorge.

"What are you all doing here?"

"Walking our dogs."

"Find any more strange frogs?" Dr. Kingfisher smiled. "I saw the photograph on the website."

"No," they said in unison. By now they were shivering. But they were not about to get out of the water as long as Dr. Kingfisher was watching them.

After a moment of silence, Dr. Kingfisher said, "Well, boys, be careful. Someone could steal your clothes. You wouldn't want to walk through town with nothing on but your sunburn, would you?"

Jaime and Jorge laughed a bit nervously. Their skinny butts were getting sore from the hard pebbles.

"You boys put on your pants and meet me at the top of the hill. We'll talk." Then he turned and walked back up the trail with Swift following.

Varry looked at Swift and then at Jaime and Jorge. He

chose to stay with his humans. Renoir nosed their clothes, took Jaime's underpants in his mouth, and followed Swift up the hill.

Jorge looked at Jaime. "What do you think Dr. Kingfisher wants to tell us?"

"I don't know. Should we call Mom and Dad?"

Jorge thought a moment. "No, we weren't supposed to be here. Let's keep this to ourselves."

The boys climbed up the bank, quickly donned their jeans, and followed in Dr. Kingfisher's tracks.

꿍꿍꿍

Jake walked into Mev's office with a frown on his face. "Big puzzle, this Withers death," he said. "I just got the report from the lab. They found no toxic substance in either the mushroom casserole or the rhubarb pie. Or in the wine."

"Well, that jibes with the Coroner's report. I was so sure Withers was poisoned."

"Maybe he was poisoned another way. Maybe he didn't eat the poison."

꿍꿍꿍

Mev looked at the clock—11:00 a.m.—and picked up her office phone. It was Rhonda.

"Mev," Rhonda said. She was crying. "I know you think that Rich killed Mr. Withers, but he didn't. And I didn't kill him either. When I baked Mr. Withers the mushroom casserole I was careful to put only the obvious morels in it. I know my mushrooms."

"Rhonda, don't be upset. I just found out that the mushrooms in the casserole were not poisonous. Anyway, I have no suspects now. I simply had to interview you all to eliminate you as suspects. I'm interviewing lots of people, including Gretchen, who sold you the morels. Don't cry."

"I'm not crying about that, Mev. I'm just crying. I cry all the time. I'm six-months pregnant at the age of fifty-three, and I'm afraid of my future. I didn't want this baby. I'm too old.

But Rich wouldn't let me have an abortion. He said it would be murder. That's why I know that Rich could not have killed Mr. Withers. He's not a murderer."

"How well did Rich know Mr. Withers?" Mev asked.

"Very well. Rich and Mr. Withers talked for a year about building a Senextra factory in Witherston. They became friends. Sort of. Mr. Withers was very old, you know. And not very talkative. But they did drink wine together. They drank Mr. Withers's fine wine."

"Why is Rich so interested in having BioSenecta build the Senextra factory here?"

"Because BioSenecta will bring jobs to Witherston and re-vitalize our town. Face it, Mev. Our town is dying. If Witherston does not bring in a big employer soon all of our young people will leave, and some of our older people too. And although you may not know it, we have a good number of unemployed and homeless people."

"Tell me, Rhonda. Did your husband sign a contract with BioSenecta?"

"Well…not exactly, though Rich and Martin Payne had an agreement. Mr. Withers had not finalized the $1 sale of his land to BioSenecta. Rich wanted to keep his negotiations with Martin secret until Friday's announcement. He knew that Lottie and Gretchen and all the other anti-progress folks around here who want to keep Witherston primitive would campaign against BioSenecta. And sure enough, they did."

"Rhonda, what's Rich's stake in BioSenecta?"

Rhonda hesitated. "What do you mean? Rich is the mayor. He wants a good future for Witherston. And Witherston needs the billion dollars Mr. Withers left our town in his will."

"Do you realize, Rhonda, that you've just offered a motive for Rich to kill Withers before Withers could change his will?"

഼ഌഌ

As she hung up the phone Mev received a text message from Paco. *ZONGXINGXING*. She loved the sound that announced a message's arrival. It signified that someone was thinking of her.

> *Hola, Mevita. Have you heard from our sons? I've been waiting here for an hour to take them swimming.*

She wrote back:

> *They haven't called me. Where could they have gone?*

Paco wrote:

> *They took Varry for a walk to the pond behind Withers Village. I'm going there myself now.*

Mev wrote:

> *Take your cell phone and call me when you find them.*

๛๛๛

In the cool shade of a large oak, Jaime, Jorge, and Neel Kingfisher sat cross-legged in a circle. Swift, Varry, and Renoir dozed nearby.

"Neel," Jaime asked. "When you became director of Withers Village, did old man Withers's values make sense to you?" Dr. Kingfisher had told the boys to call him "Neel," and they did.

"First, who's Jorge and who's Jaime?" he asked them. "I can't tell you all apart."

"I'm Jaime. He's Jorge," Jaime said. "We have different hair. My part is on the right. Jorge's part is on the left."

Neel took a moment to answer Jaime. "Do you think that Cherokee values and Withers Village values clash? If you do, you're right. The traditional Cherokee people are not at war with nature. The Withers Villagers, hooked on Senextra, are. I am Cherokee at heart. I am, as you say, conflicted."

"But you are director of Withers Village. How can you stand it? Spending day and night with those hundred-year-old people who are taking Senextra so they can get even older," Jorge demanded. "Why did you come here?"

"I came here to Lumpkin County because it's my ancestral home. My grandparents lived on this very land. One day I'll tell you who they were. But they had to leave. They were banished, you might say, eighty-five years ago. So they went to Tahlequah, Oklahoma, where I grew up. I came here to discover my roots. There was a position open at Withers Village. I took it."

"You're a doctor. Couldn't you just have a practice here?" Jaime asked.

Neel looked at the boys for a long time. "Yes, I'm a doctor," he said. "I've been trained to practice medicine, to cure humans, to ease the pain humans suffer from diseases. All kinds of diseases—genetic diseases, infectious diseases, diseases we humans bring upon ourselves, diseases we get from an environment we've poisoned with their pleasures. I've been trained to give pills and shots to humans who are fighting the forces of nature. But I'm also Cherokee. And the Cherokees, at least before the arrival of your ancestors, lived with the forces of nature."

Neel paused, and then lowered his voice. "The war of cultures that bloodied this ground almost two hundred years ago has sundered my soul. So let me tell you a secret, boys—and you must keep this secret. I'm here to observe another battle of cultural values. Another battle in the same war. The battle over Senextra. Why did I come to Withers Village? To escape sorrow, but also to accomplish something on behalf of the values of my people."

Jaime and Jorge listened, spellbound.

Neel continued. "In the nineteenth century your people believed it was your destiny to own this continent, to own the land, the rivers and streams, the lakes and mountains, and the humans who were already there. You conquered my people as if they weren't real humans because they weren't like you. You annihilated my people's civilization as if it weren't a real civilization because it wasn't like yours. You waged war to own and control, not to share. Of course, if you'd wanted to share, you wouldn't have had to wage war. I admit that my people waged war, too, to keep the land they thought was theirs."

"Wow!" Jaime exclaimed. "If we share, we don't have to fight."

"If we think of ourselves, all of us, as part of a whole in which we need each other, then we'll be more inclined to share than to fight. But that's just a dream for now. My dream. Maybe it will become your dream, and the dream of other fourteen-year-old intellectuals. It was John Lennon's dream. Google John Lennon's song 'Imagine,' and you'll see what I mean," said Neel.

"I know the song." Jaime said. "I play it on my guitar." Jaime sang: "Imagine all the people sharing all the world."

"The problem," Neel went on, "is mental, or rather conceptual. Your people, white people of European origin, for centuries defined civilization in opposition to nature. You split reality into two parts. You separated God from Earth, soul from body, humans from the rest of nature. You acted as if nature were your enemy. Now BioSenecta has developed a drug that defies nature. Senextra is humans' ultimate weapon to conquer the forces of nature, to conquer death. Your people don't think of death as natural. But death *is* natural. How well I know that. The death of individuals is necessary for the life of the planet to continue."

Neel looked up at the thunderclouds building overhead, muttered "Rain's coming," and said, "I have come to Witherston to destroy Senextra. That is my mission, boys. And that is my secret."

"Why are you telling us your secret, Neel?" Jorge asked.

"Because you can help me. You boys are sharp. You are intellectual. You are curious. And you are young. You have not yet internalized the values of your people. And you found a deformed frog in Founding Father's Creek. I am interested in that deformed frog. Very, very interested."

"You think something's wrong with Founding Father's Creek?" Jorge asked.

"Jorge and I do," Jaime said. "We didn't see any frogs or tadpoles today. Or minnows either."

"Yes, boys, I do think something's wrong. I think humans

have poisoned Founding Father's Creek, which I prefer to call Saloli Creek, or Squirrel Creek. But then, if the water is toxic, the name Founding Father's Creek is more appropriate than Saloli Creek. After all, squirrels don't have the power to bring birth defects to other species. Humans do. Humans have poisoned our planet, which is our home. No wonder we're sick. No wonder we need medicine. We need anti-toxins."

Jorge asked the question that had been on his mind all day. "Neel, are you Mr. Withers's first cousin once removed?

Neel looked startled. Then he relaxed. "Yes, I am. How did you figure it out?"

"In Mr. Withers's house we found a trunk with a lot of newspaper clippings. One of them from the *Dahlonega Nugget* had a picture of a woman named Penance Louise Withers and a man named Mohe Kingfisher getting married."

"They were my grandparents, but I didn't know them. And until I came to Witherston I never knew a Withers. But I heard stories. W. F. Withers—he was called Witty—was my grandmother's father. He disowned my grandmother because she fell in love with my grandfather, Mohe. So Mohe and Penance, with no money and no land, went to Oklahoma, where Cherokees were welcome. Unfortunately, Mohe and Penance died in a bus accident in Tahlequah in 1931, right after my father was born. My father, Neel Kingfisher, was raised in a Cherokee orphanage. He married a Cherokee woman named Ayita Nance. I'm their son, Neel Kingfisher Jr."

"Did Francis Hearty Withers know who you were?"

"I think he did, because he hired me, but he never acknowledged our relationship. I suspect he feared I'd reveal a blemish on his famous Withers heritage. Maybe he feared I'd ask him for money. Anyway, he disdained me. So I never mentioned my grandparents to him. We had little in common. I despised everything he stood for."

The rain came down hard. Lightning creased the darkening sky. Varry and Swift barked and ran to the sides of their humans. Renoir headed up the trail.

"We've got to go home, Neel. But we'll keep your secret."

"Thanks for trusting us, Neel."

"We're a team, boys."

"We're a team."

☙❧☙

Jaime and Jorge trudged home, completely soaked. The dogs pranced spiritedly alongside them, delighted with the downpour.

"Wow," said Jaime. "My head is so full of thoughts it could pop open! I wish we could tell Mom and Dad about Neel."

"But we promised Neel to keep his secret. We have to keep our promise."

"But we were going to lie to Mom and Dad about going to the creek. And keeping promises goes along with never lying."

"Let's tell them the truth," Jorge said. "But just not all of it. Let's tell them about going skinny-dipping in the creek and apologize for disobeying them. We don't have to tell them about meeting Neel there."

"Good idea. Anyway, we learned something important at the creek that we should investigate. We found no tadpoles, no frogs, and no minnows. And it's May twenty-ninth, when the creek should be full of critters."

"You know, Jaime. Growing up means thinking on your own and making important decisions by yourself."

"And knowing things that parents don't know."

"We're grown up now."

"Woohoo! We're manly!"

☙❧☙

"¡*Hijos!* Where have you been?" Paco was distraught. And drenched. "I went to the pond and couldn't find you. Your mom and I have been very worried. Where have you been?"

After changing clothes, the boys and their father had a long conversation about their worrying him and Mev.

"We're sorry, Dad. We shouldn't have disobeyed you. We just wanted to find another leggy froggy."

"We weren't thinking, Dad. We forgot about the time."

"*Hijos*, next time just explain to me why you want to go where you want to go. We can negotiate."

"Dad," Jaime said. "We did find something important at the creek. I mean, we didn't find something important. We saw no frogs or tadpoles or minnows. Zero!"

"Dad, it's like our creek is dying."

"We need to talk to Gregory when he gets better," Paco said. "We'll get the water tested." Then he called Mev. "*Hola, guapa*. The home front is okay."

∽∽∽

Mev's cell phone rang. Or rather barked. She had selected the bark option for the call signal. It was Jon.

"Mev," he said. "Are you coming back to Dahlonega this afternoon? Gregory is awake. And he's talking! At least a little. Anyway, he's going to be okay."

"Hallelujah! I'm so glad, Jon."

"Can you come down?"

"Sure. Of course, Jon. I've been waiting for Neel Kingfisher to return my call. When he does I'll come see you and Gregory."

"Thanks, sweet baby."

Mev had a couple of things to do. First she faxed the office of Martin Payne a formal request for a list of BioSenecta stockholders residing in Witherston. Then she faxed Lauren a formal request for a copy of Faith's will.

By 4:00 Neel Kingfisher had not returned her call. Mev left.

∽∽∽

Neel sat at his desk in Withers Village, contemplating his conversation with Jaime and Jorge.

They were the age his son John would have been had he lived.

He kept a picture of the boy on his desk.

Perhaps it was John's untimely death, at age ten from leukemia, that motivated him to destroy Senextra. Why should our society, he'd asked himself again and again, put so much money into keeping the elderly alive? Our future is in our children.

"If I were in charge of the country," Neel said to himself, "I'd direct the National Institutes of Health to put ninety percent of its budget into research beneficial to our society's young people."

∾∾∾

Mev arrived at Gregory's bedside at 4:30. Gregory was sitting up with a smile on his face and an IV in his left arm.

"How are you feeling, Gregory?"

"Better, Mev. Still weak, but glad to be alive. Thanks so much for coming."

"And thanks for keeping Renoir for us," Jon said.

"Renoir has made himself at home in our house. So he can stay as long as you let him."

"Mev," Gregory said. "I did hear footsteps before I was shot. Somebody heavy. A man."

"Did you turn around to see him?"

"No, I didn't. I was getting a sample of creek water to test."

"For BPA?"

"Yes, and for any other toxins. I'm thinking of BPA, of course, but also of drugs that can affect reproduction.

"Like what?"

"Estrogens, androgens, steroids, other endocrine disruptors—all stuff that people take to feel better."

"Go on, Gregory," Mev said. "I'm starting to figure out that BioSenecta will not want to build a factory where our water supply is contaminated."

"Okay. Endocrine disruptors are a class of chemicals used in lots of household products, plastics, pesticides, and drugs. They interfere with the body's hormone system. They can cause cancer in the reproductive organs, birth defects like Jaime's frog with the extra leg, feminization of males, and masculinization of females. Phthalates can make women give birth to boys with undescended testicles."

"What are phthalates?"

"Oh my god, Jon! Where do I begin? Phthalates are chemicals that are used in pills, nutritional supplements, plastics, detergents, glue, perfume, eye shadow, moisturizer, nail polish, liquid soap, shampoo, almost anything you can think of. Phthalates are probably in a lot of your hair care products. We humans, and other animals, are exposed to phthalates every day. Phthalates are in our bodies. We know, because the chemicals appear in our urine."

"Leggy Froggy was found downstream from Witherston. Maybe his mother had phthalates in her system," Mev said.

"Either phthalates or synthetic estrogen," Gregory said.

"And Varry has undescended testicles, or maybe no testicles at all."

"Who is Varry?" Gregory asked.

"Varry used to be Harry, old Withers's puppy."

"Oh. That's interesting. So Varry can't reproduce."

"Right."

"When can I go home?" Gregory asked.

"That's up to your doctor. Who's your doctor? George Folsom?"

"No, good god no! My internist is Dr. Luisa Romero, here in Dahlonega. And my surgeon, whom I met today for the first time, is Dr. Buddy Harper."

"Let's not let word get out that you are talking, Gregory. I'd like to see whether your would-be killer shows any signs of nervousness. I'll speak to Catherine Perry. And I'll order a deputy to sit by your door for your protection."

❧❧❧

The Witherston Police Department forwarded Dr. Morston's call to Mev's cell phone.

"Mev, I apologize for calling you directly, but I've found something that might be relevant to your Withers investigation."

"Hi, John. Tell me."

"I did Faith Folsom's autopsy last night. I found Senextra in her system."

❧❧❧

Gretchen was unloading cases of blueberries a local farmer had brought in when she received a text message. It was from Martin:

Would you like to go down to Founding Father's Creek tomorrow? I will pick you up at noon.

Gretchen wrote back:

Okay. I look forward to seeing you! Gandhi will go with us. Bye.

Now why does everybody on God's green earth want to go to Founding Father's Creek, Gretchen wondered.

ဧၰဧၰ

Getchen called Lottie. "Hi, Lottie. Let's have dinner together tonight. If you'll bring the wine, I'll provide vegetables and seafood."

"Perfect. See you at 6:00."

Gretchen and Lottie, both foodies, both pescatarians, enjoyed cooking together and did it often. Lottie always brought Darwin, who would spend the evening perched on her shoulder with bathroom breaks every twenty minutes or so. Gretchen always allowed Darwin to explore the table after she and Lottie had finished eating.

Darwin enjoyed the left-overs. So did Gandhi, who ate what Darwin tossed on the floor.

Tonight Gretchen produced jumbo shrimp caught off the Georgia coast near Brunswick and frozen on the boat. They sautéed the shrimp in a green onion/dill/saffron/butter sauce and served it over whole wheat penne pasta. With a side of leeks baked in olive oil, whole grain mustard, thyme, white wine, and balsamic vinegar from Modena. And a salad consisting of half of an avocado topped with pine nuts and more of that delicious balsamic vinegar. And a bottle of Barolo. For dessert, dark chocolate-covered almonds.

Darwin had dry-roasted unsalted peanuts and pine nuts. No avocado, because avocado is toxic to parrotlets, actually to all parrots. No chocolate either.

Gandhi had a turkey burger, prepared just for him. With bun.

"Lottie," Gretchen said. "Let me tell you about a dinner date and a lunch date I had with a very charming man. He's young and handsome and rich and smart, but a Republican."

Gretchen—a yellow-dog Democrat like Lottie—recounted every detail of her evening in Dahlonega with Martin Payne. Then she told Lottie about their lunch.

"Martin had a meeting Wednesday morning with Grant Griggs. He said he wanted to make sure that BioSenecta would still inherit Withers's estate. He wants the construction of the Senextra factory to start as scheduled. I, of course, don't."

"Still, it sounds like you enjoyed your time with Martin," commented Lottie. "Your eyes are all lit up."

"Then he had an appointment to see Mayor Rather late that afternoon. He didn't tell me the reason for their meeting. I'm curious."

"But you like Martin?"

"Well, I do find our conversation stimulating. And I confess to finding him attractive. But he's a decade younger than I. Why would he find me attractive?"

"Gretchen! You are beautiful, even if you use no makeup, wear your gray hair in 1970-ish braids, sport a tattoo, and dress funny. Martin must have looked past your tattoo into your soul. You have a lovely soul. And you have a great brain."

"So do you, dear Lottie," Gretchen said. "But I didn't invite you over to discuss the loveliness of our souls or the greatness of our brains. I want to know what you think of Martin's invitation to go to Founding Father's Creek tomorrow."

"Why would Martin want to go to the creek? According to recent observers, the creek offers only deformed frogs and fired-upon friends. I plan to stay away from the creek until Gregory's shooter goes into the paddy wagon."

"I wonder how much Martin knows about Witherston. I had the feeling the other night that he knew our community quite well. Funny that Mayor Rather called him so quickly after

Withers's body was discovered. Also, why would a busy CEO of a multinational corporation drop all his business to rush to Witherston for Withers's funeral? Why would he be a pall-bearer?"

"Gretchen, I don't want to hurt your feelings, but I have to ask you whether Martin might possibly be more interested in BioSenecta's prospects here than he is in you. Let's think about this. Martin approached you first when you were carrying an anti-Senextra sign at Withers's birthday party last Saturday. Then he texted you on Monday afternoon, probably immediately after he received Mayor Rather's phone call about Withers's death, to invite you to dinner after the funeral. Then he invited you to lunch, which you ended up providing. Now he wants to go to the creek with you. You've known him less than a week. Which do you think is more important to him: going to the creek with you, or going with you to the creek?"

"I know, Lottie. I've got to stay clear-headed about him. Has he fallen in love with me? Or does he need my support for building the BioSenecta plant? He should realize that he doesn't need my support for that."

"Or does he want to keep abreast of the investigation by courting you? If he courts you, he has an excuse to come to Witherston often."

"I hate to admit it, but I think he's most interested in the creek now."

༒

"Mom!" Jaime called from the boys' bedroom. "We went on the web and found a whole lot of ways to poison people!"

"*Hijos*, don't do any experimenting," Paco shouted up the stairs.

Jaime brought down his tablet. Jorge followed.

"Mom, I think that the best way to poison somebody secretly is to use potassium chloride, which causes the heart to stop," Jaime said. "Just inject it into a vein. It's very painful, and the victim might scream and yell, so the murderer would want to give the victim a sedative first."

"Potassium chloride is not noticeable in a routine autopsy,"

Jorge added, "especially if the person doing the autopsy doesn't suspect murder."

"Arsenic is also a good poison for murderers, if you give it in small doses for a long time. The victim just gets sick and dies."

"And strychnine is a good poison for murderers."

"Yes, it's used to murder rats."

"Do you know any rats?"

"Good work, boys!" Mev said. "You've been very helpful detectives."

"Woohoo!"

Before she and Paco headed upstairs to bed, Mev checked her email. She found a message from Lauren with Faith's will attached as a PDF file.

Hmmm, she thought to herself. Apparently, Faith loved animals more than she loved her husband George. She'd made the TLC Humane Society of Dahlonega the main beneficiary of her estate. That is, if her yet unborn child died before or at the same time she died.

And he did.

WITHERSTON ON THE WEB
Saturday, May 30, 2015

LOCAL NEWS

Mrs. Grant Griggs has called off the meeting of the Cele-bration Planning Committee originally scheduled for 10:00 am today in Fellowship Hall of Witherston Baptist Church. In view of the sudden and unexpected death of Francis Hearty Withers and the continued protests against the logging of Withers's land, Mrs. Griggs said she was putting on hold any plans for a Senextra factory groundbreaking ceremony.

Yesterday afternoon at 4:00, Mona Pattison took a photo-graph of Sally Sorensen nailing a KEEP NATURE NATURAL sign to a telephone pole on the northeast corner of Main Street and Ninovan Drive, across from City Hall. The sign read KNN SAYS SENEXTRA USERS' ECO-FOOTPRINTS ARE TOO BIG FOR EARTH. Miss Sorensen was arrested and fined $50. Miss Pattison claimed Mayor Rather's reward of $100 for photographing somebody putting up a KNN sign. Both young women are members of KNN.

In a possibly related incident, yesterday at 4:30, Annie Jerden took a photograph of Christopher Zurich nailing a KEEP NATURE NATURAL sign to a telephone pole on the southwest corner of Main Street and Creek Street, across from City Hall. The sign read KEEP NATURE NATURAL. Mr. Zur-ich was arrested and fined $50. Miss Jerden claimed Mayor

Rather's reward of $100 for photographing somebody putting up a KNN sign. Both young people are members of KNN.
  ~ Catherine Perry, Reporter

LETTERS TO THE EDITOR

To the Editor:

In response to Mr. Jorgensen's request: I will sign my name next time I express a sorry opinion.
  However, my opinions are seldom sorry.
  ~ Signed, Mr. or Mrs. Rude Anonymous

To the Editor:

I would like to respond to Mr. Autry's statement that "We humans need Senextra more than we need pretty trees."
  Mr. Autry had seventy-five years of living with pretty trees and no Senextra. Now he wants to live another twenty-five years with Senextra and no trees.
  Isn't Mr. Autry being selfish? I am only fifteen years old. I would like to live with trees as many years as Mr. Autry did.
  Does Mr. Autry not care if his grandchildren have only concrete to walk on and bricks to look at?
  ~ Signed, Christopher Zurich

ON THIS DAY IN HISTORY
By Charlotte Byrd

On May 30, 1838, Hearty Withers, the first Withers to take up residence in Lumpkin County, died when a Cherokee man slit his throat outside his house. Hearty Withers's wife Penance Hearty Withers (who was his first cousin) witnessed the event in the company of their eight-year-old son Harry.
  A week later, in the last entry of her diary for that year,

Penance wrote: *"Little Harry and I will never forget that young savage's murderous eyes. I can't imagine what my dearest Hearty could have done to him to make that Indian so vicious."*

Penance Hearty Withers's diary for 1838 was found in a trunk in Francis Hearty Withers's home by Detective Mev Arroyo on May 27. The contents of the trunk are being studied and will be donated to the Hargrett Rare Book and Manuscript Library of the University of Georgia.

OBITUARY
Faith Murrow Folsom

Faith Murrow Folsom, 51, died on Tuesday, May 26. She is survived by her husband, Dr. George Folsom, and her mother, Mrs. Walter G. Murrow of Savannah. Her father was the financier Walter G. Murrow, recently deceased.

Faith Folsom was known to Witherstonians for her generosity of time, energy, and money. She will be especially missed for her contributions to the TLC Dahlonega Humane Society, where she volunteered. She was famous for her creative organization of Witherston's 2015 fundraiser for unwanted pets, to which she gave the title "Fat Cats Take Care of Skinny Cats (and Dogs)."

Faith had just recently stepped down from the board of Withers Village. Faith was also a major donor to the University of Georgia, where she had obtained an M.A. in English.

In lieu of flowers, Dr. Folsom urges Mrs. Folsom's friends to make a contribution to Withers Village.

POLICE BLOTTER

On May 29, at 8:30 pm, Witherston Police officers arrested Rudy Pate, age 18, and Fen Loftner, age 18, for attempting to rob Francis Hearty Withers's grave on May 26. The officers had stopped the young men in Loftner's 2002 Toyota Tacoma for a missing tail light and discovered two muddy shovels, two *cut-off stockings, and two industrial flashlights in the back. Pate and Loftner confessed but said they were not going to steal Withers's body. They said they'd only wanted to save Withers's fancy casket from the damage it would suffer in the ground. Pate said he'd always been fond of Leonardo's "Last Supper." They were fined $100 each and released to their parents' custody.*

On May 30, at 12:15 am, Witherston Police officers ticketed Trevor Bennington, III, age 21, of Athens, for walking down Hickory Street while intoxicated. When asked for an explanation, Bennington said that his father had temporarily taken away his car keys after his May 25 traffic offense and so he had to walk.

CHAPTER 11

Saturday, May 30, 2015:

Mev was in the kitchen scrambling eggs for the men in her life when Chief McCoy called her on her cell phone.

"Does it strike you as strange that within a week Witherston has a murder, an attempted murder, and a death by stroke?" he asked. "Witherston had only 4,000 residents, and now it's down to 3,998, give or take a few good souls. What's happening here?"

"I can't believe it either, Jake," Mev replied, taking the eggs off the stove. "But I don't see how Faith's stroke could be connected to Bozeman's shooting or Withers's death. You know that Faith was fifty-one years old. Her pregnancy must have caused enormous stress on her body."

"I have big news. Dr. Morston found traces of Senextra when he did Faith's autopsy. Senextra! Now why would Faith be taking Senextra if she's only fifty-one, or was? How could she have gotten the drug?"

"That is interesting. Very, very interesting. George—Dr. Folsom—must have given it to her," Mev said. "He probably got it from Withers Village. He's Withers Village's primary care physician. He's administering the Senextra trial for Bio-Senecta. He monitors the patients' reactions to Senextra and reports them to BioSenecta."

"Could he have prescribed Senextra for Faith?" asked Jake.

"No, because the drug has not been FDA-approved for sale. Francis Hearty Withers and the residents of Withers Village were in a pilot study sponsored by BioSenecta. George was authorized to prescribe Senextra only to Withers Village residents and to Withers."

"So George broke the law."

"I guess he did. He certainly violated BioSenecta's policies and procedures."

"Well, I wonder whether old George will view the deaths of Francis Hearty Withers and his wife Faith as reactions to Senextra worthy of a report to BioSenecta."

Mev thought a moment. "He should. But then he'd have to report his use of Senextra outside the pilot study. Anyway, we still have to figure out whether the two deaths and the shooting are connected. If the deaths were related to BioSenecta, what is the relationship between those deaths and Gregory's being shot?"

"I think I'll ask to see George's patient records and his reports to BioSenecta. I'd like to know what he's reporting."

"Good idea," Mev said. "And I want to know whether anyone benefited from Faith's death. Yesterday I asked Lauren to send me Faith's will, which she'd filed in Probate Court."

"And?"

"Faith left everything but her house to the TLC Humane Society of Dahlonega."

"Wow. She must have hated George."

"Ruth Griggs witnessed the signing of the will."

✧✧✧

While Paco and the twins ate their eggs and biscuits, Mev took a morning walk in the woods.

Lately she tired easily, whether from her illness or her worries she didn't know. And although she needed the stimulation of a criminal investigation, especially now, she craved time to think about her personal situation.

Today she headed toward the creek in search of the tranquility that it always brought her. She lay down on the mossy bank and gazed up at the tops of the tall pines swaying with the breeze. Then she closed her eyes to feel nature's rhythms in her body.

Jim had given her a good prognosis. Yet Mev knew breast

cancer could be deadly, and she believed that in her case it would be. She felt sadness that she'd be leaving Jaime and Jorge without a mother when they were teenagers and disappointment that she would not enjoy more years with Paco. But she didn't feel panic. She'd never expected immortality.

She hoped only that she'd been a good mother and a good wife, and that in her forty-two years she'd done something to improve the lives of her fellow residents of Earth.

Mev shed her espadrilles and waded halfway across the creek. She felt the pebbles imprinting her toes, the cold water numbing her feet, the stream's current threatening her balance. She seated herself on a boulder that interrupted the rushing waters and created a quiet eddy for her to contemplate. As she made herself comfortable she scanned the creek water for tadpoles, as Jaime had trained her to do. And for bullfrogs. But she saw neither.

Was Founding Father's Creek polluted like so many other streams, rivers, and lakes on our continent that we humans have turned toxic with our waste? What was Gregory about to discover?

Suddenly Mev heard low voices on the other side of the creek. People were coming! She slid off the rock and hopped and skipped at her top speed to the bank where she'd left her shoes. She slipped into them and ran back up the trail. She heard someone yell, but she didn't turn around. Five minutes later she was home in the kitchen, still scared.

Paco was doing the dishes. The boys looked up from their tablets.

"Mom, what happened to you?" Jaime asked. "Why are you barefoot?"

"Because your mother is a fraidy-cat, boys," Mev replied. "Your mother runs when she hears strange sounds."

Paco rubbed her shoulders as she told them about the noises that had frightened her.

"Human voices," she said, "not the voices of the birds and squirrels I went down to the creek to hear."

Jorge rubbed her back. "Mom, we humans always drown out everybody else's voices."

"Ha! That's our destiny," said Jaime. "To make more noise than anybody else on Earth."

"With our planes, trains, automobiles," Jorge added.

"And our all-terrain vehicles."

"And our factories."

"We are all-powerful!"

"The planet is ours!"

"Boys, please," Mev begged. "I've just had the fright of my life. Let's be serious."

"Why were you so scared, Mom?"

"Because Gregory was shot at Founding Father's Bridge. I was thinking of him when I heard the men—I think they were men—coming toward me from the other side of the creek. I panicked because I thought they might shoot me."

"Why was Gregory shot?"

"Because he was getting creek water to test for the Environmental Protection Agency. He suspected that toxins in the water caused your frog's deformity. He went to Founding Father's Bridge because that's where you found Leggy Froggy, Jaime."

"My picture of Leggy Froggy was in *Witherston on the Web*, Mom," Jorge said. "So everybody in the world knew that Leggy Froggy came from Founding Father's Bridge."

"Floundering Father's Bridge." Jaime giggled. "You know, Jorge, not everybody in the world reads the *Webby Witherston*. Maybe only five hundred Witherstonians."

"Georgia's founding father begets leggy froggies! I'm going to send that story to *Webby Witherston*," Jorge said.

"Good idea, Jorge," Mev said. "Our online paper can be as good as you want to make it."

"*Hijo*, first google Abraham Baldwin and Cherokee to make sure you get your facts right," Paco said.

౸౸౸

Jorge wrote his story on his tablet while sitting at the kitchen table. After a half hour he read it aloud to Mev, Paco, and Jaime.

"Georgia's Founding Father Begets Leggy Frog
"By Jorge Arroyo

"On Sunday, May 24, Jaime Arroyo caught a bullfrog with three back legs under Founding Father's Bridge. A photograph of the leggy frog taken by his brother, Jorge Arroyo, appeared in Witherston on the Web on May 26.

"Is Founding Father's Creek sick?

"The Cherokees called the creek "Saloli" creek. "Saloli" means "squirrel." The Cherokees liked all of nature, even squirrels. They didn't consider humans more important than animals.

They wanted nature to stay in balance, like an ecosystem.

"But the Cherokees lost their gold and their land to Americans who believed that humans should control nature. And they were force-marched to Oklahoma in 1838 on the "Trail of Tears." "Trail of Tears" is the English translation of the Cherokee "Trail Where They Cried" ("Nunna daul Tsuny").

"In 1857, Harry Withers renamed the creek "Founding Father's Creek" for Abraham Baldwin, who was a founding father of the United States. He represented Georgia at the Constitutional Convention.

"Now Founding Father's Creek produces frogs with three back legs. Is the leggy frog telling us that the creek is polluted? The frog's mother lived in the creek and drank from it.

"If humans drink from Founding Father's Creek will some human mothers give birth to babies with three legs?

"How's that?" he asked his family triumphantly when he'd concluded.

"Good. Really good, *hijo*. But I suggest you take out the last paragraph." Paco said.

"But Dad, that's the most important part!"

"The last paragraph sounds like you're making a joke. And although you seem to make jokes for a living I think you have a very serious message here."

"Let him send it to Smitty," Mev said. "We can hope that Smitty will run it as an opinion piece on the editorial page, since it's not really a story. If Smitty wants to cut the last paragraph, he'll do it. Anyway, Jorge, you've written an excellent essay!"

"Hey, bro. You're becoming a journalist," said Jaime. "Woohoo!"

❦

The phone rang—the land line. That was increasingly rare. It was George Folsom.

"Hello, Mev." George sounded upset.

"Hello, George. I've felt so bad for you. I am so sorry that Faith passed away. Is there anything I can do for you?

"Well, yes, there is, Mev. You have probably heard that Faith's autopsy showed the presence of Senextra in her system. I would be grateful if you could keep the autopsy report confidential. To protect her privacy, you know."

"I work in the Witherston Police Department, George. Medical reports are not my responsibility, unless they are part of a criminal investigation. And Faith's death really seems to be an unfortunate accident of nature."

"It certainly is, Mev. So was Faith's pregnancy. Faith didn't want to end it. I wanted her to have an abortion. She'd be alive now if she had followed my advice."

"George, why was Faith taking Senextra? She didn't look her age."

George was silent for a moment. "Mev, you'll comprehend this when you get older. Faith wanted to stay young. She asked me to get her the drug, which I was administering to Withers Village residents."

"How long had she been taking it?"

"About two years. But why should that be relevant, Mev? You just said that medical reports are not your responsibility."

"Just curious."

"Mev, I'm suffering. Faith was my wife of twenty-nine years. On Monday she'll be buried at her family's grave site in Bonaventure Cemetery in Savannah. Her mother lives there. Since I'll continue to practice in Witherston I ask you to please keep Faith's medical history out of the press."

"George, I'm investigating Withers's death. Unless Faith or you had something to do with Withers's death, I've no interest in making public Faith's medical history. Don't worry."

e/ɔe/ɔ

At 12:00 noon Gretchen watched Martin park his BMW, with the top up this time, in front of her store. Despite the light drizzle, Martin looked ready for a walk to the creek: a newish navy Atlanta Braves T-shirt, newish jeans, newish sandals, designer sunglasses, and an umbrella. Gretchen was ready too: oldish black T-shirt with a peace symbol, oldish jeans, oldish sandals, not-designer sunglasses, and a headband. No umbrella, for sure.

"Hi, Gretchen," Martin greeted her as he walked through the door. "Perfect afternoon to go to the creek. Seventy-two degrees. Not too cool, not too hot."

"I've packed us a couple of tomato sandwiches, a couple of apples, and a baggy of raw cashews. Thought you might not have had time for lunch on your drive up to Witherston."

"I haven't eaten lunch, though I did get here earlier this morning to do some business. Are you going to take Gandhi with us?"

"I am," Gretchen replied. "Gandhi! Come here," she yelled at the top of her lungs.

Gandhi loped up from the woods behind her house smelling of whatever he'd just rolled in and jumped up to lick Martin's face.

Gretchen remembered her favorite old cartoon in which a similarly large dog leaps upon an unsuspecting well-dressed stranger and starts humping his face. The dog's owner says proudly to the stranger, "Rover likes you." But after noticing Martin's distress over Gandhi's affectionate kisses, she decided to not to mention the cartoon.

She got her walking stick, Martin graciously took her back-pack, and Gandhi joyfully led them along the half-mile trail to the creek. They followed the creek the two miles down to Founding Father's Bridge.

"Do you like hiking?" she asked him.

"I like walking in the woods with you," he responded.

"Yes, yes. I can see what a treat that must be," she said. "Let me ask the question in another way. Do you do much walking in the woods?"

"Not as much as I'd like, Gretchen. But the more I see of Witherston, the more I want to get out into nature."

"Even in the rain?" The warm rain had started again.

"Even in the rain."

They heard a big splash, rounded a bend, and saw Gandhi swimming downstream.

"*Gandhi*! Come here."

Gandhi had been a first-class racer, running the Bonita Springs track at 40 miles per hour at the age of two. But when he slowed down to 39 miles per hour at the age of four he was retired and put up for adoption. Lottie, who kept track of every animal on Earth in need of a home, had told Gretchen about greyhounds, taken her to the Florida adoption facility, pointed out a tall 75-pound brown male, paid the adoption fee, and said, "There, Gretchen. Now you have a running mate."

Gretchen named the sweet beast Gandhi. Gandhi was intelligent, quiet, sociable, and peace-loving, and he liked to run and swim. Gretchen believed that she and Gandhi were spiritual kin.

Gandhi turned around, swam against the current, and returned to Gretchen. She leashed him, and the three of them took shelter from the rain under the great branches of an old oak. Gretchen and Martin ate their lunch sitting on the tree's massive roots.

She was still dissatisfied with Martin's answers to her questions, so she continued. "Why are you so interested in Founding Father's Creek?"

"Dear Gretchen, why are you so full of questions? Can't we just enjoy the outdoors?"

"Martin, if you enjoy the outdoors, then we do have something in common. But I'm still curious about your interest in the creek."

"Okay. I confess. I became interested in the creek when *Witherston on the Web* posted the photo of the deformed frog. I'd like to know whether that frog has any deformed relatives."

"Go on."

"I want to know whether the creek water is polluted. If it is, then BioSenecta will probably not build a factory here. So there you have it. I'm a scout for my company."

"Did you want to go with me to the creek, or to the creek with me? I need to know that, Martin."

"I wanted to go to the creek with you, Gretchen, because you are the most interesting, attractive, intelligent woman in Witherston."

"Well, gosh, thanks. Do you mean all of Witherston, or just the downtown area?"

"I mean—Gretchen, believe me—I am attracted to you. I'd want to see you whether or not BioSenecta located here."

"Even though I must be eight or nine or possibly ten years older than you?"

"Yes, Gretchen."

"Okay, I'd like to see you again too."

He picked up her hand, held it for a moment, and then dropped it. "Let's get a water sample for me to take back to Atlanta."

He got the water sample, and they trekked back up the trail through the gently falling rain to Gretchen's store. By 2:30 Martin was saying good-bye.

ᘉᘓᘉᘓ

After lunch Jaime, Jorge, Varry, and Renoir departed for Beau's house, leaving the place quiet for Mev and Paco. Mev plopped down on the sofa, which had been temporarily vacated by Varry and Renoir. Paco plopped down beside her.

"What do you want to do this afternoon, *guapa*?"

"I hate to break the news to you, Paco, but as soon as the rain stops I'd like to go back to Founding Father's Bridge and get a water sample," Mev said. "If Gregory suspected pollution, then I suspect it too."

The rain stopped at 3:00. Mev and Paco headed toward Founding Father's Bridge with an empty Rioja wine bottle. They loved their walks together, when they could talk at leisure.

"Help me understand this, Paco. How are Withers's will, Withers's death, Gregory's interest in Founding Father's Creek, and BioSenecta all related?"

"Don't forget about Leggy Froggy."

"So how is Leggy Froggy related to the shooting of Gregory and to the destiny of Witherston?"

Paco thought for a moment. "Let's list the suspects."

"Good idea. Let's see. Mayor Rather, Dr. Folsom, Mr. Grant."

"No women?" Paco asked.

"How about Rhonda Rather? But no, Rhonda is too pregnant and too rich and too nice to kill Withers—though if she really has stock in BioSenecta she may want the Senextra factory here. Anyway, Gregory heard a man's footsteps right before he was shot. And Gregory's shooter was most likely Withers's killer."

"How about Dr. Kingfisher? He may have inherited his Cherokee ancestors' grudge against the Withers family."

"And then there's BioSenecta CEO Dr. Martin Payne, who is suddenly infatuated with Gretchen and suddenly interested in Witherston," she said.

"Wow. Witherston is full of doctors. Including Jim. Not bad for a town too small to have its own hospital."

"All of the suspects on my list want to have BioSenecta here."

"And your nature loving friends who are not on your list don't want BioSenecta here. But they benefit from Withers death. They get to keep the woods." He laughed. "Maybe Aunt Lottie killed Withers."

"Paco, Witherston is divided. We're seeing a dispute here between the defenders of nature, including the Cherokees, and the defenders of BioSenecta, which makes Senextra, which keeps people alive unnaturally long."

"*Mevita*, you're about to solve this mystery."
"If only I didn't have to have surgery next week."

☙❧❧

By the time Mev and Paco got home with their water sample, Jaime, Jorge, Varry, Renoir, and Beau had taken up most of the available space in the living room. Varry and Renoir, damp from the rain and smelling like doggy, occupied the two ends of the cloth-covered sofa. The boys sat on the carpet.

"We're going to work on Withers's documents, Mom," Jaime said.

They each carried a coke, which Mev figured they'd gotten from Lauren.

"Mom," Jorge said. "We ran into Catherine Perry. She was interviewing Beau's mother about Withers's will for *Webby Witherston*—"

"And guess what," Beau interrupted. "Jorge told Mizz Perry he'd written an essay about Leggy Froggy for *Webby Witherston*, and Mizz Perry invited Jorge to write some more."

"Woohoo!" Jorge shouted. "I'm a journalist."

"My brother is gonna be famous like Aunt Lottie," Jaime said.

☙❧❧

At 4:45, Jorge got an email from Smitty Green. Smitty had written:

> *Dear Jorge: Thank you for your column on Founding Father's Creek. It will appear on WITH-ERSTON ON THE WEB tomorrow morning. Now I invite you to write a regular online column this summer—that is, a short column like your aunt Charlotte's of 200 words or fewer. We can call it "What's Natural?" You may email me a piece whenever you like. Of course you must agree to being edited. All journalists get edited. Please send me a head shot of yourself. Best wishes, Smitty Green*

Jorge read the message and yelled "Woohoo!" for the benefit of everyone within hearing distance.

Then he wrote back:

> *Thank you very much, Mr. Green. I accept the position you have offered me. I will send you many essays this summer for my column "What's Natural?" Sincerely yours, Jorge Arroyo*

> *P.S. I attach a head shot I took of my brother. We look alike, so does it matter? If it does matter, my brother can take a head shot of me and I can email it to you later.*

☙☙☙

The twins had gone into their room with Varry and Renoir. Mev could hear Jaime quietly playing his guitar. As darkness fell, Mev and Paco sat in their rocking chairs on the back deck, enjoying the scent of the pines. An owl hooted.

Mev told Paco about her hospital visit with Gregory and Jon.

"Paco, what if Founding Father's Creek really is sick, and we've all been exposed to the same pollutants that have affected creek animals like Leggy Froggy?"

"We're getting the creek water tested, *querida,* so we don't have to worry."

"Lauren and I discussed the number of cancers in Witherston that we know about: Gretchen's breast tumor, my breast tumor, and Wanda Clement's ovarian tumor, which killed her. Then there's Faith Folsom's stroke, when she's pregnant at the age of fifty-one. Rhonda Rich is pregnant too, and she's in her fifties. Now that's *weird.*"

"You all must be drinking from the same pitcher. *Guapa,* you haven't been drinking water from the creek behind my back, have you?" Paco tried to bring fun to any conversation. Not everybody found that trait endearing, but Mev did. She loved his sense of humor. Good thing, because the twins had inherited it.

"Faith and Rhonda must have something in common," Mev said.

"Maybe they're just overly fertile. Poor Varry is underly fertile. But he's better off than his dead brothers. Maybe his mother drank creek water."

"Paco, I just realized something! Varry's mother was sixteen years old when she gave birth to Varry—or Harry, as Withers called him. So Maud Olive got pregnant as an elderly lady dog. And gave birth to a puppy with a genital abnormality. Do we have a pattern here?"

"There must be something in the water that affects sex."

"That affects reproduction. Gregory is very knowledgeable about the effect of toxic chemicals on reproduction."

"*Oye, Mevita.* Do we know anybody with undescended testicles?"

Mev ignored him. "Lauren says that Jim has several patients unable to get pregnant. I wonder if any young women have had miscarriages. I think I'll ask him."

"If Jim won't tell you, we can get Jorge to write a column on the subject for *Webby Witherston*," Paco said. "Jorge can say he's collecting information on unusual reproductive problems for his sex education class and ask Witherstonians to email him details."

They laughed.

"Just picture it," Mev said. "Men and women of all ages in our community would immediately email our fourteen-year-old son with details about their sex lives, their menstrual cycles, their ability or inability to get pregnant, their miscarriages, and their recent gynecological exams."

"And their prostate exams. And their erectile dysfunction. The men will tell Jorge if they need testosterone underarm cream," Paco added.

They were silent for a while.

He then said, "Okay. So why would somebody shoot Gregory to keep him from finding toxic chemicals in our water?"

"Either a polluter who doesn't want his excretion of toxic chemicals discovered or an investor in BioSenecta who doesn't want BioSenecta to withdraw from Witherston," she replied.

"When we discover what's in the water, we may figure out who put it there and why someone wants to keep it secret."

"And then we'll have the killer."

"Perhaps. But Paco, how can I keep up with this investigation if I'm dying?

"¡*Mevita!* You are not dying! You have a lump. It will be gone by Tuesday night. I'll kiss your breast until its well. Then I'll kiss you until you beg for more surgery!"

"Paco, I need to talk about this. Seriously. And without tears."

Paco held Mev's hands in his own. He listened.

చనచన

Jaime stopped in the middle of "Classical Gas."

"I have a text message," he said. "I think it's from Neel."

"What does it say?" asked Jorge.

Jaime read it:

"Can we meet at withers village pond on monday a.m.?
"N."

"What does he want, do you think?"

"I bet he wants to talk about Mr. Withers. Or maybe Senextra."

"Let's say yes. We can ride our bikes there after Mom leaves the house," said Jorge.

Jaime texted back:

We'll meet you there around 9

He received another text message:

Confirmed

చనచన

Neel looked around his study, suddenly aware that at the

age of fifty-five he had relatively few possessions. He'd brought little from Oklahoma other than his Cherokee bone knives, hundreds of them, and his books, hundreds of them, too.

He'd brought his medical books, of course, and his medical journals. But also an extensive collection of books about eighteenth- and nineteenth-century America, some written from the perspective of the white settlers on the continent, others written from the perspective of the people already here. And a number of art books on nineteenth-century American painting. He had a shelf of philosophy texts from his undergraduate years, a shelf of ecology texts, and a shelf of biology texts. And then several shelves of literature. He loved the epic poems of Henry Wadsworth Longfellow, the philosophical poems of Wallace Stevens, and the novels of Barbara Kingsolver, especially *Prodigal Summer*.

Neel gazed at the framed reproduction of Thomas's 1826 painting *Sunrise in the Catskill Mountains*, which adorned one wall. It was the only clue in his office to his love of art. He'd bought the poster when he took his ailing son to the National Gallery in Washington, DC.

Thomas Cole, *Sunrise in the Catskill Mountains*, 1826
(National Gallery of Art, Washington, DC)

Neel wrote in his journal:

> *Why do I like Thomas Cole's painting? It's because I understand Cole's veneration of a vast wilderness beyond civilization, beyond noise, beyond smog, where the mountains show no signs of human habitation.*

I too would find peace there, perhaps a relief from my sorrows.

Yet this painted wilderness is a fantasy. There were humans here in the Kaaterskill Mountain Range long before the Europeans arrived. Indians, as the Europeans called my people, lived there for ten thousand years. Did Cole not glimpse the Mohicans, whose ancestors dwelt in the Hudson River Valley for millennia before Henry Hudson arrived and gave the river his name? Or did Cole ignore the Mohicans in his desire for a spiritual union with an untrammeled nature? Perhaps he considered the Indians a part of nature and therefore not a part of civilization.

Why did the Europeans view nature and civilization as opponents? Was it their obsession with the individual that led them to view the forces of nature as dangerous, as necessary to overcome? Was it their fear of death that inspired their dissociation of civilization from nature—the death that comes to every individual organism on the planet?

Whoever sees civilization and nature as opponents must choose one over the other. And what's the future in that?

In my moments of despair—and they come more and more often these days—I see no change of vision in our leaders. I see only their desire to control nature, to escape nature, to live as if humans needed only technology and drugs. Senextra, Senextra, Senextra.

But then I have moments of hope when I see a younger generation discovering that we humans and nature are one, that Earth is a planetary ecosystem of which all of us organisms are interdependent parts, that what we do to our natural environment we do to ourselves.

In my dreams I see a clean planet, a healthy

planet, where humans stay healthy naturally, without drugs, without Senextra.

Jaime and Jorge give me hope. Their generation will have a vision of nature different from my generation's.

Maybe their generation will end childhood leukemia.

Maybe I will end Senextra.

PART 2

STATE OF GEORGIA
COUNTY OF LUMPKIN

LAST WILL AND TESTAMENT
OF
FAITH MURROW FOLSOM

I, FAITH MURROW FOLSOM, of said State and Lumpkin County, do make and publish this my Last Will and Testament.

ITEM I
(a) I wish my body to be buried on the Walter G. Murrow Family plot in the Bonaventure Cemetery in Savannah, Georgia. I desire and instruct that no funeral service be performed. The costs of my burial shall be paid out of my estate.

(b) All of my due and payable debts shall be paid out of my estate as soon as is practicable.

ITEM II
I give and bequeath my home in Witherston and the lot it stands upon at 3300 Mountain Pass, which I purchased in 2011 for the two of us to occupy, to my husband GEORGE FOLSOM.

ITEM III
I give and bequeath the sum of ONE HUNDRED THOUSAND DOLLARS ($100,000) to the TLC HUMANE SOCIETY OF DAHLONEGA.

ITEM IV
I give and bequeath the remainder of my estate to my yet unborn child.

ITEM V
In the event that my child precedes me in death, or in the event my child and I die at the same time, I give and bequeath the remainder of my estate, including my BioSenecta stock, to the TLC HUMANE SOCIETY OF DAHLONEGA.

ITEM VI

(a) I hereby appoint RHONDA RATHER as Executor of this Will.

(b) If for any reason Rhonda Rather should be unable to fulfill this responsibility, I appoint RICHARD RATHER as Successor Executor of this Will.

IN WITNESS WHEREOF, I have hereunto set my hand and affixed my seal to this my Will, this 25th day of March, 2015.

Faith Murrow Folsom
FAITH MURROW FOLSOM
3300 Mountain Pass, Witherston GA 30534

Signed, sealed, published and declared by FAITH MUR-ROW FOLSOM as her Last Will and Testament in our presence. We, at her request and in her presence, and in the presence of each other, have hereunto subscribed our names as witnesses the day and year above set out.

WITNESSES/ADDRESSES:
Ruth Griggs
47 Pine Street, Witherston GA 30534
RUTH GRIGGS

Mary Ellen Paisley
2432 Azalea Road, Witherston GA 30534
MARY ELLEN PAISLEY

WITHERSTON ON THE WEB
Sunday, May 31, 2015

LOCAL NEWS

Mayor Rather has confirmed that before his death Francis Hearty Withers secured and paid for the services of Hardy Loggers to clear-cut in its entirety the 31.7 acres designated as tax map/parcel 182B 007T at Saloli Falls across the creek from Withers's homestead. The logging will begin on Monday, June 16.

Mr. Withers was in the process of selling the clear-cut land to BioSenecta for the construction of a BioSenecta plant on the site. He had purchased the land in 2005.

On Friday Dr. Charlotte Byrd, on behalf of Witherston's environmentalist organization KEEP NATURE NATURAL, petitioned Lumpkin County Superior Court for an injunction to block the logging, arguing that the destruction of old-growth forest damages the environment beyond the 31.7-acre site.

After receiving a photo taken by Ada Lightfoot at 4:30 pm yesterday, Witherston police officers arrested 18-year-old Thom Rivers for leaving flyers at the bar in Rosa's Cantina on Black Fox Road.

The flyers depicted human beings wearing oxygen masks walking across a planet of tree stumps.

Mr. Rivers told police he had found the flyers by the garbage bin outside Rosa's Cantina and had brought them inside to ask Rosa whether she knew who'd printed them.

Mr. Rivers was fined $50 for littering and released. Miss Lightfoot claimed Mayor Rather's reward of $100 for photographing somebody putting up a KNN sign.

Miss Lightfoot did not say why she was in Rosa's Cantina at 4:30 yesterday.

~ Catherine Perry, Reporter

OPINION

Georgia's Founding Father Begets Leggy Frog
By Jorge Arroyo

On Memorial Day, Jaime Arroyo caught a bullfrog with three back legs under Founding Father's Bridge.

A photograph of the leggy frog taken by his brother, Jorge Arroyo, appeared in WITHERSTON ON THE WEB on May 26.

Is Founding Father's Creek sick?

The Cherokees called the creek "Saloli" creek. "Saloli" means "squirrel." The Cherokees liked all of nature, even squirrels.

They didn't consider humans more important than animals. They wanted nature to stay in balance, like an ecosystem.

But the Cherokees lost their gold and their land to Americans who believed that humans should control nature.

And they were force-marched to Oklahoma in 1838 on the "Trail of Tears." "Trail of Tears" is the English translation of the Cherokee "Trail Where They Cried" ("Nunna daul Tsuny").

In 1857, Harry Withers renamed the creek "Founding Father's Creek" for Abraham Baldwin, who was a founding father of the United States. He represented Georgia at the Constitutional Convention.

Now Founding Father's Creek produces frogs with three back legs. Is the leggy frog telling us that the creek is polluted? The frog's mother lived in the creek and drank from it.

If humans drink from Founding Father's Creek will some human mothers give birth to babies with three legs?

LETTERS TO THE EDITOR

To the Editor:

It's time somebody defended Asmund Jorgensen from the disrespectful anonymous critic of his views. Let's remember that Mr. Jorgensen left his mark on many gorgeous homes in Atlanta. He deserves to live as long as he damn well pleases. Thanks to Senextra, he is still with us.

As a doctor I believe that Senextra is mankind's greatest achievement. I can think of no more important invention in all of history. Senextra halts the aging process. It halts the onset of many diseases. If we take Senextra, we won't get old enough—or rather, our bodies won't act old enough—to contract arthritis or cancer or Parkinson's or Alzheimer's. So whose side are you on, my fellow Witherstonians: death or life?

~ Signed, George Folsom, MD

ON THIS DAY IN HISTORY
By Charlotte Byrd

On May 31, 1935, Peter Yarrow—of Peter, Paul, and Mary fame—was born. Peter Yarrow wrote "River of Jordan." Here's a stanza we may want to think about:

> *There is only one river, there is only one sea,*
> *And it flows through you, and it flows through me.*
> *There is only one people, we are one and the same.*
> *We are all one spirit, we are all one name.*
> *We are the father, mother, daughter and son.*
> *From the dawn of creation, we are one,*
> *we are one, we are one.*

CHAPTER 12

Sunday, May 31, 2015:

Sunday morning dawned sunny and warm, a perfect day for the hike Mev and Paco had planned on Saturday night. The TV weather lady predicted a high of eighty-five degrees. Mev called Lauren.

"Lauren, would you all like to come with us on a hike and picnic? We want to go to Saloli Falls, a couple of miles up the creek from Witherston, near Withers's house."

"We'll be at your place by ten," Lauren said.

Mev put a couple of loaves of whole wheat bread, a large gouda cheese, a summer sausage, a small paper bag of raw cashews, and a big paper bag of cherries in her backpack. Paco put paper napkins, a thermos of cold water, seven paper cups, a knife, a corkscrew, and a bottle of Priorat—the heavy red wine of Cataluña—in his. Jaime and Jorge put bottled water, plastic baggies, small fish nets, energy bars, and smartphones in theirs.

At 10:00 Lauren, Jim, and Beau arrived, each with a similarly filled backpack. Beau, as usual, had a fishing pole.

Jaime leashed up Varry and Renoir.

Off they went on foot. First they walked through the woods to Founding Father's Creek. Then they followed the ancient path up the creek, the path trodden by the first Americans for ten thousand years, by the deer for longer than that, and, so very recently in its history, by the white settlers who established Witherston. And now, in 2015, by Mev's and Lauren's families, who looked to the creek for signs of a killer.

Mev hiked alongside Lauren.

Mev was thinking about illness. Did the Cherokee who preceded her on this trail four hundred years ago suffer from the same diseases that afflicted her and her friends? Did Cherokee women get breast cancer? Probably, Mev figured. Breast cancer had been known to the ancient Greeks 2500 years ago. But did as many first Americans get it as modern Americans? Mev doubted it. In 2015, approximately twelve percent of American women would be diagnosed with breast cancer in their lifetimes. Mev remembered another statistic: In 1970, only ten percent of American women would be diagnosed with the disease in their lifetimes. She didn't know whether the statistics reflected a longer life expectancy in 2015 or a higher incidence of cancer.

According to Aunt Lottie, we humans toxified our environment; then our toxic environment made us sick; then we invented drugs to make us well, or at least able to continue living in the toxic environment. And then we excreted those drugs into the environment, which put them into the bodies of other humans and animals. In twenty-first-century America, everybody was on drugs.

But was there any way to return to the relatively clean environment the Cherokees enjoyed without giving up the modern conveniences she considered necessities, like air conditioning, like the surgery and radiation she hoped would destroy her cancer before it destroyed her.

Mev tried not to romanticize Cherokee traditional life. After all, the lifespan of a Cherokee before the arrival of the Europeans was under thirty years. If she'd been a Cherokee woman in 1615, she wouldn't have cancer because she'd be long dead.

Finally, Mev turned to Lauren. "What are you thinking about?" she asked.

"You, hon," Lauren answered. "You. I'm thinking that six months from now your lumpectomy will be a fading memory, as will the radiation."

"I so hope you're right, Lauren. I hope that after Tuesday's surgery I'll be much more focused on somebody else's death than my own."

"You will, dear. You know that ninety-two percent of

women treated for breast cancer these days are cured of the disease. That is, they live more than five years after their treatment, and after five years they're considered cancer-free."

"Hooray for state-of-the-art medicine," Mev said, but without enthusiasm. "If we make ourselves sick, we have marvelous doctors and miraculous drugs to make ourselves well. We twenty-first-century folks are fortunate indeed."

കൗകൗ

Paco hiked alongside Jim fifty yards ahead. "Jim, have you noticed anything weird happening with your patients? Like unusual pregnancies or miscarriages? Like young people unable to get pregnant? Mev and I talked last night. We were wondering about Faith Folsom and Rhonda Rather getting pregnant in middle age."

"Faith and Rhonda got pregnant the usual way and, according to them, by their husbands. What was unusual was their menopausal fertility. I'd never encountered that before."

"Any miscarriages lately?"

"Yes. Of course I can't give you any names, Paco. But I can tell you that there have been two miscarriages in the past year. That's high for Witherston."

"What about difficulties getting pregnant?"

"That, too. Yes, I've referred two couples to fertility clinics in the past year."

"Do you think that all these reproductive problems have a common cause?" Paco asked.

"It's crossed my mind."

"Okay. Let me add this up: Faith gets pregnant and dies. Rhonda gets pregnant and lives, at least for the time being. Plus two miscarriages and two infertility cases."

"Hmm. And Faith was taking Senextra."

Paco grabbed Jim's arm. "And there's more: A frog with three back legs. No tadpoles at Founding Father's Bridge. No mussels either. Or minnows."

"We should take a sample of the water at Saloli Falls."

"Did Beau tell you that Varry has no testicles? And his three siblings were stillborn? By the way, his mother Maud

Olive was sixteen years old—that's very old for a Chow Chow—when she had that litter."

"Varry's mother was named Maud Olive?" Jim said.

"Jim!" Paco said. "Pay attention. I'm asking you: What could be the common cause of all these weirdnesses?"

"Hormones," Jim said. "Synthetic hormones, I'd guess."

"Let's tell Mev and Lauren."

❧❧❧

"Woohoo!" Jorge shouted. "Look at the minnows!"

"And the trout!" shouted Beau. "Rainbow trout. I'm going fishing."

Jorge took off his green KEEP NATURE NATURAL T-shirt and jumped into the pool below the waterfall. Varry and Renoir jumped in after him. Jaime and Beau watched.

"*Brrrrr*," Jorge said and jumped back out of the water. "The water's cold."

The falls were spectacular, the water crashing down one hundred feet. The boys could hardly hear each other. The dogs didn't care.

Jorge, Jaime, and Beau scrambled up the bank, found a big boulder warmed by the sun, and sat down on it. After a minute Jorge put his T-shirt on.

"I want to catch a couple of those trout," Beau said. He got out his fishing pole.

❧❧❧

Having enjoyed their picnic, Jaime, Jorge, and Beau, with Varry and Renoir, went back to the falls. Beau fished for trout, Jaime looked for tadpoles, and Jorge took pictures of tiny ferns with his cell phone. Varry and Renoir chased each other.

Mev, Paco, Lauren, and Jim finished their wine. The four of them sat cross-legged on the red-checked paper tablecloth Lauren had spread on the ground.

"I just had a thought," said Mev. "While I'm here I'm going to fill our wine bottle with water from Saloli Falls. We can

take both samples to the EPA—the Priorat bottle for Saloli
Falls, and the Rioja bottle for Founding Father's Bridge."

"The EPA lab is in Athens. I'll take the samples tomorrow
to Gregory's friend Susana Pérez while you women go to
Gainesville," Paco said.

"We'll all have fun tomorrow," Mev said.

ᥱᣥᥱᣥ

Rich Rather closed the door to his home office as soon as
he realized that George Folsom was on the line. He was surprised to get the call.

"Hi, George. Again let me say how sorry I am that Faith
died."

"It couldn't be helped, Rich. She was not tolerating her
pregnancy well. I couldn't control her blood pressure. I was
expecting a miscarriage."

"How are you doing today?"

"Okay. Thanks. As well as can be expected. I'm leaving for
Savannah in an hour to be present at the burial tomorrow.
Faith's grave will be by her father's in the Bonaventure Cemetery. No place saved for me. I didn't count much to the
wealthy Murrows because I didn't come from an old Savannah
family or old money. And apparently I didn't count much to
my wife, either. She left me out of her will, practically speaking. She gave me only the house. She didn't even have the
courtesy to tell me. The TLC Humane Society of Dahlonega
gets her whole damned estate, including all her shares of Bio-
Senecta."

"I'm sorry, George."

"Did you know?"

"Faith told Rhonda a couple of months ago when she re-
vised her will. Being pregnant she wanted to take care of her
child financially. Rhonda didn't tell me till yesterday."

"Well, I have my own BioSenecta stock, thank goodness.
Anyway, that's not what I called you about."

"What did you call me about, George?"

"Faith's body was autopsied. The pathologist found the
Senextra in her system. I've asked Mev to keep the autopsy

report confidential. Have you told anybody that I've given Senextra to Rhonda?"

"No, George. Why would I do that? I don't tell anybody about the drugs I'm taking or the drugs Rhonda is taking. Not even you."

"Do you think that Rhonda has told anybody about Senextra? You know I could be ruined if word got out that I was giving Senextra to people outside the clinical trial I'm administering."

"Have you given Senextra to anybody else, George?"

George hesitated a moment. "I have. But let me explain. I have given the drug as an act of kindness for no financial gain. I believe that Senextra is a miracle drug. By halting the aging process, or at least slowing it down, Senextra will prevent the onset of many other ailments that come with aging. Senextra is a boon to all humanity."

"Wow, George."

"I am a pioneer, Rich. I am leading a medical revolution. I am changing the world."

"Now I see why you're administering BioSenecta's pilot study, George," Rich said in awe.

"Yes, Rich. My heart's in BioSenecta. So is my hope. And, I'll admit, so is my money. The pharmaceutical companies that make drugs for illnesses of the aging will go out of business when those illnesses no longer threaten human health. Their drugs will become obsolete. What use will we have for drugs that cure illnesses we no longer have?"

"Actually, I should tell you that Rhonda too has a lot of money in BioSenecta."

"Good! Once Senextra has been approved by the FDA, BioSenecta will become the largest pharmaceutical company in the world. Its stock price will make its investors millionaires, or even billionaires."

"So you and Martin Payne work together?"

"Martin is paying me well to conduct BioSenecta's study on humans. Senextra has already proven to be efficacious in mice, enabling them stay mentally and physically healthy far beyond their normal life span. If we get good results for the men of Withers Village, BioSenecta will file for FDA approval."

"How well is BioSenecta paying you, George?"

"Very well. That's all I'll say. I told Mev, who is investigating Withers's death. I had to convince her that I had no reason to kill Withers. She thinks Withers was murdered."

"Do you think he was murdered?"

"Of course not. Anyway, by administering Senextra to old men, I have proven that the drug extends their health beyond ninety years. By administering Senextra to women, which I do in secret since women are not in the clinical trial, I'm proving that the drug delays menopause and preserves youthfulness, inside and out. It also increases women's sex drive."

"I noticed," Rich said. "Does Martin know you're treating women?"

"I haven't told him. No need."

"I see the need for secrecy, George.

"It's that side-effect of menopausal fertility that we must keep quiet, Rich."

"I understand."

"And Rich, tell Rhonda not to tell Jim Lodge either, no matter what she goes through in her pregnancy. We can't have any interference from our local gynecologist."

"I understand, George. I understand. You know, I have my own reasons for keeping quiet. I've staked my political career on the construction of a Senextra factory in Witherston."

"I guess we both benefited from Withers's timely death, Mr. Mayor."

౼౿౿

Rich called Grant Griggs after his phone conversation with George Folsom.

"Grant, what can I do to raise $100,000?"

"Do you want to use Rather Pre-Owned Vehicles as collateral?"

"Yes. Please arrange it tomorrow."

"What's the rush?"

"George Folsom has just explained the future of Bio-

Senecta to me. If Senextra keeps people alive and healthy and feeling good till they're centenarians, then all the drugs the pharmaceutical companies are making for arthritis, bunions, acid reflux disease, ulcers, and even erectile dysfunction will not be needed. The pharmaceutical companies that make their money from old-age ailments will shrink, since few people will be buying their products. And BioSenecta, which has a patent for Senextra, will grow. In fact, BioSenecta will become the world's largest pharmaceutical manufacturer. And those of us with BioSenecta stock will get rich! So I want to buy $100,000 worth of shares in BioSenecta."

"You want to get rich, Rich?"

"I do, Grant. Don't you?"

"Yes, of course."

Rich then called his broker Trevor Bennington, Jr.

"I know it's Sunday, Trevor. But I have a request."

"Hi, Rich You may call me any time. What's up?"

"I'd like you to buy me $100,000 worth of BioSenecta stock first thing tomorrow. I'll get you a check for it by close of business."

"Sure, Rich. Did you get a tip?"

"Yep!"

"You want to get rich?"

"Of course, Trevor. Don't you?"

"I'm rich enough, Rich. I'll get you your stock shares, but I think I'll keep my money in the blue chips."

❧❧❧

The light on the answering machine was blinking when Jim, Lauren, and Beau walked in the door at 2:30. Lauren played the message.

"Dr. Lodge. This is Rhonda Rather. Please call me on my cell phone after 9:00 tomorrow morning. It's very important." She left a number.

Lauren had to play the message twice, because the speaker had whispered it.

"Jim," she called. "Something's up."

❦

I'll admit that Senextra may have some unanticipated side effects. Unwanted pregnancies in menopausal women, for one. I figured that out.

And if Senextra is in Witherston's water supply, everybody's drinking it. So it may be affecting reproduction in people not getting the shots. Could it be causing infertility in young women—or infertility in young men? I need to know that.

I wonder what the fertility specialists found when they examined Sandra and Phil. Fertility specialists routinely do sperm counts when determining the cause of a couple's infertility. Rhonda will tell me whether the problem is Sandra's or Phil's. She's always confided in me. Sandra would die if she knew what all her mother had told me. Anyway, fertility treatments work. She'll get pregnant.

Whatever Senextra's side effects may be, they should not keep the drug off the market. Senextra's side effects can be alleviated with other drugs. Its benefits outweigh whatever harm it may do. That will become obvious.

All drugs have effects beyond the intended. Almost any drug will do good to one part of the body and harm to another. So we just take the second drug to counteract the side effects of the first. No problem. Some drugs cause depression, so we take anti-depressants and feel just fine. If our anti-depressants cause erectile dysfunction, we take Viagra and feel just fine. If our decongestants cause insomnia, we take sleeping pills and feel just fine. Our goal as individuals with access to modern medicine is to feel just fine for a long long time, isn't it?

And that's what Senextra can do for us. It can make us feel fine for a long time. Everybody wants to feel fine for a long time.

That kid Jorge Arroyo may be a problem if he starts scaring everybody about possible birth defects. I say, if the baby you're carrying has defects, get an abortion.

I'll have to watch Jorge. I wish I could tell him apart from his brother.

Senextra's side effects must, must, must remain hidden until the drug is on the market. That's my mission: to keep the side effects hidden. It's for the benefit of the civilized world.

ფოებო

Jorge sat at the kitchen table with his tablet open. "Dad, what's an old-growth forest?"

"Look it up on the web, *hijo*," Paco said. "If you become a journalist, you have to teach yourself what you need to know. You have to do research, lots of research. Good journalists figure out what is important to their readers or viewers, and they work hard, very hard, to learn all about it."

"Okay. I do want to be a good journalist, Dad. I want to write about things that are wrong with the world to make the world better."

"What would be a better world, Jorge?"

"I guess I haven't thought about it that much. I like Aunt Lottie's idea of a better world: a world without war, a world where nobody kills anybody else. Maybe a world where nobody deceives anybody else or takes advantage of anybody else. Now I've got it! A world where honesty rules and dishonesty gets exposed."

"Wow, *hijo*. That would really be a better world than what we've got now."

"So when I'm a journalist—I guess I'm already a journalist—I am going to expose dishonesty and let honesty rule."

Paco put his hand on his son's shoulder. "Great mission, *hijo*. I'm proud of you. But your job will not be an easy one. The good journalist always tells the truth as he sees it. But remember this. Although it's not easy to tell the truth when you're facing powerful people who lie for their own benefit, you can see the truth pretty well then if you try. However, it's more difficult to tell the truth as you see it when you're facing powerful people who believe they see the truth too, only their truth is different from yours. You may think they're wrong, and they may think you're wrong. You have to remember that as a journalist you are always telling the truth from a particular point of view, yours. You're always telling the truth as you see it."

"Dad, you're not trying to discourage me, are you?"

"No, *hijo*, no. I'm trying to encourage you to be strong and brave in one of the noblest professions I know. I'm saying that different people growing up in different families, living in different cultures, speaking different languages, and inheriting different views of the world from their parents and grandparents, teachers and priests—all these different people will interpret the same set of events in different ways. For example, Neel's Cherokee ancestors and Withers's white ancestors interpreted the murder of Hearty Withers in 1838 very differently. "

"Then how can you figure out who is right?"

"No one person can, Jorge. And there's no one right way to think. But if we all converse with each other and share our ideas, then we can help each other think clearly. That's how journalists can be our society's leaders. I like to think that journalists can be our society's conscience. Journalists can remind us to look at events from different perspectives. Good journalists believe that they are making society better by giving the people the best information they can get."

Jaime jumped into the discussion. "I like the idea that sharing ideas makes us all better thinkers. Jorge, remember what Neel said? Neel said that if we share, we don't have to fight."

"*Hijos*, conversing with each other is always sharing. Shouting insults at each other is not. Shouting insults is like waging war—though without any risk. When people shout insults at each other, nobody ever backs down. Nobody ever decides he's wrong, because nobody likes to lose."

"Are you thinking of KEEP NATURE NATURAL's signs, Dad?

"No. Actually, I'm thinking about the Democrats and the Republicans in Congress."

"But, Dad," Jorge protested. "Aren't there some ideas that are just wrong?"

"Yes, son. That's why we need journalists. There are some ideas that are very wrong and very dangerous. Journalists expose those ideas for the danger they pose to society, and then society will handle the situation." Paco sighed. "But that sometimes takes a long time."

"Thanks, Dad. I think my mission will be to give the people the best information I can get."

☙☙☙

It was 10:00 p.m. Neel sat at his desk in his small apartment gazing out his picture window at Withers Village Pond. The moon was almost full, and the sky was bright with stars. He spotted a red fox coming out of the woods for a drink of water. And then he saw her four kits. He watched silently, holding his breath in awe of the beautiful animals with whom he shared the pond.

What does the world look like to the fox? Neel wondered. Fundamentally different from the way the world looked to him. Or perhaps he should ask how the fox's world was different from his, because he and the fox lived in different worlds. To the fox, the woods were not imbued with history, the woods were simply home. To him, the woods were a reminder of wrongs inflicted by Withers people on his Cherokee people. To him, the woods, Founding Father's Creek, Saloli Falls, Withers Village, all his surroundings, wherever he might go, were replete with history.

Or rather—he realized—he himself endowed everything he saw, heard, tasted, touched, or smelled with the history he'd inherited from the human community in which he lived. Humans lived in the memories their people passed on to them. Foxes didn't.

Neel wrote in his journal:

Unlike foxes, we humans tell each other stories about the way we understand things. We talk to persuade others to our own way of thinking. And we pass on what we've learned, what we think we know to be the truth, to our children, and our children's children, and our children's children's children. We humans bequeath to future generations "the look of things."

So many battles have been fought because each side believes it knows the truth, because each side believes itself to be right and the other to be wrong, because each side believes that there is only one truth, and consequently only one right way to think, only one right way to behave, only one right way to divide wealth.

In my life I have seen the world as a Cherokee, and I have developed hatred toward people like Mr. Francis Hearty Withers who see the world differently. I thought I knew the truth. And probably Withers thought he knew the truth. My hatred of Withers and his people has brought anguish to my spirit and pain to my body. It has twisted me with bitterness.

But Friday when I spoke with Jaime and Jorge that anguish and pain and bitterness began to dissipate. Those boys spoke to me with interest, respect, even appreciation. At the age of fourteen they have yet to claim they know the truth.

If only all our young people could shed the prejudices they inherit from their parents and grandparents and great grandparents, the prejudices instilled in them from infancy and reinforced at the dinner table over their lifetimes. I hope I can.

Neel remembered a poem by Wallace Stevens, "A Postcard from the Volcano." He copied into his journal his favorite lines.

> *...with our bones*
> *We left much more, left what still is*
> *The look of things, left what we felt*
> *At what we saw.*

"Now I understand that poem," Neel said to himself. "Now I understand why we humans wage war, and foxes don't."

WWW.ONLINEWITHERSTON.COM

WITHERSTON ON THE WEB
Monday, June 1, 2015

LOCAL NEWS

Mayor Rich Rather has filed a request that Francis Hearty Withers's will be probated immediately.
~ Catherine Perry, Reporter.

EDITORIAL

I am happy to announce that WITHERSTON ON THE WEB will have a new columnist for the summer. Jorge Arroyo, who has contributed photographs and notes on nature from time to time, will write a regular column whenever he likes titled "What's Natural?"

Fourteen-year-old Jorge, the great nephew of our columnist Charlotte Byrd, will enter ninth grade at Witherston High this fall.

Today Mr. Grant Griggs, one of Witherston's distinguished attorneys, writes of his unhappiness over the views Dr. Byrd expressed in her column "On This Day in History" on May 31.

I would be happy to publish a column by Mr. Griggs in WITHERSTON ON THE WEB if he should desire to write one.

Mr. Griggs need only propose a subject for a series of articles.

It is the position of WITHERSTON ON THE WEB to publish the full range of opinions that our contributors submit.
~ Smitty Green, Editor

LETTERS TO THE EDITOR

To the Editor:

I have a question for Dr. Folsom regarding his letter to the editor of yesterday: Who is "we"?
~ Signed, Rude Anonymous

To the Editor:

Charlotte Byrd's quoting that old Peter, Paul, and Mary song in her column would have made me unsubscribe from your left-wing, stuck-in-the-sixties, environmentalist Webby Witherston website if I could have.

I thought Professor Byrd was supposed to write only about the history of our region.

Obviously, Witherston has become divided into two camps: Professor Byrd's advocacy of a share-everything, live-with-nature, environmentalist, pro-Cherokee, anti-capitalist, anti-modern-medicine, anti-progress way of life, on the one hand, and Mayor Rather's advocacy of a pro-individual, pro-progress, pro-capitalist, pro-modern-medicine way of life. I'm glad Rich Rather is our mayor, and not Charlotte Byrd. (I hasten to say I don't dislike Professor Byrd. She's likable enough.)

By the way, Mayor Rather is not anti-environmentalist. He just believes, as I do, that we should use our resources to help individual humans, not frogs.

(However, I do like fried frog legs. The more legs our frogs have the more fried frog legs we'll enjoy eating.)

Webby Witherston's readers should realize that time moves in only one direction. In 2015 we have cars to take us long distances in short periods of time. In 1815 our ancestors had horses and buggies to take them short distances in long periods of time. We use fossil fuels.

I'm sure our ancestors would have if they could have. In 2015 we don't have to let nature decide our lifespan. In 1815 our ancestors did.

We have medicines. I'm sure our ancestors would have used our medicines if they could have. In 2015 we have Senextra to enable us to live long healthy lives. In 1815 our ancestors didn't even have penicillin.

So here's your choice, readers: 2015 or 1815. Do you all want to go back to 1815?

~ Signed, Grant Griggs, Attorney

ON THIS DAY IN HISTORY
By Charlotte Byrd

On June 1, 1881, Withers Francis Withers ("Witty," age 23) and Obedience Olmstead (age 20) were married in the Dahlonega United Methodist Church. In attendance were her parents Jedediah and Else Olmstead of Dahlonega and his father Harold Francis Withers ("Harry") of Witherston.

Witty and Obedience returned to Witherston, and a year later, upon the death of his father, they moved into the Withers family home on Founding Father's Creek. Their son Harold Hearty Withers ("HaHa") was born in that house in 1889.

POLICE BLOTTER

Witherston police officers responded to 911 call at 10:00 last night from Virginia Ann Casey at 435 Ninovan Road. Miss Casey said when she returned from a church supper she saw a bear leaving her porch. The bear had overturned her rocking chair. By the time the officers arrived the bear had disappeared into the woods towards Creek Road.

CHAPTER 13

Monday, June 1, 2015:

Lauren picked Mev up at 7:00 a.m. for her 9:00 a.m. appointment at the Northeast Georgia Medical Center. On the way to Gainesville they discussed Withers's death, Gregory's close call, and Faith's fatal stroke.

"Mev," said Lauren, "Rhonda left Jim a voice mail on our land line yesterday. She asked him to call her this morning on her cell phone. She was whispering. And she sounded distressed."

"Oh, my god. I hope she's not had a miscarriage."

"If she had, she wouldn't be upset about it."

"I'd like to interview her again, Lauren, without Rich around. I think she'd say much more to me if she could speak in confidence. But when can I do it? I'm going into the hospital tomorrow morning."

"You could get Chief McCoy to invite her to your office this afternoon. We should be back in Witherston by 12:00, in time for lunch."

"I'll ask Jake to call her this morning and invite her to my office at 1:30. I'll also ask Jake to set up interviews at 2:00 and 2:30 with Grant Griggs and Neel Kingfisher."

"And maybe you will feel well enough to interview George Folsom on Friday."

"I know I will."

❧❧❧

In the back seat of his ten-year-old electric blue Chrysler

PT Cruiser, Paco placed a small styrofoam cooler with two wine bottles full of creek water. The Rioja bottle was labeled "Founding Father's Bridge," and the Priorat bottle was labeled "Saloli Falls." He'd deliver them to Dr. Pérez at the EPA in Athens and then pick up a present for Mev. He was thinking of a silver pin representing a dove that he'd seen not long ago in Aurum Studios. Peace. Aunt Lottie would approve of the gift.

At 8:30, Paco left the house, telling the boys to have fun on their bike ride and to be home by lunchtime.

ⱳↄⱳↄ

"I get to go home this morning," Gregory told Jon, who'd left his hospital room only to get breakfast in the cafeteria. "Dr. Harper is releasing me from the hospital. And I don't hurt so much now."

"I'll take excellent care of you, Gregory. And Renoir will protect you from anybody who may still want you dead."

"Renoir?"

"Well, Renoir and the security system I had installed on Friday. You know, it's like saying 'God will make you well,' when you actually mean 'God and surgery will make you well.'"

"God and surgery and good friends, with maybe some good movies, good food, and good wine in addition."

"Okay! I can handle that. We'll have a dinner party on Friday! I'll cook. You can lie on the sofa and make suggestions."

ⱳↄⱳↄ

Jaime and Jorge arrived at Withers Village Pond at 9:05 a.m. with Varry and Renoir. Neel was seated at a long red-wood picnic table on the far side. In the shade of a large oak, he could barely be seen. The boys rode over, parked their bikes, and sat down across from the doctor. Varry and Renoir leaped into the water.

"Hi, Neel."

"Hi, Neel."

"Hi, boys. Thanks for coming. I hope you understand my need for secrecy."

"It's because you're director of Withers Village, right?" said Jaime.

"Right. And I don't want to be fired by the board, on which Mayor Rather sits. Not yet. Not until all the secrets of the Village are out."

"Are exposed?" Jorge asked.

"Yes, exposed. Do you all know Dr. George Folsom?"

"We know him," Jaime said. "We saw him Wednesday night at the Smith House. With his wife who died the next day."

"Well, we can talk about her later. Faith was on our board too. For now, I want you boys to help me expose Dr. Folsom for his dishonesty as the conductor of the Senextra pilot study. Scientific dishonesty, which I find as loathsome as bank robbery. Actually, more so, because its consequences can be more far-reaching and damaging."

"We're listening."

"Dr. Folsom has accepted a salary from BioSenecta to administer Senextra to the residents of Withers Village and to report to BioSenecta the effect of the drug on his subjects. There are twenty-three residents of Withers Village, all of whom are over ninety years old, all of whom are feeling good, enjoying life, and thinking clearly, all of whom have been taking monthly injections of Senextra for four years.

"Francis Hearty Withers, by the way, had been taking it for five years. To all outward appearances, the drug is doing what BioSenecta intended: prolonging healthy life significantly beyond the normal human life span."

"So what is the problem?" Jaime asked.

Neel continued. "Once a month Dr. Folsom comes to Withers Village. He always parks in the lot by the pond so that nobody will nick his fancy Jaguar. He enters through the building's back door, as if he owns the place, and takes over the infirmary. There he gives our twenty-three residents each a shot and an examination, a very cursory examination. He checks their blood pressure, their weight, and their height, and he takes urine samples. He questions them about their energy level. And those data are what he reports to BioSenecta. So from BioSenecta's perspective, Senextra achieves what it was designed to achieve, which, as Dr. Folsom always says, enables individuals to feel fine for a long time."

"Are you saying that he does not report something else?" Jorge asked.

"He does not report that those old men have enlarged breasts."

"At the age of a hundred? Gross!"

"Jorge, their age is not the point. Those guys are men!" Jaime said.

"More gross."

"Boys. Those nonagenarians and centenarians are becoming effeminized. Senextra is a hormone-based drug. It's powerful. It affects the body's endocrine system. It affects the body's sexual characteristics."

"Wow. I'm going to write about this in my *Webby Witherston* column."

"Wait, Jorge. We don't want to embarrass the Withers Villagers, who are sensitive about their breasts. And we don't want to attract photographers to Withers Village. Let's try to see the big picture."

"Okay, Neel."

"Dr. Folsom has staked his personal career on the success of Senextra. His desire for fame seems to have overridden his ethical obligations to medical science. He's even tried to persuade me to take the drug. And I'm only fifty-five. He says it will make me feel younger. In my view Dr. Folsom is guilty of scientific misconduct—deliberate dishonesty, not simply negligence.

"And because of the potency of Senextra, he may cause harm to our whole community in his maniacal—that's what I'd call it—determination to make Senextra the miracle drug of the future."

"Does he think he's doing the right thing?" Jorge asked.

"I suspect he does. That's why he's so dangerous."

"He must see the world differently from other people," Jorge said.

Suddenly Varry and Renoir returned to them soaking wet,

shook the water out of their fur, drenched their humans, and then settled down beside the boys to doze.

Neel smiled and continued. "Boys, let's first talk about why Senextra is dangerous. Here's a lesson from nature. Say, you have a very stable little ecosystem, such as a spring-fed pond. It works well and stays clean on its own, but the owner decides to make it more beautiful and more productive. So he adds some fertilizer. The aquatic plants proliferate. Wonderful, he thinks, more for the fish to eat. But then he notices that the algae are proliferating as well and that the aquatic plants are taking over the surface of the pond. Plankton, aquatic insects, and fish die from lack of oxygen. The pond stinks, and the water is no longer clear, no longer beautiful. So the owner starts looking around for something to add that will clear up the water. The bottom line is that you can't meddle with one part of a system without affecting the whole system."

"Are you comparing the body to an ecosystem, Neel?"

"Yes, Jorge. The human body, like any organic body, is a system, an organic system. I say, if we meddle with a system, we'd better know how the system works. A system is composed of parts that interact with each other to produce effects we can't predict from studying only its parts. That's why we say that in a system the whole is greater than the sum of its parts. Let me use my story of fertilizer being added to the pond as a metaphor for Senextra being added to the human body. Dr. Folsom has injected Senextra into the bodies of the old men at Withers Village with one purpose: to give them longer, healthier lives. And Senextra does that. But Senextra does more than that. It changes those men's entire bodies."

"Gee, Neel. That's so interesting," Jaime said. "When you were talking about the pond being changed by the fertilizer, I started thinking about Leggy Froggy. And what my brother wrote in *Webby Witherston* yesterday. He said that if the creek is producing frogs with three back legs it might be polluted, and it might make humans sick."

"I wrote that if humans drink from the creek women may give birth to babies with three legs."

"Jorge," Neel said. "I read your article. It was outstanding. And Jaime, you're right to draw the comparison of the polluted pond to our polluted creek. Something toxic has seeped into the creek, and I'm pretty sure it's Senextra. The Withers Villagers are excreting Senextra. That's how Senextra gets into the creek. So—and here's a big lesson, boys—when Dr. Folsom, or whoever, injects Senextra into human beings, he's injecting Senextra into the ecosystem."

"Dr. Folsom injected Senextra into Mama Froggy's home, and so Mama Froggy gave birth to Leggy Froggy," said Jaime.

"I get your point, Neel," Jorge said. "When you inject something new into a system, you change what was already there."

"Yes, Jorge. The whole system, whether it's a fish pond or a human body, functions differently from the way it functioned before. The system doesn't stop functioning, but it may not function in a way that pleases us humans. But I have one more point to make here. And you may think I'm speaking as a Cherokee. Well, I am. We humans are not separable from the rest of nature. We're not different from the other animals who walk our land. When we pollute ourselves—by introducing a foreign substance into our bodies—we pollute our land. And when we pollute our land we pollute everybody who lives here with us. We pollute Founding Father's Creek and harm Mama Froggy's reproductive system—"

"Neel, are you saying that all medicines are pollutants?" Jaime interrupted. "Because that's not what I found when I looked up pollution for my science class. The dictionary defined pollution as the presence in the environment of something that has harmful or toxic effects."

"Boys, I find that definition very anthropocentric, very human-centered. Here's the Cherokee in me speaking again. I'd ask: Harmful to whom? Toxic to whom? Do we humans not care if we introduce foreign substances in our ecosystem that harm other animals, or that harm plants that other animals eat? Do we not care what we do to the soil?"

"Wow, Neel. You're right," Jaime said. "So how would you define pollution?"

"I know that not many people would agree with me, but I'd define pollution as the introduction of any non-native substance into an organic system. Any non-native substance changes the way an ecosystem works, whether the ecosystem is a pond, a forest, or a dry desert. That's why I'd call Senextra a pollutant in our ground water. I'd call fertilizer and gasoline and plastic and birth control pills and kudzu all pollutants. We humans change every system we encounter with our pollutants, but we humans are not wise enough to predict exactly how any of our pollutants will change the system."

"Neel," Jorge said, "so a pollutant could be good or bad, depending on point of view, right?"

"A drug would be a pollutant in the body of an individual, wouldn't it?" Jaime asked.

"Yes, Jorge, and yes, Jaime. An oral contraceptive could help a woman avoid pregnancy, which she would see as a good thing, but if it gave her breast cancer because it contained estrogen, she'd see it as a bad thing. It might change her body in unanticipated ways. And since it would get into our ecosystem and affect other animals' reproduction, like your frog's mother, it could be a bad thing for us all."

"Are you saying that we should return to the Cherokee way of life? Before electricity?"

"No, Jaime. I don't think we should, or could, do that. But I admit I'm pessimistic about the future of our human species if we continue our pollution of Earth. I do think that we humans are heading in a dangerous direction."

"Me too," said Jorge.

"What we can do is to expose Dr. Folsom's scientific dishonesty. We humans are changing our world with the drugs we're inventing. If we can't trust our medical researchers to tell us the truth about what they've discovered, we may change it unknowingly into a world where we humans won't thrive. That's what I believe our use of Senextra would do."

"What do you think BioSenecta would do if they knew the truth?" asked Jaime.

"BioSenecta could either abandon plans to manufacture Senextra or do what Western society habitually does: create a fix for the problem the first fix caused. And then create another fix for the problem the second fix caused. And so forth. Boys, you can figure out where I stand."

"Ha! I just thought of how to say it," Jorge said. "We use

pollutant number one to fix problem number one, but pollutant number one creates problem number two, so we use pollutant number two to fix problem number two, but pollutant number two creates problem number three, so we use pollutant number three to fix problem number three, but it creates..."

"Okay, okay, okay, Jorge. We get it," Jaime interrupted.

"Yes, boys, you get it. And thanks for making me laugh. I haven't laughed much for four years."

"Why haven't you, Neel? We laugh all the time," said Jorge.

"That's because you're goofy, Jorge," Jaime said.

"Are you sad, Neel?"

"Boys, I lost a son four years ago, to leukemia. He was ten years old. His name was John."

"Oh, we're so sorry, Neel!"

"We were ten years old four years ago."

"I know, boys. I know. You all remind me of John. John too laughed a lot, until he got sick. I came here in 2013 because my wife divorced me after he died. She couldn't handle my depression. I got this job in Witherston because I wanted a new life. And I wanted to know the place where my grandparents once lived."

"We're so sorry you're sad, Neel! Can we help?"

"You've already helped, boys, in ways you'll never know. But there is something you, we, can do together to rectify the situation."

"What?" asked Jorge. "We do want to rectify it."

"Okay. We're going to expose the doctor, boys. Jorge, now that you're a columnist for *Webby Witherston*, would you like to interview Dr. Folsom when he comes here to give the Villagers their Senextra shots? You could also take a photograph of Dr. Folsom injecting Senextra into one of the Villagers. Maybe Asmund Jorgensen would consent. I expect Dr. Folsom to come to here Wednesday morning, after he returns from Savannah."

"Great idea, Neel! I can ask Dr. Folsom about the health of the old men, since Mr. Withers died. I can ask him why Mr. Withers died when he'd been taking Senextra for five years."

"Good thinking, Jorge. And Jaime, you're the biologist. So

would you like to document the differences you observe between Saloli Falls and Founding Father's Bridge with respect to the wildlife in the water? For example, the number of fish, frogs, tadpoles, and the like. As ecologists say, you could inventory the animals in the two places."

"Sure, Neel. I'll bet we find more fish and tadpoles at Saloli Falls, above Withers Village, than at the bridge, downstream from it. Right?"

"That's what I think you'll find, Jaime. But we need documentation. You should take pictures too. Meanwhile I'll gather what information I can to expose Senextra as the dangerous weapon against nature that it is. And boys, you all should tell your parents about our plan. Get their approval. I'm also going to allow Dr. Folsom to give me an injection of Senextra to prove he went beyond the scope of his pilot study in dispensing the drug."

ⵉⵉ

"Rhonda? This is Jim Lodge calling. How are you?" It was 9:30 a.m.

"Oh, Dr. Lodge. Thanks so much for calling me back. I really need to see you. Today. I mean, this morning. Would that be possible?"

"Can you come to my office at 11:00?"

"Yes. And at 1:30 I have to go to the police station for another interview with Mev. I don't know which upsets me more, the pregnancy or the investigation of Withers's death. Mev seems to think Mr. Withers was murdered, and I'm afraid she suspects Rich as the murderer."

"Don't worry about that now, Rhonda. You have to concern yourself with your health, yours and your baby's. I'll see you at 11:00."

ⵉⵉ

As Jaime and Jorge pedaled home, Varry and Renoir raced ahead of them, certain of their destination.

"Jorge, I just realized something. Varry has been feminized! He doesn't have any balls. Do you think his mother got polluted with Senextra?"

"Maud Olive?"

"Yes, Maud Olive!"

"Could be. Maybe that's why she had puppies at the age of sixteen," said Jorge.

"I wonder if old Dr. Folsom gave her a shot or two of Senextra."

"I think I'll ask him in our interview."

∽∾∽

Rhonda sat down in Jim's office. She looked tired.

"Dr. Lodge," she started.

"Call me Jim," he said. "We've known each other a good while."

"Jim, I have a confession to make. I did not tell you, and I should have, that George Folsom has been giving me Senextra. He told me not to tell you, and since he's such a good friend of Rich's I obeyed."

"Senextra! What in the world for?"

"George is my doctor, or was my doctor till I got pregnant and came to you. He was treating me for hot flashes, osteopenia, sleeplessness, dry skin—all the stuff that women get with menopause. Including a big belly. I hated seeing those changes to my body."

"So George prescribed Senextra for you? Just for the symptoms of menopause?"

"George didn't prescribe it. He gave it to me, for free. He's been giving it to me by monthly injection for about two years. And it worked. The hot flashes went away. So did the sleeplessness and the dry skin. And it made me look younger."

"Rhonda, you're already beautiful. Why did you want to look younger?"

"I wanted to feel younger, Jim. Not just look younger. Senextra worked magic on my body, and on my spirits too. I felt really healthy, and I was, until I got pregnant. Now I'm wondering whether Senextra made me fertile."

"And that's why you're here, Rhonda? You're not having a problem with your pregnancy?"

"No, I'm still pregnant. I've been thinking a lot these days, especially since Faith died. She was my best friend, and I told her everything. We both got pregnant at the same time. Now she's gone, and I have no one to talk to. She was taking Senextra too, by monthly injections. George talked us both into taking it. He said that if Senextra was good for the aging men in Withers Village, it would be good for us aging women in Witherston. Faith and I were happy to be part of his trial study, a secret part. We were excited to be making medical history."

"When was your last Senextra shot?"

"May first."

"So you're due for one today?"

"Yes, but George is out of town. He's in Savannah for Faith's burial. He's returning to Witherston tomorrow, and he'll probably come to my house on Wednesday to give me the shot."

"I appreciate your telling me this, Rhonda. But as long as you are my patient I forbid you to take another injection of Senextra. Period."

"But what can I tell George? I'm already disobeying my husband in telling you about the Senextra, Jim. George called Rich yesterday and asked Rich to make sure that I hadn't told you, and that I would not tell you, or anybody else. Now why would George call up Rich on a Sunday just for that?"

"I don't know."

"If I tell George that you and I have talked about my taking Senextra, he is going to be furious. So how can I stop George from giving me my monthly shot? And by the way, I found out that Rich is buying a whole lot of BioSenecta stock on a tip from George. So Rich and George will do anything to prevent bad publicity for Senextra."

"Anything?"

"What should I do, Jim? Should I just take the shot? I'm already pregnant. What else could happen to me?"

"I have no idea, Rhonda. But you have to stay healthy to have a healthy baby. I say to you: Do not, let me repeat, do not let him give you another shot."

"I wonder if Senextra caused Faith's stroke."

"I wonder too. So while you're here, let me give you a check-up. We want you and your baby both to stay healthy."

"Thanks, Jim. And I want to thank you again for sending Sandra and Phil to Athens for fertility tests. They desperately want a baby. And I want a grandchild. Just not another child from my own loins. Good god."

ↄ℥ↄ

Earth to earth. Ashes to ashes. Dust to dust. At least she's in the ground now. Away from prying eyes and hands and scalpels.

And soon I'll be away from all the superficial utterances of sympathy. "Oh, I'm so sorry, George, that you lost both your beloved Faith and your baby," "You'll always be part of our family," "Please come back to visit us." Blah blah blah. If they only knew that I had hastened Faith's entry into heaven.

I had to kill her. I had to. She was waiting in the car that evening when I got out to sample the creek water. She heard the rifle go off. I told her it must have been a hunter shooting deer off season. She believed me. But she would have guessed what I'd done if she learned of Bozeman's being shot. I couldn't let that happen.

When we got home I had a glass of scotch and she had a cup of lemon tea. We sat in the living room by the open window and listened to the rain. She asked me whether the Senextra had allowed her to get pregnant. I told her that if it had she should be grateful to me forever. Then I gave her a couple of Ambien tablets—to help her sleep, I said. I kissed her goodnight. After she fell asleep I injected her with potassium chloride. She had a stroke the next day and never recovered consciousness. The pathologist noted the Senextra in her system, but not the elevated level of potassium. I guess I'm getting good at killing. The good doctor is a good killer. Who would suspect?

But I take no pleasure in killing. I have killed in order to do good for all of humanity. And isn't that what war is about? Killing some people for the good of others? War always brings collateral damage. I am fighting a war against the process of aging. Withers was collateral damage. So was Faith. So was— or would have been—Gregory Bozeman. I will go down in history as a hero, even if I get caught.

But I won't allow myself to get caught until I ensure the future of Senexta. I'm going back to Witherston this afternoon. I have unfinished business.

ഗ്രഗ

Jon and Renoir were leaving her house when Lauren dropped Mev off.

"Mev, sweet baby," Jon greeted her. He had Renoir on a leash. "Gregory is home now! I'm going home. And Renoir is going home. We're going to have a family reunion."

"I'm so happy for you all, Jon. So Gregory is recovering?"

"He's recovering so fast that we're scheduling a big dinner party Friday night at our place. 5:30! Can you and your family come?"

"Jon, you know that tomorrow I have a little rendezvous with a knife myself. But if I can be there at your party, I will, and if I can't, I'll send Paco and the boys."

"And Varry, of course."

"Varry accepts your lovely invitation with pleasure."

Mev gave Jon and Renoir each a kiss and sent them on their way.

"Mom, Dad," Jaime said at lunch, "we had a great conversation with Neel Kingfisher today. We bumped into him on our bike ride near Withers Village Pond."

"Neel thinks—"

"You call Dr. Kingfisher 'Neel'?" asked Paco.

"He told us to. He's become a friend of ours."

"Neel thinks," Jorge continued, "that Dr. Folsom is guilty of science misconduct. And we're going to help him prove it."

"Scientific misconduct," Jaime corrected his brother.

"Yes, scientific misconduct. Dr. Folsom is not telling the truth about the effect of Senextra on Withers Villagers."

"Now why would that be?" Mev wondered aloud.

"Mom, Dad. Those Withers Villagers have grown breasts!"

"Tell me what Neel discussed with you, boys."

The boys told them.

☙❧☙

Mev learned from Rhonda that her husband Rich was buying BioSenecta stock on a tip from George Folsom. Well, that was interesting. Both George and Rich now had a financial stake in the success of the Senextra pilot study. Was it ethical for George to be buying BioSenecta stock when he was conducting the pilot study for BioSenecta? Mev thought not. Mev learned also that George had been giving Rhonda monthly Senextra injections.

"George always insisted that I not tell anyone I was taking Senextra," Rhonda said. "But after Withers's death he got adamant. That's what's been bothering me. A while back I figured that BioSenecta would fire him if they found out he was dispensing the drug to Faith and me. But now I'm wondering whether he's hiding something about the drug itself."

"What would that be?" Mev asked.

"I'm embarrassed to tell even Jim about the effect of the drug on me. I felt not just younger and prettier but also eager for sex—even with Rich, whom I haven't found attractive for years...if I ever did."

"How long were you getting these injections, Rhonda?"

"Since February of 2014. Same as Faith. Faith and I talked with each other confidentially after George first proposed it."

"And when did you get pregnant?"

"I found out for sure I was pregnant last January. I didn't understand what was happening to my body, so I went to see George, and he ran some tests. Funny coincidence. Two weeks after I found out I was pregnant, Faith found out she was pregnant. So we talked some more and decided that Senextra had made us fertile. Our bodies had changed in the same way. Oh my god. I wanted to get an abortion, and George wanted me to have an abortion—he said he'd perform it—but Rich said no, absolutely not. I guess Rich wanted all of Witherston to know that he, the mayor, the big fat mayor, was a stud. Ha, ha."

"Did Faith want an abortion?"

"No. Faith wanted to keep the baby. But George wanted her to have an abortion."

"So George wanted to hide the fertility effects of Senextra? Is that what you're saying?"

"Yes. Yes. And now Faith's dead because of Senextra. Faith was my best friend. We talked every day. She was the only person I ever confided in, and now she's gone. Because of her husband's experiment. I hate George now. I hate him, I hate him."

"When did you last talk with Faith?"

"Wednesday afternoon, after her check-up in Dahlonega. She called me on her cell phone. She was excited that her obstetrician had found her and her baby both in perfect health. Perfect health. George had gone with her to Chestatee Regional for her check-up."

"Hmmm," Mev said. "That's why they were having dinner at the Smith House Wednesday night. They'd just come from the hospital."

⁊⁊⁊

Next, Mev interviewed Grant Griggs. He was buying Bio-Senecta stock too, on a tip from Rich.

Grant was not hostile. In fact, he was downright friendly. He said that on Saturday night Withers had called him and asked him to draft a new will immediately. Grant had told him he'd work on it Tuesday morning. Withers then said he'd work on it himself over the weekend."

"You didn't see Mr. Withers over the weekend?" Mev asked him.

"No."

"How specific was Mr. Withers with regard to the instructions he gave you? And did you take notes?"

"Not very specific, and no, I did not take notes."

"Did Ruth know of Mr. Withers's intentions?"

"No, I keep my conversations with my clients confidential."

⁊⁊⁊

At 2:30 Mev began her interview with Neel Kingfisher.

"Good afternoon, Dr. Kingfisher," Mev said. "I've looked forward to this conversation. My boys have grown quite fond of you."

"Good afternoon, Detective Arroyo. I have enjoyed my visits with your boys very much. Jaime and Jorge are intelligent and wise for their age."

"Please tell me what you've told them, Dr. Kingfisher."

Neel did, except for the part about his son's death. He reckoned his personal tragedy was irrelevant to her inquiry.

ꟷ

On her cell Mev read the letter from BioSenecta's office. The list of BioSenecta stockholders in Witherston was not long. It included Faith Folsom, George Folsom, Grant Griggs, Asmund Jorgensen, Art McCrakken, Rhonda Rather, Rich Rather, and Francis Hearty Withers.

ꟷ

Gretchen had just returned from a long walk with Gandhi at 7:00 when her phone rang, her landline. It was Martin.

"Hi, Gretchen. How are you?"

"Fine, thank you, Martin. How are you?" She always found these social greetings comical. She could imagine Martin replying "Fine, thank you. How are you?" And she'd reply "Fine, thank you. How are you?" She was once critical of the how-are-yous for their meaninglessness, but that was in her long-vanished, misspent youth when she wanted every utterance to have philosophical depth, intellectual breadth, or erotic intensity. Now she recognized the importance of human connection at any level in whatever way.

"Gretchen, we have to talk."

"About us?"

"No, well, not now anyway. About the creek."

"The creek?" Then Gretchen relaxed. "I've already figured out that you like the creek better than me. But that's okay. I can't compete with a creek, or with trees either. And I should tell you, neither can you."

"Gretchen, this is serious. Remember that I took a sample of creek water back to BioSenecta with me Saturday?"

"Yes?"

"Well, it was chemically analyzed today. Founding Father's Creek water is indeed polluted. I got the news late this afternoon. The sample showed detectible traces of synthetic hormones, the same synthetic hormones BioSenecta has put into Senextra."

"Oh, my god!"

"We took the sample from the bridge, which is two miles downstream from Witherston and four miles downstream from Withers Village."

"Oh, my god. We're all polluted! All of us Witherstonians. And all of the animals in our woods. And our fish. And—oh my god—my vegetables. I want to move."

"Do you think you'll find a cleaner environment elsewhere, Gretchen?"

⌘⌘⌘

Gretchen called Lottie with the news. Lottie called Mev. Mev called Gregory. Gregory called Susana on her cell phone.

Susana told Gregory that she'd analyzed the two water samples that Paco had brought into the EPA earlier that day. She would send Mev an official report. But she could confirm that the water sample from Saloli Falls was clean, as clean as mountain streams ever got these days, and that the sample from Founding Father's Bridge contained significantly high traces of synthetic hormones.

⌘⌘⌘

"Now why would Aunt Lottie be calling us at 10:30 at night?" Mev said aloud as she answered her cell phone. "Hello, Aunt Lottie! I hope everything's okay."

"I'm not sure, dear. I couldn't get to sleep, so I went out on my deck to have a glass of wine, and I heard something in the woods. Somebody walking around. Are Jorge and Jaime in the house?"

"Yes, they're upstairs."

"Well, I heard either a prowler or Bigfoot, and I'm inclined to think the individual in the woods was fully human."

"Let me check on the boys, Aunt Lottie. I'll call you back."

Just then Jorge and Jaime descended the stairs.

"Mom, Dad, is Varry back yet? Varry went into the woods to do his business about an hour ago and hasn't come back."

"Paco, let's go get him," Mev said. "Then we'll go to bed. You and I have to get up at 5:00 tomorrow morning to drive to Gainesville."

Mev called Lottie back. Then she, Paco, and the boys donned light jackets, picked up flashlights, and headed into the woods in different directions.

"*Varry*! Come here!"

"*Varry*! Where are you?"

Mev ran into Lottie, who was also scanning the ground with her flashlight. Mev and Lottie continued their search together.

After fifteen minutes of calling, Jaime screamed. "I found him. Varry? Varry. Get up, Varry. Please. Don't die. Don't die. Mom, Dad, Jorge! Varry's here, on the ground. He can't get up. I think he's dying." Jaime started to cry.

Varry died in Jaime's arms. Jorge sat down on the ground and put his arm over Jaime's shoulder. They sat there holding their pet.

After a few minutes Paco retrieved a blanket from the house, wrapped Varry up, and carried the dead puppy back to the house. The others followed him in silent sorrow.

WWW ONLINEWITHERSTON.COM

WITHERSTON ON THE WEB
Tuesday, June 2, 2015

LOCAL NEWS

Gregory Bozeman will be released from Chestatee Regional Hospital today. Dr. Bozeman, who was shot in the back Wednesday evening while sampling the creek water at Founding Father's Bridge, underwent surgery performed by Dr. Buddy Harper to remove a bullet. Dr. Bozeman is doing well.
  ~ Catherine Perry, Reporter

LETTERS TO THE EDITOR

To the Editor:

I support KEEP NATURE NATURAL's petition for an injunction to block the clear-cut logging of the late Mr. Withers's property.

At his birthday party, Withers told us at the top of his lungs that he could log his land if he liked because the land was his. I beg to differ with the dead billionaire.

Withers controlled BioSenecta and Withers Village. Fine. But we the people of Witherston don't have to allow the deceased centenarian to control the quality of the air we breathe and the water we drink. We don't have to allow him—after his death—to deplete the biodiversity of the region that keeps our natural environment stable.

We don't have to allow him to destroy the territory of all the animals whose relatives had lived there for centuries before his relatives claimed their land as his property.

We don't have to allow him to threaten our own health and

happiness for the foreseeable future, as his clear-cutting of 31.7 acres of old-growth forest would do.

We the people of Witherston, and the birds and mammals, fish and amphibians, insects and worms, and bushes and trees on that 31.7 acres, are all interconnected, interactive parts our region's ecosystem. If part of that ecosystem is damaged we are all damaged, because our wellbeing depends on each other.

Rise up, Witherstonians! Stop the clear-cutting!
~ Signed, Gretchen Green

ON THIS DAY IN HISTORY
By Charlotte Byrd

On June 2, 1924, President Calvin Coolidge signed into law the Indian Citizenship Act, which granted citizenship to all Native Americans born in the United States.

But not until President Lyndon Johnson signed the Indian Civil Rights Act of 1968 were Native Americans in all states guaranteed all the same civil rights that white American citizens had enjoyed under the Bill of Rights.

WHAT'S NATURAL?
By Jorge Arroyo

What's an old-growth forest? We Witherstonians need to know, since Mr. Withers contracted with a logging company to clear-cut an old-growth forest on his property.

According to my research, an old-growth forest is a natural forest that has been a stable ecosystem for at least 180 years and possibly a thousand years or more.

An old-growth forest may have extremely old trees, such as some 250-year-old white oaks that UGA ecology students found on Mr. Withers's property. Imagine!

Those oaks were living here before our Founding Father Abraham Baldwin signed the Constitution. But a forest is more than just trees.

Forests are a necessary part of the planet's ecosystem. Forests are called the Earth's lungs, because trees, like all green plants, absorb carbon dioxide and release oxygen into the atmosphere. We humans need our planet's forests.

POLICE BLOTTER

At 9:30 pm yesterday, Lumpkin County Police officers responded to a 911 call from Mrs. Ida Deerfoot at 215 Old Dirt Road. Mrs. Deerfoot reported seeing a black bear at the intersection of Old Dirt Road and Hiccup Hill Road. By the time the officers arrived the bear had disappeared into the woods in the direction of Creek Road.

At 11:00 pm last night Detective Mev Arroyo called Police Chief Jake McCoy to report that her family had found their dog Varry, the Chow Chow puppy that had belonged to Francis Hearty Withers whom she had adopted, dead in the woods behind her house. Detective Arroyo said she suspected Varry had been poisoned.

CHAPTER 14

Tuesday morning, June 2, 2015:

By 6:00 a.m. Mev and Paco were on the road to Gainesville for Mev's lumpectomy. They were both exhausted from the events of the previous night.Despite the late hour, Ralph Elders had come over to examine Varry and take his body to his clinic. In front of the grieving boys he said he suspected poisoning and would do an autopsy first thing in the morning.

Then Mev had called Jake. Jake said he'd call Smitty Green and Catherine Perry. He wanted Witherstonians to know that a killer was on the loose, a killer of humans and dogs.

Mev and Paco were worried. Before leaving they'd awakened Jaime and Jorge and told them not to go into the woods. The boys could invite Beau over, but they were not to go into the woods. Under no circumstances. And they were not to let anybody into the house, other than Beau. The boys were to call their dad if they saw or heard anything unusual.

"Who could have done it?" asked Paco, who was driving.

"Who would have done it? And why?" Mev said. "Did Witherston's murderer simply want to scare me? To warn me off the investigation?"

"Maybe he wanted to scare Jaime and Jorge."

"So is it about me, or is it about Jaime and Jorge?"

"Maybe it's about Varry, *querida*. Maybe he killed Varry because Varry knew him. Varry witnessed his master's death. Maybe the killer was afraid that Varry could identify him."

"Paco, Neel Kingfisher has accused George Folsom of a very serious crime, scientific dishonesty. Now I'm starting to suspect that scientific dishonesty is not George's worst crime. Could George have murdered Withers?"

"He could have. He was a doctor. He was Withers's doctor. He had access to all kinds of drugs, and he had access to Withers. But why would he have murdered him?"

"To keep the billionaire from changing his will."

"So...for money. The motive for most murders," Paco said.

"Or for Senextra. Or for both. George had BioSenecta stock. I'm thinking that George was very interested in Senextra's success, financially and personally. He could not have been happy with Withers's threat to change his will and not build the Senextra plant."

"I wonder whether George shot Gregory."

"And killed Faith."

"Are you going to question him?"

"Paco, I'm under the weather this week."

"If we don't bring him in, he could harm someone else."

"Let me call Jake before I go into surgery. Jake can keep him in Witherston."

ও৵ও৵ও

I've told Neel Kingfisher that I'll be at Withers Village to give Senextra shots this morning. Funny that Neel is suddenly willing to get a Senextra shot. And he wants one of those twins to interview me. It's a trap. Well, I'm not surprised. I'm going to be caught. It's inevitable. But before I'm handcuffed, I'll kill myself. And maybe someone else. I'll be prepared.

Two roads diverged on Saturday, May 23. I chose the one less traveled by. Had I not killed Withers—and Faith and that damned dog—I would soon have become a father. I would have changed diapers, attended my son's football games and graduation ceremonies, and then welcomed his grandchildren. In old age I would have sat on the porch with Faith, drinking scotch, looking through old scrapbooks, reminiscing about our life together. I would never have known that I had no conscience.

And I would not have fame. I prefer fame. I want to be remembered.

❦❧❦

Jorge was still in his pajamas when he heard the familiar email beep on his phone. He read the message:

> *Can you and jaime come to withers village at 10 am?*
> *Folsom here to give shots.*
> *Plan for pix and interview.*
> *N*

Jorge wrote back:

> *We will be there*
> *Someone poisoned Varry last night*
> *We are sad*

"Jaime, get up! Neel wants us to go to Withers Village this morning. George Folsom will be there."

"But Mom and Dad told us to stay here."

"They told us not to go into the woods and not to let anybody into the house. They didn't tell us to stay home."

"I guess you're right. Should we call Beau?"

"We don't have time. It's already 9:00."

"I wish we had Varry to go with us."

"I wish we had Varry, too."

Jorge and Jaime dressed, ate their cereal, and mounted their bikes. The two-mile trip to Withers Village took them less than twenty minutes. They were on time. Neel met them at the building's entrance. Swift greeted the boys eagerly.

"Good morning, boys," Neel said. "I told Dr. Folsom when he arrived this morning that you were interested in his work and would like to interview him for *Witherston on the Web*. He said that was fine."

"Neel," Jaime said, "somebody poisoned Varry. He's dead."

"It was last night behind our house," Jorge said. "Aunt Lottie heard a prowler and called us. We went outside looking for

Varry. We found him as he was dying. He died in my brother's arms."

"We think somebody gave Varry something poisonous to eat," said Jaime.

"We think it was somebody Varry knew. Or Varry wouldn't have gone up to him."

At that moment George Folsom, wearing a white apron over his pale blue seersucker suit, emerged from the hallway.

"Hello, boys," he said, smiling broadly. "I'm complimented you'd like to interview me. Shall we go to the bench on the far side of the pond? I'm parked near there."

"First," said Jorge, "may I take a picture of you giving a Senextra shot to somebody?"

George turned to Neel. "Neel, didn't you tell me you'd like to start taking Senextra? If so, I can give you a shot right now."

Neel rolled up his sleeve. George produced a syringe from his apron picket. Jorge got the picture he wanted. George and Jorge set out for the bench.

Jaime lingered behind. First he texted his mother:

>*Mom i love you*
>*I hope your lumpectomy goes well*
>*We will fix you dinner tonight*

Then he texted his father:

>*Jorge and i are at withers village w neel and george*
>*Jorge got pix of george giving shot to neel*
>*Jorge interviewing george now*

Paco texted back:

>*Stay with Jorge.*
>*George could be the killer.*
>*Tell Neel. I am calling police.*

Jaime ran to catch up with Jorge and George. As Jorge and

George sat down on the bench, Jaime leaned against the tree and texted Neel:

> *George could be killer*
> *Dad is calling police*

Jaime watched his smartphone screen and waited for Neel to text him back. Neel didn't.

సౌఌ

Paco checked his email after Mev had been taken into the operating room. He'd received a message from Ralph Elders:

> *Hi, Paco. I have examined the contents of Varry's stomach and found nothing unusual. But his blood shows extremely high potassium. And he has a spot on his neck that is irritated from an injection. I suspect that Varry was injected with potassium chloride last night. Potassium chloride is a nearly-perfect murder weapon. When injected into a vein it causes almost immediate cardiac arrest, and it is undetectable in an autopsy. My deepest sympathies, Ralph*

Paco replied:

> *Thanks, Ralph. Please report autopsy findings to Witherston Police.*

Then Paco called Lottie. "George must be the killer. He's got access to potassium chloride and syringes," he said. "And George is with Jorge and Jaime at Withers Village right now!"
"I'm on my way!"

సౌఌ

"Why have I dedicated my life to Senextra?" George was dictating, and Jorge was taking notes on his tablet. Jaime sat down under the tree and turned on his smartphone recorder.

"Senextra will bring longevity to millions of people. I want to be a leader of this health revolution in the United States, this revolution to free individuals from the painful, protracted process of aging. Long after my death I will be thanked for what I have done as one of Senextra's earliest proponents."

"Are you yourself taking Senextra, Dr. Folsom?"

No, Jorge. I am not. I am a scientist. I have not inserted myself into my experiment. And the experiment is mine indeed. You and your readers will learn soon enough how I made BioSenecta's pilot study my own. And how I have sacrificed my own future for the future of others."

"Dr. Folsom, will it be good for our country to have so many old people?"

"Jorge, the new old people, the Senextra-centenarians, will not be like the elderly people you know. They will not look older than seventy-five. They will not feel older than sixty-five. They will enjoy their lives."

"What about the poor, who won't be able to afford Senextra?"

"The poor have always had shorter lives than the rich and the middle class. We may say that those who can afford Senextra have earned the right to longevity. Those who can't don't need to remain a burden to society. And as you must know from Sunday school, Jesus said, the poor will be with you always."

"I don't go to Sunday school, Dr. Folsom. So I don't know what to think about that," Jorge said. "But I want to ask you about Senextra's side effects. Have you noticed any negative side effects?"

Dr. Folsom paused. "If I'd noticed any I would have reported them, wouldn't I? Well, I haven't noticed any so I haven't reported any."

Jorge typed Dr. Folsom's answer on his tablet. "I heard that your patients at Withers Village had developed breasts. Is that true, Dr. Folsom?"

Dr. Folsom stopped smiling.

Suddenly the quiet was shattered by sirens. Two Witherston Police vehicles, an ambulance, Aunt Lottie's Smart Car, and Catherine Perry's old Ford sped up the Withers Village driveway.

George seized Jorge with his left hand and pulled out a loaded syringe with his right. Flicking off the needle cover, he held the syringe to Jorge's neck.

"Don't move, and shut up," George shouted to Jaime, "or I'll kill your brother."

In stunned silence Jaime watched George half-drag Jorge through the woods toward the parking lot. He heard the Jaguar roar away.

Jaime screamed, "He's got Jorge! He's going to kill Jorge!" He raced back to Withers Village.

ↄ৵ↄ

Now Jorge is unconscious. I injected him with Valium. If I have to inject him with potassium chloride, he won't feel it. I've hidden my car. So I'll have a couple of hours to complete my mission, and my life. I don't know how Jorge's life will end, not yet anyway, but I know how mine will end. I will dig a grave for myself right here. I will lie down, cover myself with brush and leaves, and then inject potassium chloride into my vein. Or maybe I'll slit my wrists with my scalpel. I will never be found. I will become a legend. A legend in human history. But first I must attend to other matters.

ↄ৵ↄ

It was 11:00. Jake put George's call on speakerphone. "Yes, Dr. Folsom? Where are you?"

Jake, Neel, Jaime, Lottie, Catherine, deputies Pete Senior and Pete Junior, Barney the ambulance driver, and Steve the paramedic had gathered together in Neel's study.

"Hello, Chief. Not where you can find me, or Jorge either."

"Put Jorge on the phone."

"Jorge is sleeping, Chief. Very comfortably."

"Have you killed him?" Jake yelled into the phone. "You monster!"

"No. But I will if you don't do as I ask."

"What do you ask?"

"That somebody—I don't care who—kill that Indian Neel Kingfisher."

"Kill Neel Kingfisher? What are you thinking?"

"Here's the deal. As soon as you text me a picture of Neel Kingfisher dead I will release Jorge Arroyo unharmed. If in one hour Neel Kingfisher is not dead, Jorge Arroyo will be."

"George, you've gone crazy. What has Neel Kingfisher done to you?"

"Neel Kingfisher betrayed me. He destroyed Senextra's future. He deprived millions of longevity," George replied. "Now text me a picture of his dead body."

George severed the connection.

⁓⁓⁓

Neel looked at the others, and they looked at him. He grabbed a Cherokee bone knife off the wall and plunged it into his left side. He sank to the floor. Blood flowed from his mouth.

Everybody screamed.

Jake snapped a picture of Neel and texted it to George.

⁓⁓⁓

Catherine Perry texted Smitty Green a short, very short story for *Webby Witherston.*

> *11:00 am. Less than thirty minutes ago at Withers Village Dr. George Folsom took fourteen-year-old Jorge Arroyo captive and said he would kill him unless somebody killed Dr. Neel Kingfisher within the hour. Kingfisher then stabbed himself in the heart. Chief McCoy texted a photo of Kingfisher to Folsom. Folsom has not replied. Jorge Arroyo has not returned.*
>
> *~ Catherine Perry, reporting from Withers Village*

※※※

Paco learned of the events from Lottie. But he couldn't leave the hospital. Mev was still in surgery, and would be for another hour. He and Mev would be in Gainesville all day.

Paco asked Lottie to put Jaime on the phone.

"*¿Hijo, cómo estás?* How are you doing?" They talked for five minutes. Jaime told him that the ambulance had taken Neel to Chestatee Regional Hospital, that Neel was not dead, not yet, and that Jake was trying to reach George on his cell phone.

Finally Jaime said, "Dad, George has not called back. And he won't answer Chief McCoy's calls. Chief McCoy has been phoning and texting George since he sent him Neel's picture."

Jake took the phone. "Hi, Paco. I'm hoping that your son will walk in the door any moment."

"We can't wait, Jake. Let's get Grant and Rich involved. They're George's friends."

※※※

When Smitty received Catherine's text-message he acted. He put Catherine's story on *Witherston on the Web*.

He sent Catherine's story and Jorge's photo to Sheriff Bearfield requesting the Sheriff to send out an Amber Alert for Jorge and an all-points bulletin for George.

He put Catherine's story and Jorge's photo on *Webby Witherston*'s Facebook page.

He repeated Catherine's story on Witherston's seldom used Emergency Alert System, which automatically called the number—cell phone and/or land line—of every Witherstonian signed up for the program. He figured he'd reach a quarter of Witherston's population immediately.

Smitty started getting calls right away.

"Hi, Smitty. This is Rich. What can I do to help?"

"Hi, Smitty. This is Grant. How can I help?"

He gave them Neel's land line and told them to do whatever Chief McCoy asked.

ඏංඏ

At 11:20 Jake got a text message from George:

> *Jorge is alive. You will have to find him. You won't find me. I will destroy my cell phone now. Good-bye.*

The message accompanied a picture of Jorge tied up with rope in the right front seat of George's Jaguar. Jorge appeared unconscious.

Jake turned to those crowded into Neel's study. "We need to start a search, without delay."

At that moment, the phone rang. Jake signaled for Lottie to pick it up.

"Thanks so much for calling, Rich," Lottie said. "Will you please organize a search party? Work with Smitty." She listened a moment and then replied, "Thank you. The search party will form here at Withers Village as soon as possible." She turned to Jake. "Rich will ask volunteers to come here as soon as possible. Rhonda will come here in an hour. She and Ruth Griggs will bring enough food for fifty people."

Ten minutes later, Grant Griggs and Gretchen Green entered the front door, together. "We've come to help," Grant said. "I thought Gretchen might like a ride."

Jake looked out and saw Grant's silver Lincoln with somebody in the driver's seat.

"Who's in your car?" he asked Grant.

"We brought Gandhi. He can help too," Gretchen answered.

Catherine texted an update for *Webby Witherston.*

Soon Jon showed up with Renoir.

Jim arrived shortly thereafter with Beau.

Trevor Bennington, Jr., arrived with his son Trevor Bennington, III.

Pastor Clement arrived.

Scorch arrived.

And a dozen other Witherstonians arrived with their flashlights, water bottles, and dogs.

Gretchen texted Martin that George had kidnapped Jorge, that she'd joined the search party to find the boy, and that she hoped he could come up. She got an instant reply from Martin:

> *I am sorry but I can't get there this afternoon. I have too much business on my desk. Regrets.*

That's odd, Gretchen thought. Has he lost interest so soon? Jaime called his dad and told him the latest developments.

"*Hijo querido,*" Paco said. "Stay with Chief McCoy. You can help him take calls. Do not go out on the search for your brother. Understand? Under no circumstances."

"I understand," Jaime said.

"Your mother is out of surgery, she's starting to wake up. I'll tell her what's going on."

"Is she okay, Dad?"

"The lumpectomy went well. She does not need chemotherapy. Radiation but no chemo. We'll be home by five, I'm hoping." Then Paco whispered, "Son, please don't call your mother or text her or email her. Let me tell her when she's fully awake. And I'll tell her you love her."

ⲉⲟⲉⲟ

There's no return for me. There's no reversal of events in time. I face either death or prison. If I have meted out death to others to further my mission, then I must willingly accept death for myself. So I will die. But I will die where no one can find me.

I am a doctor. But I am not like most doctors. I am not like the doctors who acknowledge humans' kinship with beasts, the doctors who bow to nature in caring for their patients, who accept the aging of the individual as normal, who accept death as normal. I have stood proud in my conviction that human ingenuity can overcome nature. I found my life's calling in Senextra, the epitome of human success in the battle against aging. Aging is the mark of nature on the individual organism. Senextra is, or will be, the mark of human ingenuity on the individual organism, the sign of human triumph over nature.

In the future, when individuals taking Senextra live to be 150 years old or more, I will be remembered as the doctor who made their longevity possible.

I've left my car, with the kid tied up inside, under Saloli Falls. Appropriately. That's where he played, in Founding Father's Creek. The Saloli Falls pool is shallow. He'll be safe if there's no rain upstream to raise the level of the pool. He'll be found eventually.

I won't be.

ↄ∽ↄ

At 12:30, Rhonda and Ruth drove up in Rhonda's Escalade. Rhonda opened up the back to display a huge assortment of food: sandwiches, hamburgers, cold pizzas, apples, grapes, carrots, peanuts. Fifty individual cartons of orange juice, limeade, and lemonade. And a sack of dry dog food for Giuliani, who'd come with them, and any other hungry canine wannabe-rescuers.

The searchers had a wholesome tailgate lunch.

At 1:00, Mayor Rather used his bullhorn to rally the men and women gathered behind Withers Village by the pond.

"Witherstonians, thank you for coming. I've counted eighteen volunteers, and I hear more coming up the driveway. Today we will save the life of our dear friend Jorge Arroyo, who is tied up in a 2013 F-type black Jaguar convertible. Find a partner, take your water and flashlights, and fan out. Keep your cell phones on. Text Chief McCoy if you find anything."

"And take care of each other," Jake added, seizing the bullhorn Rich held. "George may be armed. He has killed before and he may kill again. Now let's go find Jorge."

Lottie set off with Rich and Giuliani.

Grant set off with Gretchen and Gandhi.

Jon set off with Renoir and Scorch.

Jim set off with Beau.

Jaime stayed with Chief McCoy.

It started to rain.

ↄ∽ↄ

Lottie wondered why Rich had brought Giuliani on the search. Giuliani trotted obediently alongside Lottie and Rich. Lottie hoped the dog had a good nose.

Rich panted. He was unaccustomed to exercise.

"You were at your best today," Lottie said to Rich. "You got us together in no time."

"Thanks, Lottie. But what a terrible reason to get together. What a terrible reason."

"You know George better than any of us, Rich. What do you think is going through his mind now?"

"I don't know. I don't know what happened to him. I just don't know. George always wanted to do something important. That's why he hitched himself to Senextra."

"Was he a nice man?"

"I'd say he was, though when he talked about himself as a genius he got strange."

"If he was a genius, why did he come to Witherston?"

"He met Martin Payne at a medical convention in Atlanta. Martin told him about Senextra. Martin was already working with Mr. Withers, who exercised a lot of power on the Bio-Senecta board of directors. Mr. Withers wanted the pilot study to be conducted at Withers Village."

"So Martin Payne put George in charge of the pilot study?"

"Yes, after George convinced him to do it. George thought he was destined—that was his word—to bring Senextra to the world. So George and Faith moved to Witherston in 2011, four years ago last month. George may also have had some financial problems in Savannah."

"Where could he have taken my nephew?"

"I have no idea. But we'd better find Jorge soon. I don't like the look of those thunder clouds."

დოდ

Gandhi raced into the woods leaving Gretchen to talk with Grant.

Grant spoke first. "I have known George a long time. For the life of me, I can't make sense of what he's done. In ten days he's ravaged Witherston and destroyed himself. He's ended lives and damaged lives, all for the sake of a drug to extend lives. Where were the signs he'd turn into this monster?"

"There may have been signs, Grant, but nobody recognized them as such. In retrospect, however, I can see that George didn't tolerate any challenge to his authority. He needed to feel important. He needed to feel powerful."

"Well, he certainly exercised power over poor Faith. Faith once told Rhonda she feared him."

"George exercised power over Faith, Rhonda, Withers, and all the Withers Villagers by being the doctor to give them Senextra, the doctor to give them long life. George derived his self image from whatever power he managed to wield."

※※※

"I meant to email you, Jon," Scorch said. "I'm sorry that Gregory got shot. How's he doing?"

"He's recuperating at home now. He'll be okay. Thanks for asking."

"I guess Gregory was collateral damage for George."

"Maybe. The way I see it is that George wanted to test the water where the twins found that deformed frog. He wanted to find out whether the creek was polluted because he didn't want anything to block construction of the Senextra factory. When he saw Gregory taking a water sample he must have panicked and shot him. He probably used Gregory's rifle, because Gregory always kept one in his truck. It's not there anymore. I forgot to tell Mev that."

※※※

"Dad," Beau said. "Why did George go bad? He seemed okay at the Smith House last week."

"Hard to figure out, Beau. George must not have had much of a conscience. And he was always certain he was right. But George never liked me much, so I never got to know him personally."

"Do you think that George knew he was doing something wrong?"

"I don't know. I suspect that George was convinced that he could see the truth and that nobody else could, that he could see what was best for the world and that nobody else could. He may have believed that killing a few people who stood in the way of what was best for the world was justifiable."

"How scary."

"Yes, son. How scary. Anybody who thinks that he's the only one who sees the truth is scary, because he will do what he feels necessary to make everybody conform to his vision. Same goes for groups of people. That's why I'm uncomfortable with certainty."

"Do you think that most people are good, Dad?"

"I do, Beau. Look around at our search party. We are all united in our desire to rescue Jorge. We've forgotten our differences."

"Dad," said Beau, "if Jorge gets hurt Jaime will know it. They feel each other's pain. And if Jorge dies something in Jaime will die. Jaime will never be a whole person again."

They walked in silence for a few minutes. Then Beau spoke again.

"Dad, what's it like to love somebody who dies?"

"It's to lose access to a whole world, the world that was your friend, or your brother, or your mother."

❦❦❦

The rain came down in sheets. A few of the searchers turned around and hurried back to Withers Village.

But most did not. Jon and Renoir caught up with Jim and Beau.

"We've got to keep searching," Jon said. "George can't be far away. The Georgia State Patrol would have blocked off all the major roads leading out of Witherston."

"*The* road," Jim corrected him.

Renoir headed toward the creek.

Jon called him, "Renoir, come here!"

"Let's just follow Renoir," Beau said,

The sky grew darker. Lightning struck nearby. Renoir led them into the woods along the creek and up the trail.

Beau texted Jaime:

We r following renoir up creek maybe to saloli falls
Tell chief mccoy

CHAPTER 15

Tuesday afternoon and evening, June 2, 2015:

Renoir raced up the trail toward Saloli Falls, where he and Varry had enjoyed a swim the previous Sunday. Through the pouring rain Jim, Beau, and Jon followed at a slightly slower pace. As they approached the Falls, they heard Renoir bark. Beau ran ahead.

"There's George's car! In the creek! It's moving!"

The lightning illuminated the black Jaguar for a few seconds.

"Stop, Beau!" Jim shouted. "Don't go near it!"

"But Jorge is in it! I can see him!"

"Beau! Come back, now!"

Beau minded his father.

Jon called Renoir and put a leash on him. Then he phoned Jake.

"Hi, Jake. We've spotted George's car. In Saloli Falls Pond." Jon listened intently. "Please hurry! The creek is swelling and the car is starting to float downstream."

Jon turned to Jim and said, "Jake and another armed officer are coming. They've called an ambulance. Hold onto Renoir."

With that Jon jumped into the water, reached the Jaguar, and tried to open the door. It was locked from the inside. By now the water had risen to the level of the windshield. Jon tried to hold onto the car.

In minutes the three heard Jake's Chevy Tahoe with its siren blaring turn off the Witherston Highway onto the narrow dirt road that led to Saloli Falls. Jake arrived with Pete Senior, Pete Junior, and Jaime.

Getting out of the Tahoe, Jaime said to Beau, "I couldn't stay away. He's my brother."

Pete Junior had brought a sledge hammer. He waded out to the driver's side of the Jaguar, bashed in the window, and while water poured into the car he unlocked the door, pulled it open, and rescued Jorge. Pete Junior and Jon laid Jorge gently on the bank.

Holding his brother's hand, Jaime called his father. "Dad, Jorge is okay. He's here! He's been rescued. Dad, I can't stop crying." Then he gave the phone to his barely conscious brother.

"I'm okay, Dad," Jorge said, "just tired." He handed the phone to Jim.

"Hi, Paco. This is Jim. Jorge looks okay. I'll take your boys home, and I'll examine Jorge, just to make sure. Beau and I will stay at your house until you and Mev get home tonight. So Mev is okay?" He listened. "Tell her she's in our thoughts."

℘℘

Catherine texted another update for *Webby Witherston*.

℘℘

Jorge napped all afternoon on the living room sofa, which he no longer had to share with Varry and Renoir. Jim dozed in Paco's chair.

Jaime and Beau were in the kitchen making dinner for the first time. They were wearing aprons. Jaime's apron, a gift from Lauren to his mother, depicted four wine glasses and the words "Group Therapy."

"I've got to do this for Mom," Jaime had explained to Beau. "She had a bad day today."

"So did Jorge!" Beau said.

"And Neel. What an amazing man he is. He sacrificed himself for Jorge."

"Maybe he'll live. He was breathing when the ambulance took him to Dahlonega."

"I'll text him. Then if he lives he'll know we care for him."

> *Dear neel*
> *I hope you live to read this message*
> *You are an amazing man and a great teacher*
> *Jorge and i will carry out your mission*
> *We will show that senextra goes against nature*
> *and will harm life on our planet*
> *Best wishes*
> *Jaime*

"There," said Jaime. "I want Neel to know that if he dies he's passed on his ideas to our generation."

"That's what teachers do. That's why I want to be a teacher, a professor of history. I want to be like your Aunt Lottie. Now should I keep reading you the recipe, Jaime?" Beau had found a recipe for chicken stew on his smartphone.

Under Beau's direction, Jaime put into a big pot of water: red potatoes, onions, celery, carrots, fresh parsley, fresh basil, and some chicken thighs he found in the freezer. The recipe called for sage, but neither of them knew what sage was, so Jaime put thyme in the concoction instead. The recipe called for a bay leaf, but they didn't know what that was either. So Jaime just added salt and pepper and turned on the heat.

While waiting for the soup to come to a boil, Jaime and Beau talked.

"I didn't know you wanted to be a professor, Beau."

"I want to spend my life studying the history of Georgia—well, the history of the Southeast. If I'm a professor, I can try to figure out whose stories have not been told and then tell those stories to my students. And I can write those stories in books that people will read after I'm dead and gone. That's how I will pass on my ideas to a future generation."

"Whose stories have not been told, Beau? Whose story would you write first?"

"I guess if we know whose stories haven't been told then we've already been told about them by somebody, or we wouldn't know about them, right?" Beau laughed. "But I know from my father that not many stories have been written down about the black people who worked in the gold mines. I think I'd like to tell about the life of one of Dad's ancestors."

"You and Jorge are a lot alike, Beau. Jorge wants to write too. Jorge wants to be a journalist, and you want to be a scholar. You both want to find out what has really happened in our society."

"What do you want to do when you grow up, Jaime?"

"I want to be a biologist. After catching Leggy Froggy and talking to Neel, I've decided that I want to figure out how we humans affect nature with our drugs."

"Who will pay you to do that?"

"I don't know. Maybe I'll have to be a professor too. A professor of biology, or ecology."

"We'll both be professors like your Aunt Lottie!"

"I want Jorge and me to have families when we grow up, but I want us to live next door to each other. I got terrified today that I'd lose him. I don't ever want to lose him."

❧❧❧

At 5:30 Paco and Mev walked in the front door, Mev leaning on Paco's arm. Mev, Paco, Jorge, Jaime, Beau, and Jim exchanged kisses, hugs, and tears for a good five minutes. Jorge was fine, Jim reported. And Mev was fine, Paco reported.

"You know that Jon and Gregory are having a party Friday night to celebrate Gregory's survival," Jim said to Mev. "Now we have more survivals to celebrate. Will all of you be there?"

"We will," Mev said. "Please call Jon and accept for all four of us."

"Great, Mom! We'll get to see Renoir," Jorge said.

Before leaving, Jim called Chestatee Regional Hospital to ask about Neel. "Neel is stable," he reported to the others. "He's out of surgery and in intensive care, but he's expected to live. The knife went into his ribs, but not his heart."

Jaime told his parents about Neel's heroic act.

❧❧❧

After Jim and Beau had left, Paco, Mev, Jaime, and Jorge moved into the dining room for their dinner of chicken stew.

The doorbell rang. In walked Lottie, with Darwin on her shoulder, and Gretchen and Gandhi. Lottie carried a 2010 cab from Niner Wine Estates in Paso Robles, California. Gretchen carried a bag with the makings of a salad: lettuce, cucumbers, avocado, roasted sunflower seeds, virgin olive oil from Georgia and balsamic vinegar from Modena. Gandhi carried a wet tennis ball, which he promptly dropped as he settled down on the sofa.

"Hello, everybody!" Lottie greeted her family. "Gretchen and I thought we'd join you all! May we?"

"Certainly! What a nice surprise!" Mev said, inwardly groaning. "But you'll have to pardon me for not sharing your wine with you. I'm still a bit groggy from surgery."

How could she not welcome her friends, even though she'd had a lumpectomy only eight hours before and longed to go to bed.

"No problem, dear! Paco, Gretchen, and I will toast you." Lottie went into the kitchen to get three wine goblets and a couple of extra place settings.

"Here's to my dearest niece Mev," Lottie said, after pouring the wine. "May she recover quickly and completely, so she can have wine with us the next time we eat together."

"*Salud,*" said Paco. "And let it be your finest wine. Remember your promise?"

"Of course!"

"And here's to Jorge," Gretchen said, raising her goblet.
"*Salud.*"

"And to Neel," Jaime said, raising his water glass. "We can't forget that Neel's in the hospital."

"*Salud.*"

"I'm going to see him tomorrow," Gretchen said.

"Neel wanted to trade his life for my brother's. We were all shocked when he suddenly stabbed himself, but now I see that he was doing what he believed in. He'd talked to Jorge and me about how in nature old people die so that young people can live. Neel probably thought that Jorge's life was more important than his for the future."

"The death of individuals in the present makes way for the life of individuals in the future," said Gretchen.

"That's Neel's philosophy," Jaime said.

"And mine, Gretchen said. "But this morning Neel didn't spend a second thinking about things. He acted. And he acted courageously."

"I hope I have the courage when I grow up to act courageously for the good of others," said Jorge.

"*Hijos*, you both are already courageous," Paco said. Then he added, "Actually, you're much more courageous than obedient. But that's okay. When you all are adults, you will need courage and honesty to make the world better, more than obedience."

"I don't think I'd like to be called obedient," said Gretchen.

"Nobody's ever called you obedient, Gretchen, dear," Lottie said. "Or me either, I guess."

Jaime suddenly put down his fork. "Oh my gosh! Who's taking care of Swift tonight?"

"I'll go get him," Paco said, putting down his fork. "I'll go get him now. *Hijos*, don't go anywhere, okay?"

"We promise, Dad."

"I'm going to lie down," Mev said.

"That's fine, dear. We'll stay here with the boys, so they don't disobey their father." Lottie started carrying out the dishes, a goblet of wine in one hand and a dirty plate in the other.

In a half hour Paco returned with Swift, who jumped onto the sofa to say hello to Gandhi. Gandhi returned his affection. The two dogs chased each other around the living room.

After Gandhi had departed with Gretchen, Lottie, and Darwin, Swift stretched out on the sofa.

క్రిస్

In their bedroom Paco gave Mev the silver pin he'd selected for her at Aurum Studios in Athens.

"Oh, Paco! I love it! A dove—for peace!"

"Remember what Jorge wrote in *Webby Witherston*? The Cherokees used the same word for both peace and health."

క్రిస్

Mev was feeling well enough to check her email before she went to bed. She had a message from Susana Pérez at the EPA in Athens:

> *Dear Detective Arroyo: I will send you a detailed analysis of the two water samples from Founding Father's Creek in a few days. On first examination we note that the sample from Saloli Falls shows minimal levels of pollution whereas the sample from Founding Father's Bridge shows unusually high levels, especially of synthetic estrogen. I've told Gregory. Susana Pérez*

"There's the evidence," Mev said to Paco."Senextra from Withers Village has polluted Founding Father's Creek. And we Witherstonians all live downstream from Withers Village."

∞∞∞

Gretchen texted Martin:

> *Hi, Martin. Would you like to go to a party with me on Friday night? Gretchen*

Gretchen waited for Martin's response. She saw the bubble with three dots that showed he was texting her back, but she didn't get any message from him. Not until 11:00 pm. Then she got a brief message. Altogether too brief, she thought.

> *Hi, Gretchen. I wish I could. But I have a meeting Friday afternoon that will keep me working late. Have a good time. Martin.*

Gretchen didn't respond. She knew what he meant. No more dates.

She had enjoyed Martin's courtship of her. Or was it a courtship? She'd been attracted to him. He looked good, smelled good, exuded intelligence, charm, and good manners, was attentive to her and respectful of her ideas. She thought he liked her. But had he simply used her? Had Lottie been right, that he was more interested in BioSenecta's future in Witherston than in their future together? And what future could they have had together?

They had nothing in common. He was a young, ambitious CEO of a giant pharmaceutical company. She was an aging, laid-back hippy who practiced yoga and owned an organic grocery. He produced Senextra. She protested Senextra. He drove a BMW. She drove a bicycle. He felt at home in Atlanta or Chicago or any big city. She felt at home in Witherston, in the woods, as far away as she could get from a big city. He liked excitement. She liked tranquility. They had nothing in common.

Why, she asked herself, had she gotten her hopes up? Because she would like to have someone to care for her, take care of her, love her for the next thirty years. She was fifty-five now with no children, no siblings, only a few close friends who might not be around in her old age. But every time she dated someone, and that was increasingly seldom these days, she found herself subordinating her views to her partner's in hopes he'd stay with her. She'd forget who she was. She'd lose her identity. She'd become obedient. Then she'd panic and flee the relationship.

She was not like other women. Was she abnormal? Probably.

Gretchen poured herself a glass of Chardonnay, put on a sweater, and settled into a chair on her back deck. Gandhi lay down beside her. Barack occupied the other chair. The rain had stopped, the clouds had gone, and the moon shone bright. The scent of damp pine invaded her brain and lifted her spirits. This was where she belonged. She'd be okay.

Tomorrow she'd visit Neel in the hospital. She hoped he'd be conscious. She wanted to talk with him.

∽∾∽

I watched that police officer pull Jorge from my car. What was the name of that officer? Oh yes, Pete Junior. What an

*idiot. Six feet four inches of brawn and no brain. Like all po-
lice officers he enforces society's laws mindlessly.*

*Society's laws don't recognize extraordinary cases. Socie-
ty's laws don't recognize genius. Society's laws tell police officers to save everybody. Even the useless, like Faith. Society's
laws put murderers to death, regardless of their brilliance,
their vision. Society's laws are made by individuals with limited intelligence and limited vision. Society's laws don't make
exceptions for the individual who thinks a hundred years
ahead, who kills for the well-being of society a hundred years
hence. Individuals like me.*

*I should be dead by now. I am lying in my future grave,
where I'll never be found. I have a syringe of potassium chloride that I will use to kill myself. Why have I not killed myself
already? Why am I afraid? I've made my contribution to the
world. I will be famous.*

*I must inject myself. I will inject myself. I can do it. I can.
Now. I know I can.*

Now. Nobody will find me.

Now. I know I can. I must.

Now.

WWW.ONLINEWITHERSTON.COM

WITHERSTON ON THE WEB
Tuesday, June 2, 2015

LATE-BREAKING NEWS

3:00 pm. Jorge Arroyo is alive! He was found by Dr. Jim Lodge, Beau Lodge, and Jonathan Finley tied up in Dr. Folsom's locked Jaguar in the Saloli Falls pool.

The rain poured down, the water rose up past the Jaguar's window, and the car started to float.

Finley tried to get into the car but couldn't because the door was locked.

Just in time Chief McCoy and his officers Pete Senior Koslowsky and Pete Junior Koslowsky arrived on the scene. They brought Jorge's identical twin brother Jaime with them.

Pete Junior saved Jorge's life by breaking the Jaguar's window with a sledge hammer and then pulling Jorge out.

Chief McCoy thanks all the volunteers who came to Withers Village and searched for Jorge in the rain.

Chief McCoy says that he and his officers will search for Dr. Folsom tomorrow. Pete Junior was awesome.

~ Catherine Perry, reporting from Withers Village

11:25 am. Dr. George Folsom has sent Chief McCoy a photo of Jorge Arroyo alive but unconscious and tied up with a rope in the front seat of his black Jaguar.

Mayor Rather is organizing a search party. Volunteers should come to Withers Village now.

Bring flashlights, water bottles, dogs, and a waterproof jacket.

~ Catherine Perry, reporting from Withers Village

11:00 am. Less than thirty minutes ago at Withers Village Dr. George Folsom took fourteen-year-old Jorge Arroyo captive and said he would kill him unless somebody killed Dr. Neel Kingfisher within the hour. Kingfisher then stabbed himself in the heart. Chief McCoy texted a photo of Kingfisher to Folsom. Folsom has not replied. Jorge Arroyo has not returned.

    ~ Catherine Perry, reporting from Withers Village

4:15 pm. Mr. Furth Lorry, vice president of Century South Bank of Dahlonega, called Chief McCoy at 4:00 pm today to inform him that Dr. George Folsom had withdrawn all funds from his accounts at 4:20 pm yesterday, June 2. The total amounted to $57,093.

    ~ Catherine Perry, Reporter

LOCAL NEWS

Dr. Neel Kingfisher, director of Withers Village, is alive and expected to recover. Dr. Buddy Harper at Chestatee Regional Hospital, after operating on Dr. Kingfisher for a self-inflicted knife wound, made the announcement at 8:30 last night.

Yesterday Dr. Kingfisher had stabbed himself with a Cherokee bone dagger from his collection when he heard Dr. George Folsom demand that somebody kill him in exchange for Jorge Arroyo's life.

Pastor Clement said to this reporter, "Dr. Kingfisher followed Christ's example. He gave his life as a ransom for many."

Mayor Rather said to this reporter, "Dr. Kingfisher is a true hero. A true hero. He sacrificed himself to save Jorge."

Jaime Arroyo said to this reporter, "I hope Neel lives."

Jorge Arroyo has completely recovered from his kidnapping by Witherston's Dr. George Folsom. Jorge said that the last words he remember Dr. Folsom saying to him before giving him a shot were: "I will be famous one day."

Dr. Folsom is famous now. Dr. Folsom was the doctor in charge of BioSenecta's pilot study of the effect of Senextra on old men. He gave monthly injections of Senextra to Withers Villagers to make them live longer. According to gynecologist Dr. Jim Lodge, Dr. Folsom also gave Senextra shots to a few women in Witherston. Senextra contains synthetic estrogen.

Jorge had been interviewing Dr. Folsom for an article in Witherston on the Web when Dr. Folsom got angry at one of his questions and grabbed him. Jorge says that he is writing up an article about Dr. Folsom and Senextra for tomorrow's edition.

Today Witherston Chief of Police Jake McCoy and officers Ricky Hefner, Pete Senior Koslowsky, and Pete Junior Koslowsky are searching the woods near Saloli Falls for the body of Dr. George Folsom, the kidnapper of Jorge Arroyo and the alleged murderer of Francis Hearty Withers.

~ Catherine Perry, Reporter

EDITORIAL

Witherston's ten-day nightmare has ended. Allow me to piece together the story as best I can.

In 2002 the Lawrence Company, of which Francis Hearty Withers was the majority shareholder, became BioSenecta Pharmaceuticals, Inc. Mr. Withers had inherited great wealth from his family and had more than tripled it through his investments in the Lawrence Company. Withers joined BioSenecta's company's board of directors.

Two years later Withers endowed the Founding Father's Retirement Community, whose residents were men over 90 years old, and changed its name to Withers Village.

In 2010 BioSenecta developed the drug Senextra to prolong healthy life in the elderly. Having learned of the drug at board meetings, Withers, age 95, requested permission to test the drug on himself and began taking the drug orally. Withers persuaded BioSenecta to do Senextra's pilot study at Withers Village.

In 2011 BioSenecta initiated a five-year FDA-approved pilot study of Senextra in Withers Village and appointed Dr. George Folsom from Savannah to conduct the research program. Folsom moved to Witherston and set up a schedule of monthly Senextra injections for Withers Villagers and Withers. BioSenecta charged Folsom with submitting monthly reports on the effects of the drug on the men.

In 2013 Dr. Neel Kingfisher of Tahlequah, Oklahoma, was hired as director of Withers Village to replace Mr. Theodore Parsons, who had passed away.

As readers of WITHERSTON ON THE WEB know, on May 22, at a public celebration of his hundredth birthday, Francis Hearty Withers announced that he had recently finalized his will to leave $1 billion to the municipality of Witherston, $1 billion to the residents of Witherston, to be divided equally among them, and the remainder of his estate to BioSenecta for BioSenecta to build a Senextra factory on property he owned. When he felt insulted by protesters of Senextra, Withers declared he would rescind the will. He also declared he would not bring the Senextra factory to Witherston, but that he would clear-cut the 31.7 acres of old-growth forest that he had intended for the factory anyway.

On the following night, May 23, Withers died.

Now I have to speculate a bit, since Detective Mev Arroyo has not yet closed the case.

Apparently, Folsom, distraught by Withers's threat to change his will, poisoned Withers by injecting him with potassium cyanide.

Here's where the story gets interesting. On Sunday, May 24, Jorge and Jaime Arroyo with their friend Beau Lodge found a frog with three back legs under Founding Father's Bridge. Jorge took a picture of the deformed frog and posted it on WITHERSTON ON THE WEB on Tuesday, May 26. Dr. Gregory Bozeman, retired EPA ecologist, became interested in the water quality of the creek where the frog was found and went to Founding Father's Bridge to obtain a sample. He was shot and left for dead.

Did Folsom shoot Bozeman? We don't know for sure.

Did Folsom poison his pregnant wife Faith? We don't know for sure.

Did Folsom poison Withers's dog Harry, whom the Arroyos had adopted and renamed Varry? We don't know for sure.

But we do know that Senextra produced unintended side effects in the primary recipients of the drug, such as breast enlargement. Folsom did not mention this side effect in his monthly reports to BioSenecta. Dr. Kingfisher, however, did notice the change in the elderly men's bodies, and he suspected the cause to be the estrogen-rich Senextra. He told the Arroyo twins about his observations. Jaime Arroyo reported the fact to Chief McCoy.

Gretchen Green and Witherston's other environmentalists argue that the drugs we humans take into our bodies get into our environment and thereby into the bodies of other humans and animals, whom we may call secondary recipients.

The environmentalists may be right. The EPA in Athens has compared water samples from Saloli Falls upstream from Withers Village and Founding Father's Bridge downstream from Withers Village.

The Saloli Falls sample shows little pollution and no estrogen. The Founding Father's Bridge sample shows a high level of estrogen.

If the environmentalists are right, Senextra is an environmental toxin, hazardous to everybody's health.

For the sake of all humans—and for the sake of all nonhumans too, as my former wife and dear friend Gretchen would want me to say—I urge BioSenecta to abandon plans to develop Senextra.

~ Smitty Green, Editor

LETTERS TO THE EDITOR

To the Editor:

I wish to thank all the Witherstonians who came out to search in the rain yesterday for our young journalist Jorge Arroyo. We are especially grateful, most especially grateful, to Jim Lodge, Beau Lodge, and Jonathan Finley for finding Jorge, and to Pete Koslowsky, Jr., for rescuing him from drowning in Dr. Folsom's Jaguar. I am pleased to report that I was called in the evening by a reporter for the ATLANTA JOURNAL AND CONSTITUTION who was writing an article about our murders for their Sunday edition. I told him what a great community Witherston is.
~ Signed, Rich Rather, Mayor

ON THIS DAY IN HISTORY
By Charlotte Byrd

June 3, 1829, was an ordinary day in Witherston's history. Some white settlers panned for gold on Cherokee land. Some Cherokees got upset and killed a few settlers. The settlers' families got upset and killed a few Cherokees. State legislators got annoyed. They discussed the Indian problem.

POLICE BLOTTER

Dr. Ralph Elders, of Witherston Veterinary Clinic, has reported to Witherston Police that Detective Mev Arroyo's dog Varry was probably poisoned by potassium chloride. Varry was Harry, Mr. Francis Hearty Withers's Chow Chow, whom Detective Arroyo adopted when Mr. Withers was found dead.

Witherston police officers responded to 911 call at 10:30 last night from Obadiah Arnold at 415 Creek Road. Reverend

Arnold complained that a black bear had overturned his gar-
bage can, leaving a mess on his driveway. By the time the of-
ficers arrived the bear had disappeared into the woods east of
his house.

CHAPTER 16

Wednesday, June 3, 2015:

After his surgery Neel had been moved into a room on the ICU floor, where he'd spent a peaceful, heavily drugged night. But he'd awakened with the morning light as he usually did, and he'd eaten some applesauce and toast for breakfast. He was surprised to be alive, and he'd asked the nurse what had happened in Witherston the day before. The nurse said she didn't know but supposed not much.

With the remote Neel turned on WNEG-TV, News Channel 32, out of Taccoa, closed his eyes, and dozed. Then he heard a reporter speaking from Witherston. He listened.

"At a 4:00 pm news conference yesterday in front of City Hall, Police Chief Jake McCoy updated the community of Witherston on the rescue of fourteen-year-old Jorge Arroyo, who had been kidnapped by Dr. George Folsom at 10:30 am this morning. In an interview young Jorge was conducting with him at Withers Village Pond, Dr. Folsom got angry, grabbed Jorge, and held a syringe to his neck while his twin brother Jaime watched. Then Dr. Folsom dragged Jorge into the woods. After more than forty concerned Witherstonians had searched the area in the pouring rain, Jim Lodge, his son Beau Lodge, and Jonathan Finley found Jorge tied up in the front seat of Dr. Folsom's Jaguar in the pool at the foot of Saloli Falls. Officer Pete Koslowsky, Jr., extracted the boy from the car. Chief McCoy gave no reason for the kidnapping. He said that the Witherston Police Department would be aided by the Lumpkin County Sheriff's Department in their search for Dr. Folsom today. In a related incident Dr. Neel Kingfisher, director of Withers Village, was wounded and taken to Chestatee Regional Hospital. He is expected to recover fully. Now back to you, Tiffany, for today's weather."

Thank goodness, Neel said to himself. Thank goodness Jorge didn't die. Neel fell asleep. He awoke a couple of hours later when the nurse entered his room to administer his medications, check his IV bag, examine his wound, change his bandages, take him to the bathroom, and remove his breakfast tray. Neel was about to fall asleep again when he heard a knock on the door.

"May I come in?"

It was Gretchen Green. She was carrying a Catesby's Trillium and a heavily packed tan book bag marked RECYCLE.

"Good morning, Neel. I hope I'm not disturbing you."

"Gretchen, seeing you gives me great pleasure. No, you are not disturbing me."

"I brought you a plant, not a bought plant from a store but a home-grown plant from my flower garden that I put into a pot for you. I thought you might need something green while you're in the hospital."

"Something green with pink blossoms! Perfect. You are so nice. Can you stay a few minutes?"

"Yes! But first let me show you what else I brought you. I went by Withers Village and picked up your smartphone, your tablet, a couple of books that were on your desk—*Georgia Odyssey*, which my friend Jim Cobb wrote, and *Birdology*—and some clothes that Mrs. Woods packed for you. By the way, I didn't know you'd hired Amy Woods to be your assistant!"

"She is a good person, and she needed a job. I had a job for a good person. So I hired her."

"She is very worried about you."

"She's sweet. I'll call her. And you are very thoughtful, Gretchen. I do need my phone. And my tablet."

"Also, you don't have to worry about Swift. He's staying with Jorge and Jaime—and probably getting lots of attention."

"What wonderful boys. How can I ever thank you all enough?"

"You can be our friend, Neel. After your remarks at old Withers's funeral, I thought you and I might have something in common. I'm not a Cherokee, but I'm not exactly a normal non-Cherokee either. I like living with nature, eating organic foods, doing yoga, and feeling connected to all the other residents of Earth, like the birds in the sky, the fish in the sea, and the animals that walk upon the ground."

"Those are my words, Gretchen, the words I used at Withers's funeral."

"I know. I remember them."

"Let's talk, Gretchen."

They did, for an hour.

"I have an errand to run, but I'll be back shortly," Gretchen said.

After she left, Neel opened his phone and found the message from Jaime.

Oh my goodness, he thought. Maybe I do have a home in Witherston after all. Maybe I'm not alone.

Neel then slept soundly.

ᏏᎶᏏ

Jake and his deputies Ricky, Pete Senior and Pete Junior had searched since 7:00 a.m. for signs of George Folsom. It was now 9:30. They'd found nothing, and they were hungry. They sat on the eastern bank in the warm sunshine and ate the ham sandwiches Jake's wife Josephine had made for them.

"I don't think we're gonna find him here, Chief," Ricky said. "Pete Senior and I have walked all over the west side of the creek, and you and Pete Junior have walked all over the east side. We've poked our sticks into every bush, into every pile of brush within a half-mile of here. He's just not here."

"But he was on foot," Pete Junior said, "so he could not have gotten far in the rain."

"Maybe he drowned in the creek. The water was high yesterday."

"If that's the case, someone will find him before long," said Jake.

"How long must we keep searching?"

"Till we find him, boys. Dead or alive."

"Do you all think he's dead?" asked Pete Senior.

"Yes," said Jake.

"No," said Pete Junior.

"No," said Ricky.

≈≈≈

Mev awoke after 10:00 feeling sore but rested. She swallowed the pills Paco gave her and drank the apple juice he brought her.

Paco very carefully lifted Mev's nightgown over her head, took it off, examined her incision the way the nurse at the Northeast Georgia Medical Center had instructed him, and changed her bandages. He lightly kissed her bandaged breast.

"Te quiero mucho, mi amor."

Paco went to her closet, selected a pink cotton big shirt, helped her into it, and then helped her into her jeans.

Mev took his head in her hands and kissed him. "I love you too. And I thank you, Paco. How lucky I am to have you," she said.

"Querida, you are very lucky to have me. And I am lucky to have you."

They heard a knock at the door.

"And we are lucky to have our fine boys," Paco added loudly, as he opened the bedroom door to admit Jorge and Jaime.

"Hi, Mom. Hi Dad," Jorge and Jaime said in unison.

"Gosh, Mom. You look pretty good. I like your shirt," said Jaime.

"Hijos, here's a pin I bought for your mother." Paco took the silver dove pin and affixed it to Mev's collar."

"Cool, Dad!" said Jorge. "A dove for peace, and peace for health!"

"May we take Swift for a walk?" asked Jaime.

"Yes, but only if you promise—and stick to your promise—that you will stay away from Saloli Falls. Under no circumstances should you go to Saloli Falls. Promise?"

"We promise," the twins replied.

Jaime leashed up Swift, Jorge got his smartphone, and the boys left the house.

"Let's go find that bear," Jorge said to Jaime.

"Great idea! We can take the bear's picture for *Webby Witherston*."

"Say cheese, Big Bear!"

"Grrrrrrr!"

თთთ

Mayor Rather called Bill Hardy of Hardy Loggers. "Bill, we've known each other a long time. I have a deal for you. You may keep the money Francis Hearty Withers paid you before his death if you will abandon your commitment to clear-cut the 31.7 acres of his property." Rich listened and said, "Thanks, Bill."

Rich hung up the phone and turned to Grant, who had entered his office. "Now there's no need for an injunction. You may think I'm crazy, Grant, but I've been persuaded by our lefty environmentalists in town, namely Gretchen and Lottie, and by young Jorge Arroyo, that it's not good for Witherston to lose those woods."

"Will Mr. Withers's original will be probated?"

"Yes, I'm quite sure. We'll all get a pot of money, Grant. A pot of money for each of us personally. Maybe $250,000. And I have to figure out what to recommend we do with the billion dollars Mr. Withers's has bequeathed Witherston."

"Now that's good news, Rich."

"I want Witherston to do something good with that billion. Something good. I want the world to notice Witherston."

Grant smiled. "And you."

"Yes. And me. I want to be remembered as the mayor that put Witherston on the map. Now I'm going to call Lottie. She'll spread the word."

☙❧

Jon and Gregory sent out an email invitation to the Arroyos, the Lodges, Lottie, Gretchen, Neel, Grant and Ruth, Rich and Rhonda, Scorch and Abby Ridge, Pastor Clement, Smitty Green, Catherine Perry, Trevor Bennington, Jr., and Trevor Bennington, III, Jake McCoy, and all the members of KEEP NATURE NATURAL for a party to celebrate Gregory's recovery, Jorge's rescue, and Neel's recuperation.

Please come to the home of Jon and Gregory at 5:30 on Friday, June 5, for grilled shrimp, grilled chicken, grilled vegetables, and watermelon, with fine wine, courtesy of Lottie Byrd, and beer. Bring your family, friends, and pets. We will celebrate Gregory's recovery, Jorge's rescue, and Neel's recuperation. 650 Yona Road. REPLY ALL.

Gretchen replied to their email right away:

Hi, Jonathan and Gregory.
Neel will still be in the hospital on Friday, and I'll be with him at the time of your party. So could we Skype? I could set up Skype on his tablet and you could set up Skype on yours. Then our friends at your party could see Neel and wish him well.
Gretchen

Jonathan wrote back:

Of course, Gretchen. Neel sacrificed himself for Jorge. He is the true hero of Witherston. I'll set up Skype on my tablet now.

Rhonda wrote:

> *Thank you soooo much for the lovely invitation, Jon and Gregory. I hope you're serious about our bringing pets. Also children. We will bring Sandra and Phil. Also Giuliani.—Rhonda Rather*
>
> *P.S. I will bring a couple of mushroom casseroles.*

Lottie wrote:

> *Thank you, Jon and Gregory. Darwin and I accept. We'll bring Gandhi, since Gretchen will be with Neel. And I will also bring a case of Muga Rioja Reserva for us to share. Lottie*

Rich wrote:

> *Thank you very much. Rhonda and I accept with pleasure. I'll have an announcement to make. —Rich Rather*

Beau wrote:

> *My parents, Jim and Lauren Lodge, and I accept your invitation with pleasure. Sincerely yours, Beau Lodge*

Paco wrote:

> *Jorge, Jaime, Mev, and I accept your invitation. The boys will bring Swift. Gracias. ~ Paco*

Grant wrote:

> *Ruth and I are truly grateful for the invitation to join you all. We accept. Thank you very much. Grant Griggs*

Neel wrote:

Gregory and Jon: I am very happy to join you all on Skype. You honor me by your lovely invitation. My good friend Gretchen is setting it up on my tablet now. Wado. Thank you. ~ Neel

Pastor Clement wrote:

Bless you, Gregory and Jonathan. I accept your kind invitation, and I appreciate being included. I will be bringing Virginia Ann Casey. By the way, Virginia Ann recently saw a bear in your eastside woods. —Paul Clement

Catherine Perry wrote:

Thank you! I accept! ~ Catherine Perry, Reporter

Smitty Green wrote:

What fun it will be to join you! My wife Jane and I will be at your party. Thank you. Smitty Green

Jake wrote:

Thanks very much. I will be there with my wife Josephine and our son Billy. I will also bring my deputies Ricky, Pete Senior, and Pete Junior.

Trevor Bennington, Jr., wrote:

My wife Carolyn and I accept your lovely invitation. Our son Trevor III will be unable to attend because of a little fender-bender in Athens yesterday that totaled his car. Because of a minor error in judgment, Trevor III has to spend a couple of weeks in jail, unfortunately.

Annie Jerden wrote:

All the members of KEEP NATURE NATURAL accept your nice invitation. Annie Jerden, president, Thom Rivers, Sally Sorensen, Mona Pattison, Christopher Zurich, Jorge Arroyo, Jaime Arroyo, and Beau Lodge.

Scorch Ridge wrote:

Abby and I will be there. Abby will bring a couple of rhubarb pies. Thanks. Scorch

෫ଵ෫ଵ

Neel was happier than he had been in four years. Gretchen had stayed with him in his hospital room all day, disappearing only when the nurses came.

At noon she'd gone down to the cafeteria to get lunch, but she was back in ten minutes with a banana for him and an egg salad sandwich for herself.

He'd dozed on and off while she perused a vegan cookbook she'd brought. She'd read aloud to him a couple of vegan stew recipes that he thought he might enjoy with chicken or beef.

Late in the afternoon Neel received an email from Martin:

Dear Dr. Kingfisher:

As of today, June 3, 2015, I have canceled the Senextra pilot study that Dr. Folsom was conducting on the residents of Withers Village.

I have also withdrawn BioSenecta funding from all research on Senextra.

I have determined that while Senextra may provide some benefits to the aging individual who takes it to prolong his life, it may impact the environment in ways harmful to others.

I appreciate your cooperation with Dr. Folsom on this project, and I wish you well in the future.

You will receive an official copy of this letter in the mail.

Thank you.
Sincerely yours,
Martin Payne, MD
CEO of BioSenecta Pharmaceuticals, Inc.

Neel read the email to Gretchen.

"Whoopee," Gretchen exclaimed. "Martin got it."

"At least he acted appropriately. But now I have to tell the Withers Villagers they will no longer be taking the drug. Some of them—most of them, all of them—will take my announcement as their personal death sentence."

"I suppose they will. They will probably be angry. But they will have to understand that though they liked Senextra their taking it hurt other people."

"How easy is it, Gretchen, to persuade individuals to sacrifice themselves for the good of others? I'd say, not easy."

"But that's what you did, Neel. You sacrificed yourself for the good of others when you tried to kill yourself to save Jorge."

"I am fifty-five years old, with maybe twenty useful years left. Jorge is fourteen years old, with sixty useful years left to make a better world. And he and his brother Jaime will make every one of those years count, I can already tell."

"You are an unusual man, Neel. I'm proud to know you."

"I'm proud to know you, Gretchen. And thanks for your compliments. Now we have to figure out how to prevent a revolt in Withers Village."

"Senextra presents the perfect case of something being good for the individual, possibly, and bad for the whole."

"Let's figure this out tomorrow. I'm getting tired."

"We have to show the Withers Villagers the big picture. We'll tell them all about Senextra's effect on the people of Witherston. If the Villagers look at Witherston as a whole, a whole that includes our non-human neighbors in our natural environment, they will see that everybody's well-being depends on the well-being of the entire community. We're interdependent."

"Gretchen, it's time for me to sleep."

"Maybe we can bring the Villagers together, with anybody else who wants to come, to a meeting where you and I talk about living in harmony with nature. We can show what happens when a drug messes with Mother Nature."

"Gretchen, *stop*! Please! I want to go to sleep!"

"We can have the meeting in Reception Hall of Witherston Baptist Church."

"To do that you'll have to talk to Reverend Clement."

"Oh."

"Goodbye, Gretchen. Thanks so much for being with me today."

"Goodbye, Neel. I'll see you tomorrow."

∽∾∽

"Boss, it's 8:30," Pete Senior said to Jake. "It's getting dark. We haven't found a sign of Folsom. We have no evidence that he's either dead or alive. We've not heard that anyone's spotted his body downstream. Can we quit looking?"

"Yes," Jake said. "For today. We'll come back tomorrow morning."

∽∾∽

I am so tired of walking. I've got to get out of here. I'll steal a truck. I have my scalpel. And my money.

WWW.ONLINEWITHERSTON.COM

WITHERSTON ON THE WEB
Thursday, June 4, 2015

LOCAL NEWS

Dr. Martin Payne, CEO of BioSenecta Pharmaceuticals, Inc, sent an email yesterday to Dr. Neel Kingfisher, director of Withers Village, stating that he had canceled the Senextra pilot study and withdrawn all funding for research on the drug. Senextra is dead!

Mayor Rich Rather stopped the clear-cutting of Francis Hearty Withers's 31.7 acres of old-growth forest with a phone call yesterday to Bill Hardy. Mayor Rather had authority to cancel Withers's paid contract with Hardy Loggers because he is executor of Withers's estate. In other words, old-growth forest is alive! Go, Mayor!

Dr. Neel Kingfisher is recovering well from surgery following his self-sacrificial stabbing to save our friend Jorge Arroyo's life. Go, Dr. Kingfisher!

Jorge Arroyo is fully recovered from his kidnapping ordeal. He and his brother Jaime went looking for Witherston's bear yesterday. They didn't find him, but they will. Go, Arroyo twins!

Dr. Gregory Bozeman is recovering well from surgery after being shot. Dr. Bozeman was checking the water quality at Founding Father's Bridge to keep all Witherstonians safe from pollution. Go Dr. Bozeman!

Today is a good day to be a Witherstonian!
~ Catherine Perry, Reporter

LETTERS TO THE EDITOR

To the Editor:

Instead of calling the beautiful ursine visitor to our community simply "the bear," let's give him a name. I suggest Bearwithus.
~ Signed, Art McCrakken, Withers Village

ON THIS DAY IN HISTORY
By Charlotte Byrd

On June 4, 1919, Congress passed the Nineteenth Amendment to the Constitution guaranteeing women the right to vote. On August 26, 1920, after Tennessee became the 36th state to ratify it, the Amendment became law.Native Americans did not enjoy the same privilege until 1924, when the Indian Citizenship Act, also known as the Snyder Act, guaranteed Native Americans the right to vote.

WHAT'S NATURAL
By Jorge Arroyo

Today I will write about what's not natural—Senextra. If you google Senextra you will find out that it is a powerful drug with "synthetic estrogen" that has been developed to make old people live longer. Senextra is not natural. And Senextra changes what's natural.

Tuesday morning I went with my brother Jaime Arroyo to Withers Village Pond to interview Dr. George Folsom. Dr. Folsom administered Senextra to the men at Withers Village who wanted to live longer. Actually, he administered the drug to all the men there, because they all wanted to live longer, except for the director Dr. Neel Kingfisher.

I asked Dr. Folsom whether he was taking the drug himself, and he said he wasn't. But I found out later that he'd been giving it to his wife Faith Folsom, who got pregnant at the age of fifty one and died.

Dr. Folsom's eyes got crazy when he talked about the benefits of Senextra. He wanted everyone who could afford the drug to take it. I asked him whether our country would have too many old people then. He said that the old people who took Senextra would look and act young. I should have asked him instead whether our country would have too many people then.

I asked him about poor people who didn't have money for Senextra. He said they'd just die and wouldn't burden society. He also said that the Bible said there would always be poor people. So I guess he meant that there would always be rich people, because if some people have a whole lot of money they must have gotten it from some other people, right? Can you have rich people without poor people?

Dr. Folsom got mad when I asked him about a side effect of Senextra in the men at Withers Village. Then he kidnapped me.

I can't write about this side effect of Senextra because I don't want to embarrass the men at Withers Village, but it's not a good side effect.

Senextra has lots of side effects. I think that Dr. Folsom gave Mr. Withers's old female Chow Chow Dog some Senextra injections, because she got pregnant at the age of sixteen. Maybe Dr. Folsom wanted to find out whether her body would still act young. But then Maud Olive—Maud Olive was her name, isn't that funny—gave birth to Harry (who became Varry when he joined my family) who had no testicles.

When Senextra got into Founding Father's Creek and Witherston's water table it affected lots of animals and proba-

bly some people in our area. It probably made a female frog give birth to the frog my brother found with three back legs. And it may have caused a die-off of minnows.

My parents took samples of the water at Saloli Falls upstream from Withers Village and at Founding Father's Bridge downstream. The water upstream was pure. The water downstream had synthetic estrogen in it.

You can figure out how Senextra got in the water downstream. I don't like to think about it.

POLICE BLOTTER

At 5:00 pm yesterday Thom Rivers called 911 to report seeing a black bear on the front steps of Witherston Baptist Church. Other people in the vicinity at the time could not corroborate Mr. Rivers's claim.

CHAPTER 17

Thursday, June 4, 2015:

I'm back!" Gretchen looked around Neel's hospital room. It was filled with flowers and cards.

"Hello, Gretchen," Neel said. "I'm very happy to see you today, even at this early hour."

"The nurse said I could come in, that you'd already had your shower. I brought you something. Blueberry herbal tea. It's good for you."

"Thanks. And I have something to show you. But let's have tea first."

❧❧❧

Jon had finished washing, cutting, coloring, and combing out Rhonda's hair. Now he was drying it.

"I am so excited about your party tomorrow night, Jon. Thanks for inviting Rich and me."

"Well, you know I love you, girl, so I'd never leave you out. And I have to admit I now have a higher opinion of your husband than I did before he organized the search party for Jorge. Mayor Rather did great work Tuesday. So I look forward to seeing you both."

"Thanks for inviting Giuliani too. She'll enjoy playing with Renoir. By the way, do you and Gregory have any other pets, like cats?"

"No, I'm sorry to say. We started to raise fancy pigeons in a pigeon coop that Gregory built, but a fox brought his relatives to dinner there one night, and they ate up Vivien, Candace, Marilyn, Cher, and Gregory Peck. You should have seen all the feathers the next morning. Enough to make another pigeon. I cried. We've had only Renoir since then."

"I miss my work at TLC in Dahlonega. Faith and I volunteered there together. Now I'm too huge to take care of the animals, clean cages, and wash kittens and puppies. If I got down on the ground the Fire Department would have to get me back on my feet."

"Dear Rhonda, will you name your baby after Gregory and me? Jonathan Gregory Rather?" Jon laughed.

So did Rhonda. "I'd love to, Jon, but I think that Rich has another name in mind: Richard."

"Then I'd suggest you name the tot Mayor Richard Rather Junior."

"Good idea. We can call him Rather Junior for short."

✑✑✑

"Let me read you an email message I've drafted to send to the Withers Villagers—that is, if you think it's okay. I want you to help me make it good," Neel said to Gretchen.

"Let's hear it."

Neel read:

> "My dear friends at Withers Village:
>
> "Thank you for all your well wishes. I am recuperating nicely from my surgery. The knife broke a couple of ribs on my left side, but it didn't go into my heart. I guess I didn't know where my heart was. I will learn.
>
> "As you know, Dr. George Folsom will no longer give you Senextra shots. He allegedly murdered Francis Hearty Withers, and now he has disappeared. BioSenecta has canceled the Senextra pilot study, so nobody else will give you Senextra shots either. I regret having to communicate this disappointing news.
>
> "BioSenecta has stopped development of Senextra because the drug disrupts reproductive cycles in living things. Once it enters the ecosystem, of which

we humans are part, Senextra may cause effeminiza-
tion of males, sterility in males, menopausal fertility
in females, and birth defects—not just in us humans
but in all animals, human and non-human.

"We humans thought we could improve on Nature by giving ourselves longer lives with a miraculous drug, but Nature had already developed a system that worked well. When we humans injected
Senextra into Nature, Nature changed in a way not to
our liking.

"Senextra seemed to conquer death for individuals, or at least postpone it, and few of us welcome
death. But we all die. Over some 200,000 years perhaps 110 billion human beings have lived and died.
Each has had only a brief moment of time on Earth,
only a brief moment of time in which to look around,
love, reproduce, care for the young, and pass something on to future generations. You and I are fortunate to have had many more years of life than our
ancestors had ten thousand years ago, or even one
hundred years ago. Our ancestors, our grandparents,
our parents died to make space on Earth for us. We
shall die to make space on Earth for others.

"I look forward to seeing you all upon my return
to Withers Village next week.

"Neel Kingfisher, MD, Director
"Withers Village"

"That's beautiful," Gretchen said, looking over Neel's
shoulder. "You're a good writer. I wouldn't change a thing."
Neel pressed Send.

WITHERSTON ON THE WEB
Friday, June 5, 2015

LOCAL NEWS

Chief Jake McCoy announced late yesterday afternoon that he and his deputies will seek help from law enforcement agencies outside Lumpkin County in the search for Dr. George Folsom. Chief McCoy said to this reporter, "Dr. Folsom may be dead or he may be alive. But he's nowhere near Saloli Falls."

Mayor Rich Rather has approved the name Bearwithus for the big black bear that has moved into Witherston in the past week.
~ Catherine Perry, Reporter

LETTERS TO THE EDITOR

To the Editor:

What's with the damned bear? Just shoot him!
~ Signed, Paul Bunion, Withers Village

To the Editor:

This reporter for Witherston on the Web apologizes for the insertion of her own opinions into her news articles yesterday. She will try not to do it again.
~ Signed, Catherine Perry, Reporter

ON THIS DAY IN HISTORY
By Charlotte Byrd

On June 5, 1860, the town of Witherston was founded as Witherstown. There were 203 men, women, and children living on the five acres that downtown Witherston presently occupies, which the Cherokees had once called their own. The fifty-one men over the age of twenty-one voted unanimously for municipal incorporation. We can assume that Harry Withers, in the fancy house on the hill, was pleased.

POLICE BLOTTER

Witherston Police officer Pete Junior Koslowsky spotted Bearwithus on Yona Road near the home of Jonathan Finley and Gregory Bozeman at 7:30 last night. Officer Pete Junior had just stopped Sally Sorensen and Mona Pattison for speeding on Yona Road in Col. Ed Sorensen's Vietnam-era jeep. They said they were chasing a bear. Apparently they were telling the truth.

CHAPTER 18

Friday, June 5, 2015:

Welcome, all of you!" Jon greeted folks from the porch. It was 5:30. The cars were lining up on Yona Road, and the party-goers were streaming onto Jon and Gregory's front lawn. The sun was still high in the sky, and the day was warm. They would have their party outside.

Lottie, dressed in a purple cotton tunic, white jeans, and a lavender apron with a large white embroidered peace symbol, had come early, with Darwin in her apron pocket and Gandhi on a leash. She'd let Gandhi off the leash and put Darwin on her shoulder. Jon had carried the case of Spanish wine from Lottie's little car to the porch. True to form, Lottie had packed four dozen glass goblets so that folks could drink her fine wine properly.

Then came Scorch and Abby, carrying four rhubarb pies.

Then came the Arroyos, Jorge with Swift and Jaime with his guitar. Paco with Mev on his arm.

Then came the Lodges. And the Griggs. And the Benningtons. And all the others who had received an invitation.

Except for the Rathers.

Everybody had fun with everybody else, including Gregory who still wore bandages under his white cotton shirt. Gregory sat in a lawn chair by the boom box enjoying a glass of wine, talking with guests, and playing a Harry Belafonte CD, loudly.

Jon and Scorch started roasting vegetables and shrimp on the four-foot-long gas grill. Jorge, Beau, Sally Sorensen, Mona Pattison, Paco, Jim, Smitty, Pete Junior, Ricky, and Pastor Clement played touch football.

Jaime and Annie sat together under a tree. Jaime played his guitar softly.

Grant talked with Lottie. Ruth talked with Mev. Trevor Bennington, Jr., talked with Jake, probably about his son Trevor III.

Finally the Rathers arrived: Rhonda and Rich, Sandra and Phil, Giuliani, and—what else?—a couple of gray crates with the words LIVE ANIMAL printed on the sides.

"Hello, everybody!" Mayor Rather hailed the crowd heartily in his campaign voice. "What a wonderful occasion this is." He unleashed Giuliani.

"Thanks so much for including us, Jon and Gregory," Rhonda managed to say, panting from her walk up the driveway.

Phil brought the crates. Sandra brought the styrofoam cooler.

"We have presents," explained Rhonda. "And mushroom casseroles."

"But first I have a speech to make."

"You always have a speech to make, Rich!" shouted Grant.

"But this is not a campaign speech!"

"We'll be the judge of that."

"ATTENTION!" shouted Jonathan. "The mayor wants to make a speech!"

"ATTENTION!" echoed Lottie. "We have to listen to the mayor! It's mandatory."

"WOOF!" barked Swift.

The footballers stopped their game and listened. The others stopped their conversation and listened. Gregory turned down the music. Jaime and Annie kept talking.

Rich Rather unfolded a sheet of paper and started reading in his best campaign voice.

"Ladies and Gentlemen. I stand before you exactly two weeks after Mr. Francis Hearty Withers disclosed the contents of his will. He promised $1 billion to Witherstonians, $1 billion to the municipality of Witherston, and the remainder of his estate to BioSenecta for use in the construction of a Senextra factory on his land.

Today, as the executor of Mr. Withers's estate, I have the authority to tell you that when Mr. Withers's will is probated each of the present legal residents of Witherston—and at last count there were fewer than 4,000 of us—will inherit approximately $250,000. If there are two of you in your family, as a couple you'll get $500,000. If there are four of you, as in the case with the Arroyo family, you'll get $1 million."

The party-goers applauded madly.

Jaime put down his guitar. He and Annie started to take notice.

Rich continued. "You may know that I have canceled the clear-cut logging of Francis Hearty Withers's 31.7 acres of old-growth forest. As the executor of Mr. Withers's estate I have the authority to make that decision. Right, Judge Lodge?"

Lauren nodded yes, and smiled. The party-goers clapped.

"You may also have heard that Dr. Martin Payne, CEO of BioSenecta, has canceled plans to build the BioSenextra factory here."

"Woohoo!" shouted Jorge.

"Woohoo!" shouted Jaime.

The other KEEP NATURE NATURAL members went wild.

Rich continued.

"Consequently, BioSenecta will not inherit the rest of Mr. Withers's estate. The municipality of Witherston will. Now what should be done with the $1 billion plus and all the land that will go to Witherston? I've been thinking of that. On Monday morning I will recommend to the Witherston town council that Witherston use a portion of that money to create a park from Withers's 31.7 acres of old-growth forest and maintain the land in its natural state. With the big endowment we'll establish with Withers's money we can ensure that the land will never be used for any purpose other than giving pleasure to people."

Annie jumped up. "Yea!" she said. "Go, Mayor! Thanks for listening to KEEP NATURE NATURAL!"

The other KNN members chimed in: "Go, Mayor! Go, Mayor!"

Mayor Rather continued.

"The town council will decide what to do with the rest of our inheritance, but I will recommend that we bank it and use the interest to make Witherston the cleanest, healthiest, and most attractive town in the southeast."

Annie then turned to fellow members of KNN. "We won!"

"Woohoo," shouted Jorge.

"Woohoo!" echoed Jamie.

"We'll put Witherston on the map!" Mayor Rather declared.

Lottie spoke up, as loudly as she could. "Everybody won! When we save trees, we save lives!"

"Now is my turn to make a speech," shouted Rhonda.

Rich went over to a lawn chair by Gregory and sat down.

"*Hear, Hear*!" yelled Jon.

"I have brought some presents for some special people."

"Go, Mrs. Mayor," yelled Christopher.

Rhonda went on. "I would like to give Gregory a get-well gift. Gregory was concerned with the health of all of us when he went to Founding Father's Creek to get a water sample. He didn't do that just for himself. He did it for all of us. So from a grateful Witherston community, Gregory, I would like to present you with a kitten!"

While Lottie put Darwin into her apron pocket, Rhonda opened the smaller crage and took out a two-month-old calico kitten. "Her name is Felicia," she said, "for happiness. We're happy you're alive." She gently handed the kitten to Gregory. "She came from the TLC humane society in Dahlonega."

Gregory seemed overwhelmed. He kissed Felicia on her

nose. "I don't know what to say, Rhonda. Except that you're kind and thoughtful and sweet and caring and just beautiful!"

"She is all of that," said Jon. "And she's going to name her baby after us: Jonathan Gregory Rather!"

"*What?*" Rich stood up, uncertain of what to say in front of so many voters.

"Gregory is just kidding, Rich," Rhonda said. "Our baby will be named Mayor Richard Rather Junior. We'll call him Rather Junior."

"Or Mayor Junior," said Pete Junior."

"Or Junior Mayor," Pete Senior said.

Rhonda winked at Jon. "I have three more gifts to give, one to the Arroyos, one to the Lodges, and one to Dr. Kingfisher."

Jaime joined Jorge and Beau, right by Rhonda.

"Open the big crate, Phil, please."

Phil did. He brought out two terrier-mix puppies.

Rhonda smiled. "On behalf of all Witherstonians, I want to give the Arroyo family and the Lodge family each a puppy for solving Witherston's first murder and saving our community from Senextra. My little Giuliani had three puppies nine weeks ago, and I wanted the puppies to have loving families."

"And I told her she had to get rid of them by this weekend," Rich said. But he smiled.

Jaime accepted the white puppy for his family. "What's his name, Mizz Rather?" he asked.

"Whitey," she answered.

"Let's call him Mighty," said Jorge.

"Perfect!" said Jaime.

Beau accepted the black puppy for his family. "What's his name, Mizz Rather?" he asked.

"Blacky."

"I think we'll call him Sequoyah," Beau said. "Okay, Mom, Dad?"

"I do like Sequoyah better than Blacky," Jim replied.

"Sequoyah invented writing for the Cherokees." Beau said.

"Look," Jorge said. "There's another puppy in the crate."

"Yes," said Rhonda. "Jon, have you got Neel and Gretchen on Skype now?"

"Yes." Jon took his laptop over to Rhonda. "Hello, Neel," he said, as Neel entered his screen.

"Hello, Jon. Hello, Mrs. Rather."

Gretchen suddenly appeared beside Neel on the screen. "Hi, everybody!"

Rhonda looked into the laptop camera. "Dr. Kingfisher. On behalf of the town of Witherston, I'd like to give you a present. You sacrificed yourself to save the life of our Jorge. You're a Cherokee, and you still wanted to exchange your life for that of someone whose ancestors hurt your ancestors."

"You're not talking about my ancestors," Paco smiled. "My ancestors were busy hurting people in Spain."

"You're talking about my ancestors," Mev said. "They are the ones who hurt your ancestors."

"Anyway," Rhonda said, "I would like to give you my lovely Giuliani's only female puppy. Her name is Ama." Ronda held up the reddish-brown puppy for Neel to see."

"Ama is the Cherokee name for water!"

Rhonda giggled. "I know. I looked it up. Actually, it's appropriate for her."

"In Spanish it means *he loves* or *she loves*," said Jaime.

"From the verb *amar*, to love," said Jorge. You can say *ámame* and command somebody to love you."

"Wonderful," Neel said. "Thank you, Mrs. Rather. Thank you, thank you." Unaware that he was still on Skype, Neel turned to Gretchen. "Oh my god. What will Swift think?"

"Swift is right here, Dr. Kingfisher. See?" Rhonda shifted the camera to capture Swift's image.

"Woof," said Swift.

"Dr. Kingfisher, I want you to have Ama so that you will always have a tie to Witherston. We want to keep you here."

"You're a lovely woman, Rhonda. By the way, I notice that Ama has big feet. Who was her father?"

"Only God knows," Rhonda said.

"Bye, everybody!" Gretchen said, and their Skype image disappeared from the laptop screen.

Jon got up on the chair. "Now we're going to play a party game, folks. Attention! Listen, you all! This is a game I made up just for tonight. I'm calling it the 'We Are Fam-i-ly' game.

Here's how we play it. Everybody has to say one nice thing about somebody else here. Okay?"

"About anybody else?" asked Rich. "Like do I have to say something nice about somebody in KEEP NATURE NATU-RAL?"

"Yes, that's the idea, Mayor Rather!" said Jonathan. "So would you like to say something nice about someone? Someone of your choosing, preferably someone who wasn't a friend before tonight."

"Please call on somebody else first, while I try to think of something nice to say about KNN."

"Okay, Mayor. Hmmm. I call on Lottie Byrd."

"Mayor Rather has a heart after all," Lottie said,

"Woohoo!" shouted Jorge.

"Go, Mayor!" yelled Christopher Zurich.

"I call on Grant Griggs," said Jon.

"Despite being a left-wing, liberal, tree-hugging communist with an unfortunate liking for Peter, Paul, and Mary, Professor Byrd shows a tiny bit of intelligence in her *Webby Witherston* essays," Grant said. "A tiny bit."

"I want to say something," said Thom Rivers. "I have come to know Chief McCoy and officers Ricky, Pete Senior, and Pete Junior very well in the last month or so. They are nice people. I always enjoy seeing them in Rosa's Cantina."

"Stop! I've never been to Rosa's Cantina!" Jake said to his wife Josephine. "At least not for pleasure. Really, sweetie. Believe me."

"Say something nice about someone, Jake."

"Okay. I admire the KEEP NATURE NATURAL kids for their cleverness in collecting Mayor Rather's $100 rewards. They photographed each other putting up KNN signs around town."

"*What*? You're kidding!" exclaimed Rich. "That's what they were doing?"

"I call on Mayor Rather," said Jon.

"Okay, okay. Well, Gretchen Whole Grain has a nice dog."

The party lasted until 9:45 pm. It would have lasted longer if the bear hadn't come.

WITHERSTON ON THE WEB
Friday, June 5, 2015

LATEBREAKING NEWS
(5:30 pm)

ATLANTA, June 5, 2015, 5:10 pm – At 1:00 pm today, Dr. Martin Payne, Chief Executive Officer of Atlanta-based Bio-Senecta Pharmaceuticals, cashed in his stock options and sold all his holdings of BioSenecta at $83.53 per share for a total gain of over $5.7 million. Between 1:00 and 4:00, when the stock market closed, BioSenecta's price per share plumeted to $12.11. Payne was unavailable for comment.

Lloyd Hull, Chair of BioSenecta's Board of Directors, said he was shocked by Payne's actions. "I cannot predict Dr. Payne's future at BioSenecta," he said.

~Elaine Mirko, Associated Press

The Georgia Bureau of Investigation reports that an 18-wheeler carrying a load of live chickens was highjacked on Withers Highway a mile above Saloli Falls late Tuesday night, June 2, or early Wednesday morning, June 3. The driver of the vehicle, identified as Frank Hitchens, was found in Founding Fathers Creek at 4:30 pm on Friday, June 5, by two fishermen from South Carolina.

His throat had been cut with a very sharp knife, perhaps a scalpel. Southern Chickens, Inc. had reported the truck missing on the morning of June 3. The truck has not been located.

~ Micky Donaldson, Reporter

The End

About the Author

Dr. Betty Jean Craige is Professor Emerita of Comparative
Literature and Director Emerita of the Willson Center for Hu-
manities and Arts at the University of Georgia. She has lived
in Athens, Georgia, since 1973.

Craige is a teacher, scholar, translator, humorist, and writer.
She has published seventeen books in the fields of literature,
politics, art, and history of ideas. The most recent is *Conversations with Cosmo: At Home with an African Grey Parrot.* For
two years she wrote a Sunday column about animals, "Cosmo
Talks," in the *Athens Banner-Herald.*

Downstream, a murder mystery, is her first novel.

Made in the USA
Charleston, SC
08 February 2015